WAGONS WEST:
TEXAS FREEDOM!

WAGONS WEST: TEXAS FREEDOM!

Dana Fuller Ross

PINNACLE BOOKS
Kensington Publishing Corp.
www.kensingtonbooks.com

PINNACLE BOOKS are published by

Kensington Publishing Corp.
119 West 40th Street
New York, NY 10018

All Kensington titles, imprints, and distributed lines are available at special quantity discounts for bulk purchases for sales promotions, premiums, fund-raising, educational, or institutional use. Special book excerpts or customized printings can also be created to fit specific needs. For details, write or phone the office of the Kensington special sales manager: Kensington Publishing Corp., 119 West 40th Street, New York, NY 10018, attn: Special Sales Department; phone 1-800-221-2647.

PINNACLE BOOKS and the Pinnacle logo are Reg. U.S. Pat. & TM Off.

ISBN-13: 978-0-7860-2817-7
ISBN-10: 0-7860-2817-3

First printing: March 2012

10 9 8 7 6 5 4 3 2 1

Printed in the United States of America

Prologue

The Pierce-Arrow limousine had an open front seat for the chauffeur and an enclosed body for the passengers. Gliding onto the scene in a well-bred whisper, the car stopped and the chauffer got out, then hurried around to open the door to allow Fancy Darrow Nelson to step down. Applause greeted the eighty-nine-year-old lady and she smiled in appreciation. She was followed from the car by her son, sixty-five-year-old Tom Nelson, and his wife, Cindy, who also received a warm welcome from the crowd.

In addition to the Pierce-Arrow, a cavalcade of Fords and Chevrolets arrived to discard Fancy's grandchildren, great-grandchildren, and one great-great-grandchild, all of whom were honored guests for the upcoming ceremony. Uniformed policemen from the city of Amarillo led them all into a special reserved seating section.

The Amarillo High School band was playing "The Yellow Rose of Texas," as Fancy started toward the reserved bleachers, but Oscar Colquitt, the diminutive governor of Texas came to her side.

"Mrs. Nelson, if you please, there is a reserved chair for you on the reviewing stand."

Fancy walked with the governor over to an elevated stand where he helped her climb the six stairs, then led her to a comfortable, padded chair. Fancy looked out toward the life-sized bronze memorial statue of her husband, Paul Nelson. He was mounted on a horse, a position which, Fancy could attest, fit him very well, for he was always a man of action.

In front of the statue there was a plaque that read:

PAUL FRANKLIN NELSON

Texas Ranger
Soldier of Texas
Embodiment of the Pioneer Spirit
A Founder of COMANCHERIA

Governor Colquitt of Texas stepped up to the podium to dedicate the memorial.

"My fellow Texans," he began, and with an acknowledging nod toward the VIP bleachers—"honored guests"—then turning toward Fancy and with a slight bow added, "and especially our very special guest of honor, Mrs. Nelson."

He turned back toward the crowd. "It is truly an honor to be present for the dedication of this memorial to a great American, a great Texan, and a great man.

"Paul Nelson not only led a wagon train to bring settlers to this part of Texas, he was also instrumental, along with his son"—the governor turned toward Tom Nelson—"in restoring the Comancheria area of Texas to vitality after the devastation brought on by the great War Between the States. Before that he was a brigadier general in the Confederate Army, and before that a captain in the Texas Rangers, fighting Indians and outlaws. Before that he was in the Mexican-American War, and he was one of the heroes of both the Alamo and San Jacinto in the Texas Revolution."

As the governor droned on, Fancy, Tom, and all others who were gathered on this day recalled not only the life of Paul Nelson, but the history of Texas itself.

Chapter One

Medina River, Texas—Sunday, February 21, 1836

Twenty-four-year-old Captain Paul Nelson lay on his belly on a flat rock on the banks of the Medina River. Opening up his telescope, he perused the Mexican encampment on the other side of the river. There had to be two thousand or more soldiers gathered there.

One of the men, resplendent in a colorful and medal-bedecked uniform, was standing off by himself, holding a riding quirt in his right hand, slapping it casually against his left. Focusing his spyglass on the face, Paul was able to confirm his suspicion. This was General Antonio Lopez de Santa Anna. Paul was positive of that, because he had once met the Mexican leader.

Paul hurried back to his horse, mounted, then started toward San Antonio de Bexar. By pushing it, he could make the twenty-five miles in about two and one half hours. He knew that an army that large would take at least two days to reach San Antonio de Bexar if they left right now.

Horse and rider were tired when they rode into San Antonio late that afternoon. To Paul's surprise, rather than preparing for Santa Anna's advancing army, citizens and soldiers alike were enjoying a great fiesta. Music was playing, men and women were dancing, children were running about, and the air was redolent with the aromas of cooking meat.

Smelling the food intensified Paul's hunger because he had not eaten a thing except a couple of pieces of deer jerky since yesterday morning. Dismounting near one of the outdoor cooking pits, he scooped some beans and spicy beef onto a tortilla and carried it around with him, eating, as he searched for Colonel Travis. He found Travis drinking coffee at a table in front of the Mariposa Cantina.

"Captain Nelson," Travis said. "It is good to see you back. Have a seat." Travis pushed out a chair with his foot and Paul joined him at his table. "Did you see them?"

"I saw them," Paul said. "They are camped on the Medina."

"That's pretty close," Travis replied. "How many are there?"

"Two thousand, maybe as many as twenty-five hundred. They are spread out quite a way up and down the riverbank."

The two men had to raise their voices in order to be heard because the celebration was so loud. Once, when there was a woman's quick scream, followed by the laughter of men and women, Paul looked toward the sound and saw that Jim Bowie was at the center of the festivities. Though it wasn't intentional, he must have had a look of disapproval on his face, and Colonel Travis saw it.

"Yes, it is our esteemed *Colonel* Bowie," Travis said. He slurred the word *colonel*.

"I know there have been some differences of opinion between the two of you," Paul said. "Colonel, I speak not as a partisan for either side, but don't you think we would all be better served if the two of you could work out your differences?"

"There is nothing I would like more, Captain, believe me," Travis said. "But it has been impossible to find Bowie sober long enough to have a serious conversation."

"*Con este cuchillo, les quitaré el corazón de Santa Anna!*" Bowie shouted, slashing at the air with his broadbladed knife.

His comment was greeted by laughter and cheers.

"What did he say?" Travis asked, obviously irritated by Bowie's drunken and boisterous behavior.

"He said, 'With this knife I will remove the heart of Santa Anna,' " Paul interpreted.

Travis stroked his chin and nodded. "That is the most difficult of all," he said. "It isn't bragging if you can actually do what you boast. And Bowie's past history would certainly prove that he could do just that."

Travis reached into the inside pocket of his tunic and pulled out two sheets of paper. He handed both of them to Paul.

"In your absence, Captain, I wrote two letters," he said. "I have kept copies, and I would like for you to read them, for I greatly value your opinion."

Paul took the two letters, and, as the celebration continued around him, began to read.

His Excellency, General Sam'l Houston:

You have no doubt already received information by express from La Bahia that tremendous preparations are in the making on the Rio Grande and elsewhere in the interior for the invasion of Texas. Santa Anna, by the last accounts, was at Saltillo, with a force of two thousand five hundred men and guns. Sesma was at the Rio Grande with about two thousand men, and he has issued his proclamation announcing vengeance against the people of Texas, threatening to exterminate every white man within its limits.

As this is the frontier post nearest the Rio Grande, we will, no doubt, be the first to be attacked. We are ill-prepared for their reception as we have not more than one hundred and fifty men here and they are in a very disorganized state. Yet we are determined to sustain the garrison for as long as there is a man left; because we consider death preferable to disgrace, which would be the result of giving up a post which has been so dearly won, and thus opening up the door for the invaders to enter the sacred territory of the colonies.

We hope our countrymen will open their eyes to the present danger, and wake up from their false security. I hope that all party dissensions will subside, that your fellow citizens will unite in the common cause and fly to the defense of the frontier.

I fear that it is useless to waste arguments upon them. It will take the thunder of the enemy's cannon, the pollution of their wives and daughters, the cries of their famished children and the smoke of their burning dwellings to arouse them. I regret that the government has so long neglected a draft of the militia, which is the only measure that will ever again bring the citizens of Texas to the frontiers.

Money, clothing, and provisions are greatly needed at this post for the use of the soldiers.

I hope Your Excellency will send up a portion of the money which has been received from the U.S. as it cannot be better applied, indeed we cannot get along any longer without money, and with it we can do everything.

For God's sake, and the sake of our country, send us reinforcements. I hope you will send to this post at least two companies of regular troops.

In consequence of the sickness of his family, Lt. Col. Neill has left this post to visit home for a short time and has requested me to take the command of the post. In consequence of which, I feel myself delicately and awkwardly situated. I therefore hope that Your Excellency will give me some definite orders and that immediately.

The troops here, to a man, recognize you as their legitimate governor, and they expect your fatherly care and protection.

In conclusion let me assure Your Excellency, that with two hundred more men I believe this place can be maintained, and I hope they will be sent us as soon as possible. Yet should we receive no reinforcement, I am determined to defend it to the last, and should Bexar fall, your friend will be buried beneath its ruins.

> *Sincerely,*
> *William B. Travis*
> *Commanding*
> *San Antonio de Bexar*

"That is a wonderful letter, Colonel Travis," Paul said, as he handed the missive back.

"Please, read the other one, then we will talk," Travis said.

Nodding in the affirmative, Paul began reading the second of the two letters.

His Excellency, General Sam'l Houston:

I wrote you an official letter last night as commandant of this post in the absence of Col. Neill, and if you had taken the trouble to answer my letter from Burnam's, I should not now have been under the necessity of troubling you.

My situation is truly awkward and delicate. Colonel Neill left me in the command, but wishing to give satisfaction to the volunteers and not wishing to assume any command over them I issued an order for the election of an officer to command them with the exception of one company of volunteers that were previously engaged to serve under me.

Bowie was elected by two small companies, and since his election he has been roaring drunk all the time; has assumed all command, and is proceeding in a most disorderly and irregular manner, interfering with private property, releasing prisoners sentenced by court-martial and by the civil court and turning everything topsy-turvy. If I did not feel my honor and that of my country compromised I would leave here instantly for some other point with the troops under my immediate command, as I am unwilling to be responsible for the drunken irregularities of any man.

I hope you will immediately order some regular

troops to this place, as it is more important to occupy the post than I imagined when I last saw you. It is the key of Texas from the interior. Without a footing here the enemy can do nothing against us in the colonies now that our coast is being guarded by armed vessels. I do not solicit the command of this post but Col. Neill has applied to the commander-in-chief to be relieved and is anxious for me to take the command. I will do it, if it be your order, for a time until an artillery officer can be sent here. The citizens here have every confidence in me, as they can communicate with me, and they have shown every disposition to aid me with all they have. We need money. Can you not send us some? I read your letter to the troops and they received it with acclamation. Our spies have just returned from the Rio Grande. The enemy is there one thousand strong and is making every preparation to invade us. By the 15th of March I think Texas will be invaded and every preparation should be made to receive them.

In conclusion, allow me to beg that you will give me definite orders immediately.

> *William B. Travis*
> *Commanding*
> *San Antonio de Bexar*

"When did you send these letters, Colonel?" Paul asked, returning the two to Travis.

"I sent them two weeks previous," Travis replied as he folded the letters and put them back in his pocket.

"Even if Houston had all intentions to send replacements to our relief, he would not be able to do so now," Paul said. "Santa Anna is too close."

"He wouldn't send them if he could," another man said, and looking over a couple of tables beyond, Paul saw Davy Crockett sitting in the shadows. He was eating a piece of fried bread, spread with butter and jam.

"Why do you say that, Colonel?" Paul asked.

Crockett held up his hand, palm out. "I told you, I'm not a colonel. I'm what you might call a high private. But you can call me Davy."

"All right, Davy, why do you say that Houston wouldn't send us reinforcements?"

"Because he is a Jackson man," Crockett said. "An Andrew Jackson man."

"I take it that you don't like Andrew Jackson?"

"I wouldn't be here if I had any regard for that polecat," Crockett said. He chuckled. "When I left, I told him, I said, 'You can go to hell and I am going to Texas.' Yes, sir, that's what I told him," Crockett said, laughing at his own story.

"Did you hear what Captain Nelson just reported about Santa Anna and his army?" Travis asked.

"I heard. He's on the Medina River. That's not too far from here, I take it?"

"It's not far at all. It means two days, at the most," Travis said.

"Are we goin' to pull out, Billy? Or are we goin' to stay here and fight?" Crockett asked.

"You can do what you want with your Tennesseans, but I'm not leaving," Travis said.

"Oh, I reckon we'll stay and see this little fracas through with you," Crockett said.

"John," Travis called, seeing Captain John Hubbard Forsythe walking by. "Come join us."

Smiling, Forsythe came over to sit at the table with Paul and Travis.

"Colonel," he said, then turning to Paul. "You just get back from your scout?"

"A few minutes ago," Paul said.

"They are on the Medina River," Travis said. "I expect they'll be here in about two more days."

"Two more days?"

"Maybe sooner," Paul said.

Forsythe drummed his fingers on the table for a moment. "We aren't going to get any reinforcements, are we, Colonel?"

"No," Travis said.

"How many did you see?"

"At least two thousand," Paul replied. "Maybe more."

"And that's not the entire army," Travis said. "From the reports I received earlier, there are more than five thousand in Santa Anna's invasion force. I expect there will be at least that many when they attack us."

"Five thousand against less than two hundred," Forsythe said.

"Are you having second thoughts about being here, John?" Travis asked.

"For me? No. But I'm damn glad Gordon is with General Houston," Forsythe said, speaking of his brother. "One Forsythe in here is enough."

San Antonio de Bexar—Tuesday, February 23, 1836

"Captain Nelson," Travis said when Paul answered a summons to report to him. "No doubt you have noticed that the last of the civilian residents of San Antonio left early this morning."

"Yes, sir, I couldn't help but notice. Wagons, carts, and horses started passing by my quarters even before dawn."

"I would like for you to post a lookout somewhere so we could get an early warning of their arrival."

"If you don't mind, I'll be the lookout," Paul said. "I've already picked my observation post."

"Where?"

"I'm going to climb up to the top of the bell tower of the San Fernando church. That is the highest place in town, and it has a panoramic view, so no matter which direction they use for their approach, I will be able to see them."

"Good idea," Travis said. "How is Bowie? Drunk again?"

"No, sir. He is ill. Very ill."

"I know he has been ill. And I have been harsh on him because of his drinking. Perhaps he has had an excuse for his drinking."

"You had every right to be upset, Colonel," Paul said. "He should have relinquished co-command and turned the entire garrison over to you, especially seeing as he is too ill to command."

"Yes, well, at this point it no longer matters, does it? The Mexicans are here, our reinforcements are not."

"When will we withdraw to the fort?" Paul asked.

Travis snorted. "Fort," he said. "I would hardly call it a fort. We have taken an abandoned mission and done all that we could to fortify it. Its only advantage is that it is a walled mission, but the grounds are much too expansive to be defended by the few men that we have. Major Jameson has done a good job of modifying it as far as he can, but there are no loopholes in the wall through which we can fire, and there are areas of the wall that can be easily breached. If you want my honest opinion, Paul, not one of us will survive this battle."

Paul extended his hand. "Colonel, regardless of the outcome of this battle, it has been a privilege to serve with you."

After shaking hands with his commander, Paul hurried to the bell tower of the church. The only steps going to the top were a set of ladder rungs that had been set into the inside wall. Paul clambered to the top, then stepped out onto the very narrow ledge and looked toward the west. There was no need to use his telescope. The Mexicans were no more than one and a half miles outside the town. And that meant there was no need to stay here any longer.

Paul climbed back down as quickly as he could, then hurried back to give his report to Travis.

"Colonel, they are upon us!" he said. "They will be in the town by noon!"

"I'm glad all the civilians have left. Spread the word, Captain," Travis said. "We will withdraw to the Alamo Mission now."

The Texians who had been quartered in the town now began moving into the mission. Paul saw Captain Almaron Dickinson ride up to the front of his house.

"Susanna!" he called.

Susanna came outside, carrying their young daughter, Angelina.

"Give me the baby, climb up onto the horse behind me, and ask me no questions," Dickinson said in short, anxious words.

Susanna did as she was ordered, and asked no questions.

By late afternoon, everyone was inside the Alamo. When the Mexican troops marched into San Antonio, they found the town completely deserted. Their first act was to raise a blood red flag, then have their trumpeter play "The Deguello."

Travis, Bowie, Davy Crockett, Captain John Forsythe, and Paul were standing on the firing platform that Green Jameson had built for the riflemen. There were also some cannon mounted there and Captain Dickinson, the artillery officer, was standing by the largest piece in the Alamo's arsenal.

"What is that music they are playing?" Travis asked.

Bowie was sweating profusely, though the weather was cool. He wiped his face with a handkerchief before he answered.

"It is called 'The Deguello.'"

"Well, now, it's just real nice of them fellers to serenade us like that," Davy Crockett said.

"It's not exactly a serenade, Davy," Bowie said. "At least, not one you would want to take pleasure in. It's the Mexican way of telling us *Se rendir ahora, o mataremos a todos ustedes.*"

"What does that mean?" Travis asked.

"It means no quarter. Surrender now, or they will kill all of us," Bowie said.

"Colonel, what do you say we answer them?" Paul asked.

"Answer them how?" Travis replied. "We don't have a trumpet."

"No, sir, but that doesn't mean we can't make a little noise," Paul said, pointing to the cannon.

"Ha!" Travis said. "Is your cannon loaded, Captain Dickinson?"

"Yes, sir, it is."

"Fire away."

Smiling, Dickinson pointed to his cannoneers, and one of them put a flame to the touch hole. The cannon roared, and they watched as the big, black ball hurled toward the massed Mexicans.

"Colonel, that was a bit premature, don't you think?" Bowie asked.

"How so?"

"I've sent Major Jameson to negotiate with Santa Anna."

"Negotiate?" Travis replied angrily. "Negotiate what?"

"An honorable surrender," Bowie said.

"Colonel Bowie, you had no right to do that without my permission," Travis said.

"Permission? I thought we were co-commanders, Travis," Bowie said.

"All right, let me reword that. You had no right to negotiate for surrender without first discussing it with me. And I remind you, that there is nothing honorable about surrender," Travis said.

An hour later, Jameson returned from his negotiations. Travis and Bowie were still at odds over the fact that Bowie had sent him out in the first place.

"What did he say?" Bowie asked.

"Here is what he said," Jameson replied, showing the co-commanders a note.

> *I reply to you according to the order of His Excellency, that the Mexican army cannot come to terms under any conditions with rebellious foreigners to whom there is no recourse left, if they wish to save their lives, than to place themselves immediately at the disposal of the Supreme Government from whom alone they may expect clemency after some considerations.*
>
> *Jose Bartres, for His Excellency*

"So, what do you think now, Colonel Bowie?" Do you see any way remaining to salvage our honor?"

"Captain Dickinson, have your men reloaded the cannon?" Bowie asked.

"They have."

"I say, let the cannon be our answer."

Travis extended his hand toward Bowie. "Jim," he said, "may we put aside our differences now, so that we can conduct this fight, not only as soldiers of honor, but as friends?"

"Bill, I relinquish any claim I may have had for co-command of this garrison, in return for a claim of friendship," Bowie said.

"I am honored to call you my friend," Travis said. He and Bowie shook hands, even as the cannon fired again. This time the ball struck a Mexican wagon and sent the pieces of it scattering. It also left three of the soldiers lying facedown on the ground.

In response to the cannon, the Mexicans let loose a veritable barrage of cannon fire. More than twenty balls came whistling over the walls to land on the plaza where they rolled quickly across the ground until stopped by the wall on the opposite side. Not one cannonball had any effect.

The Alamo—Thursday, February 24, 1836

Paul was on the parapet along with Forsythe, Dickinson, Crockett and Travis as the sun came up. A soldier climbed the ladder to report to Travis.

"Colonel Travis, Colonel Bowie sends his regards, sir, and says he is unable to join you, as he cannot leave his bed. He says that he puts all trust and faith in any decision you may make with regard to defense of this post."

"Please return my greetings to Colonel Bowie, and express my wish that he recovers from his illness."

"He ain't goin' to get no better, you know," Crockett said after the soldier left. "What he has got is the ague. I've seen it before, and them that has it, purt' nigh always wind up a' dyin' from it."

"Yes, well, at this point it does not make very much difference, does it?" Travis replied. "There aren't any of us going to get out of this alive, except perhaps Mrs. Dickinson and the baby. And then, only if Santa Anna isn't a complete devil."

Travis looked over at Captain Dickinson, and saw the expression on his face. "I'm sorry, Almaron, I shouldn't have given voice to my thoughts."

"That's all right, Colonel," Dickinson said. "Susanna and I talked about this before she chose to stay on."

"I don't mean any disrespect, Almaron, but that seems to me like a rather foolhardy thing for her to have done," Jameson said. "I mean staying on here like she done."

Dickinson chuckled. "That's not the first fool-hardy thing she ever did. When she was fifteen, she was to be a bridesmaid at the wedding of her closest friend. But instead of being a bridesmaid, she ran off and got married the night before."

"That must have been a surprise to her friend," Forsythe said.

"Yes, sir, I reckon it was," Almaron said. "Seeing as how the man Susanna ran off with was the same man her friend was to marry."

"You?" Jameson asked. "You are the man her best friend was to marry?"

Dickinson nodded. "Yep. That's how we wound up in Texas. We didn't figure anyone in Tennessee would want anything to do with us again."

Paul laughed. "That was probably a smart move for both of you," he said.

"Hey, Davy," one of the Tennesseans called.

"Yeah, Jim, what is it?"

"There's a Mexican feller sort of sneakin' up on us. He's behind that tree yonder. Is it all right if I shoot 'im?"

Crockett looked at Travis, and Travis nodded.

"Go ahead, Mr. Rose, take your shot," Crockett called back.

The marksman, James Rose, who was also the nephew of President James Madison, licked his thumb, rubbed the front sight, then raised the rifle to his shoulder, aimed, and fired. The rifle boomed, and the Mexican scout tumbled down from behind the tree. The Texians had drawn first blood.

Chapter Two

On the morning of the twenty-fifth, Texian look-outs on the parapet reported that at least two hundred Mexican soldiers had crossed the San Antonio River in order to take cover in the abandoned buildings that were nearest the Alamo walls.

"We can't let them stay there, Colonel," Paul said. "That's way too close."

"I can get them out of there with artillery fire," Dickinson offered.

"I hate wasting the powder on so few," Travis said. "We are going to need it a lot worse, later on."

"Suppose I get a few volunteers to go with me," Paul suggested. "We can sneak out there and set fire to the buildings."

"My boys can provide cover fire for 'em, Colonel," Crockett said.

"All right," Travis agreed. "How many men will you need?"

"No more than five or six, I would think."

"I'd like to go with you, Paul," Forsythe said.

"I don't know," Travis said. "I don't like the idea of having two of my captains on the same risky mission."

Forsythe laughed.

"What's so funny?" Travis asked.

"Colonel, we're all going to be killed anyway. What does it matter if you lose one or two of your officers a few days earlier?" Forsythe asked.

Travis laughed as well. "I guess you're right," he said. "All right, you men do what you have to do."

Fifteen minutes later, Paul, Forsythe, and five other volunteers ventured outside the walls. Once outside, they used an irrigation ditch for cover and concealment, which allowed them to get to within twenty feet of the first line of huts. All were carrying burning torches, and at a nod from Paul, they darted out to the huts, set them afire, then darted back to the ditch.

Not one of the Mexicans had discovered them, and they were all the way back to the wall by the time the Mexicans had discovered the fires. As the Mexican soldiers left the burning huts, Crockett's men opened fire on them. Two of the Mexicans were killed and four were wounded as they retreated back to San Antonio.

The Texians on the wall cheered.

"Colonel, do I have your permission, sir, to send a couple more calling cards toward the Mexicans?"

"Fire away, Lieutenant Dickinson," Travis replied.

The guns boomed, the thunder of their firing rolling out across the plain toward the river. The men on the walls tracked the two balls and saw one of them hit a house that had been confiscated by several of the Mexican officers. Again, the Texians cheered.

The Alamo—Tuesday, March 1, 1836

Early that morning a company of thirty-two men arrived from Gonzales, sneaking into the Alamo by the back postern. This brought the garrison's strength to one hundred and eighty men.

The arrivals were greeted with cheers and huzzahs. Travis shook the hand of Captain Albert Martin. "We are glad you are here, Captain," he said. "When will Fannin and the others be here? Quickly, I hope, for there isn't much time remaining."

"I fear, Colonel, that my thirty-two men and I are the only ones coming."

The smile left Travis's face and his shoulders drooped. Lowering his head, he pinched the bridge of his nose and was silent for a long moment.

"Then I wish you had not come at all, Captain," he finally said.

"Why would you say such a thing?" Martin asked, surprised at the response.

"Because all you have done I fear is lead your brave men to their deaths."

"Is the situation here really that bad?" Martin asked.

"It is that bad."

Martin looked down at his men, who were now being welcomed by the other Texians inside the compound.

"It doesn't matter," Martin finally said after a long pause. "All of my men are volunteers, bound to come here and help. If we all die, at least it will be for a cause that is greater than the sum total of our lives."

Once more, the Mexicans began playing "The Deguello."

"There is that infernal tune again," Jameson said. "Almaron, you think you could find where that fella is standin' and throw a cannonball at him?"

"No tellin' where he is, Major," Dickinson answered.

"I know how to get rid of him," Travis suggested.

"How?"

"We'll get Sergeant McGregor and his infernal bagpipes, and Davy and his screeching violin and have them play a song together. We'll fight fire with fire or, in this case, noise with noise."

A few minutes later the pipes and fiddle began to play, and though many of the men often teased them about their music, they welcomed it now as it did manage to drown out the accursed Mexican trumpeter. The mood of the men improved. Several began singing along with the music, and laughter was heard.

"That was a good move, Colonel," Paul said. "It's good to hear the men laughing again."

"Yes, it is. But it is, truly, laughter from hell," Travis said.

"Well, sir, I reckon I had better get busy," Jameson said. "The Mexicans have been shelling us for more'n a week now and some of the cannonballs have done a bit of damage. I'll get some men together and start makin' a few repairs."

"I tell you what else I would like for you to do," Travis said. "I want you to put some gun emplacements inside the walls."

"Inside the walls? What good are they going to do inside the walls?" Jameson asked.

"They will do us a lot of good, Green, if the Mexicans actually breach our walls."

"Oh, yeah," Jameson said. "I guess I wasn't thinkin' none."

"I wonder how much grapeshot we have?" Travis asked.

"Ha!" Jameson replied. "I have thought about that. We'll have as much as we need."

"How so?"

"I've been cuttin' up horsehoes, bits of steel, nails, everything I can get my hands on. When we fire that at a bunch of men, it'll cut 'em down like mowin' wheat."

"Good idea, Green," Travis said.

"It won't stop them though, will it?" Jameson asked.

"Nothing will stop them," Travis said. "But their victory will be a pyrrhic one. They will pay so dearly that it will be a stain on their national memory for as long as it will be a glorious chapter of our own."

The Alamo, Friday—March 4, 1836

Word got out that Travis was going to send another courier, and this time, under the urging of some of his officers, he decided to let any of the men who wanted to, to write a letter back to their families.

"John," Paul said to his friend. "Travis is sending out another courier. Why don't you volunteer to go?"

"Why don't you?"

"You've got family," Paul said. "I don't."

Forsythe shook his head. "All I have is a brother. I'm staying."

"That's family," Paul said.

"Damn, I thought you might say something like, 'That's awfully brave of you, John.' I mean seeing as I'm volunteering to stay and all."

"That's awfully brave of you, John."

Forsythe laughed. "He is sending Major Seguin, I've already heard. Seguin is Mexican, and the colonel figures he'll have a better chance. But I am going to write a letter to my brother."

Half an hour later, Isaac Millsaps, one of the men who had come in with Captain Martin, approached Paul.

"I was wonderin', Cap'n, if you would read this here letter I wrote," he said. "I wrote it to my wife, but bein' as she's blind, she'll have to have someone else read it to her. I'm wantin' to see what someone else might think of it. What I mean is, I wouldn't want to be writin' nothin' that is embarrassin' to Mary."

"I'll be glad to read it for you, Mr. Millsaps," Paul replied.

My dear, dear ones,
 We are in the fortress of the Alamo, a ruined church that has most fell down. The Mexicans are here in large numbers. They have kept up a constant fire since they got here. All our boys are well and Captain Martin is in good spirits. Early this morning I watched the Mexicans drilling just out of range. They was marching up and down with such order. They have bright red and blue uniforms and many cannons. Some here at this place believe that the main army has not come up yet. I think they is all here, even Santa Anna. Colonel Bowie is down sick and had to be to bed. I saw him yesterday and he is

*still ready to fight. He didn't know me from last
spring but he did remember Washington. He tells us
all that help will be here soon, and it makes us feel
good. We have beef and corn to eat but no coffee. The
bag I had fell off on the way here so it was all spilt. I
have not seen Travis but two times since he told us
that Fannin was going to be here with many men
and there would be a good fight. He stays on the wall
some but mostly to his room. I hope help comes soon
'cause we can't fight them all. Some says he is going
to talk some tonight, and group us better for defense.
If we fail here get to the river with the children. All
Texas will be before the enemy. We get so little news;
we know nothing. There is no discontent in our boys.
Some are tired from lack of sleep and rest. The
Mexicans are shooting every four minutes but most
of the shots fall inside and do no harm. I don't know
what else to say. They is calling for all letters. Kiss
the dear children for me and believe as I do that all
will be well and God protects us all.*
                    Isaac

*If any men come through there tell them to hurry
with the powder for it is short. I hope you get this
and know I love you all.*

"There is absolutely nothing to be embarrassed
about, Mr. Millsaps. I think this is a fine letter," Paul
said, returning the letter to the writer.

"Only except we ain't really goin' to be gettin' no
help from the outside, though, are we?" Millsaps asked.

"What makes you think that?" Paul asked.

"'Cause we was the last ones to get here, remember? If Fannin was really comin', he woulda been

here by now." He pointed to the letter. "I just wrote that in the letter, 'cause I didn't want Mary to worry none. I don't hold with lyin', but sometimes it seems like maybe that's the best thing you can do."

Millsaps's letter, as did John Forsythe's and all the rest of the mail, went out with Major Seguin. Seguin was a Mexican, fighting with the Texians. A day earlier, one of the Mexican officers had ventured too close to the Alamo and had been shot. A couple of the defenders went outside the wall and dragged him in. Sequin donned his uniform before leaving and as Paul and the others watched from the parapet, they saw him returning salutes of the Mexican enlisted men as he rode, casually, through their ranks. Half an hour later, Paul spotted him through his spyglass, now well clear of the Alamo and the Mexican soldiers who surrounded it.

The Alamo—Saturday, March 5, 1836

Early in the afternoon Travis called for an assembly of every man in the compound. Everyone responded to his call, even Bowie. Bowie was too weak to get out of bed, but he had two men carry him out into the plaza. Out on the plaza preparations had been made for the final defensive stand: Trenches had been dug, two cannons, each one already loaded with the fabricated grapeshot were in place, as were additional stores of powder and shot.

"Gentlemen," Travis said. "I think it is now clear to all of us that there will be no troops coming to our relief. That leaves us but three choices. We can surrender to the Mexicans, we can attempt to sneak out in the middle of the night, or we can stay and fight. The red flag and the playing of the 'Deguello' suggest to me that even if we did surrender, we would, no doubt, be summarily executed. There are now five thousand Mexicans surrounding us, so any attempt of a mass breakout is likely to be futile. In my opinion, that leaves but one option, and that is to stay and fight. I wish I could tell you that that option holds some hope for us, but the truth is all I can promise you is a valiant death. But I believe, sincerely, that what we do here will inspire our fellow countrymen. Falling in battle will bring us immortality because I've no doubt but that we will be remembered for as long as there is a Texas."

Travis had been holding his saber in his hand as he was speaking, and he now drew a line in the sand, then stepped back.

"I ask that all who agree with me make their commitment known by stepping across this line."

Forsythe started toward the line but Bowie called out to him.

"No, Captain Forsythe, don't you step across that line!" Bowie shouted.

Captain Forsythe and the others looked at Bowie in surprise.

"I intend to be the first one across that line," Bowie insisted. "But I can't get out of bed. A couple of you fellas are going to have to carry me."

Two men grabbed Bowie's bed and carried it across the line, then everyone else rushed across and a loud cheer went up.

* * *

The final commitment of the men seemed to act as a catharsis. The absolute knowledge that they were going to be killed eliminated the fear of being killed and for the rest of the day the men laughed and joked. Crockett and McGregor played music and the men sang. At first the singing was raucous and off-key, but eventually four or five men found a song that they all knew and their voices blended in harmony. Recognizing the song, Sergeant McGregor joined in with his bagpipes as everyone else gathered around to listen in reflective silence.

> *Amazing Grace, how sweet the sound*
> *That saved a wretch like me!*
> *I once was lost, but now am found,*
> *Was blind but now I see.*

"Beautiful music, isn't it?" Paul said to John Forsythe.

"Yes, but it makes me think of my brother, Gordon."

"How so?"

"You should hear him sing, Paul. Gordon has a wonderful, tenor voice. Why his singing could make the angels weep."

Paul laughed. "My singing could make the angels weep as well," he said. "But for an entirely different reason."

At ten p.m. that night the Mexican artillery bombardment stopped. Paul was up on the wall with Captain Forsythe when the shelling ceased. The moon was nearly full, but it was covered by clouds so that visibility was quite limited.

"The artillery has stopped. I think they will be coming tonight," Captain Forsythe said.

"I think you are right."

"Without the artillery, though, I expect most of our men will be sleeping," Forsythe suggested.

"Let them sleep while they can," Paul said. "It isn't like the Mexicans are going to sneak into camp."

Captain Forsythe chuckled. "You've got that right," he said.

The two men quit talking for a moment, but that didn't mean they were silent. From the town, and the encampment, they could hear the conversations of the Mexican soldiers, though they were too far away to actually be able to understand what they were saying. From time to time a peal of laughter would be heard, and someone, somewhere in town, was playing a guitar. Whoever it was was quite good at it, and the music floated across the distance between them, beautiful in its melancholy.

"Paul, have you ever thought much about dying?" Captain Forsythe asked.

"No, not really," Paul replied. He chuckled. "Other than the sure and certain knowledge that we are all going to do it."

"Yeah," John said. "Only thing is, I hadn't exactly planned to do it this early."

There was another long pause in the conversation, and when John spoke again, it betrayed the fact that the subject was very much on his mind.

"What do you think happens when you die?" John asked. Then, before Paul could answer, he continued the question. "What I mean is, are you aware of when you pass over to the other side? Does an angel come get you? Are there streets of gold, like they say?"

"I don't know, I think the streets of gold thing may be a metaphor," Paul replied. "But I'm sure we will be aware of who we are, on the other side. And we'll know our family and friends, and they will know us. And something else."

"What else?"

"All right, after we are killed tomorrow, time will no longer mean anything. To those we leave behind, it will seem like a long time until they see us again, but for us, I think a thousand years will be no longer than the blink of an eye, and the blink of an eye can last a thousand years."

"It is kind of hard to wrap your mind around it, isn't it?" John asked.

"Yeah, it is."

John reached over and held his hand out to shake hands with Paul. "Knowing you has made my life fuller," he said. "What do you say, as soon as all this is over, we get together for a drink? There will be liquor in heaven, won't there?"

"Heaven is supposed to be a place of pleasure," Paul said. "And it pleasures me to have a drink with friends, so, yes, I'm sure there will be liquor there."

Outside the walls the Mexican soldiers were told to remove their overcoats, even though it was extremely cold. Then they were given ten rounds apiece for their muskets, and told to prepare to advance.

Inside, enjoying the first night free of bombardment in thirteen days, the Texians slept. On the wall, every two hours, the guard changed as the defenders kept watch through the night.

March 6, 1836

In the east, a faint streak of pink began to creep up from the horizon and the darkness turned to a dull gray.

"*Viva Santa Anna!*" The shout was followed by the blare of trumpets.

"The Mexicans are at the walls!" Green Jameson yelled down, but his alarm wasn't needed as the shouts from a thousand throats and the loud, discordant bleating of the trumpets had awakened all the sleeping Texians.

Travis grabbed his shotgun, then ran toward the wall. "Come on, boys!" he shouted. "The Mexicans are upon us and we'll give them hell!"

Paul was right behind Travis and when he reached the parapet at the top of the wall, he looked out and saw hundreds upon hundreds of Mexican soldiers coming out of the darkness to mass under the wall. That left the attackers at point-blank range, and the defenders opened fire. The cannon roared, and the cut bits of horseshoes, door hinges, and nails slammed into the charging Mexicans, cutting them down like wheat before a scythe.

The Texians' fire was deadly because every shot they fired struck one of the attackers. The problem was that as the attackers massed at the foot of the wall, the defenders had to lean over the wall to shoot down on them, and while they were leaning over to shoot, they were exposed. Colonel Travis leaned over and emptied both barrels of his shotgun, then he pulled back. But he didn't pull back fast enough, and a bullet hit him right in the forehead. He dropped his shotgun over the wall, staggered back, then fell.

"Colonel Travis!" Joe yelled.

Paul took a shot, then sat down on the parapet to reload his rifle. "Joe, how is he?" he called over to Travis's black servant, who had been fighting at Travis's side, and was now knelt down beside him.

Joe looked toward Paul, then suddenly raised his pistol and fired. Paul was startled by it, until the Mexican soldier Joe had shot fell across him.

"Thanks," Paul called. "How is Travis?"

"The colonel is dead, Cap'n," Joe said.

William Travis, the commandant of the Texians who were defending the Alamo, was one of the first to fall.

The fighting continued fiercely for several minutes and the Texian fire was deadly, killing Mexicans by the score with every volley, but eventually the number of attackers proved to be too much. Then, when the north wall was breached, and the postern opened, the Mexican troops began swarming in.

"We have to get off this wall!" Paul shouted. "Pull back! Everyone, pull back to your final defensive position!"

At Paul's orders, the defenders who were on the wall jumped down and started running toward the center of the Alamo. There were two cannons in position, and preloaded. Four of the artillerymen ran toward the two guns and, at two men per gun, they repositioned the guns so that the barrels were trained on the attackers. The guns were fired with a roar, belching smoke and fire, and hurling deadly bits of metal into the ranks of the charging Mexican soldiers. With no time to recharge and reload the guns, the artillerymen hurried into one of the barracks that had been fortified for the last stand.

Almaron had supervised the last volley. Now he ran to the chapel door and shouted in to his wife.

"Good God, Sue, the Mexicans are inside our walls! If they spare you, save my child!"

With the cannons discharged and the walls abandoned, the Texian defenders retreated to the stable, the barracks, and the chapel, where they intended to continue the fight.

Paul joined Captain Forsythe and a dozen others in one of the barracks where holes had been cut to allow them to fire. He saw a Mexican soldier scrambling up the roof of the chapel to take down the Texian flag. The only difference between the Texian flag and the Mexican flag was that the numbers 1824 in the white bar of the red, white, and green flag had replaced the Mexican symbol of the eagle, sitting on a cactus, with a snake in its mouth. The 1824 referred to the Mexican constitution of 1824, which had given Texas autonomy.

Just as the Mexican soldier reached up to take down the flag, Paul fired at him, killing him. Another soldier started up.

"John!" Paul called. "Is your rifle charged?"

"Yes."

"Shoot that son of a bitch!" Paul said, pointing toward the chapel.

Captain Forsythe took aim, fired, and brought

down the second Mexican soldier who was going after the flag. Paul got the third, then Captain Forsythe fired again.

"That's four!" Captain Forsythe shouted to Paul, who was reloading his weapon. "How many do you think . . . ?"

That was as far as Captain Forsythe got before he fell from the shooting loop with a bullet wound in his neck.

"John!" Paul shouted.

Captain Forsythe blinked a couple of times and moved his lips as if to speak, but no words came out.

Outside on the plaza, the Mexicans turned one their artillery pieces toward the barracks where Paul had taken cover, and fired. Paul saw a huge flash of light, heard a thundering noise, then felt a blow to his head.

When Paul regained consciousness, he saw that everyone around him was dead. There was still sporadic firing going on outside, and some shouting. Standing up, he felt a wave of dizziness, and he had to put his hand out to the wall to keep from falling. There was a mirror right next to his hand and as he stared at his reflection, he saw that his face was black from the blowback of all the expended powder.

Then, all the shooting stopped, and he heard loud shouts of "*Viva Santa Anna!*"

His first thought was to see if he could find a loaded weapon, and take out one more Mexican before he was killed, so he started picking up and discarding the weapons he found. But like his weapon, the rifle of every defender had fired its last round.

Then he saw the body of a Mexican soldier, one who was about his same size.

Quickly, Paul changed clothes with the Mexican soldier, not only taking his uniform, but dressing the soldier in his own clothes, lest they find one of their own undressed and get suspicious.

Now, wearing the Mexican uniform, and with his face blackened by the exploding gun powder, he might be able to pass as a Mexican soldier. He stepped over the collapsed wall and walked out into the plaza.

"¿Todos estan muertos en los barracones?" someone shouted to him, asking if all were dead in the barracks.

"Sí. Todos muertos," Paul answered, thankful that he could speak Spanish.

"Viva Santa Anna!" the one who questioned him shouted.

"Viva Santa Anna!" Paul replied, shouting the words with as much enthusiasm as the others.

Chapter Three

Outside in the plaza, he was almost sickened by the carnage he saw. There were dead Texians everywhere, and among the many that he recognized, was Isaac Milsaps, the soldier who had asked Paul to read his letter to his wife.

The Mexicans were dragging the dead Texians to the middle of the plaza where they were stacking them up on top of each other, as if they were no more than pieces of firewood.

He saw Susanna, her baby, Angelina, and Travis's black servant, Joe, being taken out of the chapel. Someone fired a shot, and Susanna cried out when the bullet struck her in the leg.

"Who fired that shot?" Santa Anna called. "Do not harm this brave lady!

"What is your name?" Santa Anna asked.

"I am Susanna Dickinson, wife of Lieutenant Dickinson."

"Your husband is dead," Santa Anna said. It wasn't a question, it was a statement.

"Yes," Susanna replied.

He pointed to the wound in Susanna's leg. "Does it hurt?"

"Yes."

"*Sí, sí*, I'm sure it does."

He signaled to one of his surgeons to treat Susanna, and as he was doing so, Santa Anna saw the baby.

"You have a baby," he said.

"Yes," Susanna replied, wincing in pain.

"You have no man, no one to protect you or support you. What will you do?"

"I will support myself and my child."

Santa Anna pointed to Joe. "You, if you want to live, identify the bodies of Travis and Bowie for me."

Joe pointed toward the north wall. "Colonel Travis is there," he said. He pointed to one of the barracks. "Colonel Bowie is in his sickbed with five dead Mexicans lying beside him."

"Bring all the Texians out here," Santa Anna told one of his officers. "We will burn them."

"*Sí, Excellente.*"

"What about them?" one of the officers asked, pointing to Susanna, her baby, and Joe.

"By the generosity of the *Presidente de Mexico*, the woman, child, and Negro shall live," Santa Anna said.

Santa Anna looked more closely at Susanna. "You are a beautiful woman, Señora. Come to Mexico and live with me. You will be one of my courtesans. It will be a good life. I will see that you are well cared for, and the little girl will be looked after and educated. Would you like that?"

"No!" Susanna replied. "I would not. I want to return to my own people."

If Santa Anna was chagrinned by having his offer spurned, he didn't show it

"Because I am a generous man, I will release you, your child, and the Negro. But before you go, I am going to read a letter to you, a letter I have written to General Sam Houston. After I read this letter to you, I want you to give it to him. Will you do that for me?" Santa Anna asked.

"Yes," Susanna said.

Santa Anna pulled the letter from his pocket, cleared his throat, then began to read in a loud voice, as if performing before an audience.

"The General-in-Chief of the Army of Operations of the Mexican Republic, to the inhabitants of Texas:

"Citizens! The causes which have conducted to this frontier a part of the Mexican Army are not unknown to you, a parcel of audacious adventurers, maliciously protected by some inhabitants of a neighboring republic dared to invade our territory, with the intention of dividing amongst themselves the fertile lands that are contained in the spacious Department of Texas; and even had the boldness to entertain the idea of reaching the capital of the republic. It became necessary to check and chastise such enormous daring; and in consequence, some exemplary punishments have already taken place in San Patricio, Lipantitlan and this city.

"I am pained to find amongst those adventurers the names of some colonists, to whom had been

granted repeated benefits, and who had no motive of complaint against the government of their adopted country. These ungrateful men must also necessarily suffer the just punishment that the laws and the public vengeance demand. But if we are bound to punish the criminal, we are not the less compelled to protect the innocent. It is thus that the inhabitants of this country, let their origin be what it may, who should not appear to have been implicated in such iniquitous rebellion, shall be respected in their persons and property, provided they come forward and report themselves to the commander of the troops within eight days after they should have arrived in their respective settlements, in order to justify their conduct and to receive a document guaranteeing to them the right of enjoying that which lawfully belongs to them.

"Bexarians! Return to your homes and dedicate yourselves to your domestic duties. Your city and the fortress of the Alamo are already in possession of the Mexican Army, composed of your own fellow citizens; and rest assured that no mass of foreigners will ever interrupt your repose, and much less, attack your lives and plunder your property. The Supreme Government has taken you under its protection and will seek for your good.

"Inhabitants of Texas! I have related to you the orders that the army of operation I have the honor to command comes to execute; and therefore, the good will have nothing to fear. Fulfill always your duties as Mexican citizens, and you may expect the protection and benefit of the laws; and rest assured that you will never have reason to repent yourselves of having observed such conduct, for I pledge you in

*the name of the supreme authorities of the nation,
and as your fellow citizen and friend, that what has
been promised you will be faithfully performed."*

He folded the letter and handed it to Susanna as he said his name as the signatory of the letter.

"Antonio Lopes de Santa Anna, El Presidente of the Republic of Mexico and General-in-Chief of the Army of Operations of the Mexican Republic."

By now a wagon had been brought up, and Santa Anna had two of his soldiers help Susanna into the wagon, then hand Angelina, her child, up to her. Joe climbed into the driver's seat and took the reins.

"You have my guarantee of safe passage," Santa Anna said.

Paul had watched it all transpire from within the ranks of the Mexican army, hiding in plain sight by virtue of the Mexican uniform he was wearing. He was glad that Santa Anna was releasing Joe for being a noncombatant, even though nothing could be further from the truth. Paul had seen Joe fighting alongside Travis when he was killed.

As the wagon started toward the open front gate, Paul turned away for fear that one of them might recognize him and, inadvertently, give him away. Shortly after the wagon left, several Mexican soldiers left as well, most of them brandishing souvenirs of the battle. Travis had not carried his saber with him up onto the parapet, but Paul knew where it was. He grabbed it, not only to preserve it, but to make him appear no different from the other souvenir hunters who were passing through the gate.

The others were yelling slogans and battle cries of victory as they left the Alamo, and Paul, not to be outdone, held the sword aloft and shouted: *"Tengo la espada del comandante!"*

For the next several days, Paul, who had neither horse nor weapon, had to dodge Mexican patrols, as well as find his own source of food and water. He was still wearing the uniform of the Mexican soldier, because he had nothing else to wear. And, at this point, the uniform made him wary of encountering Mexican or Texian. The Texians might shoot him as an enemy soldier; the Mexicans might shoot him as a deserter.

He had been out for two weeks when he encountered one of General Sam Houston's patrols. That would not have been a problem for him, had he not still been wearing the uniform of a Mexican soldier.

"Please take me to General Houston," Paul said as the two men held their pistols leveled toward him.

"Oh, we intend to do that all right," one of the two soldiers said. "Then we're goin' to hang you for what you Mexicans did at the Alamo and Goliad."

"Hell, Sergeant Forsythe, let's hang him now," one of the others said.

"Gordon? Are you Gordon Forsythe? John Forsythe's brother?"

Sergeant Forsythe looked surprised. "How do you know John?" he asked.

"John was my closest friend. I am not Mexican. I am Captain Paul Nelson of the Texas volunteers. What happened at Goliad?"

"He don't sound like no Mexican," one of the soldiers said.

"You never can tell," another said. "They's some Mexicans that can talk English as good as I can. This feller may just be a Mexican claiming that he know'd your brother."

"If I were Mexican, would I also know that you have a fine tenor voice?" Paul asked. "And that your singing could make the angels weep?"

"What the hell is he talking about?" the first soldier asked.

"He knew my brother," Gordon said.

"How do you know?"

"Because my brother is the only one who ever said that my singing would make the angels weep."

"Thank you," Paul said. "I was beginning to get a little worried."

"Tell me, Nelson, how is it that you are wearing a Mexican uniform?" Gordon asked.

"I put one on after the battle at the Alamo. It was the only way I could get away."

"You ran from the Alamo, did you? You left my brother and one hundred and eighty good men to die while you saved your own hide?" Sergeant Forsythe asked.

"Hell, mister, you would 'a been better off iffen you had been a Mexican soldier. I got more respect for one of them than I do for a coward," one of the other soldiers said.

"I didn't leave a hundred eighty good men to die," Paul said. "They were dead when I left. What happened at Goliad?"

"All of Fannin's men were killed," Sergeant Forsythe said. "That's what happened."

"In battle?"

"No. Fannin surrendered to them, and the Mexican bastards murdered them all," Gordon said. "Come on, we'll take you to General Houston and let him decide what to do with you."

"We can find out soon enough whether we have a coward or a hero in our midst," Houston said. "Sergeant Forsythe, go find Travis's man, Joe, and bring him to me."

"Yes, sir," Gordon said.

A few moments later, Paul saw the big, muscular black man who had been at Colonel Travis's side during the fight at the Alamo. When Joe saw Paul, he nodded.

"Cap'n Nelson," he said. "It is good to see that you again, sir."

"You know this man?" Houston asked Joe.

"Yes, sir, I know him. He was at the Alamo."

"Did he run?"

"If he run, Gen'rul, he didn' run till after all the fightin' was done. I seen him there durin' the worst part of the fightin'."

Houston nodded, then stuck out his hand. "It's good to have you with us, Captain Nelson," he said. "See my quartermaster. He will find something more fitting for you to wear."

"Thank you, General," Paul said. "And thank you, Joe."

"Captain, I'm sorry I suspected you," Sergeant Forsythe said.

"If I had been in your place I would have been just as suspicious," Paul replied.

"My brother spoke highly of you in his letter."

"Your brother was my closest friend," Paul said. "I was with him when he died."

"You men," Houston said to the men who brought Paul to him. "And you, Captain Nelson, and you, Joe. I want all of you to keep quiet about Captain Nelson escaping the Alamo."

"Why is that, General?" Gordon asked.

"Right now, all the men believe that everyone was killed at the Alamo. I intend to use that as a rallying cry, not only to inspire our soldiers, but all of Texas. Promise me, Captain Nelson, that you won't say anything about this to anyone else."

"Very well, General," Paul said.

The others, when charged, also responded in obedience.

"I know that, right now you do not understand. It will come out later, and Captain Nelson will get his due. But for now, I want a hundred eighty-*nine* heroes, not a hundred eighty-eight and one who escaped."

San Jacinto—Wednesday, April 20, 1836

Houston and his army crossed over and marched down the right bank of Buffalo Bayou to within half a mile of its confluence with the San Jacinto River. Here, the army was protected by timber and the bayou, while before them was an open prairie.

Later that morning, as Houston's scouts had told him, Santa Anna came marching across the prairie with drums beating and flags waving, almost as if he and his army were on parade. The only nonmilitary part of the assembly was Santa Anna himself, who was riding in a grand coach, pulled by six white horses.

With him in the coach was a young, nearly naked woman.

"There they are," Houston said. "Gentlemen, let us send them a calling card." He pointed to his artillery officer and the two cannons, named the "Twin Sisters," opened fire.

The sudden and totally unexpected artillery fire brought the Mexican column to an instant halt. Santa Anna ordered his troops back to a clump of trees where they formed a battle line.

San Jacinto—Thursday, April 21, 1836

The day dawned bright and beautiful. The plain was dotted with a colorful profusion of blue bonnets, Indian paintbrush, and Mexican gold poppies. Houston had under his command seven hundred and fifty men. They were facing a force of twice their number. The Mexican soldiers were well armed, well drilled, and flushed with pride over the victories they had enjoyed for the previous few weeks against the Texians.

Houston used a spyglass to look across the plain to the Mexican encampment. Closing the glass he turned to the man next to him.

"Deaf," he said to Deaf Smith, one of his most trusted scouts. "I want you to destroy the bridge the Mexicans crossed yesterday. That will trap them on this side, and prevent any further support from coming up."

"Yes, sir," Smith said, calling two more men to come with him.

Half an hour later, Smith returned with the report that the bridge had been burned.

"Gentlemen," Houston said to his officers who were surrounding him. "Today our nation is born. Let us advance upon the enemy."

Houston mounted a white horse and rode in front of his army. Some of his soldiers were mounted, but most were following him on foot. Paul, now wearing the uniform of a captain in the Texas army, was one of those afoot, walking in the front rank, right behind Houston, who was riding his horse no faster than his men could walk.

Across the San Jacinto Plain the Mexican army, tired from their long march, and secure enough in their strength that they couldn't imagine they would be attacked, were taking their afternoon siesta. All the officers were in tents, the enlisted men were spread out on the ground, and the weapons, unloaded, were neatly stacked. When Houston and his army approached to within seventy-five yards, Houston twisted around on his horse and looked back toward Paul.

"Captain Nelson," he said. "To you shall go the honor of firing the first shot."

At that moment, Paul saw a Mexican officer step out of his tent. Whether the Mexican had heard something, or he had some intuition, Paul didn't know, but he saw the expression of surprise on the officer's face, just before he shot him.

Paul's shot rallied the rest of Houston's army and they rushed forward with the shouts of "Remember the Alamo" and "Remember Goliad" ringing from their throats across the entire line.

* * *

Less than half an hour after Paul fired the first shot, over seven hundred Mexicans lay dead, and another seven hundred and thirty were captured. Nine Texians had been killed in the battle, and Houston had been shot through the ankle when his horse was shot from under him. The second horse he mounted was also killed, but Houston pressed the battle until the last shot was fired.

When one of the Mexicans, wearing the uniform of a private, was brought into the Texas camp, several of the Mexican prisoners, seeing him, saluted.

"*El Presidente!*" they shouted.

"I'll be damned," one of the Texians said. "We got ole Santa Anna hisself."

"Kill the son of a bitch!" someone shouted.

"Yeah, let's string the bastard up!"

"No!" Paul shouted, stepping between Santa Anna and the men.

"What do you mean no? Hell, Cap'n, I'd think you would want the son of a bitch dead more than anyone else, bein' as you was at the Alamo."

"General Houston wants him alive," Paul said. "If we kill him, we've accomplished nothing. If we keep him alive, we can end this war and gain our independence this very day."

Paul and the others took Santa Anna over to Houston who was, at the moment, lying on a blanket under a tree with his bandaged leg slightly elevated.

"How is your foot, General?" Paul asked.

"It hurts like hell," Houston replied with a grimace.

"We have something that might make the pain go

away," Paul said. He pointed toward the Mexican in the private's uniform.

The Mexican came to attention and saluted.

"I'll be damned," Houston said. "You're Santa Anna, aren't you?"

"*Sí*, Señor Houston, I am general of the army, and president of the Republic of Mexico. I expect, out of regard for my rank and position, that you will be gracious in your victory."

"As you were at the Alamo? As you were with Colonel Fannin and his men at Goliad?" Houston replied angrily.

"I can get a rope, General!" one of Houston's soldiers called. "You just give me the word and I'll string the bastard up right here and now."

"Please!" Santa Anna said. "Do you not understand? I am the president of my country! Would you treat me like a common criminal?"

"I know of no common criminal who isn't your superior," Houston said. "Sit down."

Santa Anna looked around for a moment, then remained standing.

"I said sit down!" Houston repeated, more forcefully this time.

"No one has provided a chair for me," Santa Anna complained.

"Sit on the ground."

"Surely, you do not expect the Napoleon of the West to sit on the ground like a common soldier?" Santa Anna complained again.

Houston looked around until he saw two privates. "You two men, come here," he ordered.

The two privates approached him.

"I want one of you on one shoulder, and the other

on the other shoulder of this—this contemptible piece of filth—and I want you to make certain that he sits down."

Grinning, the two privates forced Santa Anna down to the ground.

Houston presented General El Presidente Antonio Lopez de Santa Anna with a paper and pen.

"You will write and sign exactly what I dictate," Houston said.

A few minutes later, Houston read what Santa Anna had signed, then he smiled.

"Gentleman," he said. "We are no longer Texians. From this day forward, we are Texans."

He held the paper aloft.

"Men!" he shouted. "The independence of Texas is won!"

Chapter Four

Amarillo—Saturday, June 15, 1912

After the dedication of the statue, a reception was held in the ballroom of the Capitol Hotel on the corner of Fourth and Pierce Streets. The high school band had left after the dedication, but the city had hired an orchestra and they were set up on a small, raised platform at the back of the ballroom.

They were playing ragtime music and all the young people were dancing. Fancy was sitting alongside the dance floor, tapping her foot in time with the music.

"Come on, Grandma," young Tyler Chapman said, coming over to reach out to her. "They're doing the fox-trot. You can do it. It's a cinch!"

Tyler was Tom and Cindy Nelson's sixteen-year-old great-grandson.

"The fox-trot? I thought you said they were doing the kangaroo dip."

"No, that was the dance before this one. And the one before that was the Crab step."

"Heavens," Fancy said. "Is this a ballroom, or a zoo?"

Tyler laughed. "It's a ballroom," he said.

"You don't want to dance with an old woman," Fancy said. "Why don't you ask Ethel Good?"

"She won't have anything to do with me," Tyler said.

"What makes you think that?"

"Because she is so pretty, and because she has danced with just about every boy in here. She could have anyone she wants. Why would she want to dance with me?"

"Her great-grandmother and I have been friends for many years," Fancy said. "And she told me that Ethel thinks you are quite the handsome young man."

Tyler beamed. "Really?" he said. He looked over toward Ethel and saw the pretty, young, blond-haired girl standing alone.

"No one is with her right now," Fancy said. "I would think this would be the perfect time for you to ask her."

"I will!" Tyler said.

"Wait," Fancy said. She licked her fingers, then reached up to smooth an errant lock of Tyler's hair. "Now," she said.

Several minutes later, Gretchen Good, escorted by her grandson, came over to sit beside Fancy.

"Can I get you anything, Grandma?" Gretchen's grandson asked. "Punch? Tea? Coffee?"

"No, thank you, dear, I'll be just fine here with my old friend. You run along and have a good time."

"What a nice young man," Fancy said.

"He has been a joy," Gretchen said. She was holding a fan, and began fanning herself. "I swear, I don't think those overhead fans are doing a thing," she said.

"It's just warm because there are so many people here," Fancy said.

"I suppose so." She nodded toward the dance floor. "Don't Tyler and Ethel make a nice looking couple, though?"

"I think they do. But of course, I might be prejudiced," Fancy said.

"Wouldn't it be wonderful if they got married?" Gretchen asked. "That would carry on our little group of freedom pioneers for another generation."

"Yes, it would."

"It was a nice dedication to Captain Nelson," Gretchen said. "I know that my father would have enjoyed it. I like to think that Captain Nelson sort of represents all of us. Just think, one hundred years from now, in twenty- twelve . . ." she paused. "Do you think they will say twenty-twelve, or two thousand twelve?"

Fancy laughed. "Heavens, Gretchen, that's not anything I have ever thought about. And we certainly won't be here to worry about it."

Gretchen laughed as well. "No, I don't suppose we will. But, someone will be here, and in two thousand twelve, as they look at that statue, they will think about us."

"I suppose they will," Fancy said.

"Do you remember? What it was like then, I mean. Do you think about it?"

"Oh, yes," Fancy said. "I think about it quite often."

Natchitoches Parish, Louisiana—Monday, June 3, 1844

Fancy Darrow's hair was so black that, like the wings of a starling, it would sometime send off flashes of blue and purple in the sunlight. Her eyes were brown, overlaid with a matrix of gold. Her cheekbones were high, her lips full, and her skin flawless. Her exotic looks made her, in the opinion of many, the most beautiful young woman in Natchitoches Parish, if not in the entire state of Louisiana.

Fancy's father, Thomas M. Darrow, master of Eagle Lair Plantation, had so doted on his daughter that he arranged for her to be educated in Macon, Georgia, at the Georgia Female College. Tom had been devoted to his daughter, who was raised without a mother. That is why when she learned, two weeks ago, that her father had died, her grief was almost inconsolable.

The situation was made worse by the fact that she was away at school and did not get back home in time for the funeral. And when she did get home she found, to her shock, that Eagle Lair and all its property, fixed and moveable, was being sold by the parish sheriff at a court-ordered estate sale. There was already a large crowd of potential bidders gathered on the place when Fancy rode up in a hack she had hired in Natchitoches.

"But why?" Fancy asked. "Why is everything being sold? Was my father in debt?"

"He was not in debt, but he died intestate," Sheriff Cramer said. "His estate is being sold and all proceeds will accrue to Natchitoches Parish."

"But, even if he left no will, wouldn't it all come to me? I know that my father had no other living relatives."

"Even if he had left everything to you, you would not be able to own it," Sheriff Cramer said.

"What? I don't understand? Why wouldn't I be able to own it?"

"Because you are a colored girl. Now, go take your seat with the other slaves."

She felt as if the entire world had just exploded in her face.

"What did you say?" she asked, the words sounding weak, even to her own ears.

"I said you are a colored girl," the sheriff said, his words dripping with contempt. "Now, go over there with the other slaves and take your seat like I told you, or I'll have one of my deputies take you over there."

"Fancy, honey, come with me," Doney said. Doney was the big black woman who had practically raised Fancy.

Fancy, now too stunned to talk, too stunned to make any decision, allowed Doney to lead her over to one of the three long, backless benches, where the slaves of Eagle Lair were sitting.

"Doney, what was he talking about?" Fancy asked. "He said that I am colored." Fancy held her arm out and looked at it.

"Bless your heart, darlin', yo' pappy should have told you about it long ago," Doney said.

"Told me what?"

Doney put her arm around Fancy and pulled the young woman to her ample bosom. She began patting Fancy gently on her back.

"Lord, chile, when you was but a baby, there's lots of times I held you just like this, patting you on the back just after I nursed you so's you would spit up and not get the colic."

"You nursed me?"

"That I did, chile, that I did," Doney said.

"Doney . . . are you my . . . mother?"

Doney laughed. "Oh, Lawd no, chile, I sure would be proud to be, but I ain't yo' mama. I nursed you 'cause I'd just give birth to a baby that died, so I had milk. Yo' mama was a fine, beautiful lady named Tricia Mouchette. She was the most beautiful lady they was in the *Maison de Beauté*. That means House of Beauty, and ever'one there was a beautiful lady, only yo' mama, she was the mos' beautiful of 'em all."

"Everyone there? Doney, was this a house of sin?"

The smile left Doney's face and she frowned at Fancy. "Don't you be sayin' yo' mama was a sinner. She didn' have no choice. She was an owned girl, don't you see. She had to do what she was told to do."

"She was colored?"

"Yo' mama was what they call a quadroon. She wa'nt no darker'n you. You are an octoroon. You are one-eighth black and seven-eighths white."

"How did I wind up here?" Fancy asked. Her head was spinning as she tried to process the information Doney was giving her. "Was the man I called father, actually my father?"

"Yes, he was yo' pappy. He fell in love with Tricia, and she be in love with him, too, but bein' as she was a colored girl, they couldn't get married. Yo' papa tried to buy Tricia, but the House of Beauty wouldn't sell her. So, he paid enough money so she didn't have to be with nobody but him, and he come to see her most ever' day. Then, you come along. Only Tricia died while you was bein' born. Your papa bought you, and he bought me, too, seein' as I worked at the House of Beauty."

"You mean you were also a . . ."

Doney interrupted her with a laugh. "Lawd no, chile," she said. "I be as ugly then as I be now. Wouldn't no white man of means pay to bed me. I was just a house slave that looked after all the beautiful ladies. And yo' papa, he buy me just to look after you. And that's what I've done all these years."

"Oh, and I love you for it, Doney," Fancy said as she embraced the large black woman. "I have always loved you."

"And I love you, too, chile, just as if you was my own," Doney said. "I think the Lawd know'd what he was doin', allowin' me to raise you right after I lost my own baby. Here I was, filled with milk, and a mamma's love with nobody to give it to, till you come along."

Doney and Fancy's conversation was interrupted by a whistle being blown by Sheriff Cramer. He blew it several times until all conversation everywhere ceased.

"Ladies and gentlemen," the sheriff said when all were quiet. "I'm goin' to read the judge's order declarin' this auction to be legal, then we'll commence the auction itself."

Sheriff Cramer cleared his throat, then began to read.

"Now come this day, Wednesday, March 12, in the Year of our Lord 1845, I, Emil P. McMurtry, Judge of Probate in and for Natchitoches Parish, Louisiana, do hereby declare that the will left by Thomas M. Darrow be declared null and void by reason of the race of the named heiress. Therefore the estate of Thomas M. Darrow is to be the property of the parish. To that end, the sheriff of said parish will cause to be held an auction wherein all property of the Thomas M. Darrow estate will be sold in whole and in part to the highest bidder. Said property will include land and all buildings thereto attached, all furnishings, paintings, crockery, clothing, machinery and equipment, and all livestock to include slaves, horses, cows, pigs, and chickens.' "

After Sheriff Cramer finished reading the judge's order, he cleared his throat, then looked over toward Myron Beck, the auctioneer.

"Mr. Beck, you may commence the auction."

Beck nodded toward the sheriff, then stepped onto the platform to face the very sizeable crowd.

Fancy sat with the other slaves, watching numbly, as the men and women, neighbors and, she thought, friends, bid frenziedly for Eagle Lair and all her father's possessions. She could not help but stop the tears from flowing when she saw Mildred Byrd hold up one of Fancy's dresses in front of her. Mildred and Fancy had long been rivals, and this seemed the ultimate hurt.

"I saw Fancy wear this at the Christmas ball," Mildred said. "I heard her pa paid just a ton of money for it. And to think that I got it for fifty cents." Mildred looked over at Fancy and stuck her tongue out at her. "You aren't so high and mighty now though, are you, miss colored girl?"

The auction continued, but so numb was Fancy to everything that was happening, that she felt as if she were outside her body, looking on with only detached interest. After everything else was auctioned off, the auctioneer began with the slaves. When Doney was bought by Chris Malone, Fancy and Doney hugged.

"Don't you worry, Fancy," Malone said. "I'm going to make certain Doney has a good home."

Chris Malone and Tom Darrow had been the closest of friends.

Malone disappeared with Doney and was gone for quite a while as the bidding continued for the other slaves. Finally, after every acre of land, every piece of equipment, every stick of furniture, every item of clothing, and every other slave was sold, it came down to Fancy. She was the last piece of her father's property to go on the auction block, when the sheriff came over to where she was sitting.

"Come on, girl, it's time for you to get up here so all the folks can look at you," he said.

"They have been looking at me all day," Fancy said. "In fact, they have been staring at me."

"Don't give me any trouble now, girl," Sheriff Cramer said gruffly. "Get up here like I said."

Fancy got up from the long bench, the last one sitting there, then walked with the sheriff up onto the platform.

"Turn around, girl," the auctioneer said. "Turn around so everyone can get a good look at you."

"Make her strip down, Beck," someone shouted. "So's we can get a good look at her!"

Fancy felt her face burning. Good Lord in heaven, they weren't actually going to make her strip down naked, were they?

Most of the men laughed, but several of the women called out in protest.

"I'm not goin' to do that," Beck said. "She looks so much like a white girl that if I was to do that, it might offend the sensibilities of the ladies in the audience. But you can get a good look at her the way she is."

"How do we know what we're seein' is real without she strips down?"

"If you can't tell by looking at her, then it wouldn't make any difference to you anyway, because you are blind," Beck said.

Again, the men laughed.

"This girl has got a good education. She would make a good nursemaid for children, and as you can see, she is strong and in good health. She would make an outstanding personal servant for your wife. So now," the auctioneer continued, "we come to the last item of this auction. I'm going to open up bids on this colored girl, known as Fancy."

"You sure she's a colored girl?" someone asked. "She sure don't look colored to me."

"Mr. Gilmore," the auctioneer said. "Would you please explain the circumstances as to how we discovered that this girl is colored?"

A short, bald, fat man climbed up onto the little elevated platform, then turned to address the crowd.

"As many of you know, I bought Charles Dillard's law office after he died. Dillard had been Tom Darrow's lawyer. After Darrow died, I started goin' through all the files Dillard had on him when I found a bill of sale for Fancy Darrow. Well, I've known Fancy Darrow since she was just a little girl. We've all known her, and watched her grow up to be the beauty that she is. So you can imagine my shock and surprise when I found papers showin' that his daughter, Fancy, was colored. Turns out she was born to the colored prostitute Tricia Mouchette. Tricia was a slave woman belonging to the proprietor of the *Maison de Beauté* in New Orleans. When that slave woman had a baby, the baby was bought by Tom Darrow. On the bill of sale, it states that Tom Darrow believed himself to be the colored girl's father. He never granted Fancy manumission

Dana Fuller Ross

because she was his daughter and he didn't think he would have to. But according to the 'one drop rule of invisible blackness' established by law in the 1830s it clearly states that 'the issue of a slave mother is also a slave.' Therefore, Fancy is not only a Negress, she is a slave. And as such, she is property belonging to the estate of the late Tom Darrow, and thus can be bought and sold just as any other slave can be."

Gilmore sat back down as there were several murmurs of surprise and shock in the crowd.

"And to think that when she was a child, I let her sleep in the same bed as my Cora Jean," one woman said. "Why, I never would have done that if I had known she was colored."

"She don't look colored to me, I don't care what anyone says," one of the others in the crowd said. "And it don't seem right to me to sell her like as if she was colored."

"The law says she is colored, so she is colored," Sheriff Cramer said. "Mr. Beck, please get on with the auction."

"Who will open the bidding?"

"Five hundred dollars," someone shouted.

"Six hundred," another called.

Fancy recognized the voice of the second bidder, and looking into the crowd she saw Chris Malone.

"Seven hundred fifty dollars!" the first man called out, raising the bid.

"And who might you be, sir?" Beck asked. "You will pardon me for inquiring, but I know the gentleman who is bidding against you, and I know that he is good for the money. I do not know you."

"I'm Felix Connor from New Orleans," the man replied. Connor was dressed more elegantly than anyone else in the crowd. He had slicked-back, dark hair, and a pencil-thin moustache. "I am the current owner of *Maison de Beauté,* and I assure you, sir, I do have the money."

"Is it your intention to make a prostitute of this girl if you buy her?" Beck asked.

"It is."

Beck looked over at the sheriff. "We hadn't really considered anything like this," he said.

"It is legal," Connor insisted.

The sheriff nodded. "He's right; it is legal, which means he has every right to bid on her."

"It just doesn't seem right, to do something like this to his daughter," Beck said. "We all knew and respected Tom Darrow. I mean, it is one thing to make a house girl or a nanny out of her. But to make her a prostitute? That's just not right."

"She is a slave girl," Connor reminded him. "And she was born to a prostitute, to be a prostitute. Now I bid seven hundred and fifty dollars and no one has topped that, so the girl belongs to me."

"One thousand dollars," Chris Malone shouted.

Now gasps of surprise rippled through the crowd. One thousand dollars seemed an enormous amount of money.

"One thousand, five hundred dollars," Connor replied.

"Two thousand dollars," Malone said.

"Five thousand dollars!" Connor said.

The last bid shocked everyone into silence, and they all looked over at Malone to see how he was going to respond. Fancy looked at him as well, pleading with her eyes. She didn't know what Malone wanted with her, but it had to be better than the fate awaiting her if Connor won the bidding contest.

Sadly, Malone shook his head, then looked down.

"Five thousand once, five thousand twice, five thousand three times," the auctioneer said. "Sold to Mr. Felix Connor for five thousand dollars."

Several of the men gathered around Connor then, and began questioning him.

"What are you going to do with her?" one of the men asked.

"First thing I'm goin' to do is break her in myself," Connor answered. "I am going to teach her how to pleasure a man, you understand. Then, when I've got her broke in real good, I am going to put her to work. She'll draw high dollar and I expect to make my money back on her before the first month is out."

The other men laughed.

"How much are you going to charge for her, Mr. Connor?" someone asked.

"I don't know. I may have an auction for the first man. You have to admit, somethin' that pretty is worth payin' a lot for."

"Hell, I'll give you a hunnert dollars right now to let me be the first," one of the men said.

"I'll give you two hundred and fifty dollars," Chris Malone said.

"You?" Connor said. "You want to bid for her? An old man like you?"

"I do," Malone replied.

"Ha! And here I thought you were being noble. Turns out you are just a dirty old man, and you wanted her all for yourself," Connor said.

"Can you blame me?" Malone asked. "Look at her. Have you ever seen anyone more beautiful?"

"No, I haven't," Connor said. "And I have been around beautiful women all my life. Two hundred and fifty dollars, huh?"

"Yes, but when I say first, I mean first. I want her before you."

"No, I ain't goin' to do that," Connor said.

"Five hundred dollars," Malone offered.

Fancy was shocked. Malone had been her father's best friend, and had just promised her that he would give Doney a good home. Now he was bidding for her, and not to own her, but to take her to bed.

"I don't know," Connor said.

"Hell, Connor, it ain't like he's goin' to break her or anything," one of the men said. "What damage can an old man like him do? I expect she'll still be as good after he gets through with her as she was before he started."

"Do you have five hundred dollars on you?" Connor asked.

Malone took the money from his pocket.

"If you had ten people like him, you'd get your money back right away," one of the other men said.

"Yeah, you're right," Connor said. He took the money. "All right, you can have her."

"I want her overnight," Malone said.

"Where will you go?"

"Nowhere. We'll stay right here. I know the man who bought Tom's house. I can make arrangements with him."

"All right. Make arrangements for me to stay here as well, and it is a deal."

After making arrangements with the man who bought the house, Malone, Connor, and Fancy went inside. Fancy's face was burning with embarrassment as she saw the expression on the faces of all the men who were watching. Most of these were men that she had known for her entire life, but never before had she seen anyone look at her the way they were. They looked like hungry dogs being shown raw meat.

She didn't speak until she was inside the house, with the door shut behind her.

"Those men," she said with a shudder. "I did not like the way they were looking at me. Their eyes, they looked so evil."

Connor laughed. "It might look evil to you, girlie, but to me it looks like money. Every one of them will be willing to pay money to have you. Not as much as this man did." Connor held up the five hundred dollars Malone had given him. "But you'll bring a pretty penny, that's for sure."

"Are we going to stay down here and talk all day? Malone asked. "I paid for this girl, and I intend to enjoy her."

Connor laughed again. "You are a surprising old man," he said. "Who would have thought that someone as old as you would be so randy?"

"Don't let this white hair fool you, Connor," Malone said. "If the woman is young enough and pretty enough, I can match any man."

"Ha, I don't believe that for a minute. I think you wanted her all night, because it's going to take you that long to get the job done."

"I'm tired of talking about it," Malone said. "Come on, Missy, let's go upstairs."

Fancy could not keep the tears from sliding down her cheeks. This man had been her father's best friend. How could he do something like this to her?

When they reached the top of the stairs, she

started, automatically toward the bedroom that had been hers.

"No," Malone said. "This one." He pointed to a bedroom at the back of the house, the bedroom that had been Doney's bedroom.

"But that's—" Fancy started to say.

"The one I want," Malone said, interrupting her.

As soon as they got into the room, Malone turned around and locked the door behind them. Then he walked over to the window and looked down. When he turned away from the window, he was smiling.

"Dry your tears, little one," he said gently. "I'm here to help you."

"What?"

Malone took two hundred dollars from his pocket and gave it to her.

"There is a ladder up to this window," he said. "When you climb down to the bottom, my man, Harley, will be there to meet you. He is going to hide you under a tarpaulin on a wagon that is taking away some of the things I bought at the auction. Don't move, or make a sound, until he tells you it is safe."

"Oh! Oh, Mr. Malone, please forgive me! I thought . . . "

"I know what you thought, darlin'," Malone said. "I had to make you think that for it to be believable. Now, go quickly."

Fancy gave her benefactor a warm hug of thanks. Then Malone raised the window and helped Fancy climb through. A moment later, she reached the wagon, and laid down on the wagon bed as Harley spread the canvas over her.

Chapter Five

It was dark when Harley lifted the tarpaulin to let Fancy out of the wagon.

"Where are we?" Fancy asked.

"This be Mr. Byrd's place," Harley said. "You can stay here for the night."

"No, I can't," Fancy said. "Mr. Byrd was at the auction. Mildred was there, too. They wouldn't let me stay with them. They would turn me in if they saw me."

"You don' be stayin' in the fancy house with Mr. Byrd," Harley said. "My mama be one of the slaves here. You stay in her cabin."

"But I can't stay there forever," Fancy said. "Why don't you take me to town? I'll buy a stagecoach ticket."

"You gots to remember that you a runaway slave now," Harley said. "An' mos' likely the slave catchers will be lookin' on all the stagecoaches to see can they find you," Harley said. "Maybe you be lookin' white, but you a darkie, and if the slave catchers catch you, they might lay on to you with a bullwhip."

"But what will I do? Where will I go? I can't stay here forever."

"You let my mama take care o' that," Harley said.

Lights were burning brightly in the big house as the wagon passed through the front gate. A fine, white marble chip roadbed made a huge U-shaped driveway in front of the house. Fancy saw a large, spreading, live oak tree in the front yard, and remembered that when she was much younger, and her relationship with Mildred was much better, that they often played on the ground under that tree.

The wagon did not go onto the marble chip driveway, but turned left onto a dirt road that led around behind the corral, stable, and carriage house. The carriage, with the team now detached, sat in front of the carriage house. In the dark, its color could not be seen, but Fancy knew that it was green, with the letter "B" in gold gilt, on the door on each side.

Behind the barn stood a dozen or so small, unpainted cabins. Fancy had never been back here. She knew about the cabins, of course, but they were always on the periphery.

She heard singing. She had heard the singing before, had even sat out on the veranda sometimes at night to listen to the music. She had always thought it was beautiful, but never before had it seemed as poignant as this.

"Listen to the music," she said. "Isn't it beautiful?"

"They singin' about you, Miss Fancy," Harley said.

Oh! My poor Nelly Gray, they have taken you away,
And I'll never see my darling anymore.
I'm a sitting by the river and I'm weeping all the day,
For you've gone from the old Louisiana shore.

One night I went to see her but "she's gone," the
neighbors say,
The white man bound her with his chain,
They have taken her to Georgia for to wear her life away,
As she toils in the cotton and the cane.

There were lights in the cabins, but contrary to
the bright shining lanterns and crystal chandeliers of
the big house, the lights in the cabins were solitary
flames, either topping homemade candles, or a rudimentary lantern of some sort. Harley stopped his
wagon in front of one of the cabins, and an older
woman, one about Doney's age, came outside. The
moon was nearly full, and her dark skin seemed to
shine silver in the night.

"Here she is, Mama," Harley said.

Fancy recognized her from the times she used to
visit the Byrd Plantation when she was younger. She
didn't realize that she was Harley's mother.

"You are Jimmie Mae, aren't you?" she said.

"Bless your heart, chile, for rememerin' me," Jimmie Mae said. "Now, you climb down from that
wagon and come on inside. Are you hungry?"

It wasn't until that moment that Fancy realized
she *was* hungry. She had not eaten a bite since supper the day before, but this day had been so full of
unpleasant surprises, that she hadn't even thought
about eating.

"Yes, I am hungry," Fancy said. "But I wouldn't
want to be taking any food from your table."

"One thing we do have is plenty of food," Jimmie Mae said.

When Fancy went inside, she had another surprise. Doney was there, waiting for her.

"Doney!" Fancy said, running to embrace her. She had always been close to Doney, but she felt closer to her now than ever before. Doney was the only part of her life that had not been taken from her.

"Sit here and have somethin' to eat," Doney said. "We fixed ham-rice, black-eyed peas, and corn bread for you."

"Oh, Doney, you don't know how good that sounds."

"I know it's your favorite," Doney said.

"Yes. All the time I was away at school, I would think about your wonderful ham-rice and peas and corn bread."

Fancy spent the next several days in Jimmie Mae's cabin, waiting for the opportunity to leave. Because she had only the dress she was wearing when she came back from school, she wore the dull, shapeless clothes of some of the other slave women who were about her size. Then, after two weeks, Jimmie Mae came into the cabin, with a broad smile on her face.

"You will be leavin' at first light in the mornin'," she said. "Harley is takin' a wagon up to Shreveport for Mr. Byrd. You be hidin' on the wagon when he leaves."

"Oh, but what if we are caught? Won't that be bad for Harley?"

"You won't be caught. And here," Jimmie Mae said, showing her a bound bundle.

"What is that?"

"That be three of yo' dresses," Jimmie Mae said. "Miss Mildred bought them, then said she don' want to wear no dresses that's been wore by colored people. She give me the dresses and tell me to burn them."

Even before dawn the next morning, Jimmie Mae shook Fancy awake.

"Wake up, Fancy," Jimmie Mae said. "Harley is hitching up the team now. He'll come to the front of the house but he won't stop, 'cause if he do and someone from the house sees him, they'll be wantin' to know what did he stop for. You'll have to get on while the wagon is still moving."

Fancy nodded her understanding, dressed quickly, and hugged Jimmie Mae good-bye.

"I don't know where I'm going, or if ever I will be back," Fancy said. "But please tell Doney how much I love her. And thank you, for all that you have done for me."

"I will do that," Jimmie Mae said. "Be careful."

They heard the wagon rolling by slowly, and clutching the bound package of her clothes, Fanny stepped outside, threw her package into the wagon, then ran behind it for a few steps before pulling herself in.

"You all settled, Miss Fancy?" Harley asked without turning around.

"I'm all settled," she replied.

"You don't raise up till I tell you it's safe," he admonished.

Fancy didn't answer. She just lay in the bottom of the wagon, and after a few minutes, the sound of the hoofbeats and the rolling wheels, lulled her back to sleep.

"Miss Fancy? Miss Fancy, you still alive back there?" Harley called. His words awakened Fancy from an unexpectedly deep sleep.

"I'm awake," she called back to him.

"You can set up now if you want."

Fancy sat up and looked around. She recognized the area, because she had been to Shreveport before. She knew they still had a long way to go.

"We won't be there until tomorrow, will we?" she asked.

"No, ma'am," Harley said. "Not until tomorrow. We will camp out tonight, but it be all right. You can sleep in the wagon. I'll be under the wagon to per-tect you from wild animals and such."

Fancy smiled. "Thank you, Harley. You are very kind."

"Like I tol' you, Jimmie Mae be my mama," Harley said. "Somethin' happen to you, she be after me like a duck on a June bug. So they ain't nothin' goin' to happen to you."

Shreveport—Saturday, June 8, 1844

Justin Good was a lawyer. After graduating from Yale, he moved to Baltimore where he read for the law under the tutelage of Francis Scott Key.

Following the British victory in Washington, where they burned the capital and forced President Madison and his wife to flee, the British forces under Vice Admiral Sir Alexander Cochrane and Major General

Robert Ross advanced up the Chesapeake to attack Baltimore. General Ross landed at North Point and began advancing overland, while Admiral Cochrane attacked Fort McHenry from water.

Justin Good had joined the army to fight the British and he took part in the battle that defeated the British land forces, and killed General Ross. After the British land assault was defeated, Major Good was sent with his law partner, Francis Scott Key, to negotiate with the British for the release of Dr. Beanes, a civilian who had been captured during the battle of Washington. Because Major Good and Francis Scott Key overheard the British plans for the bombardment of Fort McHenry, they were made to stay aboard the British flag-ship through the night. During the night of their brief captivity, they observed the rockets' red glare, and the bombs bursting in air, and through it all, saw that the flag was still there.

During the night Francis Scott Key wrote a poem to the music of "To Anacreon in Heaven," which he called "The Defense of Fort McHenry." Later, it was changed to "The Star-Spangled Banner."

It had been Key who encouraged Justin Good to go to Texas.

"I will write you a letter of introduction to President Sam Houston," Key said. Key chuckled. "I defended him in 1832, when he was in congress. He and William Stanbery got into an argument that led to a fight. It was almost fatal for Sam. Stanbery pulled his pistol and shoved it into Houston's chest and pulled the trigger, but it misfired. I feel that my letter to him will secure his friendship. And friendship of a president is always a good thing to have."

* * *

Justin Good had that letter secure in the false bottom of his wagon, along with five thousand dollars in gold. Good had assembled a train of twenty wagons, now gathered in Shreveport for the express purpose of immigrating to the new nation of the Republic of Texas.

Two of the wagons belonged to Justin Good. One of the wagons belonged to Otto Hoffman, a German blacksmith. Hoffman had come with his wife, Helga, and his grown daughter, Gretchen. He spoke with a heavy accent, but could understand English and could make himself understood. Good didn't know exactly why Otto and his family had come to America, and were now going to Texas, but he had a pretty good idea.

"Herr Gut. A lawyer you are, jah?"

"Yes, I'm a lawyer."

"Tell to me if the law in Texas would make me go to Bavaria, if the law in Bavaria asks for me?"

"Only if Texas and Bavaria have a mutual extradition agreement," Good replied. "And I would be willing to bet that they don't."

"Jah, das ist what I think, too," Hoffman said.

"Hoffman," Justin said. "I have to ask you, out of consideration for the safety of the other members of the wagon train: What did you do in Bavaria that might make them want to come after you?"

"The man who rape my daughter, Gretchen, I kill," Hoffman said. "If Gretchen is not raped, no danger will I be to anyone in the wagon train."

One of the wagons belonged to Dale Chapman. Chapman had been a soldier, a graduate of the U.S.

Military Academy at West Point. A former captain in
the U.S. Army, he was going to Texas to offer his services to the Army of the Republic of Texas, and was
certain that he would be given the rank of colonel.
He was man of extreme discipline and order, and
Good was glad to have him along, because he felt
that Chapman would be a tremendous asset in main-
taining the order and structure of the wagon train.

When Fancy arrived in Shreveport, she was wearing one of her dresses, and carrying three more. In
addition, she still had the two hundred dollars Chris
Malone had given her. What she didn't have was an
idea of where she would go, or what she would do
next, until she learned that a wagon train was making up to go to Austin, Texas. She had to cross the
Red River to find the wagon company, which was
busily making final preparations for their upcoming
trek. Larders had been filled with bacon, flour, beans,
potatoes, coffee, and sugar. Canvas covers were being
tightened, and here and there wheelwrights were fitting steel rims onto the wheels.

It was Emma Presnell who saw the beautiful young
woman standing off to one side, looking on pen-
sively, clutching a bound package.

"Dewey, look at that girl," she said to Dr. Presnell.
"I wonder what she wants."

"There's only one way to find out," Dr. Presnell said.
"Go ask her."

Emma, who was an attractive woman in her early
forties, washed her hands because she had been han-
dling potatoes. Then wiping her hands on her apron,
she walked over to confront the girl. As she approached

the young woman, she couldn't help but be struck by her beauty. That made it even more curious as to why she was here.

Fancy saw the woman coming toward her, and she felt a moment of apprehension. Was the woman coming to tell her she must leave? She was mollified, however, when she saw that the approaching woman had a smile on her face.

"Hello, dear," the woman said. "Are you lost?"

"I don't think so," Fancy said. "Not if this is the wagon train that is going to Texas."

"That is where we are going, all right."

"I would like to go with you," Fancy said.

"Oh, well I'm sure Mr. Good would be happy to have another wagon join us. He is the wagon master."

"I don't have a wagon," Fancy said.

"You don't have a wagon?"

"No, ma'am."

Emma stroked her chin for a moment. "Well, that might make it more difficult," she said.

"I was afraid of that," Fancy said, the expression on her face showing her disappointment. "I'm sorry to have bothered you." She turned to leave.

"Wait," Emma called. "My name is Emma Presnell."

"I'm Fancy Darrow."

"Fancy? My, what an appropriate name for someone as pretty as you are," Emma said. "Come with me, I'll introduce you to Mr. Good."

Fancy could have bitten her tongue off. She had not intended to use her real name, but she spoke without thinking. Now, as her pa used to say, "The fat is in the fire." She had given her real name and she was going to have to live with the consequences.

Justin Good was packing grease into the hub of one of his wagon wheels. He was wearing a collarless shirt and buckskin trousers, held up by suspenders. The sleeves of his shirt were rolled up to his elbows, and his hands were black with grease. He was a larger than average man, and even at the age of fifty-two, he had not let the muscle turn to fat.

"My, Justin, what would your Baltimore clients think of you now?" Lucy asked. "They were so used to seeing you dressed in fine suits. And now you look like a laborer."

"I am a laborer, Lucy," Justin said. "And so is everyone else on this wagon train until we get where we are going. Are you not washing dishes, and doing laundry?"

Lucy chuckled. "I am indeed," she said.

Justin saw Emma Presnell coming toward him, with a young woman that he didn't recognize. The young woman was carrying a package.

Justin stood up and wiped as much of the grease from his hands as he could.

"Mrs. Presnell," he greeted her.

"Mr. Good, this young lady is Fancy Darrow. She wants to join our wagon train," Emma said.

"Do you have a driver for your wagon?" Justin asked.

"I don't even have a wagon," Fancy replied.

"Then I don't understand. How do you expect to join a wagon train if you don't have a wagon?"

"I don't know, I suppose I hadn't given it that much thought," Fancy said. "I thought perhaps I could pay someone to let me ride with them."

"Why do you want to go to Texas?"

"I thought there might be a need for schoolteachers there," Fancy said. "I was educated at the Georgia School for Women."

"Are you unable to get a teaching position here in Louisiana?"

Fancy's eyes welled with tears. "My father just died. I have neither mother nor any other relatives," Fancy said. "This place holds bad memories for me. I'm sorry if I bothered you. I will seek some other way."

Fancy turned away, but Lucy called out to her.

"Wait!" she said. Then to Justin she said, "We have two wagons. Ralph is driving one and you are on horseback, so I am driving the other. Miss Darrow can help with the driving, relieving one of us. She could also help with the laundry, and the kitchen work."

Lucy looked up at Fancy, who had stopped when she was called. "Would you be willing to do that?" Lucy asked. "Work for your passage?"

"Oh, yes, ma'am, I would be glad to," Fancy said.

Justin stared at her for a long moment. "Miss Darrow, by trade I am a lawyer, so I am used to asking hard questions. And I'm going to ask one of you now. Are you sure that you are going to Texas to be a teacher?"

"Yes, of course," Fancy replied. Her face registered her confusion over the question. "Why do you ask?"

"I ask, because you are an uncommonly beautiful woman. A woman like you could make a fortune as a prostitute. And while what you do once you reach Texas is none of my business, it is my business what you do as a member of this wagon train. And I am telling you, straight out, that I will not countenance any whoring on this train."

Fancy's face flamed red, not so much in anger over being asked the question, as in the awareness that if Mr. Malone had not helped her to escape, a prostitute is exactly what she would be by now.

"I am not a prostitute, Mr. Good, nor do I have any intention of ever becoming one."

"Justin," Lucy scolded. "How could you ask this young woman such a question?"

"As I said, I am a lawyer," Justin replied. "Asking hard questions is what I do. And for something like this, it is better to get it out in the open right away."

The stern expression left Justin's face, and he smiled and stuck out his hand.

"Welcome to the company," he said.

Fancy took his hand, then jerked it back when she encountered the grease.

"Oh, please, forgive me," Justin said. "I forgot."

Fancy laughed, as did the others, and the initial tension of the meeting was broken.

The next morning all the members of the wagon train gathered for a hearty, communal breakfast of flapjacks and bacon. Afterward, as the women, Fancy included, washed the dishes and packed them away, the men hitched up the teams, composed in almost a one-third mix of horses, mules, and oxen.

There were a total of twenty wagons, so Justin arranged them in two files of ten wagons each. His two wagons were the lead two in the right file. Dale Chapman had been elected—after Justin's rather forceful nomination—as the train captain, and his wagon led the left file. As the train captain he, like Justin, would be on horseback for the thirty days they anticipated they would be under way. Dale's wife, Agnes, would drive his wagon.

Fancy, who had met the rest of the members of the train at breakfast, was riding in the second wagon with Justin's son, Ralph. There were sixty-two members of the train, that number including twenty-two children from infants to Justin's son, Ralph, who was sixteen, and fifteen-year-old Nancy, who was the daughter of Riley and Mary Kemper.

Once the train was in motion, the wagons separated far enough to be free of the dust of the wagon just in front of them. The day was bright and sunny, and there was a gentle breeze from the west, which carried on its breath the aroma of Texas.

The hoofbeats of the beasts of burden made a rhythmic, almost hollow-sounding clop on the hard ground, augmented by the squeak of leather harness, the jangle of tongue and doubletree, and the hum of steel-rimmed wheels rolling across the plains.

"How long before we are out of Louisiana?" Fancy asked Ralph.

"I heard Pa say we would more'n likely spend the first night in Louisiana, and the next night in Texas," Ralph said.

Fancy leaned out and looked back along the train of wagons, almost expecting to see Sheriff Cramer galloping after them. She had one more day to be nervous.

Natchitoches, Louisiana – Monday, June 10, 1844

Chris Malone and Felix Connor were in the Sheriff Cramer's office, each of them filing a complaint against the other.

"I paid him five hundred dollars in good faith, to let me spend the night with Fancy Darrow," Malone said. "I excused myself to go to the toilet, and when I returned, she was gone. He owes me five hundred dollars and I want my money back."

"Five hundred dollars? I paid five thousand dollars for her," Connor said angrily. "Five thousand dollars. And I demand to know what Malone did with her."

"Are you saying I took her? You are free to search my place anytime you want. She isn't there because I didn't take her. And the only reason you are bringing that up is because you want to get out of paying back my five hundred dollars," Malone insisted.

Sheriff Cramer held up his hands. "I don't see as either one of you have enough of an argument for me to act on," he said. "Mr. Connor, Mr. Malone paid you five hundred dollars to have the girl for a whole night, and he didn't have her for the whole night.

"Mr. Malone, if the girl got away while she was in your custody, then I can't see as it is Mr. Connor's responsibility to pay back the money you paid him."

"There, you just said it," Connor said. "The girl was in his custody, and he let her get away."

"I was just using that as an expression," Sheriff Cramer said.

"You are the one who bought her, you are the one who was responsible for her," Malone said. "You owe me five hundred dollars."

"The hell I do!" Connor replied angrily.

Sheriff Cramer held up both his hands.

"Gentlemen, gentlemen," he said. "It looks to me like the girl outsmarted both of you. Neither one of you owe the other anything. You are both out the money. Let this be a lesson."

"I'm not going to be out for long," Connor said. "She is a runaway slave, and I am going to find her."

"I don't care what the sheriff says," Malone said, frowning. "I still think you owe me five hundred dollars."

Malone held the frown until he left the sheriff's office. He had to hold it, otherwise a big smile would have spread across his face. Fancy had made good her escape, and he was held to be blameless.

Connor went to the printer's shop directly from Sheriff Cramer's office.

"I want you to do some printin' for me," he told Curly Latham, owner of the print shop.

"I'd be glad to," Curly said. Curly was completely bald, and had been so since he was a very young man, so the nickname either referred to his locks when he had hair, or it was a purposely misleading nickname, such as calling a very large man "Tiny."

Connor got a piece of paper and wrote out what he wanted, then handed it to Curly Latham. Latham glanced at it, then back at Connor.

"Are you sure the sheriff said the parish would pay this much money to recover a runaway slave?"

"The parish ain't payin' it, I am," Connor said. "I got too much money invested in that girl not to get her back."

"The thing is, you put out a reward this big, some folks might shoot her, then bring her in."

"All right, I'll reword it," Curly said.

He took another piece of paper and filled it out, then showed it to Curly. "Can you do that?"

"Yes, certainly I can do that. Look here, this girl you're lookin' for, it wouldn't be Fancy Darrow would it?"

"It is."

"You sure she is a colored girl? I've known her for her whole life. She sure don't looked colored to me."

"Just do the posters," Connor ordered.

With a nod, Curly set the type, then put it in the frame, inked it, and brought the platen down. Taking off his first page he looked at it, smiled, then showed it to Connor.

WANTED
Alive Only

THE NEGRESS KNOWN AS
Fancy

$1500
to be paid to anyone
who returns her to her owner,
FELIX CONNOR

Chapter Six

Paul Nelson, now a captain in the Texas Rangers, held his hand up and Sergeant Gordon Forsythe and the fourteen Texas Rangers with him stopped. Paul held out his hand.

"Hand me the spyglass, Sergeant," he said.

Gordon drew the spyglass from its holder on his saddle and handed it over to Paul.

"What do you see, Cap'n?" he asked.

"I'm not sure," Paul replied. "It might not be anything more than a dust devil, but I've been seeing dust beyond that ridge for some time now. Enough to make me think that there may be a bunch of Comanche under it."

Paul extended the telescope and held it up to his right eye.

"Do you see anything?"

Paul shook his head. "Nothing but a closer look at the dust," he said, pushing the glass closed and handing it back.

"Cap'n, Kickapoo Creek is just ahead," one of the rangers said. "That would probably be a good place to water our horses."

"Yes, I'd planned to," Paul said.

Paul and the other rangers were armed with the Hall breech-loading carbines, and the Paterson Colt .36 caliber, five-shot revolvers. The five-shot revolvers were newly issued, and this would be the first time the new pistols were employed against the Indians.

They were on the scout for Indians because the Comanche had been raiding isolated farms and ranches, killing the farmers, ranchers, and their families. The result was a population that was growing more frightened of the Comanche, indeed, frightened of anyone who might come around.

They had just finished watering their horses when a dozen Comanche came out of a thicket of trees toward them. The Comanche were coming at a full gallop, and they were whooping and screaming at the top of their voices. Most of the Indians had firearms which they discharged. The other Indians had bows and they loosed arrows.

After their opening volley, the Indians turned around and retreated toward the thicket of trees from which they had come. Suddenly, more than sixty warriors rode out to confront the rangers.

"This way!" Nelson shouted, and he led them in retreat to a shallow ravine. Once in the ravine, the rangers followed the ravine at right angles to the attacking Comanche. Then, riding up to the top of the ridge that ran parallel with the ravine, they had flanked the Indians.

"Fire!" Paul shouted, and all the carbines fired as one, so that it sounded like one sustained roar.

At least four Indians went down, and a couple more were hit. But the Indians, realizing that the rangers would have to reload before firing again, turned toward the Texans and charged, again filling the air with their war whoops.

"Engage with pistols!" Paul shouted, and the rangers drew their pistols, then waited until the Indians, who were now brandishing war clubs, came to within pistol range.

"Now!" Paul shouted, and he punctuated his shout with a pistol shot. The Indian he had selected as his target tumbled from the saddle. The other rangers blasted away with their repeating revolvers. The fact that they were shooting rapid-fire guns decimated the Indians, but a chief began rallying his warriors. Sergeant Forsythe took careful aim at the chief, then fired. The chief, who was holding his right arm over his head, waving his club as he exhorted the others, seemed to jerk in his saddle. He turned toward Gordon with an expression of disbelief on his face. The bullet hole in his chest was clearly visible, and the chief looked down at it, then fell from his horse.

The remaining Comanche retreated, leaving twenty-three dead behind them.

"Magnificent shot, Sergeant!" Paul said. "What are our casualties?"

"Gowdy is kilt, Cap'n," one of the rangers said.

"So is Belshaw," another added.

"Get them on their horses, we'll take them back," Paul said.

With the wagon train

They were only four days on the trail, but already Fancy had gotten into the swing of the routine of the wagon train. She wasn't the only one who was new to traveling in such a way, so she was learning along with almost all of the others. And, because Fancy was very bright, and willing to work, she caught on quickly and was soon an asset, not only to the Good family, but to nearly everyone who was a part of the train.

Each morning the travelers would arise before the sun to begin their work for the day. The first to go out would be the fire-making detail and, since wood was relatively scarce, they had to depend upon dried buffalo dung, which they euphemistically called "chips," as a source of fuel.

Though it sounded bad, in truth it made a marvelous fuel, sustaining a great deal of heat for a long time, and without odor of any kind. The chips were gathered, primarily, by the boys, from twelve to eighteen years of age. That group included Ralph, Justin Good's son. And though he was the son of the wagon master and could have complained about the detail, he did not. In fact, he went about it cheerfully, and with dedication. His attitude, given that he was the son of the wagon master, seemed to instill more of a willingness in the other boys of the train to do their chores as well.

Once the fire was laid, the women of the train all pitched in to prepare a communal breakfast. All the chores were divided, including filling the water barrels, when a source of water was available, washing of dishes, and making the preparations for the next meal. In the meantime, the men would harness up the teams, the fires would be extinguished, and by the time the sun was a full disc above the horizon, the caravan would be under way.

At noon the train would halt for an hour or more to rest the animals, and allow a quick nap for those who could nap under such conditions. The noon meal would be something that could be prepared quickly, such as bacon, corn bread, and leftover beans from supper the night before.

After no more than an hour, Justin Good and Dale Chapman would ride through the scattered and resting travelers, calling out to them.

"Let's go! Everyone to their wagons! We can't lay around here all day!" Justin and Dale would call. The only grumbling at this point was of the good-natured kind. There were no serious questions of authority, or of the need to go on.

Scouts were sent ahead of the train immediately after breakfast each morning, and they didn't rejoin the wagons until sometime around four o'clock in the afternoon. At four, or as close to four o'clock as they could find a suitable bivouac, the train would stop for the day. Often, the scouts, who were on the lookout for Indians or thieves, would find a perfect spot to stop. The perfect spot was one that had a wide, flat area, not only to afford the wagons the opportunity to form into a circle, but would also be close to water, fuel, and a supply of game.

Clem Pace was a very lean, one might almost say, bony, man. Though he was clean shaven, he wore his black hair long and unkempt. His eyes were beady and were set under a heavy brow. His nose was long

and hooked down. His chin jutted out so that in pro-
file, it almost looked as if nose and chin could touch.

Two years ago, Pace had murdered a man and his
wife in Nacogdoches, Texas. He thought he had gotten away with it, but he was seen, caught, and would
have been hanged for the crime if he had not escaped. Now Pace was a slave chaser, and a very successful one. Over the last year he had run down
seven slaves who had tried to escape their bondage,
four men, two women, and a boy of twelve. He was in
a bar in Shreveport when he heard someone talking
about the fifteen-hundred-dollar reward for a runaway slave.

"Fifteen hundred dollars?" he said, interrupting
the conversation. He made a scoffing noise. "I don't
believe it. I ain't never heard of no reward higher
than five hundred dollars bein' paid."

"Can you read, Mister?" one of the conversational-
ists asked.

"Yes, I can read."

The man showed the reward poster to Pace. He
looked at it for a moment, then handed it back.

"I'll be damned," he said. "You're right. What the
hell is so important about this girl that someone
would pay fifteen hundred dollars to get her back?"

"I heard tell that he paid five thousand to buy her
in the first place," the man who had given him the reward poster said.

"Five thousand dollars for a colored woman? Who
in hell would pay that much for a colored woman?"

"You read his name on the poster. It's Felix Connor. You mean you ain't never heard of him?"

"Never have. Who is he?"

"He owns a high-class whorehouse in New Orleans. I think this girl is one of his whores."

"She must be somethin', if he paid five thousand dollars for her, and is willing to pay fifteen hundred dollars to get her back."

"Why are you so interested in this? Are you a slave runner?"

"Yeah, I am. You got somethin' against that?"

"I don't reckon I do, seein' as how it's legal. And I reckon if a slave runs away from his owner, why that's about the same as stealin'."

"Seems odd though, to steal yourself," one of the other men at the bar said.

"You goin' lookin' for this girl?" the first man asked.

"If it pays fifteen hundred dollars I am. Absolutely. I ain't never brought no one in that paid that much."

The slaves used word of mouth, and even songs to help them escape. The word of mouth told them that a lantern hanging on a hitching rail would show a safe place for them to stop to rest, to get food, and to get directions for moving on. These were called "depots," and the people who managed the depots were called "conductors."

One of the songs they would sing while at work had meaning to them, but no meaning at all to the white masters. In fact, the white masters encouraged them to sing because they believed that it lifted the spirits of the slaves and enabled them to work harder. They also believed that as long as they were singing, they knew where they were.

One of the "escape" songs was "Follow the Drinking Gourd."

When the sun comes back and the first quail calls,
follow the drinking gourd.
For the old man is awaiting for to carry you to freedom,
If you follow the drinking gourd.
The riverbank makes a very good road, the dead
trees show you the way,
Left foot, peg foot, traveling on, follow the drinking gourd.
The river ends between two hills, follow the
drinking gourd.
There's another river on the other side, follow
the drinking gourd.
Where the great big river meets the little river,
follow the drinking gourd.
For the old man is a-waiting to carry you to freedom,
if you follow the drinking gourd.

The "drinking gourd" in this case was the Big Dipper, and by following the Big Dipper, they would go north.

Clem Pace was very good at his job. He not only knew many of the depots of the underground railroad, he also knew which depots were authentic, and which depots had been established to trap the runaway slaves so they could be turned in for the reward.

For the next two days, after learning of the high reward being paid for the runaway slave known as Fancy, he visited all the fake depot stops.

"Yeah, I got a colored woman here," Durbin, one of the fake depot "conductors" said. "And she's a fancy one all right."

"Let me see her," Pace said.

"You can see her, but you can't have her without you pay me the fifteen dollars."

"If she is the one I want, I will gladly pay you fifteen dollars," Pace said.

"She's down there, in the cellar," Durbin said. "Just a minute, it's dark down there. You'll have to carry a candle to get a good look at her."

Pace followed Durbin out the back door to an outside cellar door that was on a forty-five-degree slant. The door was chained shut by two chains and padlocks. He unlocked both of the chains, drew them off, then opened the door. The door creaked on its rusty hinges.

"Girl," Durbin called. "Girl, you still alive down here?"

There was no answer.

"Is she dead? I'm not paying anything if she's dead."

"She's alive, all right," Durbin said. "She answers quick enough when I bring food to her. Girl, if you want your meal today, you better answer me."

"I'm here," a small voice said from a far dark corner.

As they walked toward the sound of the voice, Pace and Durbin were enveloped by the small, dim, golden bubble of light that was emitted by the candle Durbin was carrying.

There, huddled in a corner, with her legs drawn up and her arms wrapped around them, was a young black woman, approximately twenty years old. She looked up at the two men with big eyes that gleamed in the light of the candle. Her hair was disheveled, and the shapeless dress she was wearing was torn in several places.

"What's your name, girl?" Pace asked.

"Sally," the young woman answered.

"Sally? You sure it ain't Fancy?"

"Don't know nobody named Fancy," the young woman said.

"I don't think this is the one," Pace said.

"What do you mean? She's a runaway," Durbin said. "That's what you do, ain't it? You chase down runaways?"

"Yeah, but the one I'm lookin' for now is someone special."

"How special? One is about like another'n. I don't never see no difference in 'em."

"The owner is payin' fifteen hundred dollars for the one I'm lookin' for."

"Fifteen hunnert dollars?" Durbin said. "Who would pay fifteen hunnert dollars for a runaway slave?"

"It says on the reward dodger that the one willing to pay that much is a man named Felix Connor."

"Felix Connor? I never heard of him. He don't own no plantations around here, does he?"

"No. He owns a whorehouse in New Orleans."

"Ha!" Durbin said. "So the girl you lookin' for is a whore, is she? You goin' to try her out a' fore you turn her in?"

"I hadn't thought about it," Pace said. "But I might."

Durbin looked at the young woman who was still cowering before them. "You want to try this one out? I'll let you do it for five dollars."

"I ain't got time. I got to find this Fancy girl before she gets too far away."

"You want to take this one back?"

"No. I told you, I got to find the one called Fancy."

"Put the candle there in that bottle," Durbin said and he started unbuttoning his pants. "And don't close the door when you leave. Talkin' about a fancy whore has got me all riled up here. I think I may just try this one out."

As Pace left the cellar, he heard the young woman behind him whimpering in fear and shame.

After checking all the depots, Pace was fairly certain that Fancy had not used the Underground Railroad to make her escape. He began asking around in Shreveport to see if there was any other way she could have left. He started with Dugan's Mercantile Store. They advertised themselves as a store that "Sells goods for all mankind."

Pace knew that if anyone in town had any helpful information, it would more than likely be Dan Dugan.

"They was a wagon train left a few days ago," Dugan said. "They stayed around here for two weeks or more, gettin' ready to leave. They near 'bout bought us out of bacon, beans, flour, and the like."

"Was there a colored woman with them?" Pace asked.

"Not that I saw. But the truth is, they was all made up on the other side of the river, so I didn't get over there, so I don't know as they had any coloreds with 'em or not."

"She may have left with them," Pace said.

"They was quite a few of the townspeople that did get over there where they was camped, for one reason or another. I don't recall any of them sayin' anything about a colored girl."

"How long ago did the train leave?"

"It's been five days now."

"Where were they going, do you know?"

"Oh, yeah, everyone knows where they were goin'. Seems like that's all any of 'em could talk about. They was all headin' for Austin."

"Let's see, they'll be makin' about ten to fifteen miles a day. That would put 'em seventy-five miles from here. And, it'll take me two days to cover that, which will put 'em another thirty miles, so if I leave now I'll catch up with 'em in three days," Pace said.

"You need any supplies before you leave?"

"You wouldn't have any shackles, would you?"

"I've got 'em for the wrists and the ankles," Dugan said proudly. "As many slaves as we got around here, shackles is always a good sellin' product."

"I'll take 'em for the wrists and the ankles," Pace said.

Nacogdoches, Texas—Thursday, June 13, 1844

Tyler Bodine was the kind of man that made people look twice. His skin was chalky white, so was his hair and moustache. The irises of his eyes were pink. He was camped just outside of Nacogdoches, Texas, along with the Hardin brothers, Frank and James. Breakfast was coffee and jerky, and one of the riders, James Hardin, tossed the grounds of his coffee away.

"Say, Ty, how much money do you think there will be in this bank?" he asked.

"At least ten thousand, I would say," Bodine replied.

"How do you split ten thousand three ways?" Frank asked.

"I'll take four thousand, you and James will get three thousand each," Bodine said.

"How come you get more?"

"Because it was my idea," Bodine said.

"I don't have any problem with that," James said. "Three thousand is better than nothing, which is what we've got now."

"Time to quit jawin' and get to ridin'," Bodine said. "We want to get there soon as the bank opens."

Fifteen minutes later, the three men rode into town. All three were wearing long yellow dusters and sombreros with wide brims. They stopped in front of the bank and Bodine and Frank dismounted, leaving James mounted to hold their horses. Pausing for just a moment to look up and down Liano Street, the two men pushed open the door and stepped into the bank.

There were four customers inside, as well as two tellers, and one bank employee who was sitting at a desk just behind a railing.

"Hands up!" Frank shouted as he and Bodine drew their pistols.

"What's going on here?" the man behind the railing said. "How dare you come in here with drawn weapons."

"This is a bank robbery," Bodine said. "Don't anybody move unless we tell you to."

Bodine took a cloth bag from under his duster and handed it to the first teller.

"Fill this up," he said. "Empty your drawer first, then his drawer, then the vault. No Texas star money," he added. "I want gold coin."

The teller just stood there looking at Bodine. Bodine didn't know if he was being defiant, or was just too frightened to act.

"When I tell you to do something, you damn sure better do it!" Bodine said. He shot the teller and the teller fell back.

"You!" Bodine said to the other teller. "Get that sack from him, and fill it up."

"Yes, sir," the teller said, acting quickly.

A moment later, the teller handed the sack back to him. The sack was heavy with gold coin.

"Bank robbery!" one of the customers suddenly shouted, running from the door. "Bank robbery!"

Frank turned his pistol toward the customer and shot him. Then, with the money in hand, the two men left the bank, leaped into the saddles, and galloped out of town.

Although dozens of citizens had heard the gunfire from the bank, and many of them had come out of their homes and places of business to watch the bank robbers ride away, not one of them turned a gun toward the retreating outlaws

Austin, Texas—Monday, June 17, 1844

"Yes, we're certain it was Bodine and the Hardin brothers," Major Rick Miller said. Rick Miller was Paul Nelson's superior in the Texas Rangers. "Nearly everyone recognized the albino, and at least two people on the street recognized the Hardin brothers as they rode out of town."

"All right, at least I know who to go after," Paul said.

"Who do you want with you, Captain Nelson?" Miller asked.

"Right now, I'll only need one man," Paul said. "And I'll take Sergeant Forsythe."

Miller chuckled. "I thought you might. I've already sent for him."

Even as the two were talking, there was knock on the door of Miller's office.

"Come in," Miller called.

Gordon Forsythe stuck his head in through the door. "You sent for me, Major?"

"Captain Nelson is going after the men who robbed the bank in Nacogdoches last Friday," Miller said. "He wants you to go with him. How long will it take you to get ready?"

"I've got mine and the cap'n's horses out front. They're already saddled, the canteens are filled, and there's six days' rations in the saddlebags," Gordon replied. "I reckon it'll take me about fifteen seconds to get mounted."

Major Miller laughed out loud. "I take it that you had an idea that Captain Nelson was going to ask for you."

"Yes, sir, but I was goin' with him whether he asked or not," Gordon said.

Both Paul and Gordon Forsythe saluted Major Miller, then left the ranger headquarters building. True to his word, there were two horses tied up out front.

"What did you mean when you said you were going to go with me whether I asked for you or not?" Paul asked.

"I was just funnin' with the major, Cap'n," Gordon replied. "I knew you was goin' to ask for me."

"And how did you know that?"

"'Cause like you and my brother, me 'n you is tight," Gordon said as he swung into the saddle.

With the train on the Texas Trail

The train was now more than a week into the journey and everyone had established a routine that made for harmonious travel. For two hours each evening, Fancy was conducting school for all the children of the wagon train. It was actually the first opportunity she had of using her education, and she found that she enjoyed it immensely. The children enjoyed it as well and often during the long, boring rides in the wagons, the younger ones, who had no specific duties to perform, would be doing their schoolwork.

Pace had debated with himself whether or not to go into Texas after the wagon train. He was safe as long as he was in Louisiana, because there was no extradition agreement with Texas. On the other hand, if he stayed well away from any settlements, the chances were good that he would not be recognized. And for fifteen hundred dollars it was a chance worth taking. He made the decision to go.

True to his prediction, it had taken Pace three days to catch up with the train. It was midday when he reached them and found them nooning, with the wagons drawn into a circle before him. As he sloped down a long, gentle hill toward them, a couple of riders came out to meet him.

Pace stopped, so as not to give any perception of danger, and he waited until the two riders, one in his early thirties with an erect, very military bearing, and the other, who was considerably younger, reached him.

"You just passing through?" the older of the two riders asked. "Or do you have business with the train?"

"I have business with the train," Pace said. "My name is Pace. Clem Pace."

"My name is Chapman, this is Ralph Good. What sort of business?"

"I'm pretty sure that when you left Shreveport, you had a runaway slave with you. I've come to take her back."

The two men looked at each other in confusion. "What are you talking about?" the older of the two asked. "We don't have any fugitive slaves with us."

"Are you wagon master?"

"No, that would be Mr. Good."

"You?" Pace asked Ralph, obviously surprised by the response.

"My father," Ralph said.

"I wonder if you would take me to him?"

Chapman and Ralph looked at each other, then Chapman nodded.

"All right," Chapman said. "Come along, I'll introduce you to him."

Chapter Seven

"Pa, this here fella is named Pace. He's a' wantin' to talk to you," Ralph said.

All the draft animals had been turned out to forage, and Justin Good was examining the crack on a doubletree to see if it needed replacing.

"All right, I'll talk to him," Justin said. "You go on back with Chapman and keep an eye on the animals."

Ralph nodded, then rode off, leaving Justin and Pace alone.

"What can I do for you, Mr. Pace?" Justin asked. Though he was willing to carry on a conversation, he wasn't willing to waste any time during the noon stop, so even as he asked the question, he continued to study the doubletree.

"I'm what's called a slave runner," Pace said.

That got Justin's attention and he looked up at Pace. "A slave runner? You mean you are one of those men who go after runaway slaves and bring them back?"

Pace smiled. "You've heard of my line of work, I see," he said.

"I don't hold with slavery, Pace. And I have even less regard for a man who would choose slave running as his occupation."

"I know they is those that might not like what I do. But it is absolutely legal. It ain't like I'm a thief or anything like that."

"Why are you here?"

"I'm here 'cause I got reason to believe there might be a runaway slave travelin' with your train."

"We are harboring no slaves," Justin said resolutely.

"I ain't talkin' about no big buck, now. I'm talkin' about a Negress."

"We have no people of color with us, neither free nor bonded, neither man nor woman."

"You wouldn't just be tellin' me that now, would you?" Pace said. "You said yourself that you didn't hold with slavery. How do I know you ain't hidin' the colored girl I'm lookin' for?"

Justin raised up from the doubletree he had been looking at and glared at Pace. His eyes blazed and his jaw tightened.

"You wouldn't be calling me a liar now, would you, Pace?" he asked coldly. "Because I don't think I would like that. No, sir, I wouldn't like that at all."

"No, no, I ain't callin' you nothin'," Pace said, backing away. "I was just commentin' that seein' as how you said you don't hold with slavin', well, you might take a mind to hide the colored girl if she was travelin' with you."

"I told you, there is no one of color traveling with us. But if she was with us, I would not turn her over to you. Perhaps you don't realize it, Pace, but you are in the Republic of Texas. There are no extradition treaties in effect with Texas and any of the states of the United States with regard to runaway slaves."

"Maybe you'd feel different if you know'd how much this here colored girl is worth," Pace suggested. He took the reward flyer from his pocket, unfolded it, then showed it to Justin. "Most especial if I told you I'd be willin' to split half of it with you."

WANTED
$1500
FOR THE NEGRESS KNOWN AS FANCY

by her owner,
FELIX CONNOR

<u>Alive Only</u>

Justin gasped as he looked at the poster. Fancy? Surely that couldn't be the young woman who joined them just before they left Shreveport.

"You have seen her, ain't you?" Pace asked. "I can tell by the way your face looked when you read this."

"No, I was surprised that so much money would be paid for a runaway, that's all. Is that normal?"

"No, sir, and that's the thing. It ain't normal a' tall," Pace said. "That's why I'm lookin' for her. And if I find her, there don't need to be no treaties and such betwixt Texas and Louisiana, 'cause I'm just goin' to take her back."

"What does she look like?" Justin asked.

"I don' know exactly, but from what I heard she's quite a looker. An' I 'spec' she's mos' white. The feller that owns her owns a whorehouse in New Orleans, and this here girl is one of his whores. You ever been in any of them fancy whorehouses in New Orleans?"

"I have not," Justin replied resolutely.

"Yes, sir, well, I have, you see. And here's the thing. Them girls in them fancy whorehouses? Well, most all of 'em is white as you or me. Onliest thing is they are white on the outside. But inside, they got colored blood, maybe half, or only a fourth or somethin'. But that makes 'em colored."

"I assure you, the woman you are looking for is not on my train," Justin said.

"Would you mind if I took a look?"

"I said she isn't on my train. Good day, Mr. Pace."

Pace started to challenge him, then thought better of it.

"All right," he said. "I'm sorry I took up some of your time. I'll just be on my way now."

"Yes, you do that."

Justin watched Pace walk back to his horse, mount, and ride away. He looked back toward a group of women who were washing dishes from the noon meal. Fancy Darrow was standing next to his wife, and when Lucy said something, Fancy laughed. Fancy had only been with them for three days, but already she had made friends with the other women, quite an accomplishment considering that she was young, beautiful, and single.

Half an hour later, the wagons were in line ready to get under way. Justin mounted, then stayed to one side watching as the wagons drove by, looking at each wagon to ascertain that all of them were still fit for travel. When all had passed him by, he rode quickly up through the center of the two files until he reached the lead wagons. At the moment, Fancy was driving the lead wagon, and Lucy was in the second wagon with Ralph. He stared at her for a long moment, though tried not to show it.

Was it possible that this was the Fancy that Pace was looking for? She did join them at Shreveport and, though he knew the background of all the others in the train, he knew nothing about her. He thought about what Pace had told him about the woman he was looking for.

"I don' know exactly, but from what I heard she's quite a looker. An' I 'spec' she's mos' white. The feller that owns her owns a whorehouse in New Orleans, and this here girl is one of his whores."

A looker, and almost white. Justin played the words over and over in his mind.

Pace had also said that the woman he was looking for was a prostitute. Funny he would say that, since that was one of the first things Justin had been concerned about when Fancy joined the train. But she had adamantly denied it. And, she was clearly a very educated woman. Just last night over supper Justin and Fancy had discussed the philosophies of Immanuel Kant and Arthur Schopenhauer. She had more than held her own during the discussion and, because there was no other member of the wagon train who could match Justin's intellectual curiosity, he had much enjoyed the conversation.

Melrose was a bustling little community when Frank and James Hardin rode in a few weeks after having pulled off the bank robbery in Nacogdoches. They were here to meet a man named Lloyd Simms, but that meeting wasn't to be until tonight. They had the rest of the afternoon to kill, so they stopped in front of the Lucky Star Saloon, tied their horses off, and went inside.

It was mid-afternoon so the saloon was quiet, with two men sitting near the stove playing checkers, and another man sitting in a chair that was tipped back against the wall. He had a towel draped around his neck, his arms were folded across his chest, and his eyes were closed.

"Is this place open or not?" Frank Hardin asked, slapping his hand down on the bar.

"Yeah, we're open," the man in the chair said, without opening his eyes. "What do you want?"

"What do you think we want? This is a saloon, ain't it?" Frank said. "What we want is a drink."

The man in the chair got up, then strolled casually behind the bar. Reaching under the bar, he pulled out two glasses and a bottle.

"You didn't ask what kind of drink," Frank said.

"It don't matter. We got only one kind," the bartender replied. "You want it or not?"

"We'll take it."

The bartender poured the liquor into two glasses. "That'll be two dollars in star currency, or four bits American," he said.

"Two dollars Texan or half a dollar American? Ain't you got no pride in Texas?" Frank asked.

"I got pride in Texas. I don't have confidence in the money," the bartender said.

Frank slid half a dollar across the bar, then picked up the drink and tossed it down.

James looked around the saloon as he drank his whiskey. "Where are the women?"

"What women?"

"This is a saloon, ain't it? Don't you have no women here to keep your customers happy and such?"

"It's too early for any of the women," the bartender said. "Business don't start pickin' up till seven or eight tonight. That's when the women come down. They can't make no money before then."

"Yeah, they can," Frank said.

"No, they can't. There isn't enough business."

Frank took a ten-dollar gold piece from his pocket and put it on the counter.

"Yeah, they can," he repeated.

Frank and James spent the entire afternoon with the women they had hired. It wasn't that they were such prodigious performers, it was the fact that they were in a bed, a relatively rare experience for them. Frank had actually gone to sleep, ordering the woman not to leave until he woke up.

When he woke up that evening, he saw the woman sitting in a chair, reading by the light of a candle. "What time is it?" he asked.

"It's about six o'clock, I would think," the woman replied.

"I've got the time here," he said, picking up his pants and reaching into the pocket. When he didn't find what he was looking for, he reached into the other pocket and came away empty again. He looked on the floor where his pants had lain. "Where is it?" he asked.

"Where is what?"

"Where is my watch?"

"I don't know where your watch is."

"You stole it! What did you do with it?" Frank was growing angrier.

"I did not take your watch," the woman insisted.

"Oh, yeah? Then tell me this. How did you know what time it was?"

"I don't know what time it is. I was just guessing, that's all."

"I want my watch, you damn whore!" Frank shouted. He slapped her.

"Please, I didn't take your watch!"

Frank hit her again and again until her nose and lips were bleeding and one of her eyes swelled shut. She screamed the first time he hit her, then tried to cover up, whimpering in fear and pain as he continued to hit her.

"Frank, come on, we've got someone to meet," James said, coming into the room then.

"Where are we supposed to meet him?" Frank asked as he started getting dressed. The woman was lying on the floor in a fetal position, whimpering.

"What did you beat her up for?"

"She stole my watch," Frank said.

"Hell, we'll get enough money from this deal for you to buy a hundred watches," James said.

"That ain't the point. I don't like having things stole from me."

The woman who had been with James came into the room then and, seeing her friend on the floor, moved quickly to her.

"Claire!" she said, shocked at the condition of her friend. She knelt on the floor beside her.

"What did you do with my watch?" Frank asked again, once he was dressed.

"Come on, Frank. We don't have time for this," James said.

The other woman got up from the floor, wet a cloth in the basin, then sat back down and started bathing the blood away from Claire's face.

"All right," Frank said. He started toward the door, then stopped and pointed toward Claire. "Next time I come here, you better have my watch," he demanded.

Claire was still whimpering as the two men left the room, then went clattering down the stairs.

It was dark when they stepped outside, and as Frank started to mount his horse, he saw a chain dangling from his saddlebag. Opening the flap, he saw his pocket watch.

"Well, I'll be damned," he said with a chuckle. He took the watch from the saddlebag and showed it to James. "Here's my watch. I guess the whore didn't take it after all."

Fifteen minutes later, they met Lloyd Simms in the alley behind the hardware store. They were meeting in the alley at night because Simms, who was a dispatcher with the Central Texas Stagecoach Line, did not want to be seen talking with Frank and James Hardin.

"I have information on a coach that will be carrying fifteen hundred dollars in U.S. specie."

"What is 'specie'?" James asked.

"Gold eagles, no paper money," Simms explained.

"Where will this coach be, and when will it be there?" Frank asked.

"Like I told you before, that information will cost you one hundred dollars."

James took out ten ten-dollar gold pieces and

handed them to Simms. "This had better be good information," he said.

"It is good," Simms said. "I took it right off the schedule. The coach leaves here tomorrow, bound for Chireno."

Slade's Place had started as a one-room cabin, from which Emil Slade had sold groceries and dry goods. It was twenty-five miles west of Nacogdoches and fifteen miles from the nearest settlement. And because it stood alone, it had no competition in bidding for the business of the nearby ranches and farms. It also served the traveler well.

A sagging roof here, a bulging window there, a façade of logs and clapboard, it might have been mistaken for a pile of scrap lumber, except for the crudely lettered sign that perched just over the doorway proclaiming it as an inn.

There was one saddled horse tethered to a hitching rail in front of the building, and Paul and Gordon tied their horses there as well. There was one customer inside, probably belonging to the horse outside, and he was sitting at a table, eating beans with obvious relish.

Emil Slade had his back to the door when Paul and Gordon came in. He was putting items on the shelf. "I'll be right with you," he said.

"No hurry, Mr. Slade," Paul said.

Slade stopped stocking his shelf, then turned toward Paul and Gordon. "Captain Nelson and Sergeant Forsythe," he said. "What an honor to have you call on me. What can I do for you?"

"We're looking for Tyler Bodine, and Frank and

James Hardin," Paul said. "If they came this way, like as not they would have stopped here. There's no other place anywhere close by."

"You're right. This is the only place between Nacogdoches and Melrose. And you are right that they did stop here. Or at least the Hardin brothers did. Bodine wasn't with them."

"You're sure it was them?"

"I'm absolutely sure of it," Slade said. "I've seen them before."

"What did you do?"

"I served them food and beer, then I stayed out of their way," Slade said.

"What do you mean, you stayed out of the way?" Paul asked.

"My mama didn't raise no fools, Cap'n Nelson," Slade replied. "I not only know who the Hardin brothers are, I know what they are. I decided the best thing to do was just give them as much room as I could."

Even as he was talking, Slade drew two mugs of beer and set them on the counter in front of Paul and Gordon. "On the house," he said.

Paul put a dime on the bar. "Thanks, but our rules won't let us accept it."

Slade smiled as he picked up the dime. "I know," he said. "I figured this was just a good way to sell the beer."

Paul laughed as he took a long, Adam's apple swallow. Then, as he lowered the mug, he said, "You wouldn't have any idea where they went from here, would you?"

"I thought you might get around to asking that," Slade replied. "From what I could gather, they were headed for Melrose."

* * *

Frank and James Hardin were waiting alongside the pike that ran from Melrose to Chireno. The stagecoach would be coming along soon, and the Hardins believed that it would be carrying fifteen hundred dollars in U.S. currency. They had paid one hundred dollars in gold for this intelligence, so they were reasonably content that the information was correct. Though they normally operated as a gang, for this particular job, they were going to work alone. Fifteen hundred dollars, even if it was U.S. currency, wasn't enough to make a larger split.

Most of the time stagecoach holdups occurred at positions that gave an advantage to the highwayman. Generally, that was at the top of a long grade so that the coach would have to stop for a few minutes to give the team a short rest break. During those stops, the driver and shotgun messenger would be especially alert.

When the coach was on a flat stretch of road, though, and the team was moving along at a brisk, eight to ten miles per hour clip, both driver and messenger were less alert, knowing that the possibility of a robbery was less likely. And it was that very element of surprise that Frank and James Hardin were counting on, as they planned their robbery.

In preparation for the robbery they had chopped nearly all the way through a tree, holding it in place only by the last bit of trunk, and a rope that was tied off behind it. It was their plan to take the tree down at the last possible moment so it would block the road in front of the coach. In the resultant confusion, Frank and James figured they would be able to get the drop on the driver and messenger.

"Frank, what kind of bug is yellow and purple, has two big pinchers comin' out of his head?" James asked.

"I don't know. Why do you ask?"

"Because they's one like that that's just a' fixin' to climb out onto your nose."

Frank slapped at his face, hard, and James started laughing.

"What are you laughing at?" Frank demanded.

"There weren't no bug a' tall," James said. "I was foolin' with you."

"Yeah? Well . . ."

"Hush," James said holding out his hand. "I think I hear the coach a' comin'."

Both men grew quiet, then smiled as they heard the unmistakable sounds of an approaching stage-coach: the clopping of hooves, the squeak of the harness, the ring of quickly rolling wheels, and the shouts of the driver.

"Heah, hosses, heah! Git up there!"

Frank and James hurried to get into position. Frank was looking toward the road, and when he thought the timing was right, he yelled up at James.

"I'm going to give it one last hit with the ax. When I do that, let go of the rope!"

Frank swung the ax and it bit into the remaining part of the trunk, but didn't go all the way through. At the same time, James let go of the rope.

"It ain't fallin'!" James shouted.

Frank hit the tree again, and this time it did start down, but instead of falling across the road in front of the coach, it fell on the coach, striking both the driver and the messenger. It also broke the tongue and freed the horses who, frightened by the crash, galloped on down the road, leaving the wrecked stagecoach behind them.

With guns drawn, Frank and James rushed up to the coach. They saw immediately however, that they didn't need their weapons. The driver and the messenger were both dead. Inside the coach a traveling salesman was groaning in pain.

With no concern for the injured passenger, Frank crawled up on the coach and picked his way around the tree limbs until he found the messenger's pouch.

"What you got, Frank?" James called up to him.

"Gold coins, Little Brother. Gold coins just like the man said."

When Paul Nelson and Gordon Forsythe rode into Melrose, they stopped at the city marshal's office.

"Are you Marshal Harris?" Paul asked, seeing the name carved into a board that was hanging from the wall of the marshal's office.

"That's me," the marshal replied. He noticed the badges the two men were wearing. "Texas Rangers, huh?"

"Yes. I'm Captain Nelson, this is Sergeant Forsythe."

"Are you workin' on that stagecoach holdup already? I knew you Texas Ranger boys were good, but I didn't know you were that good. I just now found out about it myself, and it didn't happen no more'n five miles from here."

"Sorry to disappoint you, but we weren't aware of any stagecoach robbery," Paul said. "We are looking for Tyler Bodine and the Hardin brothers."

"You don't say. Well, sir, could be they are the ones who robbed the coach, seeing as they were here yesterday."

"I know there are wanted posters out on them. If they were here yesterday, why didn't you arrest them?" Gordon asked.

"They was here and gone before I knew a thing about it," Harris said.

"How did you know they were here?"

"One of 'em beat up a woman over at the Lucky Star Saloon. She calls herself Claire, but that probably isn't her real name. Whores pretty much always take on a fake name. I reckon that's so the folks back home never learn what they are doing."

"Where would we find Claire?"

"Like as not, at the saloon," the marshal said. "She not only works there, she lives there. She and a couple other girls have got rooms at the saloon, and sometimes they actually sleep there," he added, laughing at his own, ribald joke.

Paul didn't have any trouble identifying Claire. She was sitting at a table far in the rear, all alone, with a fat lip, one eye closed, and bruises on her cheeks. When he and Sergeant Forsythe stepped over to the table, another bar girl came over to intercept them.

"Honey, you don't want to bother her," the bar girl said. "She's had a bad time of it."

Paul identified himself and Gordon. "We need to talk to her."

"Texas Rangers? Good, I hope you catch Frank Hardin and put him under the jail for what he did to Claire."

"You called him Frank Hardin. What makes you so sure it was Frank Hardin?"

"I used to work at a saloon in Austin. He and his brother came in there often. I knew he was no good, but as far as I know, neither one of them ever beat up a girl before. It's my fault. I should have warned Claire about him."

"It's not your fault, Peggy," Claire said, though her words came out as a mumble because of her cut and swollen lips.

"Why didn't you go to the marshal right after it happened?" Paul asked.

"I was afraid to. I did tell him about it this morning, though, only they were gone."

"You must have heard them talking. Did you hear where they were going?"

Claire shook her head.

"I heard them talking," Peggy said. "I don't know where they are now, but they were talking about meeting someone last night."

"Do you know who they were meeting, or what the meeting was about?" Paul asked. "Could it have been Tyler Bodine?"

"I don't know who they met, or what it was about," Peggy answered. "But I do know where they met. It was behind the hardware store."

"You sure they were going to meet behind the hardware store?" a man sitting at an adjacent table asked. He had been following the conversation closely, and with obvious interest.

"Why do you ask?" Paul asked. "Do you have some information that I could use?"

"Well, if they met behind the hardware store sometime between six and seven o'clock last night, I know who they met."

"How do you know that?"

"Because I went out back to—uh—use the privy," the man said. "And I seen Lloyd Simms comin' from behind the hardware store."

"Did he say anything?" Paul wanted to know.

"Not exactly."

"What do you mean, not exactly?"

"He had a handful of gold coins," the helpful citizen said. "And he was clackin' them together."

"How do you know they were gold?"

"I seen the coins glintin' in the lamplight."

"All I did was tell them the stage schedule," a sweating Lloyd Simms said. He was in the marshal's office and Harris, Paul, and Gordon were interrogating him. Even though he wasn't wearing a collar, he kept pulling his shirt away from his neck. "I make up the schedule for the stagecoach runs. If anyone comes to ask me for information, I give it to them. That is my job, that's what I get paid to do."

"Do you get paid in gold every time you answer someone's question about a stage schedule?" Paul asked.

"And do you always meet with them behind the hardware store?" Gordon added.

"I didn't know they were going to hold it up," Simms said.

"Buchannan and Douglas were killed, Simms," Marshal Harris said. "You worked with those two men every day. You know their families. Can you live with yourself after that?"

Simms pinched the bridge of his nose and shook his head. His eyes welled with tears.

"Nobody was supposed to get hurt," he said quietly.

"Then you did know about it, didn't you?"

Simms shook his head again. "I didn't know anyone was going to be hurt. Nobody was supposed to be hurt."

"It would go easier on you, if you told us where to find them," Paul said.

"I don't know where to find them," Simms replied. "As God is my witness, I don't know where to find them."

Marshal Harris took Simms to the back of his office and locked him in the single cell, then came back. There was a pot of coffee sitting on the stove, and he poured three cups, then handed one to Paul and one to Gordon.

"As long as these boys have been operating in Texas, it would seem to me like the rangers would have located them by now," the marshal said as he slurped some of the coffee over the rim of his tin cup.

"Texas spreads out over 320,000 square miles," Paul replied. "We have 300 rangers. That means one ranger for just over a 1,000 square miles."

"Oh," Marshal Harris said. "I guess I didn't think of that. These men could be anywhere, couldn't they? You may never catch them."

"I'll catch them," Paul said.

It did not escape Marshal Harris's attention that Paul said, "I'll" catch them, rather than "We'll."

Chapter Eight

From Fancy's diary:

I have been accepted by the other members of the wagon train, and for that I can but give thanks to God, and to Mr. Malone, Doney, Jimmie Mae, and Harley for all that they did for me. I am also thankful to Mr. Good for taking me in.

After supper last night, Mr. Good and Mr. Chapman held a meeting where we discussed all the rules that must be followed if we are to have a safe and successful journey. After that, we broke into smaller groups. I was with the families of Mr. Good and Mr. Hoffman. Mr. Hoffman is from Europe, and speaks with an accent, but is very much the gentleman.

Ralph, who is Mr. Good's son, sleeps under the wagon, allowing me to sleep inside the wagon. Through the night I could hear the call of coyotes, the occasional bawl of one of the cows that were closed up inside the circle of wagons, and from time to time, a voice, or a laugh from those who had not yet gone to bed.

As the sun rose this morning, the oxen were driven from inside the wagon ring. The animals were yoked and hitched to the wagons. Then we had a prayer, presided over by the Reverend E. D. Owen, who is a member of the wagon train. In the prayer he asked Divine Providence to guide us.

Then the order to proceed was given and the train got under way. As we progressed across the country, the men walked alongside the wagons controlling the teams of oxen by the expert use of a bullwhip. Those wagons pulled by mules or horses were controlled by reins, handled for the most part by women or children. A wagon train under way produces its own music, the clump of hooves, the creak of leather, tongue, and doubletree, the squeak of moving wagons, and the sound of rolling wheels. There rose from the meadow a gentle breeze which carried upon its breath the sweet perfume of just blossoming flowers.

We made this morning some eight miles I am told, and now we have stopped for a noon break. We do not cook at noon, and many pass the noon meal without eating anything at all, though there are biscuits and bacon left over from breakfast. This is a time of rest for man and beast so I can use this opportunity to . . .

"What are you writing?" Ralph Good asked. Ralph was lying on his back with his hands folded behind his head. He had the root of a grass stem in his mouth and he was sucking on it, as he looked up at the sky. Although only sixteen years old, Ralph was tall for his age. He was very courteous to Fancy, and she felt lucky to be sharing his wagon.

"Nothing in particular," Fancy said. "I'm just doing a writing exercise to keep my mind alert."

"You mean like when I was in school, and the teacher wanted me to write an essay about how I spent my summer?" Ralph asked.

"Something like that, yes."

"Ha! If I was still in school I could sure write an essay about this summer," he said.

"Why don't you?"

"Why don't I what?"

"Why don't you write an essay about what you are doing now?"

"Why? I ain't in school no more."

"No, but some day, when you are an old man, you might want to tell your grandchildren about this."

"Grandchildren?" Ralph hooted. "That's a long way from now."

"All the more reason why you ought to write about it now, so you won't forget."

Suddenly one of the scouts they had sent out on horseback came galloping back to the train.

"Men, to arms!" he shouted. "Women and children, under the wagons! Injuns are coming!"

Chapman, who had military experience, moved quickly to organize the men, placing them into positions with overlapping fields of fire. Everyone was ready when the Indians approached.

There were only about ten Indians, and they were not threatening in appearance. One of them rode out ahead of the others, and threw his lance into the ground. Then, with his hand raised, he rode slowly toward the gathered wagons.

"I don't think they mean trouble," Chapman said. "I'll go out and meet him." He took off his pistol, held it up so that the Indian could see he was disarmed, then rode out to meet the Indian.

From here, Fancy had no idea what they were talking about. Then she saw both Chapman and the Indian coming toward the train. When they arrived, Chapman got down but the Indian remained mounted.

"They want to trade," Chapman said.

"What do they want to trade?"

"Buffalo meat for flour."

"How fresh is the meat?" Emma asked.

"Good question," Chapman said. He looked back at the Indian. "When kill buffalo?"

The Indian looked up at the sun and pointed. Then he moved his arm down in an arc and pointed again.

"Looks like it was about four hours ago," Chapman said.

"Some fresh meat would be good," Justin said. "Ralph?"

"Yes, sir."

"Get one pound of flour from every wagon. We can all spare a pound. We'll have buffalo roast for supper."

"Yes, sir!" Ralph said and, grabbing a cloth bag, he visited each of the wagons, then came back with it. He started toward the Indian, but Chapman held out his hand to stop him. "Wait," he said.

Then Chapman spoke to the Indian. "Bring meat here. We will give you flour." He augmented his request with signs, and the Indian nodded, then rode off.

A few minutes later he and three more Indians returned. They dropped three, buckskin-wrapped bundles. Chapman undid the bundles, then sniffed the meat.

"Give them the flour," he said to Ralph, and Ralph held up the sack.

The Indian who had been their spokesman said, "You will have safe travel." Then, taking the bag, the four of them galloped back toward the others, whooping all the way.

Fancy helped with the chores for the rest of the day. And since some of the chores were unusual when compared with their normal day, she recorded it all in her notebook.

For the rest of the day after trading flour to the Indians for buffalo meat, we set about preparing it. The first thing we did was start a long slow roast of the buffalo hump. This is a large piece of meat that is without bone, and said to be very delicious. I have not yet tasted it, but its cooking fills the camp with a most delightful aroma.

As for the rest of the meat, it has been cut up into long, thin slices, which are then draped from the wagon bows in order to make buffalo jerky. One of the members of the wagon train is from Tennessee, and he has made bear and deer jerky before. He advised the others to dip the strips of meat into brine before hanging it onto the wagon bows. The reason we hang it on bows is to enable the sun to dry it naturally. Tonight the wagons are decorated with slices of meat dangling from bows, strings, and ropes, stretching from the front to the back of the wagons. To look at them now, one would think they are but wagons, gaily decorated with red ribbons.

* * *

On the night of the tenth day out, the wagon train was hit with a storm of rain and such a severe outbreak of lightning that before one bolt would recede, another would strike, turning the night into day. The storm hit just moments after they had made camp in a large flat prairie, and all the oxen, cattle, and horses were scattered by the thunder that sounded like cannon fire. The wind was so high that Fancy thought it was going to rip the canvas covers off, then proceed to tear the wagons to pieces. At the very least, she thought the wagon would be blown over by the wind, and a couple of the wagons were.

Fancy leaned out the back of the wagon and saw young Ralph Good sitting just under it, his knees raised, and his arms wrapped around his legs.

"Ralph!" she called. "Get into the wagon!" She had to scream to be heard. "Ralph! Get into this wagon now!"

Ralph shook his head. "It wouldn't be proper," he said, screaming back against the howl of the wind.

Fancy leaned over and held her hand down. "Don't be silly!" she said. "You climb in here this minute!"

Finally, reluctantly, Ralph reached up to take Fancy's hand, and she helped him climb into the wagon.

As they sat there under the cover, the lightning continued to flash incessantly, and the thunder roared. It seemed to Fancy that the earth itself was trembling. Then the hail started. It banged against the canvas covering and slammed against the wagon itself with an intensity that sounded as if musket balls were being loosed upon them.

* * *

Fancy slept but little that night, if at all. Even after the storm passed and the wind stilled, sleep was impossible because every stitch of clothing, every blanket, and every shawl was soaking wet. When the sun rose the next morning, she stuck her head out of the wagon to behold a sky that was blue and cloudless. The rain was gone, but it looked as if they were in the middle of a lake—a clear pool of water, at least two feet deep, lay upon the ground for several hundred yards in every direction.

"The animals are gone!" Good shouted. "Men and boys, turn out! We must retrieve the animals!"

"Thank you for letting me stay in the wagon last night," Ralph said as he climbed over the back, then let himself down into water that came halfway up to his knees.

"It is your wagon, Ralph. It is I who should thank you."

It was fortunate that a few days earlier they had made buffalo jerky, for on this day that was to be their only sustenance. While all the men and boys were gone trying to locate the animals that had run away in the storm, the women and girls stayed busy back at the wagons. As soon as the sun dried the canvas tops, they were rolled back to make the bows available. Every wagon bow, the tongues and doubletrees, and strings and ropes tied from wagon to wagon were put into service. From those places were suspended every stitch of clothing, every blanket, every shawl, towel, and cloth.

"Oh, my," Edith Couch said as she saw the dresses Fancy was hanging on the line. Edith was a young woman of about Fancy's age, married to Prentiss Couch, a farrier. Prentiss, like every other man and boy, was searching for the animals.

"They are not very practical for something like this, I fear," Fancy replied.

"Why have you such clothes for a journey such as this?" Edith asked.

"My father bought them for me," Fancy said, and she reached out to touch the very dress she had seen Mildred Byrd buy, then discard like so much trash. "He died," she continued. "And these dresses, that he bought me, are all that I have left of him."

"You have not even a watch, or a lock of his hair?"

Fancy felt the tears sliding down her cheeks, and a strong lump in her throat. She shook her head. "I have nothing of him," she said again.

The sun dried the clothes quickly, and everyone's mood improved, though they were still worrying about the men. Were they all right? Did they find the animals? By early afternoon most of the water was gone, and by late afternoon, even the ground began to dry. Then, Fancy heard cries and shouts of joy.

"They are back! The men and the animals! They are back!"

Fancy joined the happy women and girls as they turned out to welcome the men, retuning now with all the animals. That night, with the animals secure, the beds dry, and the night quiet, the entire wagon train enjoyed a deep and restful sleep.

Luna, Texas

Paul Nelson and Gordon Forsythe rode into the town early in the morning. None of the businesses were open yet, though some of the early risers were already at work. The owner of Goodman's Mercantile was sweeping his front porch, already wearing the white apron that would be a part of his uniform for the whole day. A yellow dog lay on the corner of the porch, confident enough in his position that he made no effort to move, so Mr. Goodman accommodated him by sweeping around him.

Paul could smell the hot acrid aroma of lye soap coming from behind the laundry. The blacksmith was stoking his fire, and a teamster was hitching up a team. From the houses came the smell of frying ham, baking biscuits, and brewing coffee. A sign, advertising BOOTS AND LEATHER GOODS squeaked as it swung, gently, in the morning breeze.

Paul and Gordon swept their eyes from side to side, but didn't see anything that raised any alarms. Gordon pointed toward a café whose owner was just turning the CLOSED sign around to OPEN.

"Cap'n, what do you say we get us some breakfast?" he suggested.

"I'd say that was a good idea."

After tying off their horses in front of the café, the two men went inside. It smelled of coffee, biscuits, and various spices. Paul and Gordon were the only two customers, so they took a table in the back of the room, against the wall.

A middle-aged, heavy-set woman came toward them.

"Biscuits, ham, and red-eye gravy," she said. "And coffee. That's our breakfast this morning."

"Sounds good to me," Paul said.

"Me, too."

"Rangers, huh?" the woman said as she brought the coffeepot over and poured two cups.

"Yes."

"Who are you lookin' for?"

"Tyler Bodine, Frank and James Hardin," Paul said.

"I'll have your breakfast out here in just a moment," the woman said.

"Did you see the look on her face?" Gordon said. "She knows something."

"Yeah, she does."

When the woman returned a moment later carrying two plates, she put them down in front of Paul and Gordon without so much as a word.

"Miss could we ask you . . .?" Gordon started to say, but Paul held up his hand.

"Hold it, Gordon," he said. There was a folded piece of paper under Paul's plate and he pulled it out, then opened it.

I don't know nothing about Bodine, but Frank and James Hardin is hidin out at the old Tucker farm. They is some more men with thim.

The two rangers ate their breakfast without any further contact with the woman who had brought them the note. After finishing breakfast, they walked around town, watching as the various business establishments opened to conduct the commerce of the day. Without being too obvious in their questioning, they held conversations with some of the merchants.

"Are you talking about the Tucker farm?" the blacksmith asked as he pounded on a strip of metal to be used to tire a wagon wheel.

"Yes, the Tucker farm," Paul said. "Do you know where it is?"

"Sure do." The blacksmith laid down his hammer

and tongs, then stepped outside of the shop and pointed to the west. "It's about ten miles that way," he said. "You'll cross two streams. After you cross over the second stream, if you'll take a look sort of southwest, like this"— he moved his arm to show the angle—"why, you can't miss it. Ain't no house left there, though. Ain't nothin' there now but a barn, and there ain't nothin' to the barn to speak of."

"Thanks," Paul said.

"What are you lookin' for the Tucker place for?"

"No particular reason," Paul replied. "We just heard it was abandoned and wondered about it."

"Well, if you are lookin' to buy it, you might see Mrs. Gimmlin. She's been tryin' to sell it 'n ain't had no luck a' tall, so, like as not you could get it for a good price."

"Where might we find Mrs. Gimmlin?" Gordon asked.

"Oh, she ain't hard to find," the blacksmith said. "She runs the café. Ole man Tucker was her brother, don't you see. An' what happened is, why, he up 'n died 'n left it to her. And the thing is, Mrs. Gimmlin is a widder woman. Her husband died a year ago his ownself, else they mighta kept the farm. Now, she's just let it run down."

"I reckon that pretty much explains why the woman in the café knew where to find them," Gordon said as he and Paul rode out in the direction indicated by the blacksmith.

"Yes, but the question is, did she tell us where to find them as a matter of her civic duty?" Paul asked. "Or is she just wanting us to get rid of some unwanted nesters?"

* * *

A man named Perkins was up in the loft of the barn, his turn to keep lookout. Frank and James Hardin, Smitty, Doolin, and Carmichael were below. They had been there for three days, trying to decide what to do next.

Perkins stepped into the open doorway, then urinated, watching as the golden stream arced out onto the dirt below. It hit a rabbit, and the rabbit, startled, jumped up and darted off rapidly.

"Ha!" Perkins said. "Now that was one pissed-off rabbit. Or was he pissed on? Ha!"

As Perkins buttoned his trousers, he saw two riders approaching the farm. At first he paid little attention to them. It was probably nothing more than a couple of travelers. A few had come by since they had been staying there and not one had noticed their presence.

Then something caught his attention, and he stared at them for a long moment.

Yes, there it was again!

What Perkins had seen was the glint of sun off a piece of metal. Sun glinting off metal would not have been all that significant had it not been for where the metal was. It was on the chest of each of the men.

What Perkins had seen was their badges.

He walked back to the edge of the loft where he could look down on the men below.

"Hey, Frank," he called down. "We got company comin'."

"What kind of company?" Frank yelled back up.

"Law kind. I seen the badges on their shirts."

"How many?"

"Two."

Frank smiled. "What do you say we go meet them?"

Perkins jumped down from the loft. Then the six men left the barn and ran out to the road, bending over at the waist so their profiles were below the adjacent hedgerow.

"Cap'n," Gordon said.

"I saw," Paul replied. "How many were there, could you tell?"

"No. I saw a couple, but the way they were moving, I'm pretty sure there were more of them."

"Don't show any sign that we have seen them. Wait until we are shielded by the curve in the road," Paul said. "Then we'll dismount and send our horses on ahead of us."

"Yes, sir."

As soon as they reached the curve, both Paul and Gordon dismounted, then slapped their horses on the rump and sent them galloping ahead. That done, they both jumped down into an arroyo and ran toward where they thought the men were.

"Here they come!" someone shouted, and Paul and Gordon could hear the pop of gunfire. Climbing up out of the arroyo, they saw six men standing in the road, now confused as the riderless horses galloped by.

"What the hell? Where did they go?" one of the six said.

"Here we are," Paul said. "Men, we are Texas Rangers. Put down your guns. You are all under arrest."

"The hell we are!" James Hardin shouted. He and four others started shooting at Paul and Gordon, and the two rangers returned fire. Even as the bullets were zipping by their heads and snapping into the brush around and behind them, through the smoke of the gunfire, Paul could see that Frank Hardin was making a mad dash for the barn.

"Frank! You cowardly son of a bitch!" James called.

James and the other outlaws and Paul and Gordon continued to exchange gunfire. Paul felt a slug tear into his left shoulder, Gordon was hit in the right leg, but the men stood their ground and continued to fire. It was all over in less than a minute. James Hardin, Perkins, Smitty, Doolin, and Carmichael lay dead or dying in the dirt. From behind the barn, Paul could hear the sound of galloping hoofbeats as Frank Hardin made good his escape.

James was gasping for breath, the only one of the five men who was still alive. He had been hit twice, once in the stomach and once in the chest.

"I . . . never . . . thought . . . my . . . own . . . bro—" That was as far as he got before he died.

As well as they could, Paul bandaged Gordon, and Gordon bandaged Paul. Then, working through the pain, they recovered their horses, and draped the bodies of the outlaws over their own horses. They had no idea of knowing whether they had matched outlaw with horse or not, but it didn't matter.

An hour later, they delivered the bodies to the undertaker, then found a doctor to improve upon their rudimentary bandaging.

Chapter Nine

From the diary of Fancy Darrow:

Seven miles north of Austin, Texas,

Wednesday evening, June 26th, 1844

*Tonight is our last night of encampment on the
trail. Mr. Good says that we are but seven miles from
the town of Austin, which we will reach by tomorrow
afternoon. And there, we are told, the wagon train
will disband, each of us to seek our own fortune.*

*I am glad that the journey by wagon train has
ended, for it has been arduous indeed. I have come to
admire these hearty people as I have admired no
other. All are dedicated and hardworking, and all
have welcomed me as one of them. For that, I am
truly grateful.*

*But, hard though this journey has been, I have
felt a part of something, and that feeling of belonging*

*has helped to ease the pain in my heart. For not only
have I lost my father, I have lost my entire identity.
The young woman who was Fancy Darrow, secure in
her life and in her future, is no more. I still have the
name, but I no longer have the soul, or the history
that once was mine. That was all taken from me on
that terrible day that my father's home, and all that
he treasured, was sold upon the auctioneer's block.*

*The question now is, in this new place, will I
survive? I will endeavor to secure a position as a
schoolteacher. I have the education and the
knowledge to fulfill such a task, but do I have
the heart?*

I feel that I will survive, for I must survive.

"I don't reckon you'll be writing in that book
much longer, will you?" Ralph asked.

"Why do you think that?"

"Because this trip is over. You won't have anything
left to write about."

"Oh, I expect I'll find something to write about,"
Fancy said.

"What are you going to do, now that we are here?"
Ralph asked.

"I hope to get a position teaching school."

"You will."

"What makes you think I will?"

"My pa is a lawyer and an important man," Ralph
said. "Folks tend to listen to him, so I reckon if he
asks the school to let you come teach, they'll do it."

"I wouldn't want to presume upon your father,"
Fancy replied.

"Oh, heck," Ralph said with a little laugh. "You

mean you have been around Pa this long and you still think you would be presuming? Pa loves to do things like that."

There was an added sense of excitement as they made ready to get under way the next morning. Breakfast was more celebratory than functional, jellies and jams were included with the normal fare. They laughed and talked about their plans, then hurried to get started. The teams were hitched, and help was freely given to those who were slower in getting ready so that the wagons started toward town much sooner than was their normal schedule.

When they came within sight of the town, they began calling back from wagon to wagon.

"Austin is ahead!"

"We can see it!"

"We are almost there!"

Then, their long sought-after goal was achieved as the twenty wagons of the Justin Good party rolled into Austin. Because of the narrowness of the street the wagons came through town in single file, rather than the normal two abreast formation they had used while traveling cross country. That stretched the train out for nearly a quarter of a mile.

It was not only the members of the wagon train that were excited. The arrival of so many wagons was also an event for the people of town as they turned out to welcome the newcomers.

There were several hand-painted signs in the windows, and on the outside walls of the various businesses around town: COOPERS GENERAL STORE WELCOMES YOU; AUSTIN LAND AND TITLE WELCOMES YOU.

The men of the wagon train, and some of the women, were walking alongside, while most of the women and the younger people were riding in the wagons. This had been their mode of travel for nearly a month. The only difference was that instead of empty countryside to look at, Fancy could look from side to side and see houses and stores.

As they reached the middle of the town, a man wearing a badge was standing in the middle of the road, holding up his hand. The excitement Fancy had been feeling moments earlier turned now to abject fear. Were they coming after her?

"Who is the wagon master?" the lawman called out.

"I am, sir. Justin Good at your service," Justin said, riding quickly up alongside the wagons to meet the lawman.

"I am Ranger Jack Hays," the lawman said.

"Are we violating some law, Ranger Hays, by coming through town?" Justin asked. "Because if we are, I assure you, it was unintentional."

"No, no, Mr. Good, you are fine," Hays said quickly. "But if you would, please take your wagons all the way through and you'll find a field just at the edge of town. You are welcome to park your wagons there as long as need be."

"Thank you," Justin said, and even though the wagons had not stopped, he motioned them on.

"Are you folks goin' to live here?" someone shouted from the side of the street.

"That's what we plan," Dale Chapman replied.

"The farmland here, it *ist gut, jah?*" Otto Hoffman called out to some of the people on the street.

"None better this side of the Garden of Eden," the answer came back.

"If you're goin' to be buildin', I got buildin' supplies," another called out.

Town children came running out to greet the wagons, and many of the children of the train jumped down from the wagons to meet them. Within moments, friendships were born as three score and more children laughed and shouted at each other and ran alongside the train, sometimes darting between the wagons to the shouted reprimands of worried parents.

When finally the wagons stopped, they were circled automatically, not for defense against Indians or predators, but because it was the most efficient use of the space allotted them. Laughing and talking happily, the women pulled out the pots and pans and started the cooking fires. A communal supper wasn't an absolute necessity tonight. Tonight it was being done for the camaraderie as they would discuss plans for their future, a future that was beginning here and now.

The stew tonight would be augmented by potatoes, carrots, and onions, those commodities being among the first things purchased since arriving in town.

Fancy was busy peeling potatoes, laughing and joining in the conversation with the other women, when Justin Good called out to her.

"Miss Darrow?"

She still had a smile on her face when she looked around, but the expression she saw on Justin's face caused her smile to fade.

Then, when he spoke to her again, she felt her knees weaken.

"Come with me, please, would you, Miss Darrow?" he asked. "We must talk."

Feeling feathers in her stomach, Fancy started toward him. She became even more frightened when he turned and walked away, indicating that he wanted some separation between them and the others when they spoke. Surely if it had been anything routine, he would have spoken to her here. What did he want?

Justin did not stop walking until they were at the farthest point they could be from other members of the wagon train, nearly all of whom had gathered where the communal dinner would be. Then, when they stopped, Justin leaned back against one of the wagons with his arms folded across his chest. He stared at Fancy for what seemed like several minutes, though she realized that it was probably only a few seconds.

"Miss Darrow, I don't know how to ask this question, or even if I should ask it. I've considered it and I have come to the conclusion that, yes, the question does need to be asked."

Fancy braced herself.

"Several days ago, shortly after we got under way, a man came by to talk to me. It seems that he was in pursuit of a runaway slave."

Justin paused in his conversation, and studied her reaction.

Fancy felt her cheeks burning, but she neither spoke, nor looked directly at him.

"He said that the slave he was looking for was named Fancy. He said that she was a beautiful woman, and that her skin was as white as mine."

Again he paused.

"I told him we didn't have such a woman," Justin said. "And, I have kept my own counsel for all this time. But, Miss Darrow, you must admit that there are things about you that call this whole thing into question. You arrived on the very day we were to leave. You had no wagon of your own, and we knew nothing of your past, other than your report that your father had just died. Your name is Fancy and, it is obvious, even to a blind man, that you are a beautiful woman. Perhaps the most beautiful woman I have ever seen.

"I'm only going to ask you this, one time. Are you the runaway slave that man was looking for?"

With tears of fright and defeat streaming down her cheeks, Fancy nodded, but did not speak. She had no idea what was going to happen to her now, and she felt as she did on that fateful day when she learned the true story of her past.

Gently, Justin reached up and caught one of her tears with a large thumb.

"Don't cry, child," he said. "I am neither going to send you back, nor am I going to reveal your secret."

Fancy breathed in a quick gasp of joy. Now she looked up at Justin, and though her eyes were still filled with tears, there was a light of joy deep down inside.

"What I don't understand is how it is that you are so well educated," Justin said, recalling their conversations.

"My father sent me to school at Georgia School for Women," Fancy said. "That's where I got my teaching certificate."

"Your father?"

"My father's name was Tom Darrow," Fancy began. "He was master of Eagle Lair Plantation. We were very—that is, he was very wealthy. I lacked for nothing as I was raised, and when I was of age, my father sent me away to school. I was there when I learned that he had died—but I did not learn until I came home that my mother, whom I never knew, was what we call in Louisiana, a quadroon. She was one-quarter Negro, Mr. Good. And that makes me one-eighth Negro. According to the law, I not only was not able to inherit any of my father's property, I *was* my father's property. I was sold as a slave to a man named Connor who was going to force me into prostitution. A friend of my father's helped me escape so, yes, I am a runaway slave."

"You poor child," Lucy Good said, suddenly appearing from behind the wagon. She went to Fancy and embraced her.

Feeling the warmth, comfort, and genuine concern of this good woman, Fancy gave vent to the emotions she had held in check for these many days. She cried until there were no more tears. Then, amazingly, a sense of calm and well-being, unlike anything she had felt for a long time, came over her.

"I can't thank you enough for your kindness," she said as she wiped her eyes.

"You cannot be extradited from Texas," Justin said. "Nevertheless, I think it would be best for all concerned if we keep this secret among the three of us. Tell no one else, not even Ralph."

"Justin, Ralph would never tell," Lucy said, scolding her husband.

"He wouldn't tell by design," Justin said. "But he is still very young, and has not yet learned to guard his tongue. I think it would be best if we kept our own counsel."

"All right," Lucy agreed.

"Now, Miss Darrow, I believe you said something about wanting to teach school. Is that truly your intention?"

"Oh, yes," Fancy said. "I've always wanted to teach school, even long before this happened."

"I have letters of introduction to President Lamar and to Sam Houston, who many say will be the next president of Texas. I'm sure that, with their backing, we will be able to find a position for you as a schoolteacher," Justin said.

Once more, tears began to flow down Fancy's cheeks.

"Why are you crying now?" Justin asked, confused by the tears.

"Justin, for an educated man, you can be very dumb sometimes," Lucy said. She smiled at Fancy. "Those are tears of happiness."

"I will never forget you," Fancy said. "For the rest of my life, I will remember what you have done for me."

Amarillo—Saturday, June 15, 1912

Ralph Good walked up to the punch bowl and, leaning his cane against the table reached, with palsied hand, for a cup.

"Here, Ralph, let me get that for you," Fancy said.

"Thank you, Fancy," Ralph said. "Look at me now. I'm a stoved up old man. Can you believe I walked all the way here from Austin? And before that, I walked most of the way from Shreveport to Austin."

Fancy chuckled. "You walked when you weren't riding a horse, or sitting in the wagon, pestering me," she said.

"Well, you can't blame me, Fancy," Ralph said. "When we came from Shreveport I was just a boy, and you were the most beautiful woman I had ever seen. In fact, not in my whole life have I ever seen a woman more beautiful than you were, and that includes all the 'so-called beauties' in the moving picture shows."

"Hush now, Ralph, you are going to make me blush," Fancy said as she handed the cup of punch to him.

Ralph took a swallow of his punch and looked at her over the rim of his cup.

"I never told, you know," he said.

"I beg your pardon?"

"That day we arrived in Austin. Do you remember it? How excited everyone was?"

"Oh, yes," Fancy said. "How could I ever forget?"

"Pa said that I was too young to guard my tongue. But I wasn't. I never said a word. I was in the wagon when you told Pa and Ma what had happened to you, how your own pa died and you found out that you were—uh—you know. I overheard all of it, but I never said a word about it to anyone. And no one ever knew that I was in the wagon that day. No one except, now, you."

"Bless you, Ralph," Fancy said, reaching out to put her hand on his.

Ralph smiled. "And I'll tell you this, Fancy Darrow," he said. "If I had been six or seven years older, I would have come courting you, and I would have given Paul Nelson a run for his money, you can count on that."

"Oh, don't be foolish, Ralph," Fancy said, laughing. "Maggie McKenzie was a beautiful woman, and you were perfect for each other."

Ralph's eyes brightened. "She was a beautiful woman, wasn't she, Fancy?" He glanced over at her, and saw her laughing with one of their great-grandchildren. "She is still beautiful, and she has been a wonderful wife. Looking at all these young people, it makes me wonder."

"Makes you wonder what?" Fancy asked.

"If they and the people who will come after them— their grandchildren and great-grandchildren, will ever know what came before them. We thought the daguerreotype picture was a miracle, today they go to a theater and watch plays unfold in moving pictures. When we came here we averaged fifteen miles to the day. They drive one hundred miles in but half a day, and find it not unusual at all. And now there are airplanes that can go farther in one hour than we could travel in seven days. They can pick up a telephone and speak to a friend on the other side of town, or a hundred miles away, and soon, it is said, we could talk to someone in New York or San Francisco, as easily as you and I are talking now. We must be as foreign to them as those brave souls who came over on the *Mayflower* are to us."

"And yet, we remember those people on the *Mayflower*," Fancy said, "as our descendants will remember us. I think we need not fear fading into history. Why, isn't this very event today a celebration of our past?"

"Fancy, you always did have a way of making people understand," Ralph said. "That is why you were such a good teacher."

Austin—Friday, July 4, 1845

A special convention called by Sam Houston, president of the Republic of Texas, voted in favor of Texas' s entry into the United States. Though there were continuing technical and legal problems to be worked out concerning the transfer of authority to the federal government, for all practical purposes, Texas became a state on that day, a day specifically chosen because of its historical significance.

True to his word, Justin Good had gotten Fancy a position as a schoolteacher. He did it by the simple expedient of establishing his own school, and since there were no public schools in the rapidly growing city of Austin, the school took root almost immediately. In little over one month, there were fourteen students enrolled.

On that historic Friday, Fancy Darrow stood in the school yard with her students watching proudly, as the flag of the Republic of Texas was lowered, and the Stars and Stripes of the United States was raised.

"Miss Darrow, does this mean we ain't Texans no more?" one of the boys asked.

"Heavens, Jimmy, please try and pay attention to grammar," Fancy said. "Who knows the correct way of asking that question?"

"I do, I do," a little girl said, raising her hand.

"All right, Ruby, if you would, reword the question for Jimmy."

"He meant to say, 'Does this mean we *aren't* Texans *any*more,' " Ruby restated, proudly.

"That is correct."

"Well, I don't like it," Jimmy said. "I like bein' a Texan. Pa says I should be proud to be a Texan."

"I meant the sentence is correct," Fancy said. "But your premise is wrong. We are still Texans. It is just that Texas is now a state of the United States, so we are Texans, and we are Americans."

"So we can still be proud?"

"Yes, and now you have two flags to be proud of," she said, pointing to the Lone Star flag which was now flying from a second pole.

Sam Houston had succeeded Lamar as president of Texas, and everyone expected him to become governor. He surprised all his friends, though, by declaring that he would rather become one of Texas's first U.S. senators, and was elected to that position, virtually without opposition.

Despite the paper signed by Santa Anna, Mexico had never officially recognized the independence of Texas, and now that Texas was about to become a state of the United States, the situation worsened. It quickly became evident that a war was going to be fought between the United States and Mexico, with Texas as the prize.

Austin—Saturday, March 28, 1846

Paul Nelson and Gordon Forsythe were both well recovered from their wounds by the time General Zachary Taylor led a large contingent of U.S. troops into Texas. He established his headquarters near Austin, and next to the headquarters of the Texas Rangers. Paul's commander in the rangers, Lee Blake, called upon General Taylor. Blake had been detached from the rangers, and given command of a thousand Texas volunteers for the U.S. Army.

"How do your men shape up?" Taylor asked.

"Fairly well, sir," Blake replied, "seeing as my troops have never fought a battle. But they are not organized. The War Department didn't know what to do with them, so they have sort of lumped them all under my command."

"I'm not surprised," Taylor said. He drummed his fingers on the table. "What do you want to do, Lee?"

"I'm at your disposal, General."

"Well, that raises a question. I've had half a mind to make you my chief of staff, but no fighting man is ever happy with a staff post. Besides, I'd lose one of my best field commanders that way. How would you like a permanent brigade of your own? That would be two regiments of regular army infantry, and a regiment of cavalry that we'll have to borrow from the Texas Rangers. Do you have any idea who to put in command of such a regiment?"

"Yes, sir. Rick Miller."

"I would be honored to serve as Colonel Miller's executive officer," Paul said to Blake when Blake approached him with the proposition. "And if you would allow a recommendation?"

"What recommendation would that be?"

"A recommendation for Sergeant Major."

"That would be Sergeant Forsythe, I take it?" Blake asked with a smile.

"Yes, sir."

"Consider it done."

Shortly thereafter, in response to a question posed by General Taylor, Lee Blake offered to give him a demonstration of the effectiveness of the Texas Rangers as a fighting unit. He invited the general to a large open field in the middle of which was a huge square of cardboard, mounted on a pine frame. On it, someone had painted a crude figure of a man mounted on a horse.

A bugle sounded, and the parade began, with two horsemen in the lead, one carrying the American flag and the other the Lone Star banner. Behind them rode Colonel Miller, with his officers and men in formation behind him.

Watching the riders carefully, Zachary Taylor growled inarticulately, the sound indicating impatience and, perhaps, disgust. Lee Blake couldn't blame him for feeling as he did. The troops rode in loose formation, unable to keep their lines straight, and they resembled amateur soldiers rather than the trained, disciplined professionals his brigade needed. He had faith in Rick, however, and hoped the rangers would find some way to compensate for their sloppiness.

The regiment paraded the length of the field, halting at the far end. Then Rick raised his saber, signaling a charge, and the bugle blared.

Suddenly the entire regiment raced up the field at a gallop, and somehow each troop, made up of fifty men, managed to maintain its separate identity.

Rick set the example for his men. His saber disappeared into its sheath, and he unslung his rifle and shot at the cardboard figure as he raced past it at a distance of about two hundred feet. Then, as the entire unit rode past the target at a gallop, each of the cavalrymen also fired.

Lee, knowing now what Rick had in mind, grinned but made no comment. General Taylor was watching the maneuver closely, his thick eyebrows drawn together.

After the entire regiment had fired at the target, Rick joined his superiors. Saluting as he rode up to them, he said, "I hope you enjoyed our little demonstration, gentlemen."

"That depends on the results," Zachary Taylor replied curtly. "Your men held their seats nicely, I'll grant you. But how accurate was their fire?"

"That's exactly what I intend to show you, sir." Rick raised an arm, and two of his sergeants immediately rode to the target, picked it up, and carried it to the place where the three senior officers were sitting.

"The entire regiment," Rick said, "including my staff and me, consists of two hundred and eleven officers and men. General Taylor, I invite you to examine this target."

The two sergeants, sitting their mounts about six or eight feet apart, held the framed cardboard up for Taylor's inspection.

A rare twinkle appeared in the commander's eyes when he saw that fewer than a dozen shots had penetrated the unpainted portion of the cardboard. The figures of the rider and his mount were heavily peppered with bullet holes; the man's face and chest had been virtually obliterated, as had the head of the horse.

Lee was impressed. Even the newest recruits, carefully chosen for their riding ability and marksmanship, were living up to the traditions of the rangers, who quietly believed they were superior to all other cavalrymen on earth.

A slow smile creased Zachary Taylor's seamed face, and then he laughed aloud. "By God, Miller," he said, "your men may not win any prizes for precision marching, but they sure as hell can shoot. And that's exactly what we need. As of this moment, the Third Ranger Regiment is incorporated into my army and assigned to General Blake's First Brigade."*

*This scene is from *Wagons West: Texas!*

Chapter Ten

Palo Alto, Texas—Friday, May 8, 1846

General Taylor, hearing that the American supply base was under attack at Point Isabel, left Major Jacob Brown in command of 500 men, while he, with 2,300 men made a forced march toward the coast.

"Major, it isn't my position to question the general," Paul said. "But I don't think any attack has taken place at Point Isabel. I think the main contingent of the Mexican Army is right here in front of us."

"What makes you think that?" Major Brown asked.

"I sent Sergeant Major Forsythe and two others out on a scouting expedition," Paul said. "They reported a very large Mexican army in front of us. If the Mexicans had attacked Port Isabel, I don't think they would have left this many men behind. I suggest that we send a galloper after the general's army with that information."

"To what end?" Major Brown asked.

"To provide him with the latest intelligence so that he may, at his discretion, determine whether to proceed on to Point Isabel, or to return."

"And your information comes from this scout that you sent out?" Brown asked.

"Yes, sir."

"I know that you have had some experience with the military," Brown said, "so I don't mean this as a question upon your service. But, I have been in the army now for many years, and if you will, Major, allow me to share some of my experience with you. I have learned that oftentimes enlisted men, who by their own perspective think in small units, are easily intimidated by what they consider overwhelming numbers. This gives them a tendency to overestimate the size of enemy forces."

"I assure you, Major Brown, I have known Sergeant Major Forsythe for some time now, and he is not easily intimidated," Paul said sharply.

"I mean no personal attack, sir," Brown responded quickly. "But I do not feel that it is my prerogative to send a galloper after General Taylor to alter a command decision he has already made. However, if you put such fidelity in your sergeant major then, by all means, let us prepare to meet the Mexicans should they attack."

After his conference with Major Brown, Paul returned to his own troops. As Colonel Miller had proceeded to Point Isabel with General Taylor, along with three-fourths of the Third Ranger Regiment, Paul was in command of those who were left behind.

"What did Major Brown say?" Gordon asked.

"He won't send a rider after the general," Paul said. "But he has agreed to place the troops on alert."

"You do realize, Paul, that if they come across the Rio Grande after us, they will outnumber us by a ratio of ten to one," Gordon said.

Paul smiled. . "Gordon, my friend," he said. "I've been here before."

"Yes, sir, I know that," Gordon said. "I only pray that this time it turns out a little better than it did at the Alamo."

As the American troops bivouacked that night, Paul realized that very few had ever actually been in battle, and he could sense their fear. They needed something to calm them, and recalling his time in the Alamo, he remembered the calming effect of music. "Gordon," he said. "How about singing something for us?"

Gordon sang a couple of hymns, including "Amazing Grace." And though the music was beautiful, it seemed to Paul that it was having an effect exactly opposite of what he wanted. The songs were so melancholy that the men were getting even more subdued.

"Damn, Gordon, don't you know any happy songs?" Paul asked.

"How about if I sing one I wrote?" Gordon replied.

"As long as it's not one that gets everyone down," Paul said.

Gordon began singing again, his voice just as strong and just as pure, but this time there was an uplifting lilt to it.

We're Texas Rangers through and through
And if you don't like it, to hell with you.
Come one at a time, or come in mass
It doesn't matter, we'll kick your ass.

The men began to laugh uproariously and by the time the song was completed, their mood had completely changed.

As the sun rose the next morning, Paul heard a familiar sound—the thunder of artillery. The Mexican army had opened the attack with cannon fire.

At first the American troops were apprehensive. By now all knew the size of the army facing them, and the Mexicans were known for the copious employment of artillery.

But after almost two hours of cannonading, without infantry follow-up, the Americans began to gain confidence, especially given the exceptionally ineffectiveness of the artillery fire. Nearly all the cannonballs launched toward them fell far short of the target, and merely rolled and bounced along the ground toward the American troops. It was very easy to step aside as the cannonballs approached, and Gordon took off his tunic and held it out as a bullfighter would his cape.

"Olé!"

By noon, General Taylor, who had both discovered that Point Isabel was deserted, and heard the cannon fire, returned. The Mexican army, under General Arista, met him with a huge army that deployed a mile-wide front, with cavalry on the right, infantry on the left, and artillery in the center. While

Major Brown proceeded on to the Rio Grande, directly across the river from Matamoros, Paul and the remaining elements of the Texas Rangers joined General Albert Sidney Johnston.

General Arista moved to envelop the Americans and capture General Taylor's baggage train, but General Taylor sent his "Flying Artillery" to his flank.

"Major Nelson!" General Johnston called. "If you would, sir, with Major Ringgold to provide defense!"

Paul moved the part of the Ranger Regiment that was under him to provide perimeter defense of Ringgold's artillery.

Ringgold opened fire on the charging Mexicans with devastating effectiveness. The first charge was stopped with scores of Mexican cavalrymen being cut down by the artillery fire.

"Major!" Sergeant Major Forsythe shouted. "They've set fire to the grass!"

The grass was tall and dry, and made excellent tinder for the fire. Within moments, the fire had spread for several acres, and so much smoke billowed up that neither army could see the other. Despite that, the artillery duel continued, with both Mexican and American cannons firing through the smoke.

Once the smoke cleared, the fighting resumed, and the killing continued.

"Major Nelson!" Ringgold called. "Their cavalry may make another—unngh!" he shouted as both he and his horse went down. A cannonball had struck Ringgold's right leg, severing it at the thigh. Then it penetrated the horse Ringgold was riding. Both injuries sent out a shower of blood, much of it getting on Paul's uniform.

"Sam!" Paul shouted. "Sam!"

Major Samuel Ringgold looked up at Paul, blinked a couple of times, then died.

Because of the intensity of the fighting, neither army had sufficient advantage on the other to advance. Then, after sunset, the Mexican army withdrew from the field, having suffered 320 killed and over 400 wounded.

General Taylor had lost only 9 killed and 47 wounded. At first count, General Taylor thought Paul to be among the wounded, though Paul pointed out that the blood was from the cannonball that had killed both Major Ringgold and his horse.

General Johnston was among those who urged General Taylor to go in pursuit of General Arista and his retreating army.

"We have them on the run, General," General Johnston said. "I say we chase them across the river and a hundred miles down into Mexico."

"I agree with your enthusiasm, General Johnston," General Taylor replied. "But we have had two extended and forced marches within two days. I think the army may be too exhausted to continue. They need a night of rest. We all need a night of rest."

The next morning, General Taylor invited his top officers to have breakfast with him so they could discuss the situation. General Blake asked both Rick Harris and Paul Nelson to accompany him. Over a breakfast of biscuits, butter, jam, and coffee, General Taylor conducted the meeting.

"Gentlemen, there has been some question in Washington as to whether or not the United States should declare war against Mexico," he said. "But I think that we can all agree now, that such a discussion is no longer debatable. We are at war, declared not by the United States, but by Mexico when they attacked us on American soil. I think we can also agree that we realized a great victory yesterday."

The officers agreed with applause and a cheer.

"And now the question before us is what is our next move?"

"General," Colonel Boyle said, "I think that, in light of our victory yesterday, that we should consolidate our forces, dig entrenchments and fortifications in this place, and await reinforcements."

"I agree," Colonel Kleuver said.

"What do you think, General Johnston?"

"Major Brown has moved to the river, General," Johnston said. "He has less than five hundred men with him. If General Arista and his army come upon him, it will be another Alamo. And as one of my officers was at the Alamo"—he looked over at Paul—"he could attest to the feeling of abandonment those brave men felt."

"Then I am to understand that you think we should pursue General Arista?" Zachary Taylor asked.

"I do, indeed," General Johnston replied.

Taylor smiled and nodded. "Good," he said. "For that is exactly what I intend to do. Gentlemen, return to your troops and make ready in all respects to march."

"What did the general say?" Gordon asked when Paul returned to his command.

"He said we are going after General Arista."

Gordon smiled broadly. "I like a man who is decisive. Zachary Taylor would make a good president."

"Yes, well, give credit to General Johnston. He is the one who urged General Taylor to do it."

Within an hour of General Taylor's decision to pursue the Mexicans, the American army was on the march. Halfway between Palo Alto and the Rio Grande, they found them. General Arista had chosen a defensive position that was so strong that even the most confident of the Americans were given pause. He had entrenched his troops at a place called Resaca de la Palma, a dry riverbed in a mesquite field.

As soon as the Mexican army was located, General Taylor launched his attack, sending his cavalry against the center of the Mexican lines. Paul was surprised to see that one of the Mexican soldiers who was fighting bravely to defend the guns was a general. The general fired his pistol, but before he could reload, Paul leaped from his horse and held the point of his saber at the general's neck.

"*¿Quién es usted?*" Paul demanded. "Who are you?"

"*Señor, tengo el honor de se General Romolo Diaz de la Vega,*" the Mexican general answered.

"The honor is mine, General de la Vega," Paul said. "Sergeant Major, please get the general out of harm's way!"

Paul remounted and continued the attack.

By now General Taylor had committed his infantry. For the better part of an hour the two armies fought hand to hand in the chaparral, breaking up into small, disconnected units so that the officers lost command and control. The fighting was bloody and intense. Then some of the Mexicans began to fall back. That spread to other units until, suddenly, there was a complete collapse of the Mexican defense. Arista ordered a general retreat and what had been a battle became a rout.

When the final count was in, the battle of Resaca de la Palma was even bloodier than the battle at Palo Alto the day before. Arista lost several hundred of his men, while the Americans had thirty-three killed and eighty-nine wounded. The Americans captured eight heavy guns, scores of battle flags and unit standards, and more than two hundred prisoners, including fourteen officers. General Romolo Diaz de la Vega was one of the officers captured.

Austin—Thursday, February 24, 1848

The Treaty of Guadalupe Hidalgo having been signed, the war with Mexico was over. Mexico was given fifteen million dollars, but lost 529,000 square miles of territory, including California, New Mexico, Nevada, Utah, most of Arizona, and parts of Colorado and Wyoming. The Rio Grande was established as the permanent boundary between Mexico and the United States.

Following the war, the Texas Rangers were disbanded but Paul Nelson and Gordon Forsythe, as well as several other rangers, were invited to stay in the army. Paul had no interest in remaining in the army, nor did Gordon. Both men became deputy U.S. marshals, continuing their careers in law enforcement.

"What is this?" Paul asked as he took a piece of paper into the office of Marshal James Allen.

"What does it look like?" Marshal Allen replied.

"It looks like a request for me to speak at the elementary school."

"Unh-uh," Allen said, shaking his head. "It isn't a request, it's an order."

"An order? Come on, James, damn it. You know I wouldn't be any good at something like that. Besides, I'm just a deputy marshal. You are the marshal."

Allen chuckled. "Which is why my request is the same as an order. You ought to know that better than anyone, Paul. You've spent half your life in one kind of service or another."

"But why me?"

"Why you? Because, my friend, you are a genuine Texas hero, the embodiment of Texas history. Think about it. You were at the Alamo and San Jacinto; you fought in the Mexican War from Palo Alto to Mexico City."

"I'm not the only one to do all those things," Paul replied.

"Really? All right, I tell you what. You find another deputy U.S. marshal who survived the Alamo and I'll ask him to speak."

"What? You know that's not fair, James. I'm the only one that—"

"Got ya, didn't I?" Allen asked, interrupting Paul's protest.

Frustrated that he was getting nowhere with his protest, Paul ran his hand through his hair. "All right, where do I go? Who do I see? And what do I do?"

"You are going to the Justin Good Elementary School," Allen said. "There, you will meet with Miss Fancy Darrow. She is a schoolteacher there, and she will tell you what is expected of you."

* * *

In the almost four years since Justin Good had arrived in Texas, he had made his name known. A political activist, he had petitioned first Governor Henderson, then Governor Wood, to make Texas a free state.

"Consider this," he said in his appeal. "Here, at the birth of this great state, we have the unique, and I think, God-given opportunity to reverse this stain of slavery—to stand up for what is right and declare, once and forever, that the chains of slavery will be forever broken inside our borders."

Neither governor listened to his appeal and, though he was able to find a few legislators who agreed with him, he was unable to muster enough to help his cause. He considered running for governor, but Peter Bell had already made it known that he was going to run. Bell had fought at San Jacinto, had served as a captain in the Texas Rangers and as a colonel in the U.S. Army during the Mexican War. Against such sterling curriculum vitae as that possessed by Peter Bell, Justin had little to offer to the voters.

But if Justin was unsuccessful in his political aspirations, he more than compensated for it in his business life. He had established a thriving law firm, augmented by his other business interests, to include a freight line, a general store, and a brick-manufacturing company. He had also started a school which, in the three years since its inception, now had thirty-six students in eight grades. All the grades met in one room, presided over by Fancy Darrow, who had already won accolades from the parents.

* * *

Fancy looked at the information Marshal Allen had sent her about the man who would be coming to speak today. He was the only living survivor of the Alamo; a man who had fought at San Jacinto; then, as a Texas Ranger had fought against the Indians and outlaws, followed by his experiences as an officer in the U.S. Army during the Mexican War. And now he was a deputy U.S. marshal who had, within the last six months, tracked down and captured a gang of cattle thieves. Not in any novel had she read about anyone more qualified to be called a hero than Deputy U.S. Marshal Paul Franklin Nelson. *My goodness,* she thought, *if he arrives in shining armor, astride a prancing white horse, I wouldn't be surprised.*

There was a time when Fancy would have been a little nervous over coming into such close contact with a lawman. Texas was a state now, and not only a state, a slave state. That meant that, as a runaway slave, she was technically a felon, and while extradition to Louisiana from the Republic of Texas was unlikely, extradition from the state of Texas was very possible. But it had been nearly four years, and she was allowing herself the hope that Felix Connor, the only person who could possibly have an interest in her, had given up any idea of ever finding her.

"Excuse me, ma'am," a deep and resonant voice said from the door of the one-room schoolhouse.

The man who spoke had wide shoulders and long legs. He wore tan colored trousers, a black vest, and a low-crowned, black hat. A star was pinned to his vest, and he wore a pistol holstered low on his right thigh.

Fancy inhaled a quick, short breath. He may not be the most good-looking man she had ever seen, especially compared to some of the dandies she had been acquainted with back in Louisiana, but there was something about him that she found extremely appealing. There was a rugged handsomeness about him and, as he stood in the doorway, he gave the illusion of a man who is used to being in command.

"Would you be Marshal Nelson?" Fancy asked.

"Yes, ma'am, only that would be deputy marshal," he corrected her.

"Please, come in and have a seat. The students will be in shortly."

Fancy pulled a chair out from the wall, but he didn't sit.

"After you, ma'am," he said.

"Oh, heavens, if you wait until I sit, you'll be standing for a long time. I'll have to greet my students. Really, I wish you would sit. It would create less of a disturbance as they come in."

"Yes, ma'am, thank you," Paul said.

Paul sat down and looked pointedly at the woman. He had never seen anyone who looked exactly like her. Her ivory skin was without blemish, her eyes so dark that he could scarcely discern the pupil from the iris. Her lashes were long, and her lips were full. The dress she wore was prim and proper, befitting a schoolteacher, yet in the finest saloon, the most beautiful girl with the most provocative dress could not divert attention from this woman of breathtaking beauty.

"I was told," Paul started to say, but Miss Darrow was writing his name on the blackboard and she held out one hand as if asking for a moment until she completed her task.

Deputy U.S. Marshal
Paul Franklin Nelson
Hero of Texas

"I don't feel comfortable being called a hero," he said.

"Genuine heroes aren't ever comfortable with such accolades," Fancy replied.

"And I don't ever use the name Franklin."

"Why not? It is your middle name, isn't it?"

"Yes, ma'am, but . . . "

"No buts," Fancy said. "It is a perfectly lovely name. And one of our founders was named Franklin."

"Yes, ma'am, Benjamin Franklin," Paul said. "My grandfather was an apprentice in his printing shop. He gave the Franklin name to my father, who passed it on to me."

"Why, I should think you would be very proud of that name."

Paul smiled. He couldn't recall ever having discussed his middle name with anyone and yet, here he was discussing it with a woman he had just met. But not just any woman. The most beautiful woman he had ever met.

"Oh," Fancy said. "The students are arriving."

Paul sat quietly until all the students had arrived. Many of them, especially the boys, looked at him, and he could tell that they were intrigued by the pistol he was wearing. His wished he had thought to leave the gun back in the office, but it was too late now.

Fancy took the roll, made the appropriate marks in her attendance book, then stood up to address the class, or classes, as clearly there were children of several different ages here.

"Boys and girls," she said. "We have been reading stories of heroes, both real and fictional. And it came to me that many of you might think that all the heroes are of olden times, men like George Washington, Nathan Hale, or John Paul Jones. But there are also heroes that are more recent, men like William Travis, Jim Bowie, Davy Crockett. Our guest today, Deputy U.S. Marshal Paul Nelson, not only knew them, his name deserves to be mentioned right along with their names. Mr. Nelson, if you would please say a few words to the class?"

Paul felt the palms of his hands sweating, a lightness in his head, and a shortness of breath. He had faced charging Mexicans, warring Indians, and gunmen who wanted to kill him with less nervousness than he was feeling at this moment.

"I am not a hero," Paul said. "Those men she mentioned, Travis, Bowie, Crockett, and I would add a few others, like Dickerson, Jameson, and Forsythe, gave Texas their last full measure of devotion. They are the heroes."

"My pa told me that you was at the Alamo," one of the boys said. "Is that true?"

"Yes," Paul answered.

"How come you didn't die like the others?"

"Silas McCarthy!" Fancy said sharply.

"I was just wonderin' is all," Silas said.

"Well, there is certainly no need to ask the question in such a challenging way," Fancy scolded.

"It is a legitimate question, Miss Darrow," Paul said. "And it is one that I have been asked many times." He paused for a long moment. "In fact, it is a question I have often asked myself. I was prepared, as was every other man there, to give my life."

"For Texas?" one of the others asked.

"Yes, but not just for Texas," he said. "When you are in a position like that, facing death with men who you have come to love like brothers, the borders of your life take on a new dimension. It is no longer your country or your state. The borders of your life do not extend beyond the men who are with you and, in a very strange sense—one that is hard to understand and even more difficult to explain— those borders also include the men with whom you are engaged in mortal battle. In that final moment, all you have is your faith and devotion to God, your fellow soldiers, and yourself. And your honor. The thing that sustains you above all else—is your honor.

"Then, you wake up in a destroyed barracks building, surrounded by those men who have fulfilled their promise of honor, and you discover that you are still alive. What are you to do then? In my case, being the only survivor, I made the decision to try and escape. Was that decision one of honor—so that I could live to fight again? Or was it a decision of weakness made by a man who, despite his best intentions to die with the others, somehow avoided it? Yes, Silas, that is a very good question."

The class had grown very quiet during Paul's explanation. And Fancy, hoping that she had not been seen, wiped away a few tears.

"Have you ever answered that question?" Silas asked. There was no belligerence in his question this time.

"No," Paul said.

"Then, I'll answer it for you," Silas said.

Fancy had a quick intake of breath, wondering where he was going, wondering if she should stop him now. The others in the class looked at him as well.

"I think it was a decision of honor and courage," Silas said.

Paul felt an unaccustomed lump come to his throat and he nodded his thanks but, for the moment, he was unable to speak.

Somehow, he got through the rest of the presentation.

As Nelson rode back to the courthouse where the U.S. Marshal's offices were, he thought about the woman he has just met. He was quite taken by her, not only by her incredible and somewhat exotic beauty—she was far more beautiful than anyone he had ever met—but also by her intelligence and her engaging personality. He was particularly struck by the way she related to the schoolchildren, sort of a benevolent authority figure. He wondered if she was married, and if she was not, did he have the courage to ever contact her again?

Probably not. A woman like that must be besieged with suitors.

Later that afternoon, Paul was sitting in his office when Gordon stuck his head in through the door.

"Paul, there is someone out here who wants to see you," he said.

"What does he want?"

Gordon smiled and shook his head. "It isn't a he,"

he said. "And whatever she wants, you'd be a fool not to talk to her."

Curious, Paul stood up and followed Gordon out into the entrance area of the marshal's office. He saw Miss Darrow standing there.

"Miss Darrow!" he said, moving quickly toward her. "What are you doing here? I mean—uh—is there something I can do for you?"

"I just wanted to tell you how pleased the children were with your visit," Fancy said. "It is all they could talk about for the rest of the day. Of course, I hasten to add that I, too, enjoyed your visit and I wanted to come by to personally thank you."

"I certainly appreciate your dropping by, though you didn't have to," Paul said. "I was glad to speak to your class."

Fancy laughed quietly. "You didn't feel that way just before you started to speak though, did you?" she asked. "You were as white as a sheet."

"I guess I was a little nervous," Paul admitted.

"Well, I know you must be terribly busy," Fancy said, turning to leave. "But I did want to stop by and thank you."

"Would you like to go eat with me?"

"I beg your pardon?"

"I—I'm sure I didn't ask that well. I mean, I don't even know if you are married or engaged or something. I probably—no—never mind, forget that I asked. I know I must have violated every kind of protocol there is."

"Yes," Fancy said.

"I knew it."

Fancy laughed again. "No, I mean, yes, I would like to go eat with you."

Chapter Eleven

Maison de Beauté, New Orleans, Louisiana—
Tuesday, May 9, 1848

"Surely, sir, you aren't just going to turn her out?" Madame Livermore asked. Madame Livermore was a buxom redheaded woman who kept her hair red now by the skillful use of dyes. Once a "lady of the evening," she now managed *Maison de Beauté* for Felix Connor. The object of their discussion was Felicia, one of the women of the house.

"She's gotten old," Connor said. The tone of his voice was totally devoid of any compassion. "When is the last time a man asked for her?"

"Why, she is with men all the time," Madame Livermore replied.

"That wasn't my question. My question was when is the last time a man asked for her? They take her now only if there is no one else left. Feeding her, keeping her in clothes, and providing a room for her costs more than she brings in."

"But, what will you do with her?"

"She's a slave, isn't she? She's still young enough and strong enough to work. She just can't work for me anymore."

"The other girls aren't going to like it," Madame Livermore said.

"And why should I care about what the others think? They all belong to me, too. They will think what I tell them to think. Now, you have Toby clean out Felicia's room and take her down to Tomkins. He deals with people like this. Tell him to get the best price he can for her."

"Yes, sir," Madame Livermore replied with downcast eyes. She started to leave, then stopped and looked back toward him. "Oh, and there is a man waiting outside to see you."

"White or black?"

"He's white."

"Why didn't you tell me before? Hmm. Maybe he's heard that I'm wanting to sell Felicia. All right, send him in."

The man who came in to see him was scrawny looking, with long, stringy, dirty hair. He had beady eyes, a hooked nose, and a protruding chin.

"The name is Pace," he said, sticking his hand out. "Clem Pace."

Connor did not accept the proffered hand. He couldn't remember the last time he had seen anyone so dirty.

"What do you need, Pace?"

"It ain't what I need, Mr. Connor. It's what you need. And I'm the man can give it to you."

"What would that be?"

"Are you still lookin' for that runaway girl by the name of Fancy Darrow?" Pace asked.

At the mention of the name, Fancy Darrow, Connor's eyes squinted and his lips tightened. It had been almost four years, but he still remembered her. How could he not remember her? She had cost him five thousand dollars.

"Yeah," he answered. "I'm still looking for her. Do you know where she is?"

"How much money is it worth for me to tell you where she is?"

"That all depends on whether the information does me any good," Connor said. "If she's dead, I won't be paying you anything."

"Oh, she ain't dead," Pace said. "I'd go get her myself, except I ain't exactly welcome in Texas."

"She's in Texas?" Connor asked.

"Yep."

"Where in Texas?"

"Well now, that's where it's goin' to cost you a little money," Pace said.

"How about twenty-five dollars?"

"Twenty-five? That ain't even worth me comin' to New Orleans for," Pace replied with a scoffing sound. "You was goin' to pay fifteen hundred when she first escaped."

"That was to have her delivered to me. If I understand the offer you are making now, I would have to get her back here on my own."

"That's right. But I can tell you exactly where she is, so's that you won't have to be goin' a' lookin' for her."

"How do you know where she is?"

"Unh-uh. If I tell you that, why, like as not you could find out for your ownself. Then, where would that leave me? I want two hundred fifty dollars."

"I'll give you fifty dollars."

"How about two hundred dollars?"

Suddenly Connor got an idea, and he smiled. "How about seventy-five dollars . . . ?"

Pace started to reply, but Connor held up his finger to interrupt him. "Seventy-five dollars," he repeated, "and, your choice of any woman you see in the parlor."

A huge smile spread across Pace's face. "Any of 'em?"

"I'll go out there with you. You can have any woman you see in the parlor," Connor promised.

"How long can I have her for?"

"Well, how long does it take you to—uh—get your business done?"

"Oh, I'm fast," Pace bragged. "I can most always do it in no more'n five minutes."

"There's your answer then. You can have whichever woman you want for as long as it takes for you to get your business done."

"You got yourself a deal," Pace said.

Connor opened a drawer on his desk and took out a stack of money. He counted out seventy-five dollars, and held it out toward Pace. Pace reached for it and Connor pulled it back.

"Unh-uh," he said. "Not until you tell me where she is."

"She's teachin' school in Austin, Texas," Pace said, reaching for the money.

"How do you know?"

Pace reached into his pocket and pulled out an article torn from a newspaper.

COME TO AUSTIN, TEXAS!

Americans of good character are invited to move to Austin, Texas, where good land and wonderful business opportunities await those who are enterprising. Texas is a part of the United States, so there is no problem with immigration. Austin now has a booming professional population, including lawyers, doctors, and bankers. We also have a school, taught by Miss Fancy Darrow, a graduate of the Georgia Female College. Those who require more information may obtain same by writing a letter to the editor of the Austin City Gazette.

"Did you see the name there?" Pace asked. "It was Fancy Darrow. Ain't that the name of the person you was lookin' for?"

"That's the person all right," Connor said.

"Now," Pace said. "How 'bout I go out there and pick me out a woman?"

"Be my guest," Connor said. He was already making plans to go to Austin, Texas.

Austin—Wednesday, May 17, 1848

When it became obvious to Justin Good that he was not going to be able to convince Texas to renounce slavery, he began exploring other options. He sat in his office studying the bill of annexation by which Texas became a state in the United States. He was particularly interested in one provision of the bill, and he read it again to make certain there was nothing about it that he didn't thoroughly understand.

> *New States of convenient size not exceeding four in number, in addition to said State of Texas and having sufficient population, may, hereafter by the consent of said State, be formed out of the territory thereof, which shall be entitled to admission under the provisions of the Federal Constitution; and such states as may be formed out of the territory lying south of thirty-six degrees thirty minutes north latitude, commonly known as the Missouri Compromise Line, shall be admitted into the Union, with or without slavery, as the people of each State, asking admission shall desire; and in such State or States as shall be formed out of said territory, north of said Missouri Compromise Line, slavery, or involuntary servitude (except for crime) shall be prohibited.*

"And why would we wish to do such a thing?" Governor Henderson asked.

"Because that way, Governor, we can satisfy those citizens of Texas who wish to keep this a slave state, as well as those, like me, who wish to denounce slavery."

"I can tell you right now, Mr. Good, I do not favor such a proposition," Governor Henderson said. "Nor do I believe the state legislature would. Why, that would be like asking a farmer to give up part of his farm. This land is Texas, from border to border."

When it became obvious to Justin Good that he would have little success coercing the state of Texas into voluntarily giving up part of its land, he began organizing a group of followers, intending to make his own petition to the U.S. Government. At first, he had some difficulty with the "up to" in his argument, because those who opposed him believed that Texas would "have" to add four states, and that, nobody wanted to do.

"I have read the provisions very carefully. 'Up to,' does not mean that we *must* add four more states," Justin argued. "It means only that we *can* add four more states if we wish."

Justin decided to do more than merely talk about forming a new state; he funded the campaign by securing a loan of 100,000 dollars from the Philadelphia bank of his father-in-law.

One of Justin's supporters was Dale Chapman. Upon learning that Texas intended to become a state, his initial idea of becoming a colonel in the Texas Army was closed to him. Well-educated, intelligent, and ambitious, he was a great asset to Justin, and became a very successful businessman, becoming a partner with Ian McKenzie, a long-time Texas resident with a lot of influence throughout the state.

Like Justin, Dale was opposed, on principle, to slavery. He also believed that being one of the founders of a new state would present an ambitious person with great business and political opportunities. He became a strong advocate for Justin's movement to establish a new, slave-free state. He was also able to bring Ian and Jane McKenzie and their family into the program. The addition of Ian McKenzie brought more validity to the movement.

Justin Good filed papers both in Austin, and in Washington, D.C. In the file he stated:

APPLICATION
FOR THE FORMATION OF A NEW STATE

*Respectfully and concurrently submitted to the
Congress of the United States of America, and to
the Legislature of the State of Texas.*

To wit:

ARTICLE THE FIRST:

*The joint resolution and ordinance of
annexation contain language permitting the
formation of up to four additional states out of
the former territories of the Republic of Texas.
New States of convenient size not exceeding four
in number, in addition to said State of Texas and
having sufficient population, may, hereafter, by
consent of said State, be formed out of the
territory thereof, which shall be entitled to
admission under the provisions of the Federal
Constitution. This joint resolution requires that if
any new states are formed, those north of the
Missouri Compromise line will become free states
and those south of the line can choose whether or
not to permit slavery.*

ARTICLE THE SECOND:

*This petition, acting in accordance with the
above mentioned article, is that the Congress of
the United States, and the Legislature of the State
of Texas, will honor the request of those whose
signatures are hereto affixed, that a new State, to*

*be called Comancheria, be admitted to the Union
with the full rights, powers, responsibilities,
recognition, and equality of all other States
currently bound in the pact known as the United
States of America.*

ARTICLE THE THIRD:

*The State of COMANCHERIA, being located in the
extreme northwest territory of Texas, and above
the afore stated Missouri Compromise Line, will
be, and declares itself a free State, inside the
borders of which, slavery will not be permitted.*

*Justin Good–Governor Pro Tem
of the Proposed State of COMANCHERIA*

After filing the papers, Justin, Chapman, Dr. Presnell, and Ian McKenzie began actively recruiting people for the new state. To that end, Justin advertised in the *Austin City Gazette.*

MEN, WOMEN, AND FAMILIES
of Good Character

—And those who oppose slavery—

Would do well to join the FREEDOM TRAIN,

*A wagon train under command of Justin Good
That soon will journey to the
Northwest territory of Texas, there to establish*

THE FREE STATE OF COMANCHERIA

Contact Mr. Justin Good to make all arrangements

Paul was working at his desk when someone knocked on the door to his office.

"Cap'n Nelson, sir, I wonder if I could speak to you."

Looking up from his work, Paul saw a middle-aged black man standing just outside the door. He had broad shoulders and big hands. Although it had been a long time since Paul had seen him, this was someone he could never forget. This was Joe, from the Alamo.

With a broad smile on his face, Paul got up from his desk and hurried around quickly, extending his hand toward Joe.

"Joe!" he said. "Joe, how good it is to see you!"

"It's good to see you too, Cap'n," Joe said.

"What have you been doing with yourself since last I saw you?"

"Well, sir, I been doin' jobs here and there, working first for one man, then for another. I'm a free man now, seein' as Colonel Travis be dead," Joe said. "Colonel Travis, he was a good man, and I don't like it him bein' dead an' all, but I do like bein' a free man."

"I can certainly understand that," Paul said.

Joe smiled. "I got myself a last name now," he said. "It be Travis. I am Joe Travis." The smile left his face to be replaced, for just a moment, by a look of worry. "Does you think Colonel Travis would be put off by that?"

"I think Colonel Travis would be honored to have you bear his name," Paul said.

"Cap'n Nelson, I can't read as you know, but folks has been tellin' me 'bout somethin' called a Freedom Train that be goin' to a place where there won't be no slaves."

"Yes, that would be the wagon train that Justin Good is assembling," Paul said.

"Does you know Mr. Good?"

"I know him."

"I would like for you to ask him, can I go with 'em when they go?" Joe said. "I've got some money, and I've got my own wagon an' team."

"Sure, I'd be glad to ask," Paul said. "But why are you interested in it? I mean, if you are already a free man."

"I be free because the colonel be dead," Joe said. "But if someone come to ask me for papers to show that I am not a slave, I got no papers to show."

Paul nodded. "I see your point," he said. "All right. I'll talk to Mr. Good. I'm sure he will take you on."

"Thank you, Cap'n."

"It's the least I can do, Joe," he said. "After all, you saved my life, twice."

"Twice, sir?"

"Once at the Alamo, when you shot the Mexican soldier who was about to chop off my head, and again at San Jacinto, when you kept Houston from hanging me for being a deserter."

"Yes, sir. Well, shooting that Mexican soldier seemed to be the thing to do," Joe said. "And it wouldn't be right you bein' hung for a deserter, when you was right there fightin' as hard as you could."

Paul chuckled. "No, I don't think it would have been right either," he said.

*   *   *

"This man is a genuine hero of Texas," Paul said as he spoke about Joe Travis to Justin Good. "He was at the Alamo, and he was at San Jacinto. He wants to go with your wagon train and I promised him I would speak to you for him."

"Why did he come to you?" Justin asked. "Why didn't he come to me? I would have taken him, even without your endorsement which, by the way, does make me think highly of him."

"He came to me because I owe him something," Paul said.

"What do you owe him?"

"My life," Paul said easily.

Since speaking at the school Paul had gone out of his way to find reasons to be with Fancy. It was difficult to do so without raising eyebrows, for neither Paul nor Fancy had family, therefore there was no opportunity for the chaperoned visits that composed most courtships. But Paul was nothing if not ingenious, and he managed to take advantage of every opening that did present itself.

When there was a call for volunteers to come whitewash the school and clean up the yard, Paul was there. At a "meet the parents night," Paul volunteered to go to the school in his official capacity as a deputy U.S. marshal to make certain that there were no disturbances from some of the older boys who weren't in school, and who had a tendency to tease their peers who were in school.

And once he attended a lunch social given to raise money for the school. Several single women prepared a lunch for two, then put them on a long table and covered them with a cloth. The idea was for the men to bid upon the lunches with the winning bid sharing that lunch with the person who prepared it. The catch was, not one of the men had any idea who had prepared the lunches that were the subject of their bidding.

No one, that is, except Paul, who knew exactly which lunch Fancy Darrow had prepared. He knew this because Silas, one of Fancy's students, had told him. Even so, the bidding was spirited, more spirited that Paul had expected, and the lunch cost him more than he anticipated. But the cold chicken was good and the money was for the school.

And now, on Saturday, June 3, the best opportunity yet was presenting itself. This was to be a dance, sponsored by the Volunteer Firemen of Austin, for the purpose of raising money for new equipment. It had taken four carpenters two days to build a bandstand and dance floor in the center plaza of Austin. The dance was not only to be the biggest social event of the year in Austin, many said that it would be the biggest event in Austin's history.

Wives were looking forward to the dance in eager anticipation, while husbands were regarding it as a necessary duty. But to the unmarried men and women, the dance would offer the perfect opportunity for them to spend some time together in a way that was not only acceptable, but encouraged.

Because there were so many more single men than single women, the young women were requested not to allow themselves to be escorted to the dance by anyone unless that person was their fiancé. All the young women would be issued "dance cards" and the young men were advised to put their names on the dance cards if they wished to participate.

The band, like the firemen, were all volunteers, and they had spent most of the day practicing the music they would be playing tonight. All up and down the street the high skirling sound of the fiddles, the bleat of trumpets, and the thump of drums quickened the step of the townspeople as they went about their commerce.

When Paul approached the plaza where the bandstand and dance floor had been built, he suddenly had a flashback to San Antonio de Bexar in those last, fateful days before the battle.

To Paul's surprise, rather than preparing for Santa Anna's advancing army, citizens and soldiers alike were enjoying a great fiesta. Music was playing, men and women were dancing, and children were running about.

He shook his head to get that memory and image out of his mind, then looked around for Fancy. Their eyes found each other at the same time, and she smiled, then held up her dance card, inviting him to come sign it. Each dance card had room for eight names, but by the rules of the dance committee, no one name could appear more than four times. However, Paul and Gordon had worked out an arrangement between them. Gordon was now squiring Gretchen Hoffman, so he signed up for four of Gretchen's dances, and four dances with Fancy. Paul signed up for four dances with Fancy, and four with Gretchen. Their plan was to pass off to the other, so that they could have all eight dances with the partner of their choice.

The band kicked off the evening with "Turkey in

the Straw," then followed with "Blow, Ye Winds, Blow, " "Buffalo Gals," and "Black-Eyed Susan." There were a few other songs, but because it was a volunteer band, their repertoire was not all that extensive, so it became necessary to repeat many of the songs. The last song of the evening was "Black Is the Color of My True Love's Hair." There was no dancing to that song, but Paul and Fancy were standing in the shadows of the apothecary building, looking back toward the lighted dance floor as one of the bandsmen, a talented vocalist sang.

Black, black, black is the color of my true love's hair.
Her lips are like some roses fair.
She has the sweetest smile and the gentlest hands.
I love the ground whereon she stands.
I love my love and well she knows
I love the ground whereon she goes.
And I wish the day, it soon will come
That she and I will be as one.

To Paul, it was as if the vocalist was singing about Fancy, and he found himself looking at Fancy's hair, gleaming in the reflected light of more than four-score lanterns suspended on lines around the town center. He reached up and touched it, and she turned her face toward his. Then, still holding his fingers to her hair, he leaned forward, closing the distance between them. He kissed her, not hard and demanding, but as soft as the brush of a flower petal, moved by a gentle breeze.

Fancy was surprised by the kiss, but she was even more shocked by her own reaction to it. She felt a tingling in her lips that spread throughout her body, warming her blood. Reaching up, she touched her lips and held her fingers there for a long moment as she looked at him with an expression that was a cross between fear and desire.

"I'm sorry," Paul whispered in the darkness. "I had no right to do that."

Fancy moved her fingers from her own lips to his. Then they slid up to his cheek and with gentle pressure, she brought his head back down, his lips to hers, and they kissed again.

"Don't apologize for doing something that we both wanted," Fancy said. She was so close to him that he could feel her minty breath against his cheeks. He was about to reply when the band played a fanfare, and the mayor of Austin called for attention.

"Ladies and gentlemen, I want to announce that we were able to raise 326 dollars tonight. The new pumper we wanted costs 300 dollars, so we made our goal!"

There was a loud cheer and applause from the others.

It was two days later, and Paul was still remembering the kiss, when Marshal Allen stepped into his office. There was a tight, almost grim expression on the marshal's face.

"What is it, Jim? You look like you've seen a ghost. What's wrong?"

"Paul, I have someone here from Louisiana. He has a writ of extradition, and I expect it is something you need to deal with."

"Oh?" Paul replied, wondering what could cause

such a reaction in a man who was well known for his calm demeanor. "What is it about?"

"His name is Felix Connor, and I'll let him explain it."

Paul stood as a very well dressed man came into his office. The man was carrying a briefcase, and without so much as a "how do you do," he put the briefcase on Paul's desk, then pulled out a sheaf of papers.

"The marshal said I should deal with you on this case," Connor said. He pointed to one of the papers. "I am looking for a runaway slave who, I have reason to believe, is now living in Texas. As you can see, this is a deed of sale, establishing the ownership. That slave belongs to me, and as Texas is now a state in the United States, and as Texas, like Louisiana, is a slave state, this document is as legal here as it is in Louisiana. I also have a writ of extradition, so I expect you to take whatever legal action is necessary to see to it that my property is returned to me."

"Are you saying this person is in Texas, and you want me to find him and return him to you? Mr. Connor, do you have any idea how big of a state Texas is? If the person you are looking for doesn't want to be found, I could search for one hundred years and not find him, for all that he is black."

Connor smiled, but it wasn't a smile of humor. It could better be described as a sardonic smile.

"Ahh, but that is just it, Deputy," Connor said. "The slave I am looking for is neither black nor a male. To anyone who might see her, she is white. She is just as white as you are, or as I am."

"I don't understand. If she is white, how can she be your slave?"

"Her skin is white," Connor said. "But seeing as she is one-eighth black, then legally, she is all black. The Negress I am talking about is named Fancy Darrow."

Once when Paul was a boy, he had fallen from a tree and had his breath knocked out. He could still remember that moment, lying on the ground, paralyzed, trying to unsuccessfully to breathe, frightened that he might never be able to breathe again.

He felt like that now. All the breath had left his body, and he felt his knees weaken. He reached one hand down to the corner of his desk to brace himself.

"Are you sure?" he asked, finally able to breathe, and actually form the question. "Are you sure that you have the name right? You are looking for a woman named Fancy Darrow?"

"Oh, yes, I got the name all right," Connor said. "She was the daughter of a man named Tom Darrow, who was one of the wealthiest planters in Natchitoches County. He raised her as if she were a white woman. She never knew otherwise until after he died, and his estate was sold. That's when everyone found out that she was not only his daughter, she was his slave." Connor laughed. "He never took out manumission papers. Some say it was because he didn't think he had to; others say it was because he didn't want the truth coming out that her mother was a colored whore working at a house in New Orleans."

"And you say she didn't know?"

"She didn't know a thing about it until she came home from school and found herself being sold on the auction block."

Connor laughed, an evil barking laugh. "That was

when I bought her, paid five thousand dollars for her, I did."

"Five thousand dollars? Why would you pay so much for her?"

"Maybe you haven't seen her yet. She is about the most beautiful woman you will ever lay your eyes on. I own the Maison de Beauté. That's a whorehouse, Deputy, but not just any whorehouse. I have the most beautiful whores in Louisiana, if not in all America. Fancy's mother was a whore there, and so, too, will Fancy be."

"And you want me to find her and turn her over to you."

"I don't just want you to find her, Deputy. I expect you to find her," Connor said. "And you don't have to go all over Texas looking for her. She is right here, in Austin, teaching school. Only when I went down to the schoolhouse, I found out that school is out for the summer. She wasn't anywhere around."

"I see."

"How long will it take for you to find her?"

"I'm not sure. As you said, school is out, so there is no reason for her to be there. I would have to find out where she lives."

"You do that, Deputy. In the meantime, I will find suitable quarters and wait for you to contact me."

"Yes, thank you. I will be in contact with you as soon as possible."

Marshal Allen came back into Paul's office, shortly after Connor left.

"Do you see now why I wanted you to handle this?" the marshal asked.

"Yes," Paul replied.

"Well?"

"Well what?"

"What are you going to do? How are you going to handle it?"

"I don't know," Paul admitted. "I suppose I could tell him that she wasn't here anymore."

"No," Allen said. "He knows that she is teaching school here. He may not have found her yet, but he will."

"Unless I hide her."

"How do you plan to do that?"

"I don't know, yet," Paul said. "But the truth is, Jim, even if I did know what I was going to do, I couldn't tell you. The law says we would have to turn her over to him, and your badge makes you honor bound to do that very thing. And as long as I wear this badge, I am bound by that same honor."

Paul took his badge off and handed it to Marshal Allen. "But I no longer wear the badge."

Marshal Allen took Paul's badge with a simple nod of his head. "I understand," he said. "And God be with you."

Chapter Twelve

After Paul left the marshal's office, he walked around a little while, trying to decide what he was going to do next. He had been a seaman for the first three years of his adult life, settling in Texas when his ship docked in Galveston. Shortly thereafter, he wound up in San Antonio de Bexar as a captain in the Texas Army, then the Texas Rangers, and most recently as a deputy U.S. marshal.

When he awoke this morning, he had no thought of ever doing anything else, but, in a thunderclap, his structured world had come crashing down on him.

Was that true about Fancy? Was she actually a black woman? If so, why hadn't she ever told him?

Why should she? And why should it be important?

It wasn't important. He loved her and that was all that mattered.

Loved her?

Hmm, he hadn't really considered that before. He knew that even though she was the most beautiful woman he had ever seen, it wasn't just her looks that had drawn him to her. She was also thoughtful and intelligent. She was the most intelligent woman—no, the most intelligent *person* he had ever met.

And there was something else about her as well. There was vulnerability about her that made him want to protect her. And, he knew this to be true as well: He would give up his life to protect her.

As he had just given up his career.

And if that wasn't the definition of love, then he had no idea what love was.

But, and he might be a little late in asking this question, did she love him? If she didn't love him, did that mean he had just made a big mistake in quitting his job to protect her?

No. Just because you loved someone, didn't mean they had to love you back. No matter how she felt about him, he had done the right thing.

As Paul continued to roam aimlessly down the street, he looked up to find himself in front of the Excelsior Saloon. And since, of the sixteen saloons in town this was his favorite, he had to wonder if his wandering had been all that aimless after all.

Pushing open the batwing doors, he stepped inside. Though the wood-burning stove had been cold for most of the spring and early summer, there was still a slight perfume of wood smoke, intermingled with the smell of tobacco and the aroma of beer and spirits.

Four men were playing cards at a table near the

cold stove and, except for Dan, the bartender, they were the only ones in the place.

"Hello, Deputy," Dan said, coming over to stand in front of him, wiping the counter as he did so. "Beer?"

"Whiskey," Paul replied.

"Whiskey? Well now, you don't normally drink whiskey in the middle of the day. Somethin' must be troublin' you."

Paul didn't answer the bartender. Instead, he waited for his whiskey to be poured, then started toward a table as far back as he could go. He needed to think about this.

As he walked by the end of the bar, he saw a stack of newspapers, so, taking a nickel from his pocket, he picked one of them up.

New State To Be Formed

In accordance with the joint resolution by which Texas became a State, four additional states may be formed from our territory. Mr. Justin Good, a lawyer of some prominence in Austin City, and the greater environs, proposes to do just that. It is Mr. Good's intention to create a new state to be called Comancheria, said state to be a free state. To that end, Mr. Good is gathering a wagon train of like-minded pilgrims to make the trek. The wagon train has been named the Freedom Train, which seems appropriate, given its intention of establishing a state where people of color cannot be placed in bondage.

The train is currently forming on the grounds next to Walnut Creek and has, at current, sixty-three wagons. Mr. Good has let

it be known that other wagons and freedom-
minded citizens are welcome to join the train.

For the reactions of other newspapers to
this grand expedition, the reader's attention is
invited to read articles from both the Memphis and Cincinnati newspapers, brought to
us by travelers.

There were at two other stories pertaining to the
Freedom Train, one taken from other newspapers.
One article was pro-slavery, the other was opposed.

From the *Memphis Appeal*:

Unwise Attempt
to Change the Balance

With the admission of Missouri to the
Union, a compromise was reached whereby a
fair and equitable balance might be maintained among those states who support slavery and those states who oppose. More
recently, Texas has been admitted to the
Union as a slave state. This is as it should be,
as the greater land mass of Texas, indeed its
capital city, falls under the Missouri Compromise line.

However, in an ill-conceived codicil to the
act of annexation, provisions were made for
the addition of four new states to be carved
from within the Texas borders. Now a man
named Justin Good, a rabble-rousing abolitionist, is attempting to do that very thing. It
is his intention to carve out a new free state in
the Northwest part of Texas, the new state to
be called Comancheria. All who hope for a

fair and balanced peace between the anti-slavery elements of the North, and the right of personal property proposed by the South, will hope that Mr. Good's efforts, no matter how noble he may perceive them to be, fail.

From the *Cincinnati Advocate*:

GRAND ADVENTURE OF JUSTIN GOOD

The hearts of all decent people must beat now with hope and best wishes for the success of Justin Good and his gallant gathering. Mr. Good, with over two hundred followers, has stated his intention to start a new slave-free state within the confines of Texas. This venture is authorized by provisions in the Texas Annexation Bill, which brought Texas into the Union, not as a territory, but as a state. The provisions enable up to four more new states to be created. Mr. Good, a staunch abolitionist, has declared his intention that the new state, which he will call Comancheria, will be a free state.

It is the hope of this newspaper, as it should be of all fair-minded and freedom loving people that Mr. Good's venture be successful.

Even as he was reading the articles in the newspaper, Paul was deciding what might be his best course of action.

Then it came to him. He knew exactly what he was going to do. He had gone to Justin Good to talk to him about taking on Joe Travis, and was pleased when Justin agreed to do so. Now, he would go see him again, this time to see if he would take Fancy with him.

Paul rode out to Walnut Creek where, on a large, flat area known only as "The Grounds," he saw a great gathering of wagons.

These were not the general wagons used on the ranches and farms, or by the local merchants, nor were they the larger freight wagons used to carry goods from town to town. Compared to those wagons, even the freight wagons, these wagons were huge. They were Conestoga wagons with heavy wheels, broad and deep beds which were divided into two floors, the lower used for provisions and things not needed for every day, and the upper used for clothing in daily use, a lounging place during the day, and family bedrooms at night. They had high, arched, canvas roofs. In the right-hand corner in the front was a water barrel and drinking cup. Attached to the wagon bed at the back was the cupboard for food, dishes, and cooking utensils. The teams, Paul noticed, were all composed of oxen.

He saw well over a hundred people making preparations to go, some unloading and reloading their wagons in order to get the best possible use out of the space available to them. Others packed the wheel hubs with grease, while still others were working with harnesses.

Some of the canvas coverings had already been decorated with signs:

COMANCHERIA THE FREE STATE

LIVE FREE OR DIE

COMANCHERIA OR BUST

Hearing the laughter of young people, he saw several children running through the wagons, engaged in some game. The smell of cooking reminded him that he had skipped lunch. He saw Justin Good leaning back against his wagon with his arms folded across his chest, engaged in a conversation with Dale Chapman. Paul knew Chapman, though only casually.

"Do try to get someone else to do it if you can," Chapman was saying as Paul approached the two men.

"It's just that you did such a good job during our move here," Justin replied.

"I would rather not do it, this time. Not since Billy was born. Agnes wants me to spend more time with her and the baby and, well, I'd just rather not do it."

"All right," Justin replied. "But if I can't get anyone, will you do it?"

"I'll do it, only if you can't get anyone else," Chapman replied.

Both men looked up then as Paul approached them.

"Hello, Deputy. Is something wrong? Have we violated some sort of ordinance?" Justin asked.

"No," Paul said. "That is, nothing that I know of. But, I am no longer a deputy."

"Yes, I can see that now," Justin said. "At least I can see that you aren't wearing a star."

"Mr. Good, I wonder if I could talk to you for a few minutes," Paul said.

"Is it something I should stay for?" Chapman asked.

"You are certainly welcome to stay for it as far as I'm concerned," Paul said. "But I wouldn't think it would be anything that requires your attention."

"Then if you don't mind, Justin, I'm going to help Mr. McKenzie repack his wagon."

"Go right ahead, Dale," Justin said.

Paul said nothing more until he saw Chapman step between two wagons that were parked about forty yards away.

"Now, Deputy, or rather, I mean Mr. Nelson. What can I help you with?" Justin asked.

"You remember that I came to you a few days ago to ask you to take on Joe Travis, the colored man who was with me inside the Alamo?"

"Yes, of course, I remember."

"How is Joe working out?"

"He is proving to be a tremendous asset," Justin said. "He can do just about anything with his hands, and he has worked on wagons, repaired harnesses, packed wheels. As I said, he has made himself most welcome."

"Good, good. Now, I have someone else I would like you take with you."

"Who?"

"I would like you to take the schoolteacher, Fancy Darrow, with you. But I must tell you, that there is—uh—something in her background that could be a matter of some difficulty," Paul replied.

"I see," Justin said. The smile left his face. "You

have been keeping company with Fancy Darrow, haven't you?"

"Yes."

"And you think you have discovered something? Well, let me tell you this, Mr. Nelson. If a little something like that can put you off on someone who happens to be one of the sweetest and most delightful young women I have ever had the privilege to meet, then you don't deserve her."

Paul was stunned by Justin's reply, not so much by what he said, as to the fact that he seemed to know Fancy's secret.

"You know about Fancy, do you?" Paul asked.

"Of course, I know about her. She made the trip here with me, didn't she?"

"Who else, besides you, knows of her rather unique status?" Paul asked.

"I thought no one else knew it," Justin replied. "But apparently, you know it," Justin said. "Did she tell you?"

"No, she has said nothing about it," Paul said. "But there is a man in town looking for her."

"There is someone looking for her, you say? Would it be a slave chaser named Pace?"

"No. This man's name is Connor, and he has papers that say that he—" Paul paused in mid-sentence because it was very hard to come right out and say. "He claims that he owns Fancy, that she is his property."

"And how do you feel about that?" Justin asked.

"Quite honestly, Mr. Good, I wanted to thrash him to within an inch of his life," Paul replied.

"But you restrained yourself."

"Yes."

"Tell me this, Mr. Nelson. If it had been about someone else, anyone but Fancy, would you still have felt like thrashing him within an inch of his life?"

Paul thought for a moment, then nodded.

"Yes," he finally said. "Yes, I think I would have felt that way regardless of who it was."

A broad smile spread across Justin's face, and he stuck out his hand. "It's good to know that there are others in Texas, besides our little band of Freedom Travelers, who feel the same way about the evils of slavery."

"I'm sure there are many who feel that way," Paul said.

"You said you had a matter of some delicacy you wished to discuss, and I'm afraid that I leaped before I looked," Justin said. "Please, start again, and I promise I will be more considerate this time."

"As I said, a man named Connor came to Texas to look for her. He was armed with papers showing legal ownership, as well as a writ of extradition. As an officer of the law, I have no choice but to turn her over to him."

"Good heavens, man!" Justin gasped. "You aren't going to do that, are you?"

"No, of course not," Paul replied quickly. "That is why I resigned from the U.S. Marshal's office. But, not everyone who wears a badge is going to have the same sense of reticence. Soon, someone is going to come after her, and since she has been much in the public eye, it will not be difficult for them to find her."

"So what do you have in mind?"

"I'm going to get her out of town as quickly as I can," Paul said. "And the reason I came to see you is,

I was hoping you might let her hide out here with the wagons until just before you leave."

"And then what?" Justin asked.

"And then what? To be honest with you, Mr. Good, I don't have the slightest idea, though, I suppose I was rather hoping you would offer to take her on with you."

"Of course, we will take her on with us," Justin said. "But I have an even better idea. Suppose you and Fancy both join the wagon train? We will need people of your experience when we establish our new state of Comancheria. And because it will be a free state, there won't be any more Connor or Paces in Fancy's past. It is absolutely the safest place for her. I take it that you care something for her?"

"I love her, Mr. Good," Paul said.

"And what does Fancy think about that?"

Paul chuckled, self-consciously. "She doesn't know it," he said. "I've never told her. I've never told anybody. I've never even said the words out loud until just now."

"Then, if that is true, you must know that her best chance, perhaps her only chance, is for you to take her to Comancheria."

"I was hoping you might invite me. But I understand that it will cost two hundred and fifty dollars to join the train, and that isn't counting the wagon and the supplies you need. I don't have that kind of money, and I don't have a wagon."

"I can make you the same deal I made Joe Travis," Justin said. "In fact, I can make you an even better deal. I waived Joe's fee as payment for him offering to be the mechanic and handyman for the trip.

"If you will act as captain of the train, I will not

only waive the two hundred and fifty dollars, I will even provide you with a wagon. You will only have to be responsible for your own provisions. Well, yours and Fancy's."

"All right, Mr. Good. I'll do it," Paul said. "That is, I'll do it if . . ." He let the sentence hang.

"If what?"

"I will do it, if I can convince Fancy to go along with it."

"She'll go," Justin said.

"How do you know?"

"I have come to know her pretty well," Justin said, "both from the trip out here, as well as from the last few years when she has worked for me as a school-teacher. She has a lot of gumption, that woman. Ask her. She'll go."

Fancy lived at Mrs. Emma Flowers Boarding House for young women. He had called for her there once, when he took her out to dinner, but he had waited in the downstairs parlor. When he went into the boarding-house this time though, there was no one in the parlor, and when he looked back into the kitchen, he saw no one there as well. He saw a series of message boxes on the wall, and found the one he was looking for:

MISS FANCY DARROW
Suite 202

Suite 202 was on the second floor, so Paul walked up the stairs as quietly as he could, then paused at the top of the stairs to make certain it was clear before he stepped into the upstairs hallway. He didn't want to be seen there. It wouldn't be good for either his or Fancy's reputation. Seeing the door marked 202, he stepped to it quickly and tapped lightly.

A moment later, Fancy opened the door. The quick expression change on her face told of her shock at seeing him here.

"Paul!" she said. "What are you doing here?"

"Please, let me in before someone sees me," Paul said quickly.

Fancy stepped back from the door and reached out to literally pull him from the hall. She shut the door behind him.

"What is it?" she asked. "Why are you here?"

"Can we sit and talk for a moment or two?" Paul asked.

"Here, in my room? That is impossible! I would be totally ostracized if anyone saw us together in my room. And I would be fired."

"You wouldn't be fired," Paul said.

"How do you know?"

"Because Justin Good is the one who sent me here," Paul replied.

"Now you have me frightened," Fancy said.

"I'm sorry, I don't mean to frighten you," Paul said. "Though there is certainly reason to be frightened. Someone came to see me today, Fancy. Someone that I think you might know."

Fancy drew in a quick intake of breath. She had a sense now, of where this was going, and she didn't like it. She didn't like it one little bit.

"Who was it?" she asked. "And what did he want?"

"His name was Felix Connor."

"Oh!" Fancy gasped, putting her fist in her mouth quickly and biting on it to keep from screaming.

"Then it is true?" Paul knew it was true, without having to ask, but he wanted to hear it from her lips.

Fancy didn't answer him with words, but she did nod in the affirmative.

"For God's sake, Fancy, why haven't you ever told me?"

"Because I thought—that is, I knew—I would lose you if you knew," Fancy said in a very quiet voice.

"You were afraid you would lose me? Fancy, does that mean that you care for me?"

"I think—no—I know I am in love with you," Fancy said. "I know I'm being foolish. I know that, now that you know, such a thing isn't possible."

"You are right," Paul said. "You are being foolish. You are being foolish to think that this would make any difference. Fancy, did you just say that you love me?"

Fancy nodded. "Yes," she said, the word almost a sob.

A huge smile spread across Paul's face and he embraced her and pulled her to him. He felt her crying against his chest and, leaning back, he put his hand under her chin and lifted her face to his.

"Don't cry," he said. "You have just made me the happiest man in the world." Bending down, he kissed her, tasting the salt of her tears on his tongue.

"But what is going to happen to us?" Fancy asked.

"We are going to get married, raise a family, and live happily ever after," Paul said.

"How? Oh, Paul, don't you know that is impossible? We can't get married, not as long as you are white and I am . . ."

"You are the woman I love," Paul said. "We will get married."

"How?"

"You let me worry about that," Paul said. "But first things come first. The next thing we have to do is get you out of here before Connor finds out where you are."

"How did he find me here?"

Paul shook his head. "That I can't tell you," he said. "But I can tell you this. Finding you is one thing. Taking you back to Louisiana with him is quite another and that, I promise you, he will never do."

"Where do we go from here? What do we do now?"

"Now we are going to join the wagon train your friend, Justin Good, is putting together. You will stay hidden there until we leave."

"All right, Paul, whatever you say," Fancy said, glad to have someone else worrying about her, with her, and for her.

Paul had Fancy put all her clothes in a bag, then drop them out the window behind the house. After that, he went out by the same window. When Fancy left the house half an hour later, she walked through the parlor and exchanged pleasant greetings with Mrs. Flowers and her other boarders.

"Will you be taking supper with us, dear?" Mrs. Flowers asked.

"No, thank you," Fancy replied. "I'll be eating with a friend."

"A gentleman friend, I'll bet," Margie Sue said. "Fancy, find out if he has any other gentleman friends."

"You never give up, do you, Margie Sue?" Mrs. Flowers asked, and the others laughed.

                              *   *   *

"We have been talking," Justin said, "and we think it would be best if you sort of stay out of sight until we leave."

"You can stay in our wagon," Lucy added. "We'll take care of you until it is time to go."

"Lucy knows about your—situation," Justin said. "But nobody else knows."

"Once we are under way, you will have your own wagon," Justin said. "And we won't have to be so circumspect about your presence."

"How soon will we be leaving?" Fancy asked.

"We'll be leaving in about two more days," Justin said. "No more than three days, I promise you."

"*We* will be leaving?" Fancy asked Paul. "Are you going as well?"

"I have to go," Paul replied with a broad smile. "I'm to be captain of the wagon train."

Chapter Thirteen

Freedom Train Begins Journey

Readers of this newspaper have been made aware by previous articles, herein printed, of the plans of Mr. Justin Good, a lawyer of the community, to start a new free state. For the journey, Mr. Good has assembled some two hundred and fifty believers, plus a wagon train consisting of seventy-six units. He calls the train the Freedom Train.

In order to make his venture successful, Mr. Good, in addition to seeking political support in the halls of the national congress and state legislature, will have with him one hundred thousand dollars in gold. This money will be used as seed money to establish the new government, of which he identifies himself as Governor Pro Tem.

The Freedom Train, which consists of seventy-six wagons has well over two hundred pilgrims, and has drawn men and women of prominence, among them, Ian McKenzie, a businessman who is well known in Austin for his honesty and willingness to help others. He will also have, as one of the pioneers of his enterprise, Captain Paul Nelson. Captain Nelson, most readers will recognize, is a genuine hero of Texas, being the last to leave the Alamo, later to fight at San Jacinto, the battle which secured for us our independence from Mexico, and more recently, a veteran of the Mexican-American war. Captain Nelson had long been a member of the Texas Rangers, leaving that organization to become a deputy United States marshal, only when that body was disbanded. He has now resigned that position in order to go off on this new adventure.

There is no doubt but the presence of these two stalwart gentlemen in Mr. Good's enterprise will attract others who are eager for adventure, and anxious to better their lot.

San Saba, Texas—June 21, 1848

The stagecoach from Austin brought not only passengers, but a few newspapers as well. One of the newspapers found its way into the hands of Frank Hardin, who was, at the time, enjoying a beer in the *La Cabeza del Toro* saloon.

Frank Hardin read the article about the Freedom Train with great interest. He was especially engrossed by one part of the story.

In order to make his venture successful, Mr. Good, in addition to seeking political support in the halls of the national congress and state legislature, will have with him, one hundred thousand dollars in gold. This money will be used as seed money to establish the new government, of which he identifies himself as Governor Pro Tem.

One hundred thousand dollars was a lot of money, enough money to tempt Hardin. The same article had also mentioned that Paul Nelson would be a member of the wagon train party, and Hardin found that just as tempting.

Hardin folded the paper over and smiled broadly. If, somehow, he could rob that wagon train and kill Nelson in the process, he could leave Texas and go east somewhere, perhaps Philadelphia, or New York, or Boston. He would have enough money to live like a king for the rest of his life.

But it was much easier to think about than to do. At just under twenty dollars an ounce, one hundred thousand dollars worth of gold meant that it weighed over three hundred pounds. Even if he could pull off the robbery, three hundred pounds was more weight than one man could deal with, very easily. He would have to find others who would be willing to go into the operation with him and, because the risks would be high, whoever came in with him would expect a rather significant share of the gold.

"This is the way we'll do it," Ty Bodine said when Frank Hardin approached him with the idea of attacking the wagon train. "We'll get two more men to go with us, and we will pay them five thousand dollars each. That would leave ninety thousand dollars for you and me to split, half for you and half for me."

"I was thinking more like I would take fifty thousand, and you would take forty thousand," Hardin said.

"Why would I want to do that?"

"You remember the bank we robbed? You got the biggest share because it was your idea. Well, this is my idea, so I get the biggest share."

"You don't have to split with me," Bodine said. "You can do the whole thing yourself."

"I can't do it myself, and you know that."

"No, I don't reckon you can," Bodine said. "Well, I thank you for the idea. I'll take care of it and keep all the money."

"If I can't do it myself, what makes you think you can do it all by yourself?" Hardin asked.

"Oh, I won't be by myself," Bodine said. "Like I told you, I'll get a couple of people to go with me. I'll pay them five thousand apiece, and keep all the rest of the money for myself."

"No," Hardin said. "I, uh, I think your idea is good. Me an' you can split the ninety thousand dollars."

"I thought you might see it my way."

"Only thing is, I don't have no idea how the two of us, or even four of us, if you add two more people, can hit a whole wagon train which is just goin' to be full of people, when you know ever' damn one of 'em is goin' to have a gun."

"Let me think on that for a while," Bodine said. "I'll come up with an idea."

Austin—Thursday, June 8, 1848

Joe Travis pulled the canvas aside and looked into the back of his wagon. "Miss Fancy?" he called.

Fancy, who was lying down so she couldn't be seen by the casual passerby, rose up.

"Yes?"

"Cap'n Nelson has done brung his wagon into the train," Joe said. "He ask me to move you over while all the rest of the folks is havin' the big breakfast."

"Thank you," Fancy said. She started out.

"Wait," Joe said, holding up his hand. "They's a couple of town folks I don't know walkin' by."

Fancy waited in the wagon for a moment longer, then Joe called out again.

"All right, Miss Fancy, you can come now."

Gordon Forsythe had resigned his position as a deputy U.S. marshal within one day after Paul. And when Gordon learned that Otto Hoffman and his family, which included his daughter, Gretchen, were a part of the wagon train, he signed on to be one of the pioneers, after making an arrangement to drive one of Ian McKenzie's wagons. Paul, in his capacity of captain of the wagon train, had already named Gordon as his second in command.

The town of Austin sponsored the breakfast that morning as family and friends came down to the wagon park to have a last meal with the pilgrims, and to tell them good-bye. There were well over five hundred people at the wagon park, which was just over twice as many people as would be making the journey. There were seventy-six wagons, plus teams of oxen, mules, and horses, one hundred horses that were not team horses, and two hundred cattle.

Three dozen cooking fires caused the assembly area to be covered with smoke and the aroma of cooking food. The younger children were running around playing, while the older children, many of whom were telling their friends good-bye, were somewhat more subdued. Last minute adjustments were being made to the wagons: Harnesses were checked, water barrels were filled, supplies of coffee, sugar, flour, cornmeal, rice, beans, onions, potatoes, cured hams, and dried beef were loaded. The expectancy of travel hung over all.

Paul, Justin Good, Dale Chapman, Ian McKenzie, and Gordon Forsythe were talking with Charles Wood, the governor of Texas, Jacob Harrell, the mayor of Austin, and James Allen, the U.S. marshal.

"I wish you would change your mind, Justin," Governor Wood said. "I'm telling you right out, your quest to form a new state will not bear fruit. The Texas Assembly is not disposed toward giving away some of our land and, frankly, neither am I."

"I know, Charles, you have made that quite clear," Justin said.

"It's bad enough that you are leaving," Mayor Harrell said. "But you are taking Mr. McKenzie and Mr. Chapman with you. You three men are the heart of Austin's business community."

"And Paul and Gordon the heart of the marshal's office," Marshal Allen said.

"I believe that when we get to Comancheria and the U.S. Government sees the industry and enthusiasm by which we will animate the area, that they will override the Texas legislature and grant us statehood," Justin said.

"How long do you think you will be on the trail?" Marshal Allen asked.

"It is a journey of six hundred miles," Justin said. "I think we will, quite easily, make ten miles per day. That will put us there before the end of summer."

"If you gentlemen will excuse me, I'm going to check on a few things," Paul said, and after shaking hands with the marshal, mayor, and governor, he walked away leaving Justin, Dale Chapman, and Ian McKenzie to argue their position behind him. Walking over to one of the tables where food had been put out, he got two biscuits, opened them up to add a slab of ham. Then, wrapping them in a napkin, he walked through all the wagons until he reached the one he would be driving.

The canvas covering was drawn closed just behind the driver's seat, and at the back. Looking around to make certain that nobody was nearby, Paul called out quietly.

"Fancy?"

The back curtain parted.

"Here," Paul said, handing the little package to her. "I brought us breakfast."

Paul climbed into the wagon, then pulled the canvas closed behind him. Though it was darker inside the wagon, the cover was more translucent than opaque, so it let through enough light to allow them to see.

"You don't have to eat breakfast with me," Fancy said. "I know you have a dozen things to do."

"I want to eat breakfast with you," Paul said, taking one of the ham biscuits from the little package.

"Paul, I'm sorry," Fancy said.

"Sorry? Sorry about what?"

"That you are having to give up your job, that you are having to move because of me."

Paul laughed. "It isn't something I have to do, it is something I want to do. Besides, I'm looking at it as an opportunity. Who knows, Fancy? When we get to Comancheria, we may become wealthy land holders. I won't be Captain, or Ranger, or Deputy Nelson. I'll be Mr. Nelson, substantial citizen." He reached over to lay his fingers along her cheek. "And you will be Mrs. Nelson."

Paul spent about fifteen minutes with Fancy, then kissed her good-bye and left the wagon to join the others in preparation of getting under way. Finally, Ralph Good, now twenty years old, rode through the wagons, calling out to them.

"Get in your places!" he shouted. "Everyone get in line! We're moving out!"

Once they got out on the trail, Paul would spend most of his time on horseback. But until they left town, he and Jason decided it would be better if Paul drove the wagon, and Fancy remained out of sight.

It took at least half an hour for the wagons to get lined up. Then with a loud whistle, they started out on their long journey. For the first mile, many from the town rode, or walked alongside the wagons. It was not until ten o'clock that the last of the towns-people left so that the wagon train was now proceeding, unaccompanied, across the plains.

"Fancy!" Paul shouted from his position on the driver's seat. "Come on up here and see the sunlight!"

Paul felt some movement behind him. Then Fancy stepped over the seat and settled down onto it.

"Ohh," she said. "It feels good to be outside."

"Better get used to it, darlin'," Paul said. "You've got about two months of it."

When they stopped at noon, many were surprised to see Fancy with them.

"I didn't make up my mind to come along until the last minute," Fancy said, and her explanation satisfied everyone but Gordon Forsythe who, when he found some time alone with Paul and Fancy, spoke to them so quietly that no one else could hear.

"I met Felix Connor," Gordon said. "He came to see me right after he learned that you had turned in your badge. He asked me to do the same thing he asked you to do."

"Oh!" Fancy said, gasping as she brought her hand to her mouth.

"Don't worry, Fancy," Paul said. "I trust Gordon Forsythe with my life. In fact, I have trusted him with my life, many, many times."

"The only reason I mentioned this at all," Gordon said, "is because I didn't want you to always have to be worrying that you might say or do something around me that would give away your secret. I want you to be as comfortable around me as you would be with your own brother."

Fancy's look of worry turned to a smile, and her eyes welled with tears. She reached over to take Paul's hand in her own. "I am so lucky to have met such wonderful people," she said.

That night, after the supper meal, Justin called everyone together.

"Ladies and gentlemen," he said. "I have spoken to all of you, individually, many times. But this is the first opportunity I have had to speak with you en masse as it were. We are going to be together for a long time, at least two months on the trail. Then, once we reach our destination, we will be together for an indefinite length of time, no doubt, for some of us, for the rest of our lives."

"Where, exactly, are we going?" one of the men asked.

"Well, George, this is a heck of a time to be asking that question, isn't it?" his wife asked. "Don't you think that's something we might have wanted to know before we started on this adventure?"

The others laughed.

"To be honest with you, George, I have no specific idea of an exact destination," Justin replied. "I know of the general area, and that only from a map. When we get there, we will find a place with fertile land and good water. Of that, I have no doubt."

"I think we all believe that, Mr. Good, or we wouldn't be coming along on this trek," another said.

"Now, the reason I called you all together is because I am going to read to you a document I have written up called the Freedom Train Compact. We'll call it a set of laws and ordinances that I expect us all to abide by. I had copies printed, and I will pass them around, but in the meantime, I shall read the compact aloud."

Justin Good cleared his throat, then began to read.

"For the advancement of our prosperity and happiness, and for the establishment of the honor and salvation of our souls, we proclaim our abhorrence and rejection of slavery. To this end, we undertake a trek to the northwest part of the current state of Texas, hereinafter to be referred to as Comancheria, where the enforced bondage of Negroes will neither take place, nor be tolerated. We do by those present, solemnly and mutually, in the presence of God and one another, covenant, and combine ourselves together into a civil body politic, for our better ordering and preservation and furtherance of the ends afore stated. By virtue hereof, we enact, constitute, and frame such just and equal laws, ordinances, acts, constitutions, and offices from time to time as shall be thought most meet and convenient to the general good of Comancheria. To this end, we promise all due submission and obedience to those appointed or elected to lead us. In witness whereof, we hereunder subscribe out names on this, the year of the United States of America the seventy-second, and on this date, June eighteenth, in the year of Our Lord, 1848."

After he finished reading, he looked out over those who were assembled. "Now, I'm going to ask all men who are over the age of eighteen to sign this," he said. "And I want you to sign it with the understanding that your signature is your pledge to follow the ordinances I just read."

"Hold on there, Mr. Good," one of the men said. "I would like to know who wrote this?"

"I wrote it, Mr. Semmes," Justin replied.

"Uh-huh, that's what I thought."

"Do you have a problem with that?"

"Yes, I have a problem. You've already been

elected the head of this wagon train, and like as not you'll be elected governor whenever we get our new state goin'. But that's governor, it ain't king. We done fought us a couple of wars against a king. I don't think it's right that you wrote that whole thing by yourself."

"I assure you, Mr. Semmes, and all others, here present," he added, taking in everyone with his gaze, "that I did not undertake to write this document driven by any sense of self-aggrandizement. I am a trained lawyer. I have written documents such as these for my entire life. I sought only to make it easier for us to become an organization, rather than a mob."

"I, for one, am happy that Mr. Good wrote the document," McKenzie said.

"As am I," Chapman added.

"Mr. McKenzie, you are an important man," Semmes said. "It don't bother you none that he is making up all the rules we should follow?"

"First of all, Mr. Semmes, I'm not sure that you even listened to the document. At this point, there are no rules, regulations, ordinances, or even leaders. This compact merely states our willingness to abide by such rules, regulations, ordinances, and leaders, as may be established. And it clearly leaves it open for the people to establish those laws and leaders."

"Mr. Semmes, if you wish to change anything within this document, I will happily entertain those suggestions."

When Semmes looked around at the others, he clearly saw that his protest was isolated from all the rest.

"No," Semmes said. "I reckon now that it has been

explained to me, I don't have no objections. I'll be willing to sign it."

"To show that this applies to each and every one of us, I will sign it first," Justin said, as he affixed his signature to the document.

Ian McKenzie was next to sign, then Dale Chapman. Paul stood back as others rushed to sign it, then stepped up to sign his own name. After the meeting broke up, everyone returned to their own wagons.

Gordon and Gretchen came over to visit with Paul and Fancy and they talked until well after sundown. There was a full moon tonight. It was not only bright enough for Paul, Fancy, Gordon, and Gretchen to see each other quite clearly, it also bathed the countryside in textures of black and silver, so that one could see almost all the way to the horizon.

"Have you given much thought to what you are going to do when we get there?" Gordon asked.

"Ranch, I suppose. There are tens of thousands of unclaimed acres there."

"Except by the Comanche," Gordon said.

"The Comanche don't have the same concept of land that we do," Paul said. "To them, land is like air and water. It is there for everyone's use."

"So how are they going to feel when we deny them that use?" Gordon asked.

"Perhaps we won't," Paul said. "Maybe there is enough land there for us to own and them to use."

"Yeah, well, that's what I hope, anyway," Gordon said.

"I see you brought your guitar. Did you just bring it over to show us? Or are you going to sing something?"

"Do that song, Gordon," Gretchen asked.

"Which one?"

"You know the one. The one you just wrote, the one you sang to me today."

"I haven't had time to learn it well enough," Gordon said.

"Don't be silly. You did a wonderful job with it. Sing it for them."

"I don't know, Gretchen, I'm beginning to have second thoughts about it."

"Why are you having second thoughts?" Gretchen asked. "Are there any two people in the world that you love more than Paul and Fancy?"

"Besides you, you mean?"

Gretchen chuckled. "You had better say besides me."

"No," Gordon said. "There is no one in the world, besides you, that I love more than Paul and Fancy."

"Then sing the song for them."

Gordon strummed a few chords, then stopped.

"Paul, Fancy, I wrote this especially for the two of you. I hope you both like it, and neither of you take offense."

Gordon began to sing, the melody lilting, the lyrics endearing, and as he sang, Paul reached over to take Fancy's hand in his.

When the song was over, Gordon looked nervously at Fancy.

"Gordon, I think that song is lovely, and I take no offense whatever. It is who I am, and I am proud to have it immortalized in song."

For the sake of propriety, they made Fancy's bed in the wagon, while Paul threw out a bedroll below the wagon.

The canvas cover of the wagon blotted out the moon, so that inside the wagon, it was so dark that Fancy couldn't see her hand in front of her face. As she lay there in the darkness, she thought of Paul lying on the ground below her. She recalled the kisses they had shared, and now, here in the wagon, she realized that she would like nothing better than for him to be here with her, and to be swept into his arms and kissed again. With such thoughts in her head, Fancy drifted off to sleep.

She was sound asleep when, suddenly, the front canvas of the wagon was jerked open and a man stepped inside. The moon was shining on his face and his eyes glistened as if lit by some internal fire. He was smiling broadly at her.

It was Felix Connor!

"Now, girly," Felix said. "I'm going to take you back with me. But first, I'm going to show you what this is all about."

"No, please! Get away from me!" Fancy shouted out loud.

Almost instantly, the back curtain was jerked open and Paul literally leaped over the tailgate.

"Fancy, what is it?" he asked.

"It's Felix Connor!" Fancy said, her voice shaking with fear. "He's . . ." She looked toward the front of the wagon, and not only saw that Connor wasn't there, she also saw that the front curtain was closed. "I thought . . ."

"There's no one here, sweetheart," Paul said. "And no one has been here. You were just having a bad dream."

"Oh!" Fancy said. "Oh, it was so frightening!"

Fancy sat up and Paul put his arms around her, then drew her to him. He could feel her heart beating rapidly with fear, and he made a silent vow to keep her from ever being afraid again.

"I'm sorry I called out," Fancy said.

"Don't be sorry," Paul said. "I'm here for you. I will always be here for you."

Paul put his hand on her face and turned her face toward his, then kissed her.

The kiss took Fancy's breath away. She had been kissed before by him, and then his kiss had been fire and ice, sending her into dizzying heights of rapture. Always before, though, the kisses had been self-limiting because of time and circumstance. This time no such artificial restraints were in place, and she began to test the limits of the kiss, to see how far it would take her. She gave herself up to it, then, quickly, felt her self-control completely desert her. Her head spun faster and faster with dizzying excitement, and for one, frightening moment, she was afraid she was going to pass out.

The sensations so overwhelmed Fancy that for an instant she lost sight of who and where she was, and she let her body, clad only in a thin nightgown, go limp against Paul. Her breasts were mashed against his chest, and she felt his hands on her body leaving blazing trails of fire wherever they went. It was going to happen! They were going to make love now; it had gone too far for her to stop it. In fact, she didn't want to stop.

Paul had the strength that Fancy did not have, and he pulled away from her. "I'm sorry," he said. "I had no right to force myself on you like that."

Fancy wanted to tell him that he hadn't forced himself on her, that she wanted him, wanted him more desperately than she had ever wanted anything before. But she sensed that he was showing almost superhuman strength to pull away from her now, and she didn't want to do anything that would weaken his resolve. She knew, instinctively, that if she did pull down his defenses that he would be angry with himself, and would blame himself for giving in to his weakness.

"I'll—uh—be just outside the wagon," Paul said. "I promise you, nobody is going to hurt you."

Chapter Fourteen

On the trail—July 4, 1848

In order that they would have an ample supply of water, the Freedom Train followed along the Colorado River for the first fifteen days of the trip. The fifteenth day was July 3, and they made camp alongside the river, intending to stay here for the rest of this day and all day the next in order to celebrate the holiday. This was also a good time to refresh the animals, and as there was ample grass here, the cattle, horses, mules, and oxen were quite content.

Paul, Gordon, Dale Chapman, and Ralph Good went hunting on the afternoon of the third, and they came back with three deer. The children, not to be outdone, fished the Colorado River and the next day they celebrated the Fourth with roasted deer meat and fried catfish. Afterward, they enjoyed cobblers made from freshly picked blackberries.

Several of the children left the wagons to play in

an alongside open field. As they played at their various games, such as hide-and-seek, red rover, and tag, they ventured a little farther away, though they were careful not to get out of sight of the wagons.

Bodine, Hardin, and two other men, Dawson and McGee, were sitting on their horses tucked back into the tree line, looking out at the wagons.

The plan had been to sneak in during the night and force Justin Good, at gunpoint, to give them the money. But as they saw the children playing, Bodine held up his hand.

"Boys, I just got a better idea," he said.

"A better idea about what?" Hardin asked.

"A better idea about how to get the money," Bodine said. He pointed to the children. "All we have to do is grab a few of those kids and hold on to them. They'll pay us to get the kids back alive."

"How are we going to let them know that we have the kids?" Hardin said. "If one of us goes to talk to them, they might just keep whoever it is and try to trade for the kids."

"You let me handle that," Bodine said. "First thing we have to do is get the kids."

"You got 'ny ideas on how to do that? They are on the other side of the creek. If they see us comin' toward them, they'll start screamin', and runnin' back to the wagon."

"Then we need to get them over on this side of the creek," Bodine said. "And I've got an idea how to do that. Dawson, you're ridin' a palomino. I've never known a kid who wasn't attracted to a gold horse. Take the saddle off your horse and let it wander out into that open area just this side of the creek."

"Ha!" Dawson said as he took off the saddle and

bridle. "I see what you are doing. You are baiting the trap."

As soon as the saddle and bridle were removed, Dawson slapped his horse on the rump, and sent it trotting out into the open area. There was a lot of good grass there, and the horse began to graze.

"Oh, look!" young Jenny Hughes said. "Look at that beautiful horse!" She pointed to the palomino that was cropping grass just across the creek.

"Is it a wild horse?" Rachael asked.

"Nah, it ain't no wild horse," Sammy said. "You don't ever see a wild horse all by itself."

"But there's no saddle on it," Steve said.

"Maybe it's a horse that ran away," Jenny said.

"Let's go get it!" one of the others said.

"Mama told us not to go across the creek."

"It's not far across the creek. It's right there!"

Bodine, Hardin, and the other two men watched from the tree line as the six children came across the creek. As they did so, Dawson clucked at his horse, and the horse started walking toward him.

That drew the children farther away from the creek.

A few more clucks and the horse came all the way up to the tree line, and so did the children. That was when Bodine and the others jumped out toward them.

*   *   *

Back at the wagons, the others were singing songs and telling stories when one of the children came up, crying.

"What is it, Sammy?" Justin Good asked.

"They took the others," Sammy said.

"What are you talking about? Who took the other children?"

Sammy pointed back toward the creek.

"Over there, on the other side of the creek. There were four men," Sammy said. "They all had guns, and they took the others. One of them gave me this note and told me to give it to you."

Justin Good opened the note, read it, frowned, then handed it to Paul.

SEND PAUL NELSON AND ALL OF YOUR GOLD TO GORMAN FALLS. YOU CAN SEND ONE MAN WITH HIM TO HELP CARRY THE GOLD. IF HE DOES NOT SHOW UP WITH THE GOLD BEFORE NIGHTFALL, WE WILL KILL ALL THE CHILDREN.

"Oh, my God! The children! Where are they?" one woman cried out, and soon the entire wagon train was in a panic.

"I don't think, for one moment, we should send just two men," Chapman said. "You heard what Sammy said. There are only four of them."

"And you saw the note," Justin said. "If they see more than two men coming, they will kill the children."

"Like as not they have already killed the children," Chapman said.

"No! Oh, God, please no!" someone shouted.

"Dale, we don't know that," Good said. "And that kind of speculation does no one any good."

"Besides, they will need to keep the children alive as a bargaining position," Paul said.

"You're right," Chapman said, apologizing quickly. "I had no right to say such a thing. But I do think we'd be making a big mistake by just sending two men. They may not kill the children, but I believe they will most assuredly kill the two men who come to call for the children."

"Since they asked for me specifically, I have a position in this," Paul said. "And I say that I am perfectly willing to go alone."

"You won't be alone, Paul," Gordon said. "They said you could take someone with you, and that would be me."

Paul smiled. "I sort of thought you might volunteer," he said.

"What about the gold?" McKenzie asked. "Are you going to take the gold?"

"How do you have it stored?" Paul asked.

"There are ten cloth bags, each containing ten thousand dollars worth of gold ingots."

"Give me one bag with gold. Empty the gold from the other nine bags and put something in that will approximate the bulk and weight."

"What happens after they discover that?" Chapman asked.

"It will be up to Gordon and me to make certain they don't discover it," Paul said.

*　*　*

Half an hour later, Paul and Gordon were ready to go. Paul had five of the bags hanging, conspicuously, from his saddle, as did Gordon. Both men were wearing pistol belts with holsters. But both men also had a five-shot revolver hidden away in each boot, giving them a total of twenty loaded charges. If Sam was right, and there were only four of the outlaws, Paul and Gordon agreed that twenty shots should be enough.

Gorman Falls was about three miles from where the wagons had camped for the last two days.

"I see no reason for us to be riding up in plain view," Paul said shortly after they got under way. "They'll be looking for us to come across the prairie from the wagons. What do you say we go down into the creek and follow it?"

"Good idea," Gordon said, agreeing with the plan.

As Paul and Gordon rode along the creek bed, they could hear the falls even before they reached it. The sound got louder as they approached until, at the end, the roar of the tumbling water was louder even than the sound of the splash of their horses' hooves in the water.

Then, suddenly after rounding a bend in the creek, they saw five of the wagon train children sitting on the ground by the edge of the creek. Three of the children were boys, two were girls. The youngest was about nine, the oldest, Jenny, was thirteen. There were two men down with the children, and one more up behind a large rock, looking out toward the prairie over which they were expecting Paul and Gordon to advance. None of the outlaws saw or heard Paul and Gordon as they came riding up behind them.

They would have gotten away with it cleanly, if one of the children, upon seeing their two rescuers had not called out.

"Captain Nelson! Mr. Forsythe!"

The two rescuers had been noticed too soon for them to achieve an element of surprise. All three outlaws, upon hearing the child call out, spun around to face them.

"Hold it right there!" one of the men called.

"Frank Hardin," Paul said.

"You recognize me, do you, Nelson?" Hardin said. He smiled, showing a mouth full of broken and discolored teeth. "Well, I'm flattered."

"I've been chasing you for over four years," Paul said. "Why shouldn't I recognize you?"

"Ah, but you aren't a ranger now. And you aren't a deputy U.S. marshal. You aren't even a deputy sheriff. You ain't no lawman of no kind," Hardin said. "So you ain't chasin' me no more, are you?"

"I guess that is correct," Paul said. He waved at the seated children. "This seems a little low though, even for someone like you."

"Well, now, no more of us than there is, you didn't expect us to attack the wagon train, did you?"

Paul knew the name of the boy who had called out when he and Gordon arrived, and he looked over toward him. It was Steve Cramer.

"Are you and the others all right, Steve?" he asked. "Have they hurt any of you?"

"They've sure scared us," Steve answered. "But they haven't hurt us, yet."

"Do you see how nice we have been?" Hardin asked. "Now, let me ask you this. Did you bring the money?"

"We brought it," Paul said, patting one of the bags hanging from his saddle.

"How do I know that it's real?"

Paul loosened the drawstring that had the top of the bag closed, then reached down inside to pull out one of the gold ingots. He held it up, and it flashed brilliantly in the sun.

"Here it is," he said. He put the ingot back into the bag.

"Bring it over to us."

Paul and Gordon rode across the creek. Paul didn't go directly toward Hardin and the others. Instead, he went about twenty yards upstream from them. Following his lead, Gordon rode alongside him. Paul began dropping the bags on the ground, one by one then, and Gordon did as well. Paul purposely chose the bag with the real gold as the last one to drop, doing it in such a way that some of the gold spilled out.

Bodine wasn't with the others, because a moment earlier he had gone back into the trees a short way to relieve himself. When he came back, he saw Nelson and Forsythe talking with Hardin and the others, so he stopped, just out of sight, to see how it all played out.

"Send the children across the creek," Paul said. "Steve, when you all get over on the other side, get away from here as quickly as you can. Get back to the wagons."

"Yes, sir, Mr. Nelson," the boy answered.

"Wait a minute," Hardin said. "Them four can go." He pointed to the three boys and youngest girl. Then he pointed to Jenny. "We're goin' to keep this one around for a while, just till we are sure we've got away."

"You aren't keeping any of them," Paul insisted.

"Well now, seein' as we got you outnumbered here, don't seem to me like you got much say in the matter, does it?" Hardin said. "In fact, before they go, why don't you two just drop your pistols there in the water? That would sure make us feel more comfortable, because I figure with wet powder, you won't be no trouble to us."

"Let them go, first," Paul said.

"All right, you brats go on across the creek," Hardin said, waving at them with his pistol in his hand.

All five started across, but Hardin called out to Jenny.

"Not you, girl," Hardin said. "You're goin' to stay with us for a while."

Jenny was crying, but not out loud. She came back, and sat down again.

"Now, I believe we had agreed that you two would drop your pistols into the water," Hardin said to Paul and Gordon.

The two former rangers pulled their pistols, then dropped them into the water.

"You two, come over here and sit on the ground next to the girl," Hardin said. Then, to the other two men with him, he said, "Boys, let's get the gold."

All three men ran toward the ten cloth bags that were lying on the ground. Not one of them looked back toward Paul or Gordon, considering them no longer dangerous since they had dropped their guns in the water. Their only interest was in getting to the gold.

"Darlin', get over there, behind that rock," Paul said quietly. "And do it fast."

Jenny did as directed, and even as she was getting herself out of danger, Paul and Gordon were pulling their two spare pistols from their boots.

"Hey, Hardin, what is this? There ain't nothin' in this bag but rocks!" one of the outlaws called out in disgust.

"They tricked us!" another said.

Bodine started to call out a warning, but he knew that the warning would be too little and too late. He knew also that once Nelson and Forsythe killed the other three his own life wouldn't be worth a nickel.

"What the hell is this?" Hardin shouted in anger. He and the other two outlaws turned toward Paul and Gordon. When they did, they were shocked to see that both men were holding revolver pistols pointed at them.

"Drop your guns, all of you!" Paul shouted.

"The hell we will!" Hardin shouted back. "Shoot 'em, men! Shoot 'em!"

Triggers snapped, firing caps popped, and charges exploded as five guns began firing. For the few seconds of the concentrated gunfire the little creek valley was filled with the roar of exploding gunpowder. The outlaws were frightened and out of control, and their shooting reflected that. Not one of their bullets found its mark, though Paul could hear the whistling of the bullets passing close by.

In direct opposition to the outlaws, Paul and Gordon were shooting calmly, and with deadly accuracy. Every bullet they fired hit flesh, and little mists of blood flew from the bullet impacts as the outlaws twisted and jerked, their bodies forced into a death dance as the balls ploughed into their body.

For just a second, Bodine watched the men writhe under the impact of the bullets. Then he ran back to his horse, mounted it, and rode off, even as he could hear the gunfire behind him.

In little more than the blink of an eye, all three outlaws were down, the rapid flowing water now carrying away whirling currents of blood, like long, bubbling bubbles of red. Cautiously, the two former soldiers, rangers, and deputy U.S. lawmen, approached the three men. It wouldn't do now for one of the outlaws to suddenly turn on them.

That was no problem. Paul kicked at all three of them, and was convinced that they were dead. "They are all . . ."

"Dead," Gordon said, who had come to the same conclusion.

"Jenny, darlin', you can come out," Paul called over his shoulder to the young girl. "You can't be hurt, now."

Cautiously, Jenny came out from behind the rock.

"There was another one," Jenny said. "He had white hair, but he wasn't old. And he had"—she made a motion across her eyes—"funny looking eyes. They were pink."

"Bodine," Gordon said.

"Where is he now?" Paul asked Jenny.

"I don't know. He rode off that way."

Paul and Gordon searched the tree line in the direction Jenny had pointed, but they saw nothing.

"He must have run when he saw their plan wasn't going to work," Gordon said.

"That's what I figure," Paul agreed. Paul lifted Jenny onto his horse, then he mounted behind her, and he and Gordon started back toward where the wagons were camped. This time they went back across the prairie. Since this was the quickest way to return, they overtook the other children more than halfway back. Then Paul set Jenny down with the others. He and Gordon dismounted, and walked the rest of the way back, which was a distance of about a mile.

Parents, grandparents, brothers, and sisters had a joyful reunion with the returned children and, with a big smile, Justin Good had a joyful reunion with his returned gold.

It was a week later, when Ralph Good and Ian McKenzie came galloping back to the wagon train, which was then in motion. Ralph and Ian had been scouting ahead of the train, when they spotted a war party of Comanche.

"Get the wagons in a circle!" Justin called, and with Paul, Gordon, Ralph, Ian, and Dale assisting, it didn't take too long for the wagons to form a circle. They left one wagon out of place, providing a wide enough opening to bring in the cattle and horses. Then, with the hastily constructed corral filled with their animals, they pulled the last wagon into place, making their "fortress" secure.

All of this happened in less than half an hour. Paul was pretty sure the Indians could have been there within that time, but for some reason they waited outside, about a quarter of a mile away. They remained sitting on their horses on top of a little rise, looking back down toward the wagons.

"Why don't they come?" McKenzie asked. "Why don't they attack?"

"They are trying to make up their minds as to

whether or not they have the advantage," Paul said. "Indians never attack unless they are sure they have the advantage."

"You mean Indians are cowards?" McKenzie asked.

Paul shook his head. "No, I would hardly call them cowards," he said.

"Well then, if the only time they will ever attack is when they think they have the advantage, and they aren't cowards, just what would you call them?" McKenzie asked.

"I would call them battlefield tacticians," Paul said.

McKenzie chuckled. "Battlefield tacticians," he said. "All right, I'll go along with that. It makes sense to me."

Paul, Gordon, and Chapman took a walk all the way around the inside of the hasty fortress, checking the firing positions of the defenders, and the cover of the others. Each man had two rifles, one to shoot, and one to be loaded by his wife, or parent, or child.

Paul decided that the Freedom Train was ready for whatever might happen.

One of the Indians, yelping and whooping, came forward from the others. When he got close enough, he loosed an arrow which flew toward Paul, then buried itself in a wagon only inches away. As the Indian pulled a second arrow from his quiver, Paul raised his rifle to his shoulder and fired. The Indian fell from his horse.

At that, four more Indians charged.

"Fire when they come in range!" Paul shouted and shortly after his shout, several rifles barked from within the circle of wagons, and all four Indians went down.

"Gordon?" Paul called. Gordon was clearly the best shot of any on the wagon train. In fact, he was one of the best marksmen Paul had ever known, clearly as good as the sharpshooting Tennesseans who were at the Alamo with Davy Crockett. "You see the one there, holding the crooked staff?"

"Yeah, I see him."

"I expect he's the leader of the bunch."

"Want me to see if I can hit him from here?"

"No, he's the one we are going to have to talk to. They are Comanche, and if we are going to live out here with them, we are going to have to make peace with them."

"Can you speak Comanche?" Justin asked. "Because I wouldn't expect them to speak English."

"Most of them can speak Spanish, and so can I," Paul said. "Gordon, if you can, I want you to shoot the one that's next to the chief."

"All right," Gordon said.

Gordon picked up a tuft of grass and dropped it, then watched what the wind did with it. Then he loaded his rifle with a double charge of powder. The others watched as he stepped to the back of his wagon, then rested the rifle on the side of the wagon as he took aim.

He fired, the rifle roaring louder than usual because of the double charge. First flame, then a huge puff of white smoke issued from the muzzle.

Running Wolf saw the flash, then the puff of smoke billowing from the rifle of one of the white men who fired from a distance that was many times more than an arrow could travel. Running Wolf was sure it was a show; he did not think the white man could hit anyone from that far.

"Uhhn!" Afraid of Bears grunted, and looking toward him, Running Wolf could see blood pouring from the black wound in his chest, even as the sound of the firing rifle reached him.

Afraid of Bears fell from his horse.

"Ayiee . . . the white men are devils!" one of the other warriors said, and all began to get nervous.

"We must attack now!" Stone Eagle said.

"No," Running Wolf replied.

"Would we stay here and let the white men with their guns kill us all?" Stone Eagle asked.

"Wait," Running Wolf said, holding up his hand. "I think we will talk."

Running Wolf saw one of the white men leave the circle of wagons and start riding toward him. The rider was holding one hand over his head to show that he was unarmed.

"We can kill him," Stone Eagle said.

"No," Running Wolf repeated. "I will speak with him."

Holding his staff over his head, Running Wolf started out across the ground toward the white man who was riding toward him.

"*¿Habla usted Espanol? Vengo en paz.*"

"*Sí, entiendo Espanol. ¿Que quieres que te hable?*"

Paul continued speaking in Spanish.

"I wish to speak of peace between us," Paul said. He pointed to the wagon train. "We have come to make our home here. We do not want to be enemies with the Comanche. We want to be good neighbors with the Comanche."

"Where will you make your home?" Running Wolf asked.

"We will make our home where we can raise cattle and grow food."

"You will live on our hunting ground," Running Wolf accused him.

"We will hunt only what we can eat," Paul replied. "And when we raise our cattle and grow our food, we will hunt less. Every season we will present a gift of cattle, horses, and food to our neighbors. We will be allies, and if someone attacks the Comanche, we will fight on the side of the Comanche."

"You are chief of the white man? You can make this promise?"

"I am not the chief, but I can speak for the chief," Paul said. "He will honor any promise I make. Can you speak for all Comanche?"

"How are you called?" Running Wolf asked.

"I am called Paul. How are you called?"

"I am called Running Wolf. I cannot speak for all Comanche, but I will speak to the Comanche." Running Wolf switched his staff to his left hand. Then, with his right hand, he made a fist, brought it to his chest, then raised it up, opening the fist. "And I will be good friend to Paul."

Paul repeated the gesture Running Wolf made, and held up his own hand.

"And I will be good friend to Running Wolf," he said.

"Eeeeeyaaahhhh!" Running Wolf screamed at the top of his lungs. Then he turned and galloped back to those who were waiting on the hill behind him.

Paul returned to the wagons, where he was met by the anxious pioneers.

"What did he say?" Justin asked. "Will there be peace?"

"There will be peace," Paul said.

*   *   *

There were no more encounters with Indians or outlaws, but that did not mean that the trip was without danger of any kind. They learned that when they reached the Colorado River. At the point where the river was joined, it was relatively deep with a rapid current and high, abrupt, soft banks.

"Damn," Justin said as he and Paul examined the obstacle before them. Seventy-six wagons were stretched out behind them. "Anyone have any ideas?"

"First thing we need to do is dig through the bank to make a point of entry, then again on the other side as our exit point," Dale said.

"Good idea."

"This is a good place for an entry point," Dale said. "But it doesn't look all that good on the other side of the river."

"We don't want the exit point there, anyway," Paul said. "Look how rapid this stream is. Once we go in, the current is going to carry the wagons and animals downstream. In fact, we can probably use the momentum to help get us across."

"Yeah, I see what you mean," Dale said. Looking across the stream, he pointed to a place on the opposite bank, about fifty yards downstream. "Right there would be a good place."

After further discussion, they decided to disconnect the animals and let them get across on their own. Then they tied a rope to the tongue of the first wagon, and a second rope to the rear. Paul, Gordon, and Ralph Good crossed the river, taking one end of the rope with them. Then when they were in position, they grabbed the rope and pulled the wagon into the water. With Justin, Ian, and Dale on the backside, holding on to the trail rope to keep the wagon from being swept below the exit point, the wagon was pushed into the river.

It took them all day long, but by the end of the day, all seventy-six wagons, and all the people and animals were across.

It was two days after they crossed the Colorado that they lost their first member. Nate Connor, a thirty-five-year-old man from Ohio, shot himself accidentally while cleaning his pistol. He left behind a twenty-nine-year-old widow, and three children. Then the wife of Ted Rittenhouse and her two children died of cholera, as did the entire Coleman family, husband, wife, grandmother, and four children. Five-year-old Andy Garner fell under the wheels of his family's wagon, and was run over and killed. Four more died along the way, though nobody knew for sure what malady had laid them low.

Funerals were held and the victims were buried en route. They buried them in the tracks of the wagons. They weren't able to leave markers directly over the graves that way, but the thinking was that burying them in the actual tracks of the wagons would prevent any wild animals from digging them up.

Chapter Fifteen

As the celebration continued in the hotel ballroom, Gretchen Forsythe sat quietly on one side of the room. Gretchen was born in Germany, and when she was fourteen years old she was raped by Ludwig von Schillinger who was *Burgermeister* of the small Bavarian village of Niederwern. Because Schillinger was both the mayor of the town, and a wealthy man, the police refused to bring charges against him. Gretchen's father, Otto, took matters into his own hands, confronting Schillinger. Schillinger drew his pistol and shot at Otto, but missed. Because the pistol held but one round, Otto was able to defend himself before a second shot could be fired. Otto defended himself by killing Schillinger.

After that, Otto and his family had no choice but to leave Germany, so they came to America. In the sixty-eight years since that time, Gretchen had wanted to go back for one final visit to the country of her birth, though she knew that it would probably never happen. Then, Gordon had surprised her with the news that they were going to Europe for a grand tour of the Continent.

It had been a wonderful visit, and Gretchen even found a first cousin with whom she had been close, many years ago. Then, when it came time to return, Gordon bought first-class passage for them on the newest, largest, fastest, and most luxurious liner on the ocean. It was the pride of the White Star Line and, as Gordon explained, excitedly, they would be making history, for they would be on the maiden voyage of the *Titanic.*

Two months earlier

Captain Edward Smith was resplendent in a white dress uniform that was festooned with colorful decorations. He was seated at the head of the table in the first-class dining salon of the *Titanic,* joined by Mr. and Mrs. John Jacob Astor of New York, Mr. and Mrs. Walter Clark of Los Angeles, Mrs. Molly Brown of Denver, and Mr. and Mrs. Gordon Forsythe of Amarillo, Texas.

A uniformed waiter came to the table. "Ladies and gentlemen, for dinner this evening we have *pigeon-neau rôti, asperges, filet mignon au bacon, et pommes de terre rôties.*"

"What are we having?" Gordon asked.

"Pigeon, honey. He's talkin' about pigeon and steak," Molly Brown said.

"Squab," John Astor said.

"Well, that'll be all right then," Gordon said. "I've

eaten both of 'em. But why didn't you say it in English? This is an English boat, isn't it?"

The others around the table laughed.

"I'm told, Mr. Forsythe, that you were a participant in the battle of the Alamo," Walter Clark said.

"No, I wasn't at the Alamo," Gordon said. "My brother was, and he was killed there. I was at San Jacinto."

"And Palo Alto, during the Mexican-American war, and Shiloh, Antietam, and Gettysburg, during the War Between the States," Gretchen added.

"War Between the States," John Astor said with a chuckle. "You are a true lady of the South, referring to the Civil War in such a way."

"Captain Smith, you may not be aware, sir, but we are sharing the table tonight with a true figure of American history," Molly Brown said.

Captain Smith raised his glass toward Gordon. "It is indeed an honor, sir."

"No, sir," Gordon replied. "The honor is all mine, to be dining at the table with the captain of the most magnificent ship ever built."

Captain Smith's eyes sparkled. "The *Titanic* is a wonderful ship, isn't she? She is a marvel of engineering, and a testimony to the greatness of man."

"I'll give you this, Captain," Gretchen said. "It's a lot more comfortable than traveling by wagon train."

During the meal, the ship's orchestra performed in the dining salon and when some of the passengers began to dance, Gordon reached over to take Gretchen's hand.

"If we were thirty years younger, I would ask you to dance," Gordon said. "But at this age, I think holding hands is enough."

"Now look what you have done," John Astor said. "You have forced me to have to take Madeleine's hand, too, so as not to be outdone."

"John!" Madeleine said, slapping his hand, playfully. "You mean you have to be forced to take my hand?"

"Never would I have to be forced, my dear," John said, lifting his wife's hand to his lips and kissing it. "Taking your hand is always a delight."

Again, the table laughed.

Much later that night, after they had gone to bed, Gretchen was sound asleep when she was awakened by a strange, shivering motion of the ship. Not at any time on the way across, nor in the few days onboard this ship on the way back, had she experienced such a thing. Nervous about it, she got out of bed and walked over to the porthole. Looking through it though, she saw nothing but the night, and the few, almost luminescent, feathers of white on the sea.

Behind her, Gordon was sleeping peacefully, his snoring measured, but not too loud. Opening the door to their cabin, Gretchen looked up and down the companionway, but saw no confusion, nor did she hear a noise of any kind. Satisfied that there was no danger, Gretchen got back into bed, and snuggled up against the warmth of her husband.

As she lay there in bed, however, she continued to feel a sense of unease and, again, she got up and opened the door to look out into the companionway. This time she saw that she wasn't the only one concerned, because there were others now, who were also sticking their heads out of their doors to look around as if by that way they could discern something.

Gretchen saw a steward hurrying by, and she called out to him.

"Has something happened to the ship?"

"Oh, I think not, madam," the steward replied. "If something had happened, we would have been told by now."

"But I heard something," Gretchen said. "More than that, I felt something. I'm sure the ship hit an object of some sort. Another ship, perhaps?"

"More than likely, madam, it was nothing but an errant wave," the steward replied. "I've been to sea many years and that happens from time to time."

"But, if it is anything serious, you will tell us?" Gretchen asked.

"Of course, I will. But I'm sure it is nothing to worry about," the steward said.

Not quite satisfied, Gretchen returned to the bed, but instead of getting in under the covers, this time she just sat on the edge.

"Is something wrong, darling?" Gordon's sleepy voice asked.

"I don't know," Gretchen said. "I felt something a short while ago. It felt like the ship hit something. And I think others felt it as well, for when I looked out into the passage, I saw others enquiring."

"Do you think we should get dressed?" Gordon asked.

"I don't know."

"Would you feel better if we got dressed?"

"Yes," Gretchen said. "Yes, I think I would."

"All right," Gordon agreed.

Over the next few moments, Gordon and Gretchen got dressed, and by the time they were dressed, they could hear movement and voices out in the passageway. Gordon opened the door and saw one of the ship's officers, recognizing him as an officer by the hat he was wearing.

"Officer, there seems to be some confusion aboard this ship. Has there been an accident? Is there some danger of any kind?"

"None, so far as I know, sir," the officer replied.

"What do you think?" Gretchen asked when Gordon closed the door and turned back toward her.

"I still don't know."

"I heard his answer. It was courteous, quiet, and reassuring," Gretchen said.

"Yes, exactly the kind of answer he would be trained to give under such circumstances," Gordon said.

"Now, you've got me worried."

Gordon chuckled. "You started it," he said. "I was sleeping peacefully in my bed."

She laughed, too, though it was a nervous laughter.

Gordon opened the door again, and this time he saw the officer talking to one of the other members of the ship's crew. And what he heard that time made his blood run cold.

"We can keep the water out for a while. But I fear it has involved too many compartments," the other crew member said.

Gordon closed the door quickly, then turned around and looked at Gretchen. The expression on his face frightened her.

"Gordon, what is it?"

"Get your warmest coat on," he said. "Wrap yourself in a scarf. Put on your warmest shoes."

"Gordon, what is it? Oh, pray, tell me."

"I think this ship may be sinking," Gordon said in a tight, but controlled voice.

A few moments later, after they were dressed in coats, there was a tap on the door. Gordon opened it quickly. It was a ship's steward, the same steward Gretchen had spoken to a few minutes earlier.

"I apologize for the intrusion, but I'm afraid I am going to have to ask you to get your life vests on quickly," the steward said. "Then go to the main deck, please."

Outside the stateroom the corridor was filling rapidly. But unlike the laughter and gossip heard when passengers filled the companionway heading for the wonderful meals served during the voyage, this time there was no laughter and very little conversation. Instead, everyone seemed to stand around quietly, as if waiting for further instructions on what to do. And strapped around the torsos of all, including the stewards, were the life vests.

When they reached topside, the deck was crowded, at least as crowded as it had been when they left Southampton where everyone had come aloft to wave good-bye. It was also very cold, and Gretchen began shivering uncontrollably. She knew though, that the shivering was not entirely driven by the cold, and she moved closer to Gordon.

Gordon put his arms around her. For the last sixty-four years, Gordon could soothe her fears or ease her pain with his embrace. But that comfort wasn't there now. All Gretchen could feel now was a numbing fear that penetrated to her very soul.

"Women and children to the lifeboats!" a ship's officer was calling as he passed through the throng on the deck. "Women and children to the lifeboats, please."

"If you don't mind, I prefer to wait and go into the same boat as my husband," Gretchen said.

"Sorry, madam, but the women and children are being taken off first."

"Don't I have the right to choose to wait?"

"No, ma'am. Don't worry about your husband. As soon as we get all the women and children loaded, we'll get the men."

"No, I'll—"

"You'll get into the boat," Gordon said, gently but firmly.

"Gordon, no, please. I want to wait and go with you."

"Don't you understand, Gretchen? There are no boats for the men. Now, please do what the officer says."

Gretchen gasped, and raised her hand to her mouth. "Gordon?"

Gordon embraced her, pulling her to him as hard as he could. Then he kissed her. "I'll see you again," he said. "I'll find us a nice place in heaven. I'll see Paul. And knowing him, I'll bet he already has a place staked out for us." Gordon smiled. "Hey, I'll even get you that screened-in porch you have been wanting." Gordon chuckled.

"How can you laugh at this?"

"Sweetheart, I told you a long time ago, if you can see the humor in it, you can take anything."

"There is no humor in this."

"Then humor me," Gordon said. He put his finger

under her chin and lifted it slightly. "Go with the steward."

"Gordon, no, please, I'm not going," Gretchen said. "I'm staying with you."

"No," Gordon said. "You need to stay alive long enough to tell all our children, grandchildren, and great-grandchildren good-bye for me. Please, darling, go. Don't you understand? The only thing I have left now will be the knowledge that you survived this."

"Gordon, I . . ." Gretchen started, but she couldn't finish. Tears were streaming down her face as Gordon reached out to put his hands on her shoulders. Then he gently turned her so that she was facing the direction the ship's officer wanted her to go. Gretchen followed the officer across the deck, almost as if she were in a trance.

When she reached the rail, there were two crewmen helping the women and children into the boat. The crewmen were both strong, handsome young men, reminding Gretchen of her Gordon when he was that age. And though Gordon had lived a full and very productive life, she knew these two young men were just starting life, but would end it, here on this ship. The sailors knew it as well, but this was the life they had chosen, and the knowledge that they were soon to die did not stop them from performing their duty with courage, strength, compassion, and dignity.

Gretchen's lifeboat had thirty-six people in it as it was swung out from the davits, and began to be lowered down to the sea. At first, only one side of the ropes worked, and the lifeboat started to tip sharply to one side. Some of the women called out, and

Gretchen feared they would panic and cause the boat to tip over, dumping all into the sea.

"Quiet! Sit still!" one of the sailors on deck ordered, and finally, they got the ropes working together so that the boat went down smoothly and evenly. Even now, Gretchen was not convinced that the ship would really sink. A part of her felt sure that this must be only a drill, and soon they would all be taken back onboard and returned to their staterooms to sleep the rest of the night away in their warm beds.

But the boat was rowed away, and the outline of the *Titanic* was growing less and less. Also, the bow of the ship was getting black, as light after light began to wink out. It was not until now, as she watched the progressive darkening of that great ship that Gretchen was able to accept that she had parted from Gordon for the last time.

Gretchen searched the deck she had just abandoned, and she saw Gordon standing at the rail. He smiled and waved at her, and her heart broke.

Sitting by Gretchen in the lifeboat were a mother and daughter. The mother had left a husband and son on the *Titanic*, and the daughter a father, husband, and brother.

As the forward portion of the ship sank deeper, Gretchen could see passengers' futile scrambling to the stern. Gordon, who was already near the stern, stayed in place, bracing himself against the increasing angle of the ship by holding on to the rail.

The almost fifteen hundred people still aboard broke up into groups, clinging in clusters, only to fall in masses, pairs or singly, as the great stern of the ship, two hundred and fifty feet of it, rose into the sky 'till it reached a sixty-five or seventy-degree angle.

Below the decks of the great ship, Gretchen could hear the sliding of furniture, the crashing of glass and the loud twisting of metal. As the first funnel went underwater, it burst open with a huge, explosive gasp of gleaming white steam and smoke. Then, slowly, majestically, almost as if in a ballet, the *Titanic* slid beneath the water.

"Two hours and forty minutes since we hit the iceberg," someone said, as if they felt it necessary to give an historical marker to this disaster.

They rowed on through the night, discovering to their horror that they had not one quart of water and not one biscuit among them. Would they drift about on water until they died of starvation? Would it not have been better to have gone down with the ship, in the company of their loved ones?

Overhead the stars slowly disappeared, and in their place came the faint pink glow of another day. Then someone called out, "I see a ship! We are saved!"

Amarillo—Saturday, June 15, 1912

Gretchen shook her head to clear her mind of such horrendous memories. Then she got up and walked over to sit beside Fancy.

"Hello, Gretchen," Fancy said. "How are you doing, dear?"

"Some days, I do better than others," Gretchen said. "It's almost three months now—eighty days since I sat in the boat and was rowed away as the *Titanic* went down."

Fancy reached over to take Gretchen's hand in hers.

"I tell people that I could see Gordon, standing on the side of the ship, holding on to the railing as he watched the lifeboats pull away. I tell people that I kept my eyes on Gordon until the very end. I tell them that, but I don't know if it is true or not. We were so far away from the ship by then, and it was so dark."

Tears began streaming down Gretchen's face. "I should have stayed onboard with him, Fancy. I begged him to let me stay with him, but he said I had to go, for the sake of our children and our grandchildren."

"He was right, Gretchen," Fancy said. "Can you imagine what a blow it would have been to your family if they had lost both of you? I know what a blow it was to me to have lost an old friend like Gordon. I don't know if I could have stood losing you as well. You are my oldest and dearest friend."

"Why didn't they have enough lifeboats, Fancy? You would think it would have been a simple thing. As big as that ship was, there was plenty of room for lifeboats, enough that they could have rescued everyone onboard."

The song that had been playing ended with a flourish. Then after a pause of less than a minute, another started. As soon as the next song started, the young people began dancing again, and Gretchen, with a concerted effort to erase such melancholy from her mind, smiled at Fancy.

"Are you enjoying the dance, Fancy?" Gretchen asked.

"I'm too old for the dance," Fancy said. "But I am enjoying the music."

"You know who would have really enjoyed the music," Gretchen said. "It would have been my Gordon."

"Yes, I know he would have."

"He loved music," Gretchen said. "And I'm sure you remember, Fancy, that Gordon was quite the musician himself."

"Oh, how well I remember," Fancy said. "He would play his guitar and sing for us on that long trip up from Austin."

"And do you remember the song that he wrote for you and Captain Nelson? The song that was dedicated to you?"

"Yes. 'The Yellow Rose of Texas,' " Fancy said.

"That song has become a part of the lore of Texas now," Gretchen said. "It was played by the band at the dedication today, but I'm sure that, of the thousand or more people who were there, not more than half a dozen know the real story of the song. They don't know who wrote it, and they don't know that it was written especially for you."

"I suppose they don't," Fancy said.

"How does it make you feel, when you hear that song?"

"It makes me feel sad and happy at the same time," Fancy said. "It makes me sad because my Paul, your Gordon, Mr. Good, Mr. Chapman, Mr. McKenzie, so many are gone now. But it makes me happy because when I hear it, I recall those times when we were all together, trying to build something new and wonderful."

"We did more than try," Gretchen said. "It didn't

come about exactly as we had planned, and it took a lot longer than we planned but, Fancy, it is here, and we did it. Look around at this auditorium, at all the young people who are enjoying the benefits of what Paul, Gordon, Mr. Good, Mr. Chapman, and Mr. McKenzie created."

"It wasn't just them, though," Fancy said. "It was all of us."

"I have something for you," Gretchen said. She reached down into her purse. "I wanted to give this to you, on this special day, and I've been waiting for the right moment." She pulled out an envelope and handed it to Fancy.

"What is it?"

"You'll see what it is when you open it."

Fancy opened the envelope, then pulled out a folded piece of paper. There was something written on the outside of the folded paper.

This song was written for my friend
Captain Paul Nelson, and the beautiful lady
at Captain Nelson's side.
   Gordon, Forsythe, on the trail, June 18th, 1848.

"Is this the original?" Fancy asked.

"It is. Gordon and I kept it, all these years."

"Oh, no, Gretchen, I can't take this." Fancy handed it back to Gretchen. "I especially can't take it now, not after what happened to Gordon. This will mean so much to you."

Gretchen refused to accept it.

"I want you to have it," she said. "Gordon wanted you to have it. In fact, we spoke about it during our trip to Europe. Gordon knew that there was going to be a statue and dedication to Paul, and he was very much looking forward to giving this to you on this day."

"Gretchen, are you sure you want to part with it?"

"I'm not parting with it," Gretchen said. She put her hand over her heart. "I will always have it here. And as long as you have it, I will always know where I can go to see it. Please, take it now. I know that Gordon and Paul are in heaven looking down on us right now, right this moment. Don't disappoint them."

"Of course, I will take it," Fancy said. "And I will protect it, and hold it dear for the rest of my life."

Fancy unfolded the paper and saw the lyrics, the ink faded brown by time, but still clearly legible.

The Yellow Rose of Texas

There's a yellow rose in Texas,
That I am going to see,
Nobody else could miss her,
Not half as much as me.
She cried so when I left her,
It like to broke my heart,
And if I ever find her,
We nevermore will part.

She's the sweetest girl of color
That Texas ever knew,
Her eyes are bright as diamonds,
They sparkle like the dew;
You may talk about your Clementine,
And sing of Rosalee,
But the Yellow Rose of Texas
Is the only girl for me.

"I know that when some recall that long wagon trip," Gretchen said, "they think only of the hardship. But it was during that trip that Gordon and I were married. You and Paul, too. So when I think of it, I remember only the joy."

"Oh, yes," Fancy said. "It was quite memorable in so many ways."

Cindy Nelson came over to join Gretchen, her mother, and her mother-in-law, Fancy.

"Hasn't this been a wonderful day?" she said. "Everyone is having such a wonderful time."

"They are, aren't they?" Gretchen said. "And can you believe that we actually have five generations here? Of course, Margaret is here in body only. Bless her little heart, she is sound asleep. It is amazing how she can sleep with the noise, the music, the talking and all."

"Children have an amazing facility to block everything out when they want to sleep," Cindy said.

Chapter Sixteen

Texas Panhandle—Thursday, August 24, 1848

Sixty-seven days after leaving Austin, Paul Nelson, Gordon Forsythe, Justin Good, Ian McKenzie, and Dale Chapman held a conference on the banks of the Canadian River.

"For the last two days we have been passing through flat, fertile land," Justin said. "Also, there have been many creeks, streams, and tributaries from the river, meaning that this area is well watered." Justin smiled, broadly. "Gentlemen, I think we have reached Comancheria."

"How big is Comancheria to be?" Ian asked.

"I don't want to be greedy."

"It isn't a question of greed, Justin," Dale said. "It is a matter of having enough room for our new state to be viable."

"Gentlemen, I submit to you that it doesn't take

that much room," Justin said. "Look at Rhode Island or Delaware."

"That's true," Paul said. "It doesn't take a whole lot of room to be a state. But because I know this area, having been here several times while with the Texas Rangers, I could make a suggestion if you are interested."

"Yes, by all means, do make a suggestion," Justin replied.

"I would suggest that the Canadian River be our southern border. Our northern and our eastern border will be the Indian Territories, and our western border will be the western border of Texas."

"And what is that western border?" Ian asked. "As I'm sure all of you know, the western border of Texas is now in dispute."

"I think it is going to be settled by the establishment of the territory of New Mexico. The line that is being proposed is the 103rd longitude. If we go beyond that line, we are going to get embroiled in bickering with the state of Texas and the federal government. As well as New Mexico."

"I agree," Justin said. "Most of the studies I've seen place the compromise western boundary of the panhandle at the 103rd longitude."

"I don't have a problem with that," Ian said. "But the Canadian River is too far north," Ian complained. "I think we should go well south of that, all the way down until we take in the entire panhandle."

"That could cause us trouble," Paul suggested. "Especially, seeing that our purpose is to establish a free state."

"Why would that cause trouble?" Dale asked.

"As I understand it, the article of Congress that authorizes statehood for Texas, and allows for additional states, declares that only that portion north of the Missouri Compromise line will be declared a free state. That line is the thirty-sixth parallel, and to be honest, the Canadian River is slightly south of that line, but if we do choose that as our southern border, I think that, with the majority of the state north of the thirty-sixth, we will have no trouble in declaring ourselves a free state."

"I agree with Paul," Justin said. "I've no wish to do anything that could cause difficulty with our prime objective."

"I agree with Ian," Dale said. "I think we should extend our border all the down to the bottom of the panhandle."

"What do you think, Gordon?" Justin asked.

"That isn't fair," Ian interrupted.

"What do you mean it isn't fair?"

"Asking Gordon what he thinks. He is Paul's best friend. He is naturally going to agree with him."

Gordon chuckled. "You are probably right, Ian," he said. "Ninety-nine times out of a hundred, I will agree with Paul, no matter the question. But it just so happens this time that I would agree with him, even if I didn't know him. However, I do have a suggestion for our dilemma."

"What would that suggestion be?" Justin asked.

"I suggest that we put the question to the members of the wagon train and let them vote on it. After all, they are the ones who are going to have to live here. They certainly should have some say in the matter."

"I think Gordon is right," Dale said. "I think we should put it to a vote."

"All right," Justin said. "Let's do that."

Although the five men had been conducting their conference out of the hearing of the rest of the members of the wagon train, the others had followed it as best they could from a distance, knowing that a decision of great importance to them were being made. As the five men walked back toward the wagons, the pilgrims began gathering around them.

Justin chuckled. "I thought I was going to have to call a meeting," he said. "Evidently, that won't be necessary."

Justin waited a moment longer as the others, those few who had not gathered out of initial curiosity, joined the group. When everyone was there, Justin cleared his throat, then began to speak.

"Ladies and gentlemen of the Freedom Train, let me begin by saying the Freedom Train is no more. We have reached our destination, our trip is completed!"

Justin's announcement was met with loud cheers and huzzahs.

"You mean this is Comancheria?" one of the men asked.

"Yes."

"Where are we?" another asked. "What I mean is what are the borders of Comancheria?"

"Funny you should ask that, Walter," Justin replied. "Because that is just exactly what we were talking about. Where should we establish our borders?"

"What did you come up with?"

"We haven't come up with anything yet," Justin admitted. "Since this concerns all of us, we think everyone should have some input as to the final decision. Now we have two proposals, so I'm going to ask Ian to speak for one proposal, and Paul to speak for the other. Afterward, we will take a vote."

Ian spoke first.

"Ladies and gentlemen, you all know me," Ian said. "And you all know that I am not a person who thinks small. It is my suggestion that the state of Comancheria encompass the entire panhandle of Texas. There are several advantages to that. First we would only have to draw one border line, that being the one at the bottom of the panhandle that would go from the Indian Territories to the 103rd longitudinal line. It would make the state of Comancheria larger than any existing New England state, and on a par with most of the other states in the country. And," he added with a smile, "it would form an almost perfect square. Think how easy it would be for our children in school to learn to draw a map of our state."

The others laughed at that.

Ian finished his presentation, and Justin stepped up again. "Now, when we vote, we will refer to this as the McKenzie plan. Paul Nelson will speak for the Nelson plan."

"There is much to be said for the McKenzie plan," Paul began. "But I would like to offer my plan for your consideration. I think we should establish our southern border at the Canadian River. Having a river for a border is always advantageous, since it is clearly defined, thus avoiding any future border disputes. Also, one of the articles of statehood which grants the right to carve additional states, says, specifically 'and having sufficient population.' At this point, we have a population of just over two hundred people. The area of the panhandle that Mr. McKenzie is proposing is over twenty-five thousand square miles.

That breaks down to one hundred twenty-five square miles for every man, woman, and child. I do not think our petition would be well received if we attempted to claim such a large area.

"And finally, and most importantly, I ask you to consider the stated purpose for our founding the state of Comancheria. We have come here inspired by the universal commitment to establish a slave-free state. If we have the entire state north of the Canadian River, we will have enough territory north of the thirty-sixth parallel to make certain that our status as a free state not be questioned."

When Paul finished his presentation, Justin addressed the people again.

"Now I'm going to give you folks about half an hour to discuss this among yourselves," he said. "Then we will vote on it, and after that vote is taken, we will abide by the results, with no further argument."

After a lively discussion, a hat was passed around. Those who wanted to vote for the McKenzie proposal were asked to drop a black bean into the hat. Those who wanted to vote for Paul's proposal were to drop a white bean into the hat.

Justin, Ian, and Paul counted the results as the members of the wagon train looked on, anxiously. Finally the count was concluded.

"Ladies and gentlemen," Justin said. "By a fair vote, the Nelson proposal is adopted. Welcome to the new state of Comancheria!"

Again, the cheering was loud and enthusiastic.

"Now, I have two duties to perform," Justin said. "Though as I intend to do both at the same time, I suppose you can really say it is only one duty.

"I have been asked to perform the marriage ceremonies for some of our people. And while you have ratified me as governor pro tem of Comancheria, such a state does not yet, officially, exist. Therefore, to make certain that these marriages are valid, I will perform the ceremonies under the power granted to me, and which authority I still hold, by the state of Texas.

"Paul Nelson and Fancy Darrow, would you please come forward? And Gordon Forsythe and Gretchen Hoffman, I would ask you to come forward as well."

Because they had known about this, and had made plans for it, both Fancy and Gretchen were wearing wedding gowns that they had made during the trip out. When they appeared in the wedding dresses, the rest of the assembly applauded.

Neither Paul nor Gordon was wearing suits, but they were wearing clean trousers and shirts.

Justin began performing the ceremony. At the point where he said, "I require and charge you both, and all here present, as ye will answer at the dreadful day of judgment when the secrets of all hearts shall be disclosed, that if any know any impediment why Paul and Fancy, and why Gordon and Gretchen may not be lawfully joined together in matrimony, ye do now confess it. For be well assured, that if any persons are joined together other than as God's Word doth allow, their marriage is not lawful."

Paul heard Fancy draw a quick breath of apprehension at the charge, and he felt her tighten up. He put his arm around her and drew her closer to him.

With the charge unanswered, Justin continued the ceremony until, finally, he pronounced Paul and Fancy husband and wife, and Gordon and Gretchen, husband and wife.

After the wedding ceremony, there was a great

dinner of celebration, not only of the weddings, but of the successful completion of their journey.

The first thing the new residents did was build houses. Initially they built small, one-room cabins, meant to serve as shelter from the coming winter. With everyone working together, it took less than a month to build the little community of Comancheria. Once the town was built, they set about establishing land claims for those who wanted to ranch or farm. Some, like Ian McKenzie, preferred to enter the mercantile business and as he had brought three wagons on the journey, two of them filled with goods for his store, he was able to set up his business rather quickly, though for the first winter he did business mostly on credit.

Comancheria City— May 5, 1852

The state of Comancheria did not come into being. The application for admission as a state was turned down, both by the United States Congress and the legislature of the State of Texas. Texas did not want to give up any of its territory, and the United States Congress declared that there were not enough people in the Comancheria area to justify a new state.

Having their application denied did not come as a complete surprise to everyone, because they knew the battle was an uphill fight anyway. And, in the long run, it didn't make that much difference to them. Within the first four years they built farms, a church, and a school. Though the settlement that would, within thirty years, become Potter County had not yet been established, there were few who didn't believe that that day would come.

Although Paul Nelson had title to over thirty thousand acres of land, he was making effective use of much less. Like his neighbors around him, he was growing cotton on about five hundred acres. That was as large a farm as he could manage with the shortage of manpower. However Paul, like Gordon, who owned the neighboring ranch, and all the others who had made the long wagon train trip up from Austin, had absolute faith that the area would grow, and they would grow with it. He named his place "Longtrail" and burned it into a board, then hung the board from an arch over the road that led up to the house.

"The sign is as big as the house," Fancy said with a lilting laugh.

"It is now," Paul said. "But I promise you that one day, Longtrail will be a place that you are proud of."

Fancy wrapped both her arms through Paul's arm. "What a silly man you are, Paul," she said. And before Paul could respond, she added, "I am already very proud of it."

Although they had been unsuccessful in establishing the state of Comancheria, they did succeed in building a town by that name. Thanks in great part due to the entrepreneurialism of Ian McKenzie, who built stores and a bank, the leadership of Justin Good, who built a school and a courthouse, and the evangelical zeal of the Reverend E. D. Joiner, who built an interdenominational church, civilization came to the panhandle. And, with the promise of land, new settlers arrived so that the community began to grow.

Joe Travis was a skilled carpenter who prospered

by building many of the buildings in the town. Within a year after arriving in Comancheria, Joe returned to Austin where he found a wife by buying the freedom of a woman who was indentured to Mirabeau B. Lamar, former president of the Republic of Texas. Joe brought Wanda back to Comancheria, where he built them a house on ten acres of property just out of town.

Wanda turned out to be as good a gardener as Joe was a carpenter, and she raised enough vegetables, not only to feed them, but to sell to the growing number of residents of the community.

Part of the growth in population was the new children who were being born. One year after Paul and Fancy were married, their son, Thomas William, named after Fancy's father and Colonel William Travis, was born. Tommy was three years old now, and the absolute joy of Fancy's life. He had his mother's dark hair and eyes, but was already big for his age and everyone said that he was going to be as big a man as his father.

Gordon and Gretchen had a daughter, Sally, who was one year younger than Tommy, and Paul and Gordon accused Fancy and Gretchen of matchmaking.

One day Fancy had just given Tommy a bath and he seemed unusually fidgety as she was dressing him.

"Hold still, Tommy," she said as she tried to slip a shirt down over him.

"There is a man outside, Mama," Tommy said.

"What man? Hold your arms up."

"There is a man," Tommy said again.

"Is it Mr. Forsythe?" Fancy slipped his shirt down over him.

"No. There is a man," he said again.

"Tommy, sweetheart, I don't know what you are talking about. What man?"

Tommy pointed toward the door and Fancy looked around, then gasped out loud in fear. "Felix Connor!"

"I am flattered that you recognized me. Did you think you could escape, Fancy?"

"Why are you here? After all this time?"

"What difference does time make to us, my dear?" Connor said. "After all, I bought you. That means you will belong to me until the day you die."

"I'm married. I've nothing to do with you now," Fancy said.

"Ha," Connor said. "The same law that says you belong to me says you aren't married."

"But I am married, and as you can see, I have a child now. Please, I beg of you. Just go away and leave us alone."

"Yes, I can see that you've whelped. And the law says that the child of a slave is a slave. Looks to me like I'll be gettin' two for one," Connor said. "Come on, it's a long way back to Louisiana."

"I'm not going anywhere with you," Fancy said defiantly.

Pulling his pistol, Connor pointed it at Tommy.

"Oh, I think you will. You'll either come with me, peaceably, or I'll kill the brat."

"No!" Fancy said. She stepped in front of her child. "You'll have to kill me first."

"Rest assured, my dear, if I can't take you back to Louisiana, I will kill you," Connor said.

Connor pulled the hammer back on his pistol, and Fancy closed her eyes, bracing for the impact of the bullet.

"Connor!" a loud, angry, and authoritative voice called.

"Paul!" Fancy called out.

Connor spun toward Nelson, shooting as he turned. Fancy saw Connor shoot, and heard only one shot. Then, to her horror, Connor turned back toward her, with a broad, evil smile on his face. He took two steps into the room, then, on the third step, he stumbled and fell, with his gun clattering to the floor. That was when Fancy saw the exit wound in his left shoulder blade. She heard quick footsteps from outside. Then Paul ran into the room, uninjured, and holding a smoking pistol.

"Fancy!" he shouted.

She rushed to him—and they embraced.

"Oh, Paul, he was going to kill the baby," Fancy said.

"You don't have to worry, Fancy, never again for the rest of your life," Paul said.

Tommy had not spoken a word since Connor confronted them, and now he stood looking at his parents, confused as to why his mother was crying. Paul reached down and picked him up.

"None of us have to worry again," Paul said.

Commerce, Texas—1860

One hundred fifty miles southeast of Comancheria was the town of Commerce. Despite a name suggestive of business and prosperity, Commerce was little more than a fly-blown speck on the wide open range. Railroads were just being built in Texas and one early plan called for a railroad to pass through Commerce. No such railroad developed, but on its promise,

Commerce did manage to build a few saloons and bawdy houses.

Two young men, passing through the town, stopped in front of the Blind Pig Saloon. Swinging down from their horses, they patted their dusters down.

"Whoa there, Denny, all that dirt rising around you, you look like one of them dust devils comin' across the plains," his partner said.

"Yeah, well, I tell you, Jake, you ain't exactly squeaky clean your ownself," Denny said. "What do you say we go inside and get us a beer?"

The two young men went into the saloon, then stepped up to the bar. The saloon was relatively quiet, with only two men at one table, and a third standing down at the far end of the bar. The two at the table were engaged in conversation, while the one at the end of the bar was nursing a drink. The man nursing the drink had a face that was almost totally devoid of color. The hair was white, but it wasn't the white of age, it was the white of one who has a total lack of melanin. The irises of his eyes were so pale a pink as to be practically colorless. The lack of color was especially vivid due to the fact that he was dressed in black. A turquoise-and-silver band around his short-crowned black hat provided the only deviation in the drab scheme.

Neither of the boys had ever seen anyone who looked quite like this and they stopped in mid-conversation to stare at him. He looked back with an unblinking stare of his own.

"What'll it be, gents?" the bartender asked.

One of the two boys continued to stare.

"Jake?" Denny said. "The bartender asked what'll we have."

"Oh," Jake said, breaking away from his fascination with the albino. "I'll have two beers."

"Two beers it is," the bartender replied. He turned to draw the beers.

"I'll have two beers, too," Denny added.

The bartender laughed. "You boys sound like you've got a thirst."

"Yes, sir, we have," Jake said. "We have ridden hard for about six days now. We're headin' up into the panhandle."

"Are you now?" the bartender replied. "Well, you got a ways to go yet. You headin' for any place in particular up there?"

"Yeah, a place called Comancheria."

"Comancheria, huh?" the bartender said as he put the beers on the bar. "Well, I've never been there, but I know there are some good people who have moved up there."

"We was told we should meet with someone named Justin Good. You ever hear tell of him?" Jake asked.

"I've heard of 'im. They call him the governor of Comancheria."

"Governor? Don't you mean mayor?"

The bartender chuckled. "Well, I reckon he is a mayor, but at one time, or so I'm told, they was goin' to make that into a state, and he was goin' to be the governor. Only that didn't never happen, 'cause it wasn't never made into a state."

"What are you meeting with Justin Good about?" the albino asked.

"Excuse me, sir. Are you Mr. Good?" Denny asked.

"No."

"Then, no disrespect, mister, but I reckon what

we're meeting with Mr. Good about is between Mr. Good and us."

"It don't matter none," the albino said. "Good, McKenzie, Nelson, Forsythe, all those people up in Comancheria are nothing but trash. And if you two boys go up there, you won't be nothin' but trash either."

"Mister, you've got what they call a belligerent attitude, did you know that?" Jake asked. Then he ameliorated his comment with a smile. "But to show that there ain't no hard feelin's, suppose we drink a toast to Comancheria?"

The albino smiled, but the smile just made his pale face look even more grotesque.

"Go on up there if you want to. But if you do, you'll just be trash like the rest of 'em up there."

Denny had less patience than Jake. "You got something stuck in your craw, mister?" he asked, bristling now at the man's comment. He turned away from the bar to face the man at the other end.

"Easy, Denny," Jake said, reaching out for his partner. "I'm sure he doesn't mean anything personal by that remark."

"Yeah, I do," the albino said, his voice little more than a sibilant hiss. "I mean it just real personal."

Denny glared at the albino, but the expression on the albino's face never changed.

"I got me an uneasy feelin' about this, Denny. Let's leave it be."

"I just don't like being insulted by some maggot-looking son of a bitch who's got no more sense than to butt into someone else's business," Denny said.

"We promised our folks we wouldn't get in no trouble, remember?" Jake said. "We're just up here to see if we can claim some land of our own."

"You're plannin' on claiming some land of your own?" the albino asked. He laughed, a short, mirthless laugh. "You two wouldn't even make good farm or ranch hands, let alone land owners. If you want my advice, you'll turn around now, and get back to wherever it is you came from."

"That's it, Mister! I'm going to mop the floor with your sorry hide!" Denny said. He put up his fists.

The albino smiled, a smile without mirth. "If we're going to fight, why don't we make it permanent?" he asked. He stepped away from the bar and flipped his jacket back, exposing a pistol which he wore low, and kicked out, in the way of a gunfighter.

Denny realized now that he had been suckered into this, and he stopped, then opened his fists and held his hands, palm out in front of him.

"All right!" he said. "Hold on, wait a minute here. I reckon I sort of let this go further than I intended. I'm sorry if I offended you. I don't see no need to carry this on any more'n I've already done. This isn't worth either one of us dying over."

"It's too late for that. You've done got my dander up, so I'm going to have to kill both of you."

"No, you won't, 'cause neither one of us have any intention of drawing on you," Jake said. "If you shoot us, you are going to have to shoot us in cold blood, in front of these witnesses."

"Oh, you don't need to be worryin' none about witnesses," Bodine said. "You see them boys over there?" Bodine pointed to the table. "Both of 'em ride with me. Boys, how about you say hi to these two young fellas?" Bodine called out.

The two men at the table smiled and nodded toward Denny and Jake.

Jake's knees grew so weak that he could barely stand, and he felt nauseous.

"And the bartender knows that if he don't say what I want him to say, I'll kill him, too."

"Please, we don't want any trouble," Jake said. "Why don't you just let us apologize and we'll go on our way?"

Bodine shook his head. "You boys brought me to this ball, now you're goin' to have to dance with me," he said. "Pull your guns."

Jake and Denny looked at each other. Then, with an imperceptible signal, they started their draw. Though the two young men were able to defend themselves in most bar fights, they were badly over-matched in this fight. They made ragged, desperate grabs for their pistols.

So bad were they, that Bodine had the luxury of waiting for just a moment to see which of the two offered him the most competition. Deciding it was Denny, Bodine pulled his pistol and shot Denny first. Jake, shocked at seeing his friend killed right before his eyes, released his pistol and let it fall back into his holster. He was still looking at Denny when Bodine fired a second time, this one so close to the first one that some who were outside thought they heard only one report. Jake fell on top of Denny.

Bodine whirled his pistol around on his finger, then blew away the smoke that was still curling out from the muzzle.

"Bartender," he said in the same, low voice.

"Yes, sir?"

"Slide them un-drunk beers down the bar to me. Ain't no sense in lettin' 'em go to waste."

Chapter Seventeen

Austin—January 10, 1861

For many southerners, the election of Abraham Lincoln in the fall of 1860 was equivalent to a declaration of war on the South. That was no less true in Texas, but there were those who argued against it, including Paul Nelson and the aging Justin Good, who traveled to Austin to see if they could exert some influence.

Governor Sam Houston poured brandy for the two men when they called on him in his home.

"Colonel Nelson, it has been a long time," he said. "And, Mr. Good, how well I remember your arguments to allow the state of Comancheria to be born." Houston took a swallow of his drink, then wiped his lips with the back of his hand.

"I wish I had joined with you in your fight," he said. "That would have at least prevented Texas from the folly of secession. I have argued the benefits of mediation and compromise."

"But you've had no success?" Justin asked. "You can't find any who will support your position?"

"None," Houston said. "I even made the suggestion that if we do secede from the Union, that we return to our pre-statehood status. I believe we would fare far better as an independent republic than we would as a member of this abominable Confederacy."

"But surely, Governor, the people of Texas will listen to you," Paul suggested. "You are to Texas what George Washington is to the United States."

"I'm afraid my views carry little weight among the secessionists in the state, who are clearly in the majority," Houston said. "I have done what I can—I have refused to call the legislature into session. For the time being that has blocked the secessionists from any official action."

"Well then, that clearly is the solution, isn't it?" Justin said. "How can they do anything without a session of the legislature?"

"I'm afraid the sons of bitches have called upon the people of Texas to elect delegates to a Secession Convention to meet in Austin. Their purpose is to consider what action Texas should take on the secession issue in light of the recent sequence of events."

True to Sam Houston's prediction, a total of 177 delegates were elected, representing two members from almost every county. Paul and Justin represented the Bexar District. The convention met on January 28, 1861. Four days later, on February 1, its members voted by a margin of 166 to 8 to secede, Paul and Justin being 2 of the 8 who voted against secession

They drafted and signed an Ordinance of Secession, which "repealed and annulled" the Texas annexation laws of 1845. Then, though Houston pleaded that if secession is to be, that Texas be declared a republic, the convention adopted another ordinance uniting Texas with the Confederacy. Sam Houston refused to take the oath of allegiance to the newly organized Confederate government. Undaunted, the convention declared the governor's office vacant and administered the governor's oath of office to Edward Clark, who had previously served as lieutenant-governor.

Reluctantly, Paul and Justin returned to Comancheria to share with the people there the results of the Declaration of Secession.

We hold as undeniable truths that the governments of the various States, and of the confederacy itself, were established exclusively by the white race, for themselves and their posterity; that the African race had no agency in their establishment; that they were rightfully held and regarded as an inferior and dependent race, and in that condition only could their existence in this country be rendered beneficial or tolerable.

That in this free government all white men are and of right ought to be entitled to equal civil and political rights; that the servitude of the African race, as existing in these States, is mutually beneficial to both bond and free, and is abundantly authorized and justified by the experience of mankind, and the

*revealed will of the Almighty Creator, as recognized
by all Christian nations; while the destruction of the
existing relations between the two races, as advocated
by our sectional enemies, would bring inevitable
calamities upon both and desolation upon the fifteen
slave-holding States. By the secession of six of the
slave-holding States, and the certainty that others
will speedily do likewise, Texas has no alternative
but to remain in an isolated connection with the
North, or unite her destinies with the South.*

*For these and other reasons, solemnly asserting
that the federal constitution has been violated and
virtually abrogated by the several States named,
seeing that the federal government is now passing
under the control of our enemies to be diverted from
the exalted objects of its creation to those of oppres-
sion and wrong, and realizing that our own State
can no longer look for protection, but to God and her
own sons—We the delegates of the people of Texas, in
Convention assembled, have passed an ordinance
dissolving all political connection with the government of the United States of America and the people
thereof and confidently appeal to the intelligence and
patriotism of the freemen of Texas to ratify the same
at the ballot box, on the 23rd day of the present
month.*

*Adopted in Convention on the
2nd day of February, in the year of our Lord
one thousand eight hundred and sixty-one and
of the independence of Texas the twenty-fifth.*

"What does that mean as far as our colored folks
are concerned?" one of the men in the audience
asked.

"It has no bearing on them whatsoever," Justin replied.

"It has to. We've got near twenty colored people living here now."

"And every one of them, like Joe Travis, a free man," Paul said.

"Yeah, but, what I mean is, once we secede from the union, why, we'll be a slave state. I don't know that it would be right for us to have that many coloreds among us, and not one of 'em be a slave."

"Consider this, Arnold," Paul said. "We have been a slave state from the time we became a state. You were not with the original settlers, but our intention of coming here was to make Comancheria a free state. We failed in that. We are still a part of Texas, and Texas is a slave state. But, and this is an important distinction, through it all, we have remained an enclave of freedom in the state, and we will continue to do so.

"Joe Travis is one of us in every way you can measure. He was at the Alamo, he was at San Jacinto, and he came here as part of the Freedom Train. And I would like to ask now, by a show of hands, how many of you are living in houses that Joe Travis built."

More than one third of those who had assembled for the reading of the declaration held up their hands.

"There will be no further questions as to the status of our colored neighbors," Paul concluded.

After the reading of the declaration, the citizens of Comancheria wandered around for a while, not exactly sure what this all meant. Would there be war? And if so, would it come to them?

"Cap'n Nelson?" Joe said coming up to him then. Joe's daughter, Beulah, was with him. "I want to thank you for what you said at the meeting."

"No thanks needed, Joe," Paul replied. "I just said what needed to be said, is all."

"Yes, sir. Well, to tell you the truth, some of us was fixin' to leave. We was goin' to go north, 'cause we didn't have it settled in our minds what it meant, with Texas breakin' away from the Union and all. But after hearin' you talk, we decided to stay. This is our home, too."

"Yes," Paul said. "It is very much your home."

Comancheria—July 4, 1861

There was some discussion throughout the rebellious states as to how the Fourth of July should be celebrated. It had been, traditionally, one of the most gala celebrations of the year, complete with music, parades, flags, tableauxs, and fireworks.

Finally it was agreed that the Fourth of July was a celebration owned by Northerners and Southerners alike, since all shared the heritage of the War of Independence.

"Do not think," Justin Good said in his speech to those who had gathered for the Fourth of July celebration in Comancheria, "that we shall be cheated of this hallowed possession. The Confederate States of 1861 are acting over again the American Revolution of 1776. To us, therefore, belongs the most sacred right of property in the memory of Independence Day as the loyal inheritors of its principles and its glories. We trust the day may never come when the people of the Confederate States will no longer celebrate with becoming marks of respect and reverence this glorious anniversary."

The town square—for Comancheria had been specifically designed to have a town square—was gaily decorated in red, white, and blue, both in bunting and flags. The red, white, and blue flags, however, were not the Stars and Stripes, but the Stars and Bars of the Confederate States of America, as well as the Lone Star Flag of the state of Texas.

In addition to Justin's speech, there was music from the volunteer fire department band, fireworks, a parade, and a town picnic to which everyone in town made a contribution.

Paul, Fancy, Tommy, Lucy, John, and Susanna were sharing a table with Justin, Lucy, and Ralph Good, Ian McKenzie and his family, Gordon and Gretchen Forsythe, with their daughter Cindy, and Dale and Agnes Chapman and their son, Billy.

Dale Chapman was wearing the gray-and-gold uniform of the Confederacy because he had recently been appointed to the rank of lieutenant colonel, attached to Greer's Texas Regiment. Greer's Texas was garrisoned at nearby Fort Adobe. They had participated in the parade, and many of them were now wandering through the town, enjoying the food and the company. Most of them, officers and soldiers alike, were wearing flowers in the lapels of their uniforms, and many had a bit of ribbon laced through a button hole, given them by some young woman who wished to show her patriotism in such a way.

This celebration was bittersweet for them, though, because on the next day they would be departing for

a long march up through Arkansas, where they
would join with General Benjamin McCulloch, who
was not only a Texan, but a former Texas Ranger.

Dale Chapman was not the only resident of Co-
mancheria who had joined the army. In addition to
Dale, Silas McCarthy, the young man who had been
Fancy's student and had questioned Paul about the
Alamo, was wearing the gray. So were Peter McKenzie
and Bobby Rittenhouse, son of Ted Rittenhouse.

Wilson's Creek, Missouri—August 9, 1861

Shortly after General Benjamin McCulloch and
the troops with him reached Wilson's Creek, the
general ordered all commanders forward to discuss
the plans for battle. As the officers were gathering,
McCulloch noticed Dale Chapman standing to one
side, and he walked over to speak with him.

"How was your march up from Texas?" he asked.

"It was made with little difficulty, General," Dale
replied.

McCulloch smiled. "Well, you are a West Point
graduate, after all," he said. "I would expect no less.
You are from the Comancheria area, I believe?"

"Yes, sir."

"Two of the finest men I ever served with, during
the Texas War of Independence, the Texas Rangers,
and the Mexican War live there, I believe."

"You would be talking about Paul Nelson and Gordon Forsythe."

"I am, indeed," General McCulloch said. "Paul, of
course, was at the Alamo. I would have been, too. I
left Tennessee with Davy Crockett, but I got the

measles en route and couldn't finish the march to San Antonio with him. Strange how history can turn on such small events," he said.

"Yes, sir, it is."

"General," Colonel Churchill said then. "The commanders are gathered."

"Good, good," McCulloch said. He walked out away from the tree where he had been in conversation with Dale to address his officers.

"Gentlemen, the Yankees are not too far on the other side of the creek. It is my intention to engage them in battle on this very night. We will wait until nine o'clock. It will be dusk then, and I don't think the Yankees will be on guard. We will hit them hard, and with everything we have."

"Well, now, General, you've just raised the issue here," Colonel McRae said. "When you say everything we have, my boys have less than ten bullets apiece."

"We've got near forty," Colonel Greer said. "I could have my boys give your men maybe fifteen rounds apiece."

"That would be most generous of you, Colonel," McRae said.

As General McCulloch began laying out the plans for the attack, it started to rain. At first, the rain was relatively gentle, but then it began raining very hard.

"General, my men don't have cartridge boxes," Colonel Hebert said. "They're all havin' to carry their cartridges in their jacket pockets, and in this rain, that powder is goin' to get wet and won't fire."

"I'm afraid we're in the same boat, General," Colonel McRae said.

Now the rain turned into a thunderstorm, with high wind, roaring thunder, and flashing bolts of lightning.

"Gentlemen!" McCulloch said, finally giving up. "Find shelter for your men! We will meet again tomorrow morning to plan the attack!"

The troops pitched tents and stayed out of the rain as much as possible, though it rained hard enough for the water to seep into the tents, even though they had all dug little diversion trenches to prevent that. Finally, at about midnight the rain stopped, but the misery didn't. Now the air was hot and humid, and filled with mosquitoes.

After a fitful, and mostly sleepless night, General McCulloch sent for Dale when dawn arrived. Unlike the small, two-man tents occupied by the soldiers, the general's tent was large enough to allow a person to walk around upright inside. When Dale reached the general's tent, he saw that the general had a map spread out on a small field table.

"Dale," he said, looking up. "Our last scout was late yesterday afternoon. We believe that the enemy is here." He pointed to an area. "I would like for you to send someone out to scout."

"I won't send them, General. I will lead them," Dale replied.

Comancheria—September 4, 1861

From the *Comancheria Bulletin:*

A SAD REPORT

Word has been received of the death at Wilson's Creek in Missouri on August 10th, of one of Comancheria's own gallant soldiers, Colonel Dale Chapman of the Greer's Texas Regiment. This newspaper herein prints the article exactly as it appeared in the *First Division Proclamation*, a paper published by the Yankee troops, First Division of the Department of the West.

This editor neither adds nor detracts from the copy, preferring to let the words stand as they might in order that our readers may see for themselves the cruel nature of the Yankee troops, and the callous disregard they hold for life and human dignity.

CIRCUMSTANCES OF THE DEATH OF THE REBEL DALE CHAPMAN

This paper has the pleasure, and it is indeed a pleasure, to report to our readers the news of the death of Dale Chapman, who was killed on the tenth instant about seven miles south of the Wilson Creek camp. The circumstances are as follows: In company with three other officers, Chapman was approaching our fortifications with a view of making a reconnaissance. Secreted in a bush by the roadside were a number of the 17th Missouri regiment, and as Chapman and his companions came up the road, the Missouri boys arose from their place of concealment and fired.

Chapman fell from his horse on the first round, having received three bullets, two of which passed entirely through the body, entering at the right breast, and one of the remaining quartet was also hit, but the two remaining unhurt managed to get him away by supporting him on his horse.

The body of Chapman was conveyed to the quarters of Colonel Wagoner where he lived for the space of half an hour, never speaking save to utter the words, "Duty, honor, Texas."

In Chapman's pockets were found one hundred dollars in United States gold currency and a splendid gold watch. His uniform was new and of a most elegant make, gray broadcloth coat and pants with yellow piping, and a yellow satin vest. His collar insignia denoted him to be a lieutenant colonel—one of Texas's offerings.

The settlement of Comancheria had grown considerably since the arrival of the Freedom Train pioneers. The two hundred now numbered over one thousand, and every original pilgrim, and at least half of the more recent settlers, attended the memorial service for Chapman, his body having been buried in Missouri.

Paul and Fancy had done their part to make Comancheria grow. In addition to their son Tom (he was now thirteen years old and no longer considered "Tommy" appropriate), there was Lucy, who was ten and named after Lucy Good; John, who was six, and named after John Forsythe; and Susanna, four, named after Susanna Dickerson. The house at Longtrail had grown in order to accommodate the enlarged family, and was now a two-story brick house, with a full, columned porch across the front and dormer windows that glistened gold in the rising and the setting sun.

The entry gate had been rebuilt with larger, more

substantial posts on each side of the road, and a wide spanning arch, from which hung the same sign Paul had created when first they arrived in the area.

After the memorial service, Justin Good asked Paul to please visit him in his office.

"You folks go on ahead," Paul said. "I'll walk home."

"Daddy, you won't forget that we are having my birthday cake tonight, will you?" Susanna asked.

"Now, how could I forget the birthday of one of the prettiest girls in all of Texas?" Paul replied and Susanna beamed under the praise.

"Yes, sir, the three prettiest girls in all of Texas are Fancy, Lucy, and Susanna."

"Mama's not a girl," John said.

"She's not? Well, what is she?"

"She's a mama," John explained.

"Oh, of course, how could I have forgotten that?" Paul asked, leaning over to kiss Fancy. He stepped back as she snapped the reins against the back of the team to drive the country wagon back to the spreading, five bedroom Spanish Colonial home that had replaced the first house they had built.

Justin Good's office building was the largest and most grand building in Comancheria. Paul was ushered into Justin's office, which spread all the way across the back of the building.

"Paul, there is someone here I would like for you to meet," Justin said. "In fact, I believe he is an old friend of yours, since the two of you fought together during the Mexican-American war."

There had been someone sitting in a chair who,

because the back of the chair was to the door, had not been seen by Paul. Now he stood, then turned to extend his hand.

It was General Albert Sidney Johnston. Though while he had been a general in the U.S. Army the first time Paul met him, he was now a general in the Confederate army.

"Hello, Paul," General Johnston said. "It's a pleasure to see you again."

"Hello, General," Paul said.

"I'm very sorry to hear about your friend Colonel Chapman. He was a good officer."

"Before that, he was a good friend, a good husband, and a good father," Paul said.

"Yes, the tragedy of war is that it takes our best men from us," General Johnston said. "The good of war is that it brings out the best in us. It was not merely by accident that Colonel Dale's last words were 'duty, honor, Texas.' But, of course, I don't have to tell you that," Johnston added. "After all, you fought at the Alamo, at San Jacinto, and again at Palo Alto, during the Mexican-American war."

"Paul, General Johnston has a proposition for you," Justin said.

"I think I know what your proposition is, General, and I'm not interested," Paul said.

"You haven't heard the proposition yet."

"You want me to join the Confederate army," Paul said. "Am I right?"

"Not just join, Paul. I am authorized to offer you command of a regiment. That offer comes with the rank of lieutenant colonel."

"I'm flattered," Paul said.

"I would hope you would be more than that," General Johnston said.

"I am also honored."

"Now, we are getting closer to what I want to hear," General Johnston said. "When one says they are honored, that means they have a sense of honor and responsibility. Of course, that isn't a challenge, for you have already proven that you have a sense of honor, responsibility, and a sense of duty, as well as a love for Texas, time and again.

"I would call upon that same sense of honor, duty, and devotion to Texas again."

"General, I was very much opposed to the secession of Texas," Paul said. "And I am very much opposed to slavery. Were I to accept this commission, I would be in direct opposition to those principles."

"Would it help if I told you that General Robert E. Lee is vigorously opposed to slavery? He is fighting for the principle of state's rights and personal freedom. Those are principles you could support, are they not?"

"General, would you excuse us for a moment?" Justin said. "Let me talk to Paul."

"Very well," General Johnston said. "I will take a walk around your town."

Justin waited until General Johnston was gone before he spoke.

"Paul, let me ask you a question. If it were not for Fancy's rather unique situation, would you accept this commission?"

"I don't know," Paul said. "I suppose I would."

"Then put your mind at ease. I have already spoken to Fancy about this."

"What? Excuse me, Justin, but what gives you the right to do something like that? To talk to my wife about this?"

"I assumed the right of friendship," Justin said. "And the fact that outside of my own son, Ralph, I consider you and Fancy to be as close as my own children. I'm sorry, Paul, if my talking to Fancy about this upsets you. But you know how firmly I stand against slavery, and yet, my feelings for state's rights and individual freedom are even stronger. If I were young enough, I would apply for the position that General Johnston is offering you."

"General Johnston spoke of a sense of responsibility. And he is right, I do have a sense of responsibility, but not just to Texas. I have a sense of responsibility to my family and to one other."

"One other?"

"Joe Travis," Paul said. "I have a bond with Joe that is stronger than the bond I have with any other human being outside my own family."

"I know you are friends, but . . ."

"It goes much deeper than friendship, Justin. Our relationship was irreversibly bonded during those long, anxious days and terrible last hours of the Alamo. It was cemented in the fires of San Jacinto when, for the second time, Joe Travis saved my life.

"I will make no commitment unless I have the blessings, not only of Fancy, but of Joe Travis."

"All right, Paul," Justin said. "Do what you feel you must do." Justin reached out and put his hand on Paul's shoulder. "And know this, my friend. Whatever decision you make, you will have my one-hundred-percent support."

Paul smiled. "I don't doubt that for a moment, Justin," he said.

Joe Travis and three of the men who worked for him, for he was now a very successful contractor, had just dug a well, and now they were building the stone wall around the well. Joe and Andy were putting mortar between the stones, while the other two men were building the scaffold which would stretch over the top of the well, to hold the winch.

When Joe saw Paul coming toward him, he picked up a cloth to wipe his hands, then walked out to meet Paul.

"I think I know why you are here," Joe said.

"How do you know?"

"Because I seen Gen'rul Johnston, and I know he wouldn't be comin' here unless he could find someone to replace Mr. Dale. And that someone he's lookin' for is you."

Paul nodded.

"Paul," Joe said. It wasn't the first time Joe had ever referred to him by his first name, though he had never addressed him so in public. "I also know what you are worryin' about. You are worryin' that if you go off to fight for the Confederacy that you would be turnin' your back on me, bein' as I'm a man of color, and this war is bein' fought to keep people like me down."

"That's what I'm worrying about, all right," Paul said.

"Well, stop worryin' about it," Joe said. "The way I look at it, this war is being fought for Texas. Texas is

my home, same as it is your home. And the truth of it
is, if they would let me go fight I'd do it, just like I
done twice before."

Paul nodded, then stuck out his hand to grasp
Joe's hand in his.

"You are a good man, Joe Travis. As good as any
man I've ever known."

"I don't want you to go to war because I don't want
to think about losing you," Fancy said. "And to be
honest with you, and myself, until I learned the truth
of my own situation, I never had a strong feeling
about slavery one way or the other. I didn't think of
them as slaves, I thought of them as people. I loved
Doney as much as I did anyone else in the world. I
don't want you to let my circumstances affect your
decision. We are Texans, Paul. And our friends and
neighbors are involved in this war. I don't see how we
can avoid it."

"I love you, Fancy," Paul said.

"Stay safe, my darling," Fancy said.

The next morning Fancy and the children stood
in front of the house as Paul, wearing the gray-and-
gold uniform of a Confederate officer, swung into
the saddle of his horse. With a good-bye wave, he
turned and rode away, wondering if he would ever
see any of them again.

Fancy was having the same thoughts as she watched
him ride away. She could remember, six months earlier, attending a going-away party when Dale Chapman
and at least half a dozen other men from Coman-

cheria had left to go to war. There had been a gala dance then, with the band playing, and flags waving. Now Dale and two others who had left that day were dead.

"Please, Lord," she said, quietly. "Watch over him and keep him safe. Bring him back to me."

"Bring him back to us," Tom said, somewhat surprising Fancy, who had not even realized that she had prayed aloud.

"To us," Fancy amended.

Chapter Eighteen

General Albert Sydney Johnston had established his headquarters in the house of W. M. Inge, in Corinth, Mississippi. The house was known locally as the "Rose Cottage," because it was painted pink. Shortly after Lieutenant Colonel Paul Nelson brought his regiment into Corinth, he was asked to report to General Johnston at his headquarters.

"Lieutenant Colonel Nelson, who is your second in command?" General Johnston asked, when Paul reported to him.

"Major Gordon Forsythe, sir," Paul said.

"Is he a good man? What I mean is could you entrust command of your regiment to him?"

"Yes, sir," Paul replied, resolutely.

"Good. Then I am promoting him to lieutenant colonel, and I would like him to take temporary command of your regiment. I am promoting you to

full colonel, and I would like for you to be attached
to my staff until further notice. Please go pass command on to him, then return here to headquarters."

"Yes, sir," Paul said.

Leaving the general's headquarters, Paul rode
back to his regiment's encampment.

"Has anyone seen Colonel Forsythe?" he asked.

"Sir, Major Forsythe is over there with Cap'n
Caleb's company," a sergeant said.

"I'm not looking for Major Forsythe, I'm looking
for Lieutenant Colonel Forsythe," Paul said. "He's
been promoted."

After a round of congratulations, repeated when
Paul told them that he had been promoted to full
colonel, Paul passed command of the regiment over
to Gordon. Then he returned to the Rose Cottage.

"Are you hungry, Colonel?" Johnston asked.

"Yes, sir, a little. I haven't had my supper."

You can dine with me," Johnston said.

"Thank you, sir."

Shortly after they finished their dinner, the other
generals arrived for a scheduled meeting in the living room of the house. Although he wasn't specifically invited, neither was he told that he could not
attend. So Paul got a second cup of coffee, and
leaned into the door frame of the door between the
living room and dining room so he could see and
hear, watching as Generals Beauregard, Bragg, Polk,
Hardee, and Breckinridge arrived.

There were not enough places for all the generals
and their executive officers to sit, so Beauregard,
who was second in command only to Johnston, dis-
dained a chair or a place on the sofa, to sit on the
floor near the fireplace. When several officers of

lesser rank offered their own seats, Beauregard waved them off, insisting that he was quite comfortable where he was.

"Gentlemen," Johnston said when all were assembled, "while I have guarded against an uncertain offensive, I am now of the opinion that we should entice the enemy into an engagement as soon as possible, before he can further increase his numbers."

"General, I think we should strike at Pittsburg Landing right now, while the Yankees are engaged in offloading their boats," Bragg suggested. "They haven't built any fortifications, and my scouts tell me they've set up tents, just as if they were on parade."

"An attack of the kind you propose is exactly what the Yankees are counting on," Beauregard said.

"What do you mean?" Bragg asked.

"Think about it, Braxton," Beauregard replied. "Why are they setting up tents? Why have they built no fortifications? Because they are hoping to draw us out in a bold and foolish attack."

"Do you equate boldness with foolishness?" General Johnston asked.

"No, sir, not always. But under these circumstances, I would urge some restraint upon audacious action."

"Please, be more specific," Johnston invited.

Beauregard stood up, then leaned back against the fireplace mantel and crossed his arms across his chest as he elaborated on his point.

"I think we should occupy the field in a way that would compel the enemy to display his intentions to attack. Then, when he is within striking distance of us, we should go on the offensive and crush him, cutting him off, if possible, from his base of operations at the river. If we could then force a surrender from such a large army, the North would have no choice but to sue for peace. We could win the entire war, right here, right now."

The others all began speaking at once, and Johnston had to hold up his hand to quiet them.

"Gentlemen, gentlemen, I appreciate your suggestions and ideas, but as I am in command here, the ultimate responsibility rests with me. General Beauregard, your contention that we could win the war right here is a good one. That is why we must not let the opportunity slip out of our grasp. But I believe General Bragg's suggestion offers us the greatest chance for success. I believe it is imperative that we strike now, before the enemy's rear gets up from Nashville. We have him divided, and we should keep him so if we can."

Johnston's word was final, so there was no further argument on that subject. The discussion then turned to the plan of battle, and in this, Johnston decided to form the army into three parallel lines, the distance between the lines to be one thousand yards. Hardee's corps was to form the first line, Bragg's the second. The third would be composed of Polk on the left and Breckinridge on the right.

"As second in command, General Beaurgard will coordinate your efforts. Gentlemen, please have your elements in position by seven o'clock in the morning. We shall begin the attack at eight."

There was a buzz of excited conversation as, for a few moments, the generals discussed the orders with each other.

"And now, I am certain that you all have staff meetings to conduct, so I release you to return to your units," Johnston said by way of dismissal.

The assembled officers stood then and, as one, saluted. After that they trooped outside, clumped across the porch, then mounted their horses to return to their units. Beauregard stayed behind.

Johnston stayed in the front door for a long time after the others left. He hung his head, almost as if praying, and during that time Beauregard said nothing. The only sound in the room was the popping and snapping of the wood fire burning briskly in the fireplace.

Paul realized now, that except for the two generals, he was the only one left, and he knew that he probably should leave—but the drama of the moment kept him there. But if he thought he would be privy to something of historical significance, he was wrong, for after a long moment of silence, Beauregard left as well.

As Johnston's army maneuvered into position early the next morning, an abrupt April thunderstorm broke over the winding columns. The rain filled hat brims, then spilled over to run down the soldiers' backs. It slashed through the trees, and turned the dirt roads into paths of deep, sticky mud. Wagon and artillery wheels cut through rain-soaked quagmires causing the mud to cake up on the wheels and gather in great mud balls on the shoes of the marching soldiers. This made every step a chore, causing the calves and ankles of the men who were struggling forward to ache with a debilitating pain.

The army did not advance smoothly, but in awkward, erratic movements which barely advanced the columns. Periodically, they would stop for long periods of time while the men stood, made miserable by the falling rain. Then the army would lurch forward again, causing a ripple effect down the line that would inevitably cause the trailing columns to have to break into a difficult and exhausting trot just to keep up.

As the march grew more wearisome, the sides of the road began to fill with discarded personal items, from overcoats and shovels to newspapers and even letters.

Finally the army was called to a halt so that General Johnston's orders, which by now had been transcribed into a score or more copies, could be read to the various regiments. Paul had ridden back to check in on his regiment, so he read General Johnston's proclamation to the troops himself, shielding it from the rain by holding his hat over the piece of paper on which the orders were written.

"'Soldiers of the Army of the Mississippi,'" he read. Then clearing his throat, he moved into the body of the orders:

"'I have put into motion to offer battle to the invaders of our country. With the resolution and disciplined valor becoming men fighting, as you are, for all worth living and dying for, you can but march to a decisive victory over the agrarian mercenaries sent to subjugate and despoil you of your liberties, property, and honor. Remember the precious stake involved; remember the dependence of your mothers, your wives, your sisters, and your children on the result; remember the fair, broad, abounding land, the happy homes and the ties that would be desolated by your defeat.

"'The eyes and hopes of eight millions of people

rest upon you. You are expected to show yourselves worthy of your race and lineage, worthy of the women of the South, whose noble devotion in the war has never been exceeded in any time. With such incentives to brave deeds, and with the trust that God is with us, your generals will lead you confidently to the combat, assured of success.' "

After he finished reading, Paul looked up. "And it is signed by A. S. Johnston, General."

"Hip, hip!" someone shouted.

"Hoorah!" his call was answered.

"Hip, hip!"

"Hoorah!"

"Hip, hip!"

"Hoorah!"

Having read the orders, Paul once more took leave of the regiment, and returned to General Johnston's headquarters.

Although it had been General Johnston's intention to have the men in position by seven, and begin the attack by eight, that was not to be. At eight o'clock, when they should be beginning their attack, the Southern columns were still bogged down in the stop-and-go slogging progress along the muddy roads.

Of all the generals present, General Bragg was the most frustrated. One of his divisions was lost somewhere in the rain on the jammed, muddy roads. That caused his entire corps to be late, and that caused the carefully planned operation to fall apart.

Beauregard, who was second in command, was holding Bragg personally responsible for the delay, even though Bragg had done everything within his power to keep to the schedule. Bragg held no animus toward Beauregard, though. Bragg was a West

Point graduate and veteran of the War with Mexico, and he realized that the ultimate responsibility lay with the commander.

Not until the men reached their positions, did the sun finally show itself. However, when the sun did appear, it was already high in the sky, for the eight o'clock deadline imposed by Johnston was long past. Also, to the chagrin of the officers, the soldiers, fearful that the rain may have dampened the powder in their rifles, began testing the powder by shooting their rifles. As a result, all up and down the line their muskets popped and banged, well within earshot of the Federal outposts. In addition, some of the men took advantage of the protracted delay to shoot at game, from rabbit to deer, to cook for their lunch.

Generals Johnston and Beauregard stood by through the long morning as Bragg continued to bring up his corps. By now it was noon, and the corps had yet to appear.

"General Bragg," General Johnston said, "we are waiting."

"Yes, sir. I'm sorry, sir. The mud, the crowded roads . . . it has made passage impossible."

"General, may I remind you that everyone else has been subjected to the same conditions," Johnston said. "But they are here. Only your corps is not in position."

"Yes, sir."

General Johnston took out his watch and looked at it.

"It is twelve-thirty," he said. He snapped the watch shut and put it back in his pocket. "This is perfectly unacceptable."

It took two more hours for Bragg's lost division to

come up front, and two more hours beyond that for it to be put into position. By that time it was four-thirty in the afternoon and the shadows were growing longer.

Suddenly there was the unmistakeable sound of a drummer giving the long roll. General Beauregard put his hand to his head in anger and frustration. "What is going on here? Do we have an army? Or is this a bunch of Sunday schoolchildren going to a picnic?"

Looking around, he saw Paul standing nearby.

"Colonel Nelson, I do believe that drummer is in your regiment. Would you be so kind as to silence him?" Beauregard said.

"Yes, sir," Paul replied.

Mounting once more, Paul rode quickly down the line toward his regiment and the sound of the beating drum. When he reached the regiment, he called out to Lieutenant Colonel Gordon. "Colonel, send someone to find out who is beating on that drum and take the damn thing away from him!" Paul ordered.

"I'm afraid that is going to be difficult," Gordon replied, with a big smile on his face. "In fact, it might well be impossible."

"Impossible to take a drum away from a drummer boy? What are you telling me, Colonel?"

"I'm telling you that the drummer is over in the Yankee camp."

"The Yankee camp?"

"Of course, I guess I could yell over at him and tell him to stop, but I doubt he would listen to me," Gordon suggested, then laughed at his joke.

Paul laughed as well. "Then he probably wouldn't listen to me either, would he?"

"No, sir, for all that you are a full colonel now, I don't think he would listen to you," Gordon said.

"All right, carry on," Paul said.

When Paul returned, he told General Beauregard that the drummer they were hearing was in the Yankee camp.

"Well, that does it, then," Beauregard said. "If we can hear them, there's no doubt they have heard us."

General Johnston was speaking with General Polk. Polk had been Johnston's roommate at West Point, but more recently had been ordained an Episcopal bishop; as a result, he was referred to as "the Bishop" fully as often as he was called "General."

"There is no longer any chance of surprise. By now the Yankees will be entrenched up to their ears," Beauregard said.

"So, what are you telling me, Gus?" Johnston asked.

"I'm suggesting that you might want to reconsider the attack order, General. Perhaps we would be better served by withdrawing to Corinth to strengthen our own defenses and let the Yankees bring the fight to us."

"No, no, I strongly disagree," General Polk said. "Our troops are most eager for battle. Consider this, gentlemen. They left Corinth to fight, and if they don't fight, they will be as demoralized as if they had been whipped."

"I totally agree," General Bragg said. "We can't even consider withdrawal now."

"Funny you should say that, General Bragg, since it was your delay that has put us into this situation," Beauregard reminded him.

"I apologize for the disruption in plans my corps caused," Bragg said. "I make no excuses, but I do apologize."

General Breckinridge rode into camp then and, when he dismounted, was surprised to learn that the impromptu war council he had happened upon was even contemplating withdrawal.

"What is your opinion, General?" Johnston asked Breckinridge after outlining the situation for him.

"Gentlemen, I say we attack. Speaking for myself, I would as soon be defeated as retire from the field without a fight."

"Well, that leaves us only Hardee to hear from," Beauregard said.

Breckinridge chuckled. "Hell, Gus, you know where Bill stands on this. He's already deployed, and anxious for battle. If he were here, he would vote to attack."

"Then it looks to me as if the vote is in," Johnston said. "And there's no doubt as to the way it has gone. The attack is still on."

"Now? With darkness nearly upon us?" Beauregard asked. "Do you intend to launch a night attack?"

"No, we would have no means of control during such an attack. We will go at first light, tomorrow," Johnston said. "Gentlemen, once all your troops are in position, put them at ease and have them sleep on their arms in line of battle. At least tomorrow we will have no unexpected delays in arrival."

"General, there is one more thing you should consider," Beauregard said, not yet ready to give up his argument.

"What is that?" Johnston asked.

"General Buell," Beauregard said. "He has, in all likelihood, joined with the others by now, and if so, that would bring the number of men arrayed against us to nearly seventy thousand or more."

"The attack order stands," Johnston replied.

"Very good, sir. I will see that everyone gets the word," Beauregard said.

Beauregard and the other generals left to attend to their various duties. Johnston watched them ride away, then turned to Paul, who had listened with great interest to the entire discussion. Paul could see the look of determination in General Johnston's eyes.

"You were listening to our conversation?" Johnston asked.

"Yes, General."

"You understand, don't you, Colonel? We have no choice but to attack. We have given away too much ground as it is, and now the Yankees are on our very doorstep. If we don't stop them here, they will occupy all of the South within six months including your Texas. General Beauregard is worried because their numbers may be seventy thousand."

"Do you think there are that many, General?" Paul asked.

"I would attack if there were a million. Actually, the numbers aren't important, because the Yankees are spread out between Lick Creek and Owl Creek. That means they can present no greater front between those two creeks than we can. In fact, the more men they crowd in there, the more difficult it would be for them to maneuver, and the worse we can make it for them."

Johnston was silent for a long moment, then

spoke again. "I'm glad you decided to come," he said. "When I went to Texas to recruit you, I wasn't sure you would."

"It was a difficult decision for me to make," Paul said.

"But ultimately, you did come," Johnston said. "That means you believe in this war."

"That is why the decision was so difficult for me to make, General. If I thought the only reason I am fighting was to preserve slavery, I wouldn't have come. I hate slavery. I think it is the most despicable act one man can inflict upon another. But I am convinced that this war is for more than the right to own slaves. I think it is for something like honor and duty, and love of one's land. It's more complicated than I can understand, but here I am."

"Were there bands playing, flags flying, and pretty girls waving when you left?" Johnston asked.

"We've had our share of parades and bands and pretty girls waving," Paul agreed.

"I'm going to tell you something, Paul," Johnston said. He was quiet for a long moment as if trying to gather his thoughts. "After this battle, the country's mood is going to change. Never again will men go off to war with bands playing, flags waving, and women throwing flowers at marching troops. We are in for a day or two of bloodletting the likes of which this nation has never seen. And it will change our way of looking at this war, perhaps all war. Forever."

Though the day had begun with rain, it was ending now with a clear, red sunset shining through oaks

that were green with new growth. The moon, in cres-
cent, rose in a dark blue twilight. Then, finally, the
sky darkened and the stars came out. Standing on
the porch of the Rose Cottage, Paul could hear faint
bugle calls in the distance, and he felt a strange sense
of deprivation over not being able to bed down with
his own regiment. He thought of the men he had
brought to battle, many of them barely older than his
son, some of them, like Lieutenants Silas McCarthy
and Steve Cramer, were but children on the wagon
train up. Lieutenant Cramer had been one of the
children taken by Hardin. He was married now to
Jenny Hughes, who had been among the same group
of children captured that day.

Paul looked toward the dark woods that separated
the two armies. On the other side of the woods was
the enemy. There, men dressed in blue were bedding
down for one last night before the killing began. He
thought of how pastoral the scene was. He could
hear whippoorwills calling in the night, the birds totally innocent of the slaughter that would take place
the next day as men who shared the same language,
history, and culture would be killing each other.

The next morning, on Sunday, April 6, 1862, on
the Mississippi-Tennessee border, near a small church
meeting house called Shiloh, General Johnston com-
menced the battle that would, ever after, bear the
name of the little meeting house.

The attack met with immediate, initial success as
the Union lines sagged and crumpled, and Federal
troops fled to safety under the bluff along the river. A

few brave Union soldiers held on at a place called the "Hornets' Nest," though at a terrible cost in terms of lives lost.

Shiloh campground had been General Sherman's place of bivouac during the night before, but now General Beauregard made the little log church his personal headquarters. From it, he issued orders and dispatched reinforcements where they were needed, thus affording General Johnston the freedom to move up and down the line of battle, giving encouragement to the men.

As the general's chief of staff, Paul rode with him. To those who needed a calming influence, Johnston spoke quietly. "Easy, men, make every shot count. Keep calm, don't let the Yankees get you riled."

To those he felt needed more spirit, he injected a note of ferocity to his words: "Men of Arkansas, you are skilled with the Arkansas toothpick. Let us use that skill with a nobler weapon, the bayonet. Use it for your country! Use it for your state! Use it for your fellow soldiers! Use it well!"

General Johnston was well mounted on a large, beautiful horse, and his presence among the men, whether he was speaking or not, was all the inspiration they needed. His progress along the line could be followed easily through the rippling effect of hurrahs shouted by the soldiers.

"Hey! Lookie here!" one of the men shouted as they came across what had been a Yankee camp. "These damn Yankees left their food still a-cookin'!"

"Yahoo!" another shouted, and to Paul's frustration, nearly half of the army broke off its pursuit of the fleeing Union soldiers to sit down and eat the breakfast the Yankees had so recently abandoned.

"You men!" Paul shouted. "We've got the Yankees on the run! Let's finish the job. Then you can come back to it!"

"We do that, Colonel, and there won't be nothin' left," a corporal said, grabbing a couple of biscuits and a hunk of salt pork.

"Colonel, let the stragglers be," General Johnston shouted to Paul. "We have more important things to do! We're losing cohesion here!"

The underbrush, gullies, twisting roads, as well as pockets of stiff Union resistance had disrupted the orderly progress of the attack. The three lines of battle, so carefully sketched out on the battle map, bore little resemblance to the way the troops were deployed in the field. Divisions, brigades, and regiments became so intermingled that men found themselves fighting side by side with strangers, and listening to commands given by officers they didn't even know. Over it all was the cacophonous roar of battle: thundering cannon, booming muskets, shrieking shells, screams of rage, curses of defiance, fear, and pain, the whole enshrouded in a thick, opaque cloud of noxious gun smoke.

"Colonel Nelson, get back to Beauregard as quickly as you can. Tell him I wish to reorganize into four sections, Hardee and Polk on the left, Bragg and Breckinridge on the right!"

"Yes, sir," Paul replied. "Where will you be, General?"

"I will be here," Johnston said.

Paul galloped back to Shiloh Church. Some of the wounded had straggled back as far as the church and many were sitting or lying on the ground, attended to by doctors and their orderlies. Beauregard was in conversation with two colonels when Paul reported to him.

"General Johnston's compliments, sir," Paul said, saluting.

"Yes, yes, what is it, Colonel?" Beauregard asked, obviously displeased at being interrupted during this critical time.

"The general wishes you to reorganize into four sections, Hardee and Polk on the left, Bragg and Breckinridge on the right."

"Reorganize in the midst of battle?" Beauregard replied. "And how am I supposed to do that, did the general say?"

Paul shook his head. "I'm sorry, General, he didn't say. He just said to reorganize into four—"

"Sections, Hardee and Polk on the left, Bragg and Breckinridge on the right, yes, yes, I heard that," Beauregard said interrupting Paul in mid-sentence. Sighing, he stroked his Vandyke beard. "Very well, Colonel, you may tell General Johnston that I am complying with his order."

"Yes, sir," Paul said as he turned to ride back. When he returned from his mission, he saw General Johnston heading toward a peach orchard that was occupied by several pieces of Confederate artillery. The trees were in full bloom, and each time one of the guns would fire, the concussion would cause the flower petals to come fluttering down in a bright pink blizzard.

When the attack began, the Confederate troops carried the field, breaking the Union lines and driving them back. But this was not without terrible loses. The Sixth Mississippi lost 300 men out of its total of 425, and the Eighteenth Louisiana lost 207.

Paul's regiment suffered heavily, too, but the attack continued without letup.

Because of the lay of the land and the logistics of keeping the men supplied with ammunition it was not a sustained attack, but rather a series of thrusts where ground would be taken and held, lost and regained. Then another thrust, first on one end of the line, then the other, then in the middle.

At about half past two o'clock that afternoon, General Johnston turned to Paul. "Colonel Nelson, with your permission, I should like to lead your regiment in the next charge."

"It is Colonel Forsythe's regiment now, but I am sure he would be honored, General," Paul said.

The two men rode to where Paul's regiment was, and General Johnston asked Gordon's permission to lead the regiment in its next charge.

"General, we will follow proudly!" Gordon said.

General Johnston, who was mounted, held his saber aloft, then started forward, advancing no faster than the troops behind him. They had gone little more than one hundred yards when Johnston grunted in pain.

"Uhnn!"

Paul, who was just behind him, saw a little pink mist of blood squirt from his leg where a bullet hit. Johnston halted his advance.

"General, are you all right?" Paul shouted, riding over to him.

"It is just a nick, I think," General Johnston replied. "But they nearly rendered me *hors de combat* in that charge."

Paul left the general to join with Gordon and his regiment as, running now, and shouting at the top of their voices, they routed the enemy from the orchard.

"We did it, General, we carried the field, thanks to you!" Paul called, turning back toward the general. That was when he saw General Johnston looking ashen faced and reeling in the saddle. Paul rode toward him. "General! Are you all right, sir?"

"I have been wounded," General Johnston said. "And I fear seriously so."

Dismounting quickly, Paul helped General Johnston down from his horse, then laid him on the ground beneath a peach tree. Not until then did Paul look more closely at what the general had initially called "just a nick."

The wound was, in fact, much more than that. The bullet had severed an artery and Paul could see blood spilling out of the general's boot.

"I've got to get you back to the field aid station," Paul said.

"No, Colonel, there will be others with worse wounds. Just let me rest for a few moments."

Paul was certain that the wound was worse than General Johnston believed, and he was about to insist that he be taken back when he saw two soldiers returning from the front with Captain Ralph Good. Ralph had been struck by a Minié ball and his knee was shattered.

"Ralph!" Paul shouted.

"I guess I zigged when I should have zagged, Colonel," Ralph said.

"Get him to the aid station, quickly," Paul said.

"Yes, sir."

"General, I'm going to get you back there, too, no matter what you say," Paul said.

But General Johnston couldn't hear him, because the Confederate commander was dead.

With Johnston dead, command now fell upon the shoulders of General P.G.T. Beauregard. Paul, after arranging to have General Johnston's body removed from the battlefield and returned to the Rose Cottage, hurried to tell General Beauregard that he was now in command.

Beauregard, who had expressed some hesitancy before the battle, was now fully committed to it, and even as Paul approached him, the general was issuing orders to a colonel.

"Tell General Bragg that we will continue our attacks against the Sunken Road. The Yankees are holding there and we must dislodge them."

"General, we have already launched twelve separate attacks against that road, all without success," the colonel said. His smoke-blackened face validated that he had been a participant, and not merely an observer of the battle. "And the toll has been terrible," he added. "Each time we make an attack, we must climb over the bodies of the men who were killed in the previous attack."

"Then we will launch attack number thirteen," Beauregard insisted. "And this one will not fail. I have ordered artillery support."

Paul watched as the heavy guns were brought up from other places on the field. One by one the caissons were unlimbered, swung around, then anchored in place. The gun crews went about their business of loading the guns with powder, grape, and canister. Then, at nearly point-blank range, sixty-two guns opened up on the defenders in the Sunken Road. The Hornets' Nest, as both armies were now calling this place, was enveloped in one huge crashing explosion of grapeshot, shrapnel, shards of shattered rock, and splintered trees.

Finally, the artillery barrage stilled and the Confederates launched their attack, not running and screaming across the field, but marching as if on parade. Paul, who for the last two days had been a member of General Johnston's staff, now returned to take command of his regiment, and as his men advanced, he rode in front of them, his saber drawn.

Now, the cannonading had stopped, no muskets were being fired, and no challenges were being issued. After a full day of thunder, an eerie quiet descended over the battlefield, the only sound being the measured and muffled beating of the drums, the jangle of equipment, and the brush of footsteps. It was so quiet that conversation could be heard in the Yankee lines.

"Looks like the Rebs are comin' at us again," someone said, and the fear Paul could hear in that voice mirrored the fear he was feeling, but managing to keep subdued.

"How many of them fellas do we have to kill a'fore they quit?" another said.

The Confederates continued their advance. There were no challenging Rebel yells, no cheers, no conversation of any kind. Scattered throughout the first rank were the drums, whose cadence not only kept the men marching as one, but relayed the officers' orders. The drummers were young, some as young as twelve, but already their eyes were glazed over with the same hollow stare as those of their older comrades.

Paul led his men down to the creek, then into it.

The backwater slough was knee deep with mud and stagnant, standing water, and it slowed the attackers' advance even more.

"Fire!" the Yankee artillery commander shouted.

In one horrendous volley, more than sixty cannons fired, belching out flame, smoke, and whistling death. The artillery barrage was followed almost immediately by a volley of deadly accurate rifle fire. Hundreds of attacking soldiers went down in the withering fire, and the attack was stopped in its tracks. The remaining Confederate soldiers turned and scrambled back out of the water, up the embankment and into the wood line beyond, leaving their dead and dying behind them.

One of the dead left on the field was Lieutenant Steve Cramer of Comancheria.

Considerably less aggressive than Johnston, Beauregard halted the advance that evening, rather than carrying through as Paul was certain Johnston would have.

"We need to give our men an opportunity to catch their breaths," Beauregard said. "And," he added, "to allow them to enjoy the largesse that has fallen into our hands."

Beauregard was talking about the food the Union soldiers had abandoned when they left the field. That night many of the Southern soldiers ate better than they had eaten in the previous six months.

But the pause proved to be a very costly one, for during the night the Federal gunships were able to move far enough up the Tennessee to bring the Confederate troops under fire. The cannonading continued all night long, shot and shell screaming through the night, leaving long sparkling fuse trails against the dark sky. It also rained again, a cold, bitter rain, which increased by tenfold the suffering of the wounded who lay, by the thousands, bleeding and in pain among the dead on the battlefield.

More significant than the gunships, though, was the fact that General Buell was able to bring his troops up in support of General Grant during the night. When fighting resumed the next morning, the Union forces not only greatly outnumbered the Confederate forces on the field, but more than half of them were fresh, un-bloodied, and well supplied. On this, the second day of a most horrendous battle, the Confederate army was severely crippled in body and spirit. The Confederates had also depleted most of their powder, shot, and shells. Although the day before had clearly belonged to the Confederates, the Federal troops carried this day. Beauregard withdrew his army leaving victory, pyrrhic though it was, to the Union.

Chapter Nineteen

After Shiloh, Paul's regiment was detached from Beauregard and attached to General Hood. There, they took part in the Battle of Gaines Mill, then Antietam. Silas McCarthy was killed at Antietam.

After Antietam, Paul was promoted to brigadier general, and given a brigade. He brought Gordon along with him as his second in command.

Then, Lee turned his army north, to invade the Union. They marched into Pennsylvania.

Gettysburg, Pennsylvania—July 2, 1863

The battle had begun a day earlier when Confederate General Heth, not realizing that Gettysburg was occupied by Union soldiers, led his own division into town, partly in search of shoes. There, General Heth and his men encountered Union General Buford, and the fighting began as a general skirmish. But the skirmish quickly brought in supporting units so that, by nightfall of the first day, what had started as skirmishing was beginning to develop into a full-blown battle.

Brigadier General Paul Nelson was in command of the Texas Third Brigade. The Texas Third was attached to General Hood, who was himself attached to General Longstreet.

The next day, Paul and his executive officer, Colonel Gordon Forsythe, reconnoitered the field where they had fought the day before, and discovered that though the Union forces had fortified their positions, they had left two hills, Little Roundtop and Big Roundtop, unoccupied. This was critical because those two hills had commanding views, not only the battlefield, but the approaches to the battlefield.

"Tell me I'm not seeing what I think I'm seeing," Gordon said.

"Well, if you think you are seeing those two hills unoccupied, then you are seeing exactly what I'm seeing," Paul said. "Come on, we need to report this to General Lee."

General Robert E. Lee was only fifty-six years old, but with his snow-white hair, white beard, and somewhat frail appearance, one could easily have guessed that he was twenty years older. On the other hand, Paul Nelson, who was only eight years younger than Lee, still had a look of youth about him. His hair was dark, his skin weathered, but not wrinkled, his eyes vibrant, his physique strong.

Paul found the general leaning back against a gun caisson, with his arms folded across his chest.

"General Lee, there are no Yankee soldiers on either one of those two commanding hills," Paul said when he reported to the general.

"That seems odd," General Lee replied. "Do you trust the report?"

"I reckon I do, General, seeing as I'm the one that's making the report. I saw those hills with my own eyes."

General Lee smiled broadly, then hit his hand in his fist. "Then, by golly, General Nelson, we have them. Go back and tell General Longstreet that I repose full faith and trust in him, and that I intend for him to occupy both Little and Big Roundtop."

"Will the general be supporting my efforts?" Longstreet asked after Paul delivered the message.

"It would not be my place, General Longstreet, to make assumptions about General Lee's intentions," Paul replied. "I am but delivering his instructions to you."

"Yes, of course," Longstreet said. "Good job of scouting this morning, and I thank you. You may return to General Hood, now."

"Thank you, General," Paul said.

General Longstreet decided to make his attack a surprise, and surprise meant stealth. That required his corps to march back up Chambersburg Pike, then head south for over three miles, and then turn east to attack the Union's left flank . . . all the while trying to avoid Union detection. But, in trying to avoid detection and awaiting reinforcements, Longstreet did not reach his position and become ready to attack until four o'clock that afternoon.

In the meantime, Paul acted as liaison between General Hood and General Lee. General Lee was not a person who was often demonstrative of his feelings, especially when he was angry, but Paul could tell that he was becoming increasingly frustrated with Longstreet's lack of progress.

General Hood was also frustrated with Longstreet's slow pace, and he made no bones about it.

"It's four-thirty. We have been tarrying here all day long. What in the hell is Longstreet trying to do?" Hood asked Paul. "Does he think that if he will just delay long enough, the Yankees will get tired and leave?"

"Longstreet is a methodical man," Paul said.

"Yeah, well, believe me if Jackson hadn't gotten himself killed, we wouldn't be waiting around like this," Hood said.

Hood had barely gotten his comments out when the ground literally shook with the sound of artillery fire. Longstreet had begun his attack with a concentrated artillery attack on the peach orchard. A courier arrived from Longstreet at that moment, and he reported to Paul.

"General Nelson, General Longstreet's compliments, sir, and he asks that General Hood's division take the right side and attack the two Round Tops and Devil's Den. McLaw's division will attack through the wheat field and the peach orchard."

"Very good, Courier," Paul said, returning the salute. He took the message to Hood.

"It is about time," Hood said. "General Nelson, to

you goes the honor of commanding the first element. Please proceed as soon as you can position your Texans."

"My Texans are in position, General Hood," Paul replied.

An anxious Colonel Forsythe met Paul when he returned to the brigade's command post.

"What is the word?" Gordon asked.

"We are to attack," Paul said. "Now."

A broad smile spread across Gordon's face as he moved into position. Paul drew his saber—the same saber Colonel Travis had carried at the Alamo— and moved to the front of his men. He held the saber up, high over his head for a long moment, until he was certain that not only his subordinate commanders, but every man in the brigade saw him, then he brought it down sharply. Fifteen hundred men, with a roar of defiance in their throats, started forward.

They crossed Big Round Top with little resistance, but came to a halt on Little Round Top when the Union forces offered a stronger defense. And there, despite fierce fighting, the Union was unable to hold Devil's Den and were forced to vacate the position. After that, the fighting continued northwest along the line, through Rose's Woods, the wheat field, on the Stony Hill, and up to the peach orchard. Attack and counterattack were made until about six o'clock that evening. By then, the Confederates had reached as far as Plum Run and victory seemed well in their grasp. But there, darkness fell and they were forced to halt the advance.

* * *

The next day the battle continued with neither army realizing any advantage until General Lee, thinking this would be the time for an act of boldness, ordered a frontal attack, calling for nearly twelve thousand men to march over a thousand yards across open ground. Pickett's division of Longstreet's corps would be the southern wing.

Paul's brigade was held in reserve, as over one hundred Confederate guns began the contest by firing barrage after barrage into the Union lines. The attack started from Seminary Ridge with Pickett's and Trimble's divisions slowly marching eastward, the line of attackers stretching out more than one mile from end to end.

Union batteries from Cemetery Hill to Little Round Top immediately opened fire on the advancing line, creating temporary gaps in the units. The Confederates kept coming and, after crossing Emmitsburg Road, re-formed their lines to fill in the gaps left by those who were killed or wounded. As the Confederate forces came closer and closer to the Union lines, the cannon barrels were depressed, and solid balls were replaced with canister, grapeshot, and explosive shells. They were brought to bear against the Confederate lines with devastating effect.

"My God," Paul said, as he watched the attack through binoculars. "It's like the Mexicans at the Alamo. Only instead of one-tenth their number, these brave men are marching into a fortified position of at least equal, and maybe even greater numbers."

Paul remembered seeing the Mexican soldiers being cut down in waves as they attacked the Alamo, and he was seeing the same thing again. At the Alamo, the Mexicans so outnumbered the defenders that there were enough attackers to carry through despite the slaughter. That wasn't the case here. The numbers of defenders and attackers were nearly even, with the defenders well fortified behind rock walls, while the Confederates were in the open.

By now, the attacking soldiers were also well within Union rifle distance. As the men in the charge saw their friends around them falling, the natural tendency was to come together to keep the line solid. As the body of men continued their advance, the lines converged, with Pettigrew moving to his right and Pickett moving to his left. The attacking Confederate line, which had been one mile long at the start of the charge, was now compacted to about one-half mile long.

Brigadier General James L. Kemper's brigade formed Pickett's lead right-front brigade. To his left was Brigadier Richard B. Garnett's brigade, followed by Brigadier General Lewis A. Armistead's brigade. Pickett ordered his men to turn to the northeast in order to link with Pettigrew's division. The maneuver exposed his right flank to the artillery on Little Round Top and the southern portion of Cemetery Ridge, allowing the Union artillery to fire along the Confederate line with little chance of missing a target.

The Confederate line continued to bunch toward the center until they became a disorganized mass of men fifteen to thirty deep. Opposite the main assault was the "Angle"—a point in the Union line where it formed a ninety-degree angle. As the Confederates pushed forward, the men and artillery in the Angle poured devastating fire into the approaching units. Still, the Confederates came, this time reaching the stone wall of the Angle.

Here, the Union forces halted the Confederate advance and forced many of the enemy to seek cover behind the western side of the stone wall. Hand-to-hand fighting raged in the Angle and Union reinforcements rushed into the Angle to drive the Confederates out.

The Confederates were now outnumbered and cut off from any reinforcements. Soon, anyone left in the Angle was either captured or killed. The remaining Confederate units near the Angle slowly retreated and made their way back toward Seminary Ridge.

As Paul scanned the field between his position and the furthermost point reached by the charge, he saw a battlefield so strewn with bodies that one could walk the entire thousand yards without his feet having to touch the ground.

"General Pickett," Lee called out as General Pickett and what was left of his division came back into the relative safety of the Confederate lines at Seminary Ridge. "Please hold your division ready for a possible Union counterattack!"

"What division would that be, General?" Pickett replied. "I no longer have a division."

Comancheria—June 11, 1864

Tyler Bodine stood in the stirrups and rubbed his sore behind as he looked down from a small hill onto the house and buildings below. There were six other men riding with him.

"Well now," Bodine said. "Looks to me like Nelson has got hisself a real nice-lookin' spread down there. You know that a house like that, big and fancy as it is, is goin' to have gold and silver all through it."

"You know Nelson, do you?" the rider on his right asked.

"Yeah, I know Nelson," Bodine said. "Me 'n him is old friends."

"Old friends?"

"Yeah, well, only in a manner of speakin'," Bodine said. "Let's just say that we've run across each other from time to time over the years. Get the flag out, we're goin' to pay 'em a visit."

"Which flag we want to use? Rebel or Yankee flag?"

"The Yankee flag," Bodine said. "We are the Independent Union Raiders, remember?"

"Last month we was raidin' in Kansas under the Rebel flag."

Bodine chuckled. "Well now, that's the beauty of bein' independent, ain't it? We can be Rebels one time and Yankees the next. And no matter what we do, it's an act of war, don't you see?"

Joe Travis had come over to Longtrail to make some repairs to the roof of the barn. He had been a frequent visitor during Paul's absence, making repairs when necessary, running errands when required. He had just cut a piece of board and was about to put it in place on the roof when he saw several riders on a ridgeline, looking down at them. They were too far away for Joe to recognize any of them, but he didn't have a good feeling about it.

Moving quickly, he climbed back down the ladder, then ran to the house.

"Miz Nelson, Miz Nelson!" he called.

"What is it, Joe?" Fancy asked.

"I think it might be best if you and the children came out to the barn with me and climbed up into the loft."

"Why, what is it?"

"Looks to me like you are about to have some visitors, and I don't think they're goin' to be friendly ones."

"Children!" Fancy called. "Come quickly."

"Do you have any guns here?"

"A couple of pistols and a couple of rifles," Tom said. "The rifles are Henry repeaters."

"Grab 'em, boy," Joe said. "And plenty of bullets. I think we're goin' to need 'em."

Tom grabbed the weapons. Then he, his mother, brother, and two sisters hurried back outside to the barn.

"You folks climb up into the loft, and hide behind some hay bales," Joe said. "The boy and me will go over to the machine shed. That way when they start shootin' back at us, you and the others won't be in the line of fire." Joe handed one of the pistols to Fancy. "This is just in case you need it," he said.

"Tom, can you shoot that thing pretty good?" Joe asked.

"I've killed a lot of rabbit and squirrel," Tom said.

"You ought to be all right then," Joe said. "Rabbits and squirrels is a lot smaller than a man." He pointed to the windmill. "See if you can climb up that thing. Lay down on the platform up there, nobody will see you. You can shoot through the gap in the windmill blades. It'll be a lot harder for 'em."

"Where will you be?"

"I'll be right here in the machine shed. If they get folks shootin' at 'em from two directions, they will likely get all a'feared and run off. Leastwise, that's what I'm hopin' they'll do."

Dividing up the ammunition, Tom took the pistol and rifle with him, then climbed up the windmill. He had just gotten into position when the riders came in through the arched gate.

"Ha! Longtrail," one of the riders said as they came into the yard. "Ol' Paul Nelson has got hisself quite a layout here, don't he?"

Tom had never seen anyone quite like this rider. He was so pale as to be chalk white. His hair was white, too, but Tom didn't think it was because he was old. Then he remembered hearing about such people. They were called albinos.

"Is Nelson here?" one of the others asked.

"He ain't here, he's off fightin' the war," the albino said. "But his wife and kids is here." The leader of the group raised his hand to his mouth, and called out loudly.

"You in the house!" he shouted. "Come on out here! Come out now, or we'll burn the house down with you inside!"

Tom drew aim on one of the riders, but he didn't know if he should shoot yet or not. The question was answered for him, when he heard a shot fired from the machine shed. One of the riders went down. Tom pulled the trigger then, and man he was aiming at went down as well.

"What the hell? Where are they shooting from?" one of the riders called.

Another shot from the machine shed hit another rider, and though he didn't fall, he slumped forward in his saddle.

"I'm gettin' out of here!" someone shouted, and he turned and galloped back toward the gate. Everyone but the albino followed. Tom shot at him, and saw a spot of blood appear on his shirtsleeve. The blood was deep red, all the more vivid because of the pale skin of the would-be raider. The albino spurred his horse and left the grounds at a gallop.

From his position atop the windmill, Tom had a good view of them as they departed. He stayed up there watching, until they were at least two miles away, and still riding hard. Not until then did he climb down and call out to the others.

"It's all right, you can all come out now!" he shouted. "They're gone!"

As the others came from the barn and the machine shed, Tom hurried over to look down at the two men who had been hit. One of them, the one Joe had shot, was still alive, though just barely so. He was still gasping for breath as the others came over. Tom was looking at the man he had shot. He was dead, and Tom felt a terrible sense of awe over having killed him.

"Don't you be worryin' none about that," Joe said. "They's some folks in this world that just needs killin'. And these folks was goin' to burn down your house, an' ain't no tellin' what they had in mind for yo' mama and sisters."

"It would be easy, he said," the rider who was still

alive said. He gasped for breath. "Nelson was gone, he said, wouldn't be trouble 'tall."

"Who told you that?" Joe asked. "Who was that pasty-lookin' man that was leadin' you?"

"The albino, you mean?" He coughed.

"Yeah," Joe said. "Who was that?"

"Bodine. Tyler Bodine," the raider asked. He coughed a few more times and this time Tom noticed that blood was coming from his mouth. Then, after one last, gasping breath, his head fell to one side, and even though his eyes were still open, Tom knew that he was dead.

"I reckon I've done murder now," Tom said, awestruck by what he had done.

"No, you ain't, boy," Joe said. "What you was doin' was defendin' your own family. That ain't murder."

"Joe is right, honey," Fancy said. "You did what you had to do."

"What—what are we going to do with them?" Tom asked.

"You don't worry none about 'em," Joe said. "I'll get 'em out of here."

"What are you going to do with them?" Tom asked.

"I'll bury 'em somewhere," Joe said.

Tom nodded. "I'll come help," he said.

Fancy felt a lump come to her throat. Today, her boy had become a man.

Chapter Twenty

Virginia—April 1, 1865

After a series of defeats and military setbacks, the Confederate army was now hanging on tenuously to an ever-decreasing area of operation in Virginia. General Robert E. Lee ordered Pickett with his infantry division and Munford's and Rosser's cavalry divisions to hold the vital crossroads of Five Forks at all hazard. But while Sheridan's cavalry pinned the Confederate force in position, the V Corps under Major General G. K. Warren attacked and overwhelmed the Confederate left flank, causing Five Forks to fall into Union hands.

Loss of Five Forks threatened Lee's last supply line, the South Side Railroad, and it fell to Brigadier General Paul Nelson to tell Lee of the defeat.

"They've turned our flank, General," Paul said.

Lee looked stunned, then put his left hand down

on the table that held his situation maps, lowered his head, and closed his eyes for a long moment.

"We have no choice now, but to evacuate our position," Lee said. He looked at the situation map for a moment. "We will try to reassemble and resupply our men at Amelia. Then, perhaps, we can link up with Johnston's Tennesseans and go on the offense."

Lee sighed. "I just wish it was Albert Johnston instead of Joseph Johnston. You were with Al when he was killed, weren't you, General?"

"Yes, sir," Paul said. "And I was with him at Palo Alto during the Mexican War."

"I was there as well. So was our adversary. We were all wearing the same uniform then," Lee said, almost wistfully.

"Yes, sir."

"Please get the word out, would you, Paul?" Lee said. "We will pull out tonight."

"I'll spread the word, General," Paul promised.

"We're pulling out tonight?" Colonel Gordon Forsythe said.

"Yes, we have no choice."

"It doesn't look good, does it, Paul?"

"No, it doesn't look good at all."

During the night of the second and third of April, the Army of Virginia abandoned the trenches they had held, steadfastly, for ten months. Slipping out, and leaving the field to the Union troops, they made a forced march to Amelia, arriving on April fourth. There, they had expected to find provisions, but nothing was there.

Paul sent Gordon out with wagons to forage from the surrounding countryside.

"We have nothing left," a woman told Gordon when the three wagons arrived at her farm. "You already took our last two pigs and all but three chickens. Would you have us starve to death?"

"I'm sorry, ma'am," Gordon said, touching his eyebrow in a casual salute. "We will leave you with what you have." He reached down into the wagon and pulled out a sack. "Here is some corn meal," he said.

The woman, who but a moment before had been pleading to keep what little she had, was shocked at Gordon's beneficence.

"God bless you," she said. "And God bless our army, though I pray that this war will end soon."

When Gordon returned, the foraging had been so fruitless that what little food they had managed to find, did not compensate for the loss of a day of marching. The next morning, the army headed west to Appomattox Station where a supply train awaited them. By now Lee's army was composed only of the cavalry corps and two small infantry corps. Lee had less than fifteen thousand effectives in the field— ragged, incomplete units, poorly armed, poorly clothed, and starving, opposed by ninety thousand well-armed and well-fed Union soldiers.

En route to the station, on April sixth at Saylor's Creek, nearly one-fourth of the retreating Confederate army was cut off by Sheridan's cavalry and elements of the Federal II and VI Corps. Two Confederate divisions fought the VI Corps along the creek. The Confederates attacked, but were driven back, and soon after the Union cavalry cut through the right of the Confederate lines. Most of the 7,700 Confederates surrendered, including Lieutenant General Richard S. Ewell and eight other generals. Of all the generals assigned to Ewell, only Paul Nelson managed to avoid capture.

A little before noon on the seventh of April, 1865, General Grant, with his staff, rode into the little village of Farmville, on the south side of the Appomattox River, establishing his headquarters on the piazza. He drew up in front of the village hotel, dismounted, and established headquarters on its broad piazza.

At two o'clock that same afternoon, advance units of the Union II Corps attacked Paul's entrenched troops at Cumberland Church. They attacked twice, and were repulsed both times. Union General Thomas Smyth was killed in the battle, which ended with the Union forces withdrawing from the field.

Back at the Union Headquarters, Generals Ord and Gibbon visited Grant at the hotel. They brought with them General Ewell, who was now Grant's prisoner. Because General Ewell had lost a leg at the second Battle of Bull Run, he had to brace himself on one leg and a peg that extended from his knee.

"General Grant, General Ewell has something to say that you might want to hear," General Ord said.

Grant was enjoying a supper of roast beef, baked potatoes, and corn bread. The potatoes and corn bread were courtesy of the Confederate supply train they had captured.

General Ewell looked down at the food with a barely concealed craving.

"Oh, excuse my bad manners," Grant said. "Sergeant Martin, please set a plate for our guest."

"Thank you, General," Ewell said, sitting gratefully, when a chair was offered.

"General, I am told that you spoke highly of me to General Lee, when the war began," Grant said. "You said, I believe, that there is a West Pointer, little known, that you hoped the North did not discover. You said you knew me well at the academy and in Mexico and that you thought the South should fear me more than any other officer. Did you make such a statement?"

Sergeant Martin set a plate, well provisioned, in front of Ewell.

"Yes, sir, I did make that statement," Ewell said.

Grant chuckled. "As I recall my days back on the plains of West Point, when you were a senior classman and I was a plebe, you had no such illusions about me."

"I apologize, sir, if you found my hazing offensive back at the academy."

"Not at all, General, not at all," Grant said. Noticing that Ewell had yet to take a bite of his food, Grant pointed to it. "Please, General, enjoy."

"Thank you, sir," Ewell said, attacking his plate with gusto.

"Now, what is it, General Ewell, that General Ord thought I should hear?"

"Our cause is lost, sir," Ewell said between bites. "It was lost when we crossed the James River, and I considered it General Lee's duty to negotiate for peace then, while he still has a right to claim concessions. Indeed, for every man killed from this point on, someone should be held responsible, for it will be little better than murder."

"Dick, have you spoken of this to Lee?" Grant asked, using the name he had addressed General Richard Ewell with when they had served together.

"I can't tell Lee what to do, Sam," Ewell said. "I can only hope that he will at once surrender his army."

"Is it your suggestion then that I reach out to him?" Grant asked.

"Yes, sir, it is," Ewell replied, though his words were muffled as he ate a large bite of corn bread.

That night, under a flag of truce, a Union colonel approached Paul Nelson's lines. When he was brought to Paul, he stated his mission.

"General, I have a note from General Grant for General Lee, and beg your indulgence, sir, in being able to present it."

"Colonel Forsythe," Paul called to his second in command. "Be ready to repulse should the Yankees make any attempt to violate the truce."

"Yes, sir," Gordon said.

"I assure you, General, we will not violate the truce," the Union officer said.

"We will see," Paul said. "What is your name, sir?"

"Hardesty, sir. Colonel Hardesty of General Grant's personal staff."

"Come along, Colonel, I'll take you to General Lee."

General Lee was having his own supper when Paul and Colonel Hardesty approached him. Lee's supper consisted of a square of hardtack and a cup of coffee. The hardtack could only be eaten by soaking it for a long moment in the coffee.

"General Nelson, have you read the note?" Lee asked.

"Yes, General, I have," Paul replied.

"Let me see it," Lee said, extending his hand.

Paul gave General Lee the note, then studied the expression on Lee's face as the general read it.

HEADQUARTERS, ARMIES OF THE U. S.
5 P.M., April 7th, 1865

GENERAL R. E. LEE, Commanding C. S. A.:
The results of the last week must convince you of the hopelessness of further resistance on the part of the Army of Northern Virginia in this struggle. I feel that it is so, and regard it as my duty to shift from myself the responsibility of any further effusion of blood by asking of you the surrender of that portion of the Confederate States army known as the Army of Northern Virginia.

U. S. Grant, Lieutenant-General

Lee sat down and opened his case to remove a sheet of paper and a pen. Knocking the pen point against the blotter, he replied to the letter in large, bold strokes.

April 7th, 1865
LIEUTENANT-GENERAL U. S. GRANT

GENERAL: I have received your note of this date. Though not entertaining the opinion you express of the hopelessness of further resistance on the part of the Army of Northern Virginia, I reciprocate your desire to avoid useless effusion of blood, and therefore, before considering your proposition, ask the terms you will offer on condition of its surrender.

R. E. LEE, General CSA

"If you would, General Nelson, escort Colonel . . ." He looked up at the Union colonel.

"Hardesty, Sir. Terrence J. Hardesty."

"Hardesty back to the nearest point to his lines, and see to it that he has safe passage thereto," Lee said.

"Yes, sir," Paul replied. "Colonel, this way please."

When Paul returned sometime later with the news that Hardesty was on his way back to his own lines, Lee mused out loud.

"With our supplies at Appomattox destroyed, I fear our only hope now is the railway at Lynchburg. We'll have supplies waiting for us there, and right now, all that is between us and Lynchburg is their cavalry. Is your brigade ready to move?"

"Yes, sir," Paul said. In truth, Paul dreaded ordering his men into battle one more time. They were exhausted, physically, mentally, and spiritually. And they had so little ammunition left that they would be unable to sustain any battle for more than a few minutes.

By the time Colonel Hardesty returned to Grant with Lee's response, Grant had a throbbing headache, and he rubbed his temples as he read the note.

"It looks as if Lee still means to fight," he said. "I expect he is going to make a move toward Lynchburg. General Ord, move your corps up to support Sheridan's cavalry. If we can prevent Lee from resupplying his troops, we can end this thing now."

"Yes, sir," Major General Edward Ord replied.

"While you are doing that, I'll answer General Lee," Grant said.

Leaving Grant to draft his reply to Lee, Ord returned to his corps and sent them on a midnight march. By four a.m., they arrived to support the U.S. Cavalry under Sheridan. Sheridan then deployed three divisions along a low ridge to the southwest of Appomattox Courthouse

The next morning, Lee received Grant's second letter.

April 8th, 1865
GENERAL R. E. LEE,
Commanding C. S. A.:
  Your note of last evening in reply to mine of the same date, asking the conditions on which I will accept the surrender of the Army of Northern Virginia, is just received. In reply, I would say that, peace being my great desire, there is but one condition I would insist upon—namely that the men and officers surrendered shall be disqualified from taking up arms against the Government of the United States until properly exchanged. I will meet you, or will designate officers to meet any officers you may name for the same purpose, at any point agreeable to you, for the purpose of arranging definitely the terms upon which the surrender of the Army of Northern Virginia will be received.

  U. S. GRANT, Lieutenant-General

Lee responded immediately.

LIEUTENANT-GENERAL U. S. GRANT
  GENERAL: I received at a late hour your note of

today. In mine of yesterday I did not intend to propose the surrender of the Army of Northern Virginia, but to ask the terms of your proposition. To be frank, I do not think the emergency has arisen to call for the surrender of this army, but, as the restoration of peace should be the sole object of all, I desired to know whether your proposals would lead to that end. I cannot, therefore, meet you with a view to surrender the Army of Northern Virginia; but as far as your proposal may affect the Confederate States forces under my command, and tend to the restoration of peace, I should be pleased to meet you at 10 A.M. tomorrow on the old stage road to Richmond, between the picket-lines of the two armies.

R. E. LEE, General, CSA

Grant replied.

April 9th, 1865
GENERAL R. E. LEE
    GENERAL: Your note of yesterday is received. I have no authority to treat on the subject of peace. The meeting proposed for 10 A. M. today could lead to no good. I will state, however, that I am equally desirous for peace with yourself, and the whole North entertains the same feeling. The terms upon which peace can be had are well understood. By the South laying down their arms, they would hasten that most desirable event, save thousands of human lives, and hundreds of millions of property not yet destroyed. Seriously hoping that all our difficulties may be settled without the loss of another life, I subscribe myself, etc.

U. S. GRANT, Lieutenant-General

Lee's response:

> *April 9ᵗʰ, 1865*
> *LIEUTENANT-GENERAL U. S. GRANT*
>   *GENERAL: I received your note of this morning
> on the picket-line, whither I had come to meet you
> and ascertain definitely what terms were embraced in
> your proposal of yesterday with reference to the sur-
> render of this army. I now ask an interview, in ac-
> cordance with the offer contained in your letter of
> yesterday, for that purpose.*
>
>   *R. E. LEE, General, CSA*

Now the messages were moving between the generals with increasing rapidity.

> *GENERAL R. E. LEE,*
> *Commanding C. S. Army:*
>   *Your note of this date is but this moment (11:50
> A. M.) received, in consequence of my having passed
> from the Richmond and Lynchburg road to the
> Farmville and Lynchburg road. I am at this writing
> about four miles west of Walker's Church, and will
> push forward to the front for the purpose of meeting
> you. Notice sent to me on this road where you wish
> the interview to take place me.*
>
>   *U. S. GRANT, Lieutenant-General*

When it was decided that the surrender would
take place at Appomattox, General Lee asked Paul if
he would go ahead and find a place suitable for the
meeting. When he reached the village, he met one of
its residents, named Wilmer McLean.

"What's going on, General?" McLean asked.

"I'm here to find a meeting place for General Lee and General Grant."

"Why are they meeting?" McLean asked. "Is Lee going to surrender?"

"That is not for me to say," Paul said.

"Well, hell, General, they can meet in my house," McLean said. "The war may as well end in my house as it started in my house."

"What do you mean?"

"When the war started, I lived at Manassas. General Beauregard used my house as his headquarters."

"Really?" Paul said.

"Yes, indeed," McLean said. "Therefore, I consider it only proper that the war which started in my house, end in my house."

The house had a comfortable wooden porch with seven steps leading up to it. A hall ran through the middle from front to back, and on each side was a room having two windows, one in front and one in the rear. Each room had two doors opening into the hall. The building stood a little distance back from the street, with a yard in front, and to the left was a gate for carriages and a roadway running to a stable in the rear.

"Yes," Paul said. "This will do nicely."

After making arrangements with McLean, Paul rode back find General Lee, then escorted him to the house where the surrender would take place.

"Yes," Lee said, looking around. "This will do nicely. Mr. McLean, my thanks, sir, for your courtesy and generosity."

"It is my honor, General," McLean said.

McLean led them into the parlor which was commodious enough to accommodate several people.

"General, here comes Grant," Colonel Babcock said.

"That would be General Grant, Colonel," Lee corrected him, gently.

"Yes, sir, General Grant," Babcock said.

General Grant mounted the steps and entered the house. As he stepped into the hall, Colonel Babcock opened the door of the room on the left, in which he, General Lee, Colonel Marshall, and Paul had been waiting. General Grant and those who had accompanied him came in. It was now half past one, on Sunday, the ninth of April.

Paul, acutely aware that he was once again at center stage for a significant historical event, fixed the room in his mind. Grant sat at a marble-topped table in the center of the room. Lee was sitting at a small oval table near the front window, in the corner opposite to the door by which Grant had entered, and facing General Grant. Colonel Marshall, General Lee's military secretary, was standing at Lee's left.

The officers with Grant came in, quietly, and took places around the room from which they could witness the ceremony. Some found chairs, some sat on the sofa. Most just stood around near the walls to watch.

As Paul looked at the two commanders, he couldn't help but notice the contrast. General Grant was five feet, eight inches in height, with shoulders slightly stooped. His hair and full beard were brown, without a trace of gray. He was wearing a single-breasted, dark blue jacket, unbuttoned to display a white vest. His trousers were tucked down inside his boots, trousers and boots spattered with mud. He was not wearing a sword, and had it not been for a pair of shoulder straps to denote his rank, he could have been taken for a private.

General Lee, on the other hand, was fully six feet in height, and quite erect. He had silver gray hair and a full beard, which nearly matched the color of his uniform. At his side he was wearing sword, with a jewel-studded hilt.

"I met you once before, General Lee, while we were serving in Mexico," General Grant said. "You came over from General Scott's headquarters to visit Garland's brigade. I was then attached to that brigade. I have always remembered your appearance, and I think I should have recognized you anywhere."

"Yes," General Lee said. "I know I met you on that occasion, and I have often thought of it and tried to recollect how you looked, but I have never been able to recall a single feature."

"I believe I met you during the Mexican War as well, did I not, General?" Grant said to Paul.

"You may have, sir. I was with Johnston at the time," Paul said.

"This might interest you, General," Lee said. "General Nelson was also with William Travis at the Alamo, and with Sam Houston at San Jacinto."

"You have certainly been an eyewitness to history, General," Grant said. "And now, you are onstage to witness it again."

"So he is," Lee said. "And to that end, may I suggest that we proceed? I suppose, General Grant, that the object of our present meeting is fully understood. I asked to see you to ascertain upon what terms you would receive the surrender of my army."

General Grant replied, "The terms I propose are simple. That is, the officers and men surrendered to be paroled and disqualified from taking up arms again, and all arms, ammunition, and supplies to be delivered up as captured property."

"Yes, those are about the conditions which I expected would be proposed," General Lee said. "I presume, General Grant, we have both carefully considered the proper steps to be taken, and I would suggest that you commit to writing the terms you have proposed, so that they may be formally acted upon."

"All right, if you wish, I'll write them out," Grant replied. He looked over at General Ord. "General, my manifold order book please."

Ord responded quickly. Grant opened it on the table in front of him, then began writing. When he had finished the letter, he called Colonel Parker, one of the military secretaries on the staff, to his side.

"Would you take a look at this, Colonel?" Grant asked.

Colonel Parker read through it quickly, then pointed to a word. "You repeated this word," he said.

Grant looked at it, nodded, then marked through the word "their" which he had written two times. When this was done, he handed the paper to General Lee for his perusal.

Lee took it and laid it on the table beside him, while he drew from his pocket a pair of steel-rimmed spectacles and wiped the glasses carefully with his handkerchief. Then he crossed his legs, adjusted the spectacles very slowly and deliberately, took up the draft of the letter, and proceeded to read it attentively. It consisted of two pages.

APPOMATTOX CT. H., VA.,
April 9th, 1865
GENERAL R. E. LEE,
Commanding C. S. A.

    GENERAL: In accordance with the substance of
my letter to you of the 8th instant, I propose to receive
the surrender of the Army of Northern Virginia on
the following terms, to wit: Rolls of all the officers
and men to be made in duplicate, one copy to be
given to an officer to be designated by me, the other
to be retained by such officer or officers as you may
designate. The officers to give their individual
paroles not to take up arms against the Government
of the United States. Each company or regimental
commander to sign a like parole for the men of their
commands. The arms, artillery, and public property
to be parked, and stacked, and turned over to the
officers appointed by me to receive them. This will not
embrace the side-arms of the officers, nor their private
horses or baggage. This done, each officer and man
will be allowed to return to his home, not to be dis-
turbed by the United States authorities so long as they
observe their paroles, and the laws in force where they
may reside.

        Very respectfully,
        U. S. GRANT, Lieutenant-General

When he reached the top line of the second page,
Lee looked up, and said to General Grant, "After the
words 'until properly,' the word 'exchanged' seems
to be omitted. You doubtless intended to use that
word."

"Why, yes," said Grant. "I thought I had put in the
word 'exchanged.'"

"I presumed it had been omitted inadvertently," General Lee said. "With your permission I will mark where it should be inserted."

"Certainly," Grant replied.

Lee felt in his pocket as if searching for a pencil, but did not seem to be able to find one. Seeing this, Paul handed him his pencil. Lee took it and, laying the paper on the table, made the notation. As he continued to read, he kept twirling this pencil in his fingers and occasionally tapped the top of the table with it. When he was finished, he looked up again.

General Grant then said, "Unless you have some suggestions to make in regard to the form in which I have stated the terms, I will have a copy of the letter made in ink and sign it."

"There is one thing I would like to mention," Lee replied after a short pause. "The cavalrymen and artillerists own their own horses in our army. Its organization in this respect differs from that of the United States. I would like to understand whether these men will be permitted to retain their horses?"

"You will find that the terms as written do not allow this," General Grant replied. "Only the officers are permitted to take their private property."

Lee read over the second page of the letter again, and then said, "No, I see the terms do not allow it; that is clear." His face showed plainly that he was quite anxious to have this concession made.

Grant said very promptly and without giving Lee time to make a direct request, "Well, the subject is quite new to me. Of course, I did not know that any private soldiers owned their animals, but I think this will be the last battle of the war—I sincerely hope so—and that the surrender of this army will be followed soon by that of all the others. Also, I take it that most of the men in the ranks are small farmers, and as the country has been so raided by the two armies, it is doubtful whether they will be able to put in a crop to carry themselves and their families through the next winter without the aid of the horses they are now riding. I will arrange it in this way: I will not change the terms as now written, but I will instruct the officers I shall appoint to receive the paroles to let all the men who claim to own a horse or mule take the animals home with them to work their farms."

"I thank you, General Grant," Lee said. "This will have the best possible effect upon the men. It will be very gratifying and will do much toward conciliating our people."

He handed the draft of the terms back to General Grant, who called Colonel T. S. Bowers of the staff to him and directed him to make a copy in ink.

"General, if you don't mind, I will turn this over to Colonel Parker," Bowers said. "He has much better penmanship than I."

"Very well, Colonel Parker may do it," Grant said.

Parker sat down to write at the table which stood against the rear side of the room.

"Colonel Marshall," Lee said. "If you would, sir, please write a letter accepting the terms of surrender. I will then sign it."

It took but a few minutes for Colonel Marshall to draw up the letter, which he then handed to General Lee.

HEADQUARTERS, ARMY OF NORTHERN
  VIRGINIA,
April 9th, 1865
LIEUTENANT-GENERAL U. S. GRANT
  GENERAL: I received your letter of this date
containing the terms of the surrender of the Army of
Northern Virginia as proposed by you. As they are
substantially the same as those expressed in your
letter of the 8th inst., they are accepted. I will proceed
to designate the proper officers to carry the
stipulations into effect.

R. E. LEE, General, CSA

"Is there anything else to be discussed?" Grant
asked.

"Yes. I have a thousand or more of your men as
prisoners, General Grant, a number of them officers
whom we have required to march along with us for
several days. I shall be glad to send them into your
lines as soon as it can be arranged, for I have no provisions for them. I have, indeed, nothing for my own
men. They have been living for the last few days prin-
cipally upon parched corn, and we are badly in need
of both rations and forage. I telegraphed to Lynchburg, directing several trainloads of rations to be
sent on by rail from there, and when they arrive, I
shall be glad to have the present wants of my men
supplied from them."

"I am afraid, General, that General Custer, one of
my officers, captured those trains last night, near Appomattox Station," General Sheridan said.

"I see," was all Lee said.

"General Lee, I should like to have our men returned as soon as possible," Grant said. "I will take

steps at once to have your army supplied with rations, but I am sorry we have no forage for the animals. We have had to depend upon the country for our supply of forage. What is the current strength of your army?"

"Indeed, I am not able to say," Lee answered after a slight pause. "My losses in killed and wounded have been exceedingly heavy and, besides, there have been many stragglers and some deserters. All my reports and public papers and, indeed, my own private letters, had to be destroyed on the march, to prevent them from falling into the hands of your people. Many companies are entirely without officers, and I have not seen any reports for several days, so I have no means of ascertaining our present strength."

"Suppose I send over rations for twenty-five thousand men? Do you think that will be a sufficient supply?"

"Thank you, General. I think it will be ample, and a great relief, I assure you," Lee replied.

Chapter Twenty-one

East Texas—June 10, 1865

Paul Nelson and Gordon Forsythe were tired. It wasn't just the tiredness of the long ride back to Texas from Appomattox, it was a bone-deep, butt-tired exhaustion from four years of war.

"There's a building ahead," Gordon said. "Maybe we can get something to eat there."

"A drink wouldn't be bad, either," Paul said.

The building may have started its existence as a stage stop for one of the many stagecoach lines that had been put out of business by the war. A crudely lettered sign nailed to one of the porch supports read:

FOOD, DRINK, GOODS.
BEDS TEN CENTS, BLANKETS FIVE CENTS.

The building was old and so badly in need of repair that it looked as if the slightest puff of wind might blow it down.

There were two men sitting on a bench out front. One was a big man, with dark hair and a scraggly beard. The other was small and wiry, clean-shaven, or as clean-shaven as he could be under the circumstance. Neither man was in uniform, so Paul had no idea if they were veterans or not or, if they were, which army they had served. If they had served, had they been honorably discharged? Or were they deserters?

Of course, Paul could also ask that same question about himself and Gordon. There had been no formal orders releasing them from the army, though as the surrender declared that the Confederate Army no longer existed, it was reasonable to assume that their departure was not an act of desertion, but an act of reality.

The two men studied Paul and Gordon as they dismounted. What they saw were two men in gray—men whose eyes reflected the death and horror they had witnessed over the last four years.

Paul and Gordon were both wearing gray jackets, and though they had removed the insignia which would identify one of them as a colonel and the other as a general, it was obvious by the shadows on their collars, that they had been officers.

The big man on the porch scratched his beard while the other spat a stream of tobacco juice onto the dirt. Neither man spoke as Paul and Gordon tied off their horses.

The interior of the inn was a study of shadow and light. Some of the light came through the door, and some came through windows which were nearly opaque with dirt. Most of it, however, was in the form of gleaming dust motes which hung suspended in the still air, illuminated by the bars of sunbeams that stabbed through the cracks between the boards.

The proprietor came out of one of the back rooms then, wiping his hands on an apron that may, at one time, have been white.

"What can I do you for?"

"We thought maybe we could get a beer here, and something to eat," Gordon said.

"I've got beer. Beans, bacon and biscuits the only thing we got to eat. The beans is good though, my woman made 'em up no more'n two days ago."

"That'll do fine," Paul said, and he and Gordon took a table over in the corner of the room.

"Here you go," the proprietor said a few minutes later, putting the food on the table in front of him. "If you don't mind my askin', who was you with?"

"Nelson's Brigade, Hood's Division," Gordon said. He didn't identify Paul as the "Nelson" of Nelson's Brigade.

"I got a boy in the Texas Nineteenth Infantry," The proprietor said. "But we ain't heard nothin' from him for near 'bout six months now. His ma and me, we're gettin' some worried about him."

"I wouldn't be too worried about him yet," Paul said. "There are hundreds, probably thousands still out on the roads, coming back home. If he was a long way off and afoot, it is going to take him quite a while to get here."

"But he ain't mailed us no letter or nothin', tellin' us he's comin' home."

"If you think about it, sir, why would he mail a letter? He'll get here as fast as the letter would," Paul said.

The proprietor smiled. "Yes, sir, that's right, ain't

it? No need to be mailin' a letter when, like as not, he'll get here just as fast."

"I'll keep your boy in my prayers," Paul said. That wouldn't be hard to do. He was praying for all the soldiers now—to get home and start a new life.

"Hey, you, Rebs!" a gruff voice called.

Looking up from their meal, Paul and Gordon saw that the two men who had been lounging on the porch had stepped inside. It was the big, bearded one who yelled at them.

"Something we can do for you, friend?" Paul asked.

"Me an' my friend been wonderin' 'bout you two. Them's mighty fancy uniforms you are wearin'. Looks like maybe you was Reb officers. Onliest thing is, the war is over and we was wonderin', that is, me an' my friend, why you are still wearin' them uniforms?"

"That is an easy enough question to answer," Paul said. "We're wearing them because, at the moment, we don't have anything else to wear."

"We was also wonderin' about your horses," the man said.

"What about them?"

"Both of 'em is wearin' a U.S. brand. Now, seein' as you two is Rebs, what we're wonderin' about is, how'd you come by them two U.S. horses?"

"That's an easy question to answer as well," Paul said. "We took them."

"What?" the big man replied, surprised by the answer. "You mean to tell us that you admit to stealin' these horses from the Union Army?"

"I didn't say we stole them," Paul said. "I said we took them. There's a difference."

"What is the difference?"

"Turns out that the Yankee soldiers that were riding them at Franklin didn't need them anymore," Paul said.

"How come they didn't need 'em anymore? There don't nobody just give up a horse 'cause he don't need it anymore."

"You want to explain the situation to them, Gordon?" Paul asked. Paul had passed the conversation over to Gordon, not merely to be inclusive, but to draw the attention of the two men away from him.

"The Yankee soldiers that were riding them didn't need them anymore, because we killed them," Gordon said. "There were a lot of good men killed at Franklin, good men from both sides, men that didn't need to die because we had already lost the war. And after the carnage of that battle, we picked out the two best horses that remained."

"And so out of all the Rebel soldiers on the field, you two come up with the two best horses? How did you manage that?"

"Quite easily," Gordon said. "My friend here was the commanding general of the brigade. I was the colonel who was second in command."

"I don't believe that," the smaller of the two men said.

"Whoa, wait a minute," Paul said. "Are you calling my colonel a liar?" While Gordon had been occupying the men's attention, Paul had slowly, and unobtrusively, pulled his pistol from its holster and now he brought his hand up from under the table. When he did, there was a pistol in it. He cocked the pistol, making a deadly-sounding click as the sear engaged the cylinder. "Because if you are, I don't think I would find that too friendly."

"No," the smaller of the two said, holding his hands out as if to stop Paul. "I didn't mean nothin' like that. We was just curious, that's all."

"Both of you, take your pistols out, and put them here, on the table in front of us. Then go sit at the table over there. When is the last time you two boys had a good meal?"

"What? I don't know, yesterday, I guess. Some farm lady fed us."

"A Texas farm lady?"

"Yeah. Uh, I mean yes, sir. You bein' a general and all."

Paul chuckled. "I'm not a general anymore, but I do have a pistol in my hand, don't I?"

"Yes, sir, you do have that," the bigger of the two men said.

"Mr. Innkeeper, I want you to give both these boys a good meal, and a drink on us," Paul said.

"Yes, sir," the innkeeper replied.

Paul watched as the two men took a seat at the table he indicated.

"Were you boys in the war?" Paul asked.

"Yes, sir, we was," the bigger of the two said. "We was with the Sixth Missouri."

"Missouri had regiments on both sides," Paul said. "Which side was the Sixth Missouri?"

"We was Union," the big man said. "Look, we didn't mean nothin' by talkin' to you 'bout your horses an' all. You ain't goin' to shoot us, are you?" he asked nervously.

"The war's over, boys," Paul said. "We can keep on killing each other, I guess, but to tell the truth, I've had about enough of the killing. Haven't you?"

"Yes, sir, I reckon we have," the big, bearded man said.

"We got nothin' ag'in you personal, Reb," the other one said.

Paul lifted his glass toward them. "Then, I'd say we've made a good beginning," he said, toasting them.

Comancheria—Friday, August 11, 1865

As Paul rode up the lane that led to his ranch house, a rabbit jumped up from the edge of the road, ran alongside for a moment, then darted on ahead. When he came over the crest of the ridge, he saw the archway over the road and from it, the sign he had made so long ago: LONGTRAIL.

Passing under the sign, he heard the sound of an ax hitting wood. From this point, because of a bend in the road, he still couldn't see anything except the chimneys of his house. Once he rode around the bend, the house came into view. He stopped for a moment, just to look at it. Every night for the last four years, just before he went to sleep, he had called up this image in his mind, and looking at it now, he was almost overwhelmed with emotion.

He was also surprised to see it looking as well as it looked. The wood trim around the brick was a shining white, as if just recently painted. The lawn was well trimmed, not a window shutter was out of place. The barn and machine shed looked as well as the house. For a moment, he felt an odd sense of disappointment. It was almost as if he wanted it to look run-down, as evidence of his importance to the place.

He saw the source of the sound of the ax, because there was young, powerfully built man chopping wood. Paul could only see him from the back, but he noticed that the man was naked from the waist up. He had wide shoulders, and the muscles flexed in his arms as he swung the ax.

"Who the hell is that?" Paul said, speaking to his horse, but not speaking loudly enough for the ax man to hear him. Had Fancy hired some man to come work the place?

As Paul drew closer to the house, the young man with the ax either heard or sensed his presence. Holding the ax by his side, he studied the man on horseback for a moment, then a huge smile spread across his face.

"Dad!" he shouted, throwing the axe aside. "Mom! Dad is here!"

"Tom?" Paul said, shocked by the appearance of his son. When Paul left, Tom had been a thirteen-year-old boy. Now he was big, and in every respect, was a young man.

Paul dismounted as Tom ran to him and the two embraced. Even as he was embracing his son, Fancy came outside, ran down the steps and up the brick walk with her arms open wide. The other children were following behind her. The reunion was heart-felt, with tears and laughter, hugs, and kisses until they moved inside.

"I have to tell you, Fancy, I was a little jealous when I first rode up to the house," Paul said as he filled his plate with chicken and dumplings, his favorite, and a meal he had not enjoyed for nearly four years now.

"Jealous?" Fancy asked, confused by the comment.

"Yes, jealous," Paul said. "I saw this handsome young man chopping wood and I wondered just who it was."

The others laughed.

"Tom, you certainly grew up since I left home."

"Well, Pa, I'm seventeen," Tom said. "If the war hadn't ended when it did, I was going to join."

"Oh? Well, in that case, I'm glad it did end when it did."

"What about me, Pa, have I grown up?" John asked.

"Yes, all of you have. And you, Lucy, my, but you are a beautiful young woman. I'm going to have to get a shotgun to keep the boys away from you," he teased.

"It's too late, Pa," Tom said.

"What do you mean too late?"

"Billy Chapman has been sniffing around her for the past year."

"Aren't you a little young for him?" Paul asked. "What is he now, eighteen? Nineteen? And you are only fifteen."

"You were eleven years older than Mama when you and Mama were married," Lucy said.

"Good heavens, don't tell me you are talking about getting married!"

"No, it's nothing like that," Fancy said. "But if that happened some day, it would not be a bad thing. Billy is a wonderful young man."

"I'm sure he is. How is Mrs. Chapman getting along now? I mean since Dale was killed."

"She is doing well. She and Lucy Good look out for each other."

"She and Lucy look out for each other?"

"Yes, since Justin died. Agnes and Lucy are old

friends, you know, so it seems like a natural thing for them."

"Oh," Paul said. "I didn't know that Justin was dead."

"It happened just before Christmas. I sent you a letter about it."

"Did you? Well, for the last several months mail has been practically nonexistent. There is no telling where the letter is now. How is Ralph doing? Did he lose his leg?"

"No," Fancy said. "But he must use a cane to walk, now. And with Justin gone, he's having to manage the farm by himself. Such as it is."

"Such as it is?"

"With everyone gone, we had no way of working the farms. I doubt that there has been over five hundred acres of cotton grown in the last four years, and even when it is grown, we've had no market for it because of the war," Fancy said. "Don't get me wrong, we weren't in danger of starving or anything. We have been doing all right. We've got a couple of milk cows, some pigs, chickens, and we had a good garden this year. But we certainly don't have what you would call a farm. None of us do."

Longtrail ranch—Thursday, December 7, 1865

> WHEREAS it has pleased Almighty God during the year which is now coming to an end to relieve our beloved country from the fearful scourge of civil war and to permit us to secure the blessings of peace, unity, and harmony, with a great enlargement of civil liberty; and
> WHEREAS our Heavenly Father has also dur-

ing the year graciously averted from us the calamities of foreign war, pestilence, and famine, while our granaries are full of the fruits of an abundant season; and

WHEREAS righteousness exalteth a nation, while sin is a reproach to any people :

NOW, THEREFORE, be it known that I, Andrew Johnson, President of the United States, do hereby recommend to the people thereof that they do set apart and observe the first Thursday of December next as a day of national thanksgiving to the Creator of the Universe for these great deliverances and blessings.

And I do further recommend that on that occasion the whole people make confession of our national sins against His infinite goodness, and with one heart and one mind implore the divine guidance in the ways of national virtue and holiness.

In testimony whereof I have hereunto set my hand and caused the seal of the United States to be affixed.

Done at the city of Washington, this 28th day of October, A.D. 1865, and of the Independence of the United States of America the ninetieth.

The presidential proclamation had been printed in the *Comancheria Bulletin*, the newspaper started and operated by Ralph Good. There were some who said that the declaration did not apply to them, but most, Paul among them, said that we were one nation now, and we had one president. He proclaimed that he would celebrate Thanksgiving, and he invited many of his friends and neighbors to come to Longtrail to celebrate the holiday.

Young Lucy was upset that she couldn't sit with the adults, but Fancy told her that someone needed to look out for the children.

"I'll help you keep an eye on them, Lucy," Billy Chapman said. Billy had come to the dinner with his mother.

Gordon and Gretchen were there with their three children. Gretchen's parents, Otto and Helga Hoffman, were there as well.

Ralph Good, who had come home from the war with a shattered knee, had bought the *Comancheria Bulletin* and married Maggie McKenzie. They had come to the dinner with their two small children. Lucy Good came with them. Ian and Jane McKenzie had also come to the dinner.

And finally, Joe Travis, his wife Wanda, and their three children had come. While their presence may have caused some talk at other gatherings in town, Joe was most welcome here. All present for the dinner knew that Joe had been a part of the original wagon train and was, like Paul, a veteran of the Alamo and San Jacinto. It was also well known that Joe had helped fight off the raid against Longtrail while Paul was away at war, which made him most welcome.

Extra tables had to be put up in order to accommodate all the guests. But if they had to scramble for tables and chairs, there was no shortage of food. The tables were spread with roast wild turkey, baked chicken, dressing, and, especially for Paul, dumplings. In addition, there were vegetables of every hue, from green beans to yellow squash, to orange sweet potatoes, to purple beets.

"This reminds me of the meal we had just before Appomattox," Gordon said.

"What?" Gretchen asked. "You ate like this during the war?"

"Oh, no, uh, what we had there were corn dodgers made from corn meal and sawdust," Gordon said. "When I say this reminds me of that, I mean, while I was trying to get the corn dodgers down, I was *thinking* of a meal like this."

The others around the table laughed, though Gretchen and Fancy both wiped away tears.

"That's awful, to think of you and all the other poor soldiers suffering so," Gretchen said. "And you can laugh about it?"

Gordon reached over to lay his hand on Gretchen's. "Sweetheart, if you can see the humor in it, you can take anything."

After the dinner, which everyone declared was the most wonderful meal ever eaten, the assembly broke up into four groups. The women worked together to clean up, the younger children engaged in parlor games. The older children, Tom Nelson and Cindy Forsythe, Billy Chapman and Lucy Nelson, sat over to one side of the parlor, keeping an eye on the children as they talked among themselves.

The men gathered in the living room to smoke their cigars, pipes, and cigarettes.

"Gentlemen, we need to discuss the future," Tom said.

"What future?" Ian asked. "Do you have any idea how many farms have been abandoned, and how many businesses have been closed over the last two years?"

"Ian, when we came up here, you were one of the

wealthiest men in Texas," Ralph said. "Where are you now?"

Ian chuckled. "Well, I have over a million dollars in Confederate money," he said.

"That's exactly what I mean," Ralph said. "The entire South converted their cash into Confederate money, and that's all gone now."

"Now that the war is over, maybe the federal government will redeem Confederate dollars," Gordon suggested. "I mean, after all, didn't the Confederate government have gold backing the currency? What happened to that gold? No doubt the federal government confiscated it, which means they should redeem Confederate dollars with Yankee greenbacks."

Ralph shook his head. "The Supreme Court has already ruled on that, and I quote, 'That which in fact and law is money is gold or silver coin. This in law is money, and nothing else.' "

"What does that mean, exactly?" Joe asked.

"It means, exactly, that the millions in Confederate dollars that people all over the South hold are worthless," Ralph said.

"Which is exactly why we need to talk about the future," Gordon said. He glanced over at Paul. "And Paul has come up with an idea."

"What is your idea?" Ian asked.

"A cow hunt," Paul said.

"What?"

"A cow hunt," Paul repeated. "There are millions of Longhorn cattle roaming through Texas, tens of thousands of them up here, in the panhandle. I think that next spring we should round up as many as we can, keep them for a year, then drive them up to Dodge City, Kansas."

"Why Dodge City?"

"Because, Dodge City has a railhead that can ship the cattle to the slaughterhouses back East. We aren't the only ones facing a shortage. The big cities back East have a shortage of beef. We can supply that beef."

"Hey," Ian said. "That's not a bad idea. Where did you come up with it?"

"I got the idea from Ralph," Paul said. Getting up from his chair, he walked over to a rolltop desk and pulled out a copy of the *Comancheria Bulletin*. "Here, Ralph, read this aloud," Paul said, putting his finger on one of the articles.

Ralph took the paper from Paul, cleared his throat, then began reading aloud.

"The title of the piece is: 'Demand for beef is great in northern states,' " Ralph said. Then he read the article.

" 'The recent War Between the States interrupted not only the commerce in cotton, but the commerce in beef cattle as well. While cotton fields lay fallow in the beleaguered South, the Northern mills were able to satisfy their demand for cotton by importing the fiber from Egypt. No such source existed for beef cattle, for it is well known that Texas produces more beef than anywhere else in the world.'

" 'This condition of no beef in the North continues as the restaurant owners and homemakers petition the butcher for this commodity, only to be turned away. The once great cattle ranches in the South fell into disuse when the men needed to work the ranches were called to war. What happened to the cattle, one may ask? In Texas, the unattended cattle left the ranches and now roam freely, by the millions it is said, upon the vast and empty Texas plains. This paper believes that these free roaming herds of cattle could provide an untapped source of money for the enterprising. Cattle that can be had for the taking here, will bring fifty dollars a head at the meat processing plants in the East.' "

Ralph lay the paper down and looked out at the others, who had paid particular attention to his reading.

"Cap'n Nelson," Joe said. "If you'll have a black man along with you, me 'n my son Leroy would be pleased to come along."

"I'm counting on you coming along," Paul said.

"Pa, I hope you aren't planning on leaving Billy and me out," Tom said. Tom and Billy had come into the room when he heard Ralph reading the article.

"May I make a proposal?" Ian suggested.

"Sure."

"I propose that we organize the Comancheria Cattle Company, for the purposes of this operation."

"I think that is a good idea," Ralph said.

"And I nominate Paul Nelson as president of the company," Ian added.

"I second that," Gordon said.

Paul was elected by unanimous vote.

Chapter Twenty-two

The cow hunt in the previous year had been exceptionally successful, and there were now grazing upon the land owned by Paul Nelson and his next-door neighbor, Gordon Forsythe, fifteen thousand head of cattle. Planning for the drive began in the previous fall when Paul began putting together everything they would need for the drive: two chuck wagons, because this would be a much larger drive than normal; two cooks; and four hoodlum wagons, needed to carry the equipment, from axes and shovels to extra ropes, ammunition, canvas, and bedrolls.

From the first time he ever saw one, Paul was intrigued by chuck wagons. He was fascinated with the construction of the chuck box. The chuck box sat at the rear of the wagon, with a hinged lid which let down onto a swinging leg to form a worktable. Here, the cook stored his utensils and whatever food he might use during the day: such things as flour, sugar, dried fruit, coffee beans, pinto beans, tobacco, "medicinal" whiskey and, on occasion, hard candy.

When Paul had settled in Comancheria, he had grown cotton because the lack of cowhands had made his real ambition of becoming a cattle rancher very remote. He never gave up the dream though, and during the war ranching had become his connection with home. Around a thousand campfires in hundreds of bivouacs and dozens of battles, he thought of ranching. And as he thought of ranching, he thought of the chuck wagon, building one in his mind. That chuck wagon became his connection between the horror of war and the longed for tranquility of home

Calling on those memories, he had gone to a wagon builder and drawn out the design for him. These two wagons were the result of those long hours of contemplation, and seeing them actually being built gave him more personal satisfaction than he could explain.

With all the material gathered, his next job was to hire enough cowboys to handle a herd this large. He needed at least thirty men, and when he couldn't get enough experienced cowboys, he hired young men, most of them so young that they had not even been in the war.

Ownership of the fifteen thousand head of cattle had been apportioned according to individual investment in time and money. As it worked out, there were at least eight owners, including Ralph Good, Ian McKenzie, Otto Hoffman, and Gary Cramer, one of the original wagon pioneers, and the father of Steve Cramer, who had been killed at Shiloh.

Four of the eight owners—Paul Nelson, Gordon Forsythe, Joe Travis, and Billy Chapman—would be making the long trail drive up to Dodge City. Paul's son Tom, Gordon's daughter Cindy, and Joe's daughter Beulah were also going. Cindy and Beulah would cook and drive the two chuck wagons.

The first thing they had to do was gather enough horses to make up the remuda. Most of the horses were half wild and the cowboys had to break them. Tom proved to be an excellent horseman and he broke more animals than did anyone else, though Billy Chapman wasn't far behind. Once the horses were broken, the cowboys had to choose their string, selecting the most reliable for the horse they would ride at night. The rest of the remuda had to be trained to stay in a makeshift corral, which consisted of several lariats tied together and attached to trees or wagon wheels on the hoodlum or chuck wagon. It wasn't in any way substantial, but once the horses were trained, they would stay within the rope corral.

In late May, when everything was ready, Paul sent a telegram to the cattle broker in Dodge City to inquire as to how much cattle were bringing per head in Dodge. The reply, which came within two hours of sending the telegram caused a huge smile to spread across Paul's face, and when he showed it to the other owners, they smiled as well.

CHICAGO CATTLE EXCHANGE WILL PAY THIRTY
DOLLARS PER HEAD DELIVERED TO DODGE CITY.

"Gentlemen," Paul said. "Assuming we can get the cattle safely delivered to Dodge City, we have a net worth of four-hundred-fifty thousand dollars."

"When do we get under way?" Billy Chapman asked.

"Everything is ready," Paul said. "I see no reason why we can't get started Sunday morning."

Father Chris Sharkey of St. Paul's Episcopal Church, which was the only church in town, agreed to hold the Sunday services at Longtrail ranch. Practically everyone in Comancheria showed up for the communion, blessing, potluck dinner, and to see the herd depart. Although not everyone had a direct financial connection to the herd, everyone had a vested interest in it, for, in a real way, the survival of the town depended on the success of this venture.

Father Sharkey conducted the service, then ended it with a collect.

"Oh, most merciful Father, who hast blessed the labors of the husbandmen in the returns of the fruits of the earth, we give Thee humbly and hearty thanks for this Thy bounty; beseeching Thee to continue Thy loving kindness to us, that our effort may be fruitful. Bless these men as they undertake this long and dangerous cattle drive, to Thy glory and our comfort, through Jesus Christ our Lord. Amen."

All of the women had brought dishes to share at the huge potluck dinner that was being held on the lawn of Longtrail. Cattlemen and cowboys, merchants and professionals from the town, and all the children were gathered for the service, the meal and, most exciting of all, to see fifteen thousand head of cattle start the long drive to Dodge City.

If they were going direct, it would be only a three-hundred-mile drive, but in this case the shortest distance between two points was not a direct line. The direct line would carry them through Comanche territory, and there had already been several incidents between Indians and whites. The direct route also had long stretches of no water. And, because there were many in Kansas who believed that Texas cattle would bring "Texas Tick Fever" to Kansas cattle, there were several groups of armed Kansans who formed vigilante committees to make certain that no Kansas cow would be infected with the Texas Tick Fever.

Those difficulties would not be entirely eliminated by avoiding the direct route between Comancheria and Dodge City, but they could be greatly lessened by making the drive on the Chisolm Trail, an already established route with adequate water, supply points, good grass, less chance of encountering hostile Indians, and a greater chance of encountering supporters.

The problem with going way of the Chisolm Trail was that it added a hundred miles to the drive. It was decided by all, though, that the Chisolm Trail would the best way to go.

After the meal, Paul, who was not only president of the Comancheria Cattle Company, but also trail boss for the drive, let out an ear-piercing whistle. The whistle, as he thought it would, secured everyone's attention.

"All right, men, kiss your sweethearts good-bye. It's time to go," Paul announced.

With good-byes said, the cowboys and cattle owners mounted their horses and moved out into the field to start the herd north. It was necessary to push rather hard at the beginning, as the cattle were used to this as their home, and their inclination was to stay put. With that, the cattle drive of the Comancheria Cattle Company got under way.

Though the actual drive could be said to have started earlier that morning, when the four wagons, two chuck wagons and two hoodlum wagons had started north from what was a comfortable setting for man and beast. What lay ahead for them, nobody knew.

For the next few days, they pushed the herd as hard as they could, doing so for two reasons. One was to get them far enough away from their customary ranges that their attachment switched from geographic place to their relationship with the others in the herd. The other reason they were pushed so hard was so that they would be so tired at night that there wouldn't be any trouble in getting them to bed down. After a week on the trail, cattle and men settled into a routine.

Earlier this year, the Kiowas, Comanches, Southern Cheyennes, and Arapahoes had been persuaded to accept the treaty of Medicine Lodge Creek, in which they gave up the right to roam and accepted the idea of being, more or less, confined to their reservations.

Not all the Indians had agreed with that, and many of them stated they would rather die fighting than starve to death on the reservations. That caused some apprehension when they crossed the Red River into Indian Territory, even though they would be crossing the panhandle, an area designated on the maps as "public land" and would only be there for two days.

The herd crossed the Indian Territory's Cimmaron Strip without incident and, as each day passed, they grew more comfortable with the trail experience, establishing a rhythm that enabled them to work exceptionally well together, drawing upon the strength of each other.

Midway through the afternoon of the second day of being inside the Indian Territory, Tom, who had been riding scout, came back at a rapid trot. He rode up to Paul before he reined in.

"Pa, we might have trouble ahead," Tom said.

"What kind of trouble?"

"Indians," Tom said. "There are a lot up ahead, gathered in an arroyo."

"How many?"

"A lot of them," Tom said. "Maybe as many as a hundred."

"Did they see you?"

"No, sir, I don't think so."

"Not thinking so isn't good enough," Paul said. "I need to know if they saw you or not."

Tom hesitated for a second before he answered. "They didn't see me," he said.

"Were they just a group of Indians going somewhere? Were they armed?"

"Yes, they had rifles and bows."

"Go round up Gordon, Billy, and Joe. We need to talk this over."

"Were their faces painted?" Joe asked.

"Yes."

"What color was the paint?"

"What color?" Billy Chapman asked. "Why does that matter?"

"I spent some time with the Comanche after the Alamo," Joe said. "The color they use makes a difference. Was it black and white? Or red and yellow?"

"It was red and yellow," Tom said.

"That's not good," Joe said. "Black and white means peace. That means they would meet with us, and most likely bargain for a few cows. But red is war paint, and yellow means they are not afraid to die. They aim to take as many cows from us as they can. Is there water nearby?"

"Yes, there is a small lake real close."

"That's where they are going to stay, then. They figure that we'll have to water the cattle and that's where they will jump us."

"All right, Tom, I want you and Billy to select the five youngest cowboys that we have. You will stay here with the herd. The rest of us will deal with the Indians."

"I'm coming with you, Pa," Tom said.

"No, you aren't."

"Pa, think about it," Tom said. "How is it going to look to the others if you leave me behind where it is safe, when you will be taking some men with you who are younger than I am?"

Paul took his hat off and ran his hand through his hair, then sighed. "It's hard to argue with you when you are right," he said. "All right, you can go."

"How do we want to do this?" Gordon asked.

"If they are waiting for us, that means they know we are coming," Paul said. "So the best thing is not to do anything that will make them suspect that we know they are there. They will probably send a scout out to see where we are, so we'll just bed the cattle down here for the night, and go about our regular routine," Paul said.

That night, as they had every night so far on the drive, Cindy and Beulah prepared supper, the frying salt pork sending out its signature aroma. The cowboys gathered around the fire to have their dinner and coffee and conversations as if everything was normal.

"Gordon," Paul said. "Why don't you sing something for us?"

Nodding, Gordon retrieved his guitar from the hoodlum wagon, then began playing and singing the ballad "Lorena."

Finally, Paul sent the night riders out to keep watch over the herd, and encouraged the others to crawl into their bedrolls to get some sleep. Within half an hour, there was absolutely nothing that would tip an Indian scout off that the cowboys were aware of them.

Paul awakened everyone at one o'clock in the morning, including Cindy and Beulah.

"Joe, you are in charge here," Paul said. "We'll keep four men watching herd, and you'll have six more here with you, counting Cindy and Beulah. If the Indians get through us, they'll be coming here. Don't try to defend the herd. Let them take as many as they want. What's more important is that you don't get anyone killed."

"All right," Joe said.

The twenty men Paul would be taking with him

gathered in the dark. All were carrying repeating rifles, either Henrys or Winchesters. They were mounted on the best horse in their string, and with Tom leading the way, they rode five miles to where the Indians were camping. As soon as they got there, Paul realized that he could take up a position that would deny the Indians access to the water, and that's what he did, concealing his men in a willow grove that was halfway between the arroyo and the lake.

They waited there until dawn. At dawn, the Indians began milling around, cooking their breakfast, relieving themselves, laughing and talking among themselves. That was when Paul gave the order to fire.

The cowboys fired and several of the Indians went down. Then, realizing that the cowboys had discovered them, the Indians regrouped, then charged toward the willow thicket. Again the cowboys fired in volley, and because all the cowboys were armed with repeating rifles, they were able to keep up a heavy volume of fire, even though they were badly outnumbered. Again, several of the Comanche went down.

The Indians tried a new strategy, attacking from at least two different directions, trying to make their way into the thicket, but the fire from the cowboys was just too heavy.

The Indians withdrew to the arroyo and shot high into the air, trying to drop arrows down onto the cowboys, but that didn't work either. Now the Indians realized that the easy access they had to the water was no more, and they began to grow more desperate, charging, being beaten back, and charging again.

Then the Indians' war chief rode close to the willow thicket, and turned to urge his warriors to follow him in yet another attack. As he turned, though, the thick buffalo hide shield shifted enough for Paul to take a shot. He hit the chief in the side and knocked him off his horse. Then, before Paul could stop him, Tom leaped into the saddle and rode out toward the fallen Indian. He lassoed him, and dragged him back into the willows.

"That was a dumb thing to do!" Paul scolded.

"Sorry, Pa, the idea just came to me," Tom said, smiling at his father even as he was being scolded.

The Indians, furious by the action, made one more charge, but they were beaten off again.

As it turned out, the chief Paul had shot was only slightly wounded in body, though much depressed in spirit, as a result of his ignominious retrieval from the field of battle.

"Do you speak English?" Paul asked. "*¿Habla usted español?*"

"I speak English," the Indian said.

"If we let you go, will you and your warriors guarantee our safe passage through the territories?" Paul asked. "If you will do this, I will give you ten of my cattle." Paul held up his hands, showing ten fingers.

"This many," the Indian chief said, flashing both hands twice.

"This many," Paul countered, holding up two hands, then one hand.

"Done," the Indian chief replied.

"Bring two warriors with you," Paul said. "Three of you should be able to handle fifteen cows."

True to the chief's word, the Indians allowed the herd to pass through without any further trouble.

Paul had heard that sometimes cattle herds were met at the Kansas border by armed groups of men determined to keep Texas cattle from coming into the state, but they encountered no such obstacle and entered Kansas without difficulty.

For the next several days they proceeded north with ease. Each day the entire outfit ate breakfast together, those who had been riding since midnight, and those who had just been awakened to start the new day. Then, one morning while they were having their breakfast, Paul saw Joe walking around, pulling stems of grass and sucking on the roots, snapping twigs and smelling them, and scooping up a handful of dirt to examine it very closely.

Finally, Paul's curiosity got the best of him

"Joe, you want to tell me what you doing?" he asked.

"What's the name of that river you say we'll be crossing next?" Joe asked.

"The Arkansas."

"How far would that be?"

"I'd say another seventy to eighty miles. Five days."

"Cap'n, I'm afraid we are in for some very dry trailing," Joe said. "From the looks of things, there hasn't been a rain here in quite a spell. That means that, like as not, any watering holes between here and the Arkansas are likely to be dried up."

"Oh, damn, that's not good," Paul said. "That's not good at all. Five days without water? The cattle won't make it."

"It may not be that bad," Gordon said. Gordon had listened in on the conversation. "This is an established trail, so there are bound to be some year-round streams or creeks between here and the river. Otherwise people wouldn't be coming this way."

Paul shook his head. "I don't know, Gordon, there's nothing on the map, and I've never been up here myself, so I don't know."

"How accurate is the map?" Gordon asked. "Didn't we come across a good stream down in the territories that wasn't even marked on the map?"

"Yeah," Paul said. "Yeah, we did, didn't we?"

"You want a suggestion? I think we should send a couple of scouts out, one going east and one going west. See if they can find any water."

"Good idea," Paul said. "If either of them find water, that's where we will go."

Although they normally started moving before the cattle began grazing, they changed their routing this morning, letting the cattle graze before the sun could dry out what little moisture the grass had absorbed during the night. The cowboys let them eat their fill before pushing them on. Before the wagons left, the cowboys filled their canteens with water. The remuda was kept with the herd and four changes of mounts were made during the day in order not to exhaust any one horse.

Several times for an hour or more, the herd was allowed to lie down and rest; but by the middle of the afternoon thirst made them impatient and restless, and the point men were compelled to ride steadily in the lead in order to hold the cattle to a walk. A number of times during the afternoon, they attempted to graze the cattle, but the cattle would not eat until twilight.

* * *

After the fourth change of horses was made, Paul sent a couple of his riders on ahead with the remuda to overtake the wagons. Paul instructed him to tie up all the night horses, because if the cattle would not graze, he intended to continue the drive until at least ten o'clock, and that would require all hands to be present.

The two riders who had gone out looking for water rejoined the herd without reporting success.

As expected, the cattle grazed easily after nightfall, but thirst was beginning to affect them so that barely half of them lay down that night. Paul doubled the night riders, and very few of the cowboys managed to get any sleep. Cindy and Beulah took turns so that they kept coffee and food available for the cowboys all through the night.

The next morning, they started the cattle forward an hour before dawn, and were five miles into the second waterless day by sunrise. By now the thirst was beginning to effect the drovers as well, for the water barrels carried by the chuck wagons were running low, and Paul established a rationing to the water that remained.

The wagons were sent on ahead, and told not to stop until they reached water. In the meantime, the cattle were pushed on through another day of torrid heat. The cattle were a pitiful lot, their tongues hanging out, their lowing a desperate appeal for water.

At noon they reached a line of timber which suggested a creek. The wagons were parked there, but before they got there, Cindy rode out to meet them.

"There's no water there," Cindy said.

"None?"

"Not enough to water the herd," Cindy said.

"There's just a small pool of water. We filled the water barrels and there may be enough for the horses, but not for the cows."

"Damn!" Paul said. "We are going to lose this entire herd."

"Pa, why don't we hold the herd here while Billy and I go on ahead until we find water?"

"All right," Paul agreed. "In the meantime, I'll send riders ten miles upstream and ten miles downstream to see if there is water anywhere in this creek."

"Paul, if there is enough here for the horses, I think we should let them water," Gordon said. "They are going to have to stay healthy if we are going to be able to control the herd."

"Good idea," Paul said.

The water that was available was in a small pool that had sprung up from a well. The pool had a diameter of no more than three feet across, which meant it was only big enough to handle no more than two horses at a time. The men took the horses down two at a time until finally all were watered. By the time they were finished, the two riders who were exploring the dry creek bed returned with the news that they had not found water.

The cattle continued their piteous bawl.

"Oh," Cindy said to Beulah, as the two women prepared supper. "Listen to the poor things. This is just breaking my heart."

"I know what you mean," Beulah said. "I almost feel guilty drinking in front of them."

By nightfall, Tom and Billy returned from their

scout with a big smile. "It's fifteen miles ahead," Tom said. "But we found water."

"Fifteen miles," Joe said. "That's one more night and day that they will be without water."

"It's bad," Paul said. "But I think they'll make it. They have to," he added.

None of the cowboys got any sleep that night, because on this third waterless night, the cows wouldn't even lie down. Instead, they tended to drift away, and riders were constantly moving through the herd to bring back groups that had wandered off to the main herd. Sometimes the errant cows would get as far as a mile away from the herd, but by the light of the moon and stars, and because every cowhand was involved, the herd was kept fairly intact.

It would have helped if it would rain, or even if it had been a cloudy day, but the next morning broke without a breath of air, promising another day of sizzling heat. As they got the herd under way, the heat was almost unbearable, not only for the cattle, but for the men. The men suffered enough, even though they now had full canteens, but the cattle were becoming feverish and ungovernable. The lead cows kept trying to turn back, no doubt to return to the last watering hole, and it was difficult to keep them moving ahead.

"You dumb cows!" Tom shouted at them in frustration. "Don't you know that the closest water is in front of you!"

Cindy heard Tom's shout and she laughed, then called out to him. "Do you expect them to answer you?" she asked.

There was ample evidence along the trail that this

was not the first time in which a herd had been caught in a waterless drive, for the bones of many a fallen animal lay bleaching along the trail.

By now the herd was strung out nearly five miles in length, and they were moving forward at about a three-mile-per-hour gait. At this speed, if they could be kept on course, they would reach water by mid-afternoon. The problem was in keeping them on course, because there was still embedded in their collective memory, the thought of water behind, and they continued to try and break the course to go back. Only because the horses had been well watered, and could be used to their fullest advantage, were they able to continue pushing the cattle in the right direction. The cowboys raced out to intercept those cows who had turned, firing pistols in front of them, hitting them in the face with ponchos which were being turned to ribbons by that use.

Finally, the lead cows arrived at the water, where they began to drink.

The trailing cows, now aware that water was before them, quickened their pace until the entire herd was there, spread out up and down the stream for fully five miles, drinking their fill. As the herd drank, Paul sent out riders, searching the countryside for miles in all directions to bring in those stragglers that had not yet found the water.

By nightfall, every cow had been watered, had grazed, and now lay down to sleep the sleep of the exhausted. The men were just as exhausted and they stayed right here, with good water and grass, for three more days until man and beast were fully recovered.

Chapter Twenty-three

From the *Dodge City Times:*

CATTLE BUSINESS.

An enormous herd of cattle has arrived from Texas. The cattle, belonging to the Comancheria Cattle Company, number upwards of fifteen thousand head, and are expected to bring thirty dollars a head. Though no one broker is expected to take the entire herd, three brokers have united their efforts and will be taking five thousand head apiece, making the total transaction $450,000. This is the biggest single transaction since Dodge City became the terminus for Texas cattle.

It is said that the cattle so recently arrived do not belong to one rancher, but to a consortium of ranchers in the panhandle of Texas. The trail boss for the cattle drive, and indeed one of the owners, if not the biggest owner of the cattle is Paul Nelson.

Paul Nelson, late a Confederate general in the recent unpleasantness, is one of the founders of a small community in Northwest Texas called Comancheria, from whence the name of the cattle company is derived. That this is a family affair can best be illustrated by the fact that Paul Nelson has brought his son, Tom, on the drive, while Gordon Forsythe, also one of the Texas businessmen engaged in this operation, brought his daughter, Cindy.

The money is being paid in cash, Comancheria being much in need of that commodity. The cowboys will be paid out here, in Dodge City, so it is expected that much of the money generated by the drive will stay here as the cowboys, no doubt long deprived from libation and female companionship, will likely leave much of their money with the 16 saloons doing business in our fair community.

The man sitting at a table in the back of the Long Branch Saloon was an unusual looking man, with his pink eyes, white hair, and chalky white skin, but he had been a habitué of the saloon long enough now that his appearance seldom garnered a second glance.

Though originally from Texas, Tyler Bodine had severed all connections with that state when he established a group of Union raiders. After the war, he had come to Kansas where his raiding activities were regarded not as treasonous, but as heroic.

In truth, it had not been patriotism that motivated his guerrilla activities. It had been his opportunity to rob homes, stores, and trains without violating the

law. What, under normal circumstances, would be regarded as outlaw activity was, under cover of the war,
military action.

Bodine recognized the names of Paul Nelson and
Gordon Forsythe, having encountered both of them
when they were Texas Rangers, and later, when they
were U.S. marshals. Now they were cattlemen and,
according to the article in the newspaper, rich cattlemen.

Rich cattlemen, ripe for the picking.

"Do you have any idea how many men it took to
bring up a herd of fifteen thousand head?" Will
Jarvis asked.

"I'd guess around twenty-five to thirty," Bodine
said.

"I'd say closer to thirty, and maybe even more,"
Jarvis said. "There are four of us, going up against
thirty? I don't like those odds."

Will Jarvis and Jim Meeker had ridden with Bodine in some of the last raids he had made during the
war. And like Bodine, they had come to Kansas, be-
lieving it to be a safer environ for them.

"We aren't going up against thirty men," Bodine
said. "We are going up against one woman."

"What do you mean, one woman?"

"Trust me," Bodine said.

Cindy and Beulah had gone into town after the
herd reached Dodge City. But unlike the men, they
had come to town only to buy supplies for the long
trip back home. Now, with a fresh supply of flour,
cornmeal, cured bacon and ham, potatoes, onions,

and dried apples and peaches, they were back at the chuck wagons, cleaning, rearranging, and putting away the groceries.

"You think five apple pies will be enough?" Beulah asked. The two had planned making apple pie as a surprise for the men before they started back.

"Normally, I would say yes," Cindy said. "That would be six pieces per pie. But I know that Tom could probably eat half a pie all by himself."

"Papa could eat the other half," Beulah replied with a little laugh. "What did we do with that flour sifter?"

"I think it is in the other wagon," Cindy said.

"I'll get it."

The two women were standing behind the chuck box of the first wagon, with the drop leaf down. Beulah started up the side of the wagon, then stopped short. She would have screamed, if she had not been so shocked. She was face to face with the whitest man she had ever seen in her life. There were two others with him, and all three were holding pistols.

Joe Travis was just coming away from the blacksmith shop holding a new draw pin he had made for one of the hoodlum wagons when he saw Beulah running toward him. He was surprised to see her, and shocked to see tears streaming down her face.

"Beulah!" he said. "What is it, girl?"

"They took her, Papa, they took her!" Beulah said.

"You're not makin' sense, girl. Who took who?"

"Cindy," Beulah said. "Three men came with guns and they took her! They gave me this." She held out a sheet of paper.

*WE TOOK THE GIRL. IF YOU WANT TO SEE
HER ALIVE AGAIN, BRING FIFTY THOUSAND
DOLLARS TO THE OLD RED BARN WEST OF
TOWN.*

"I asked about it, Pa," Tom said. "I found out
where the barn is."

"I expect I had better go by myself," Paul said. "If
they see a lot of people coming, they might hurt her."

"Cindy is going to be my wife," Tom said. "I am
going."

"She's my daughter," Gordon said. "I've followed
your orders for thirty years, Paul, but no order is
going to keep me back from this one."

"All right," Paul said. "I guess the first thing we
need to do is get the cash ready."

"Are we going to pay them off? Do you really think
they will follow through with their end of the bargain?" Tom asked.

"No, I don't expect them to keep their end of the
bargain. At least not willingly. And yes, we are going
to pay them off. Temporarily."

"Temporarily?"

"The most important thing to do is to get Cindy
back. Then, after we know she is safe, we'll get the
money back."

Bodine was standing by the window of the loft of
the barn, though he was keeping himself to one side
so he couldn't be seen.

"Do you see anyone yet?" Jarvis asked.

"No."

"Do you think they'll come?"

"They'll come," Bodine said.

"Yeah, but how many of 'em?" Meeker asked.

"He's smart enough to know better'n to come with a whole bunch of men with him," Bodine said. "He knows that if he does, we'll kill the girl."

Cindy was sitting on the loft floor, leaning against the wall with her hands cuffed behind her and her feet tied together. There was also a gag around her mouth, so she couldn't speak. She looked on at the three men with her eyes open wide in fear.

"Hey, Bodine," Jarvis said. He reached down to rub himself. "How about we have us a little fun with the girl before we let her go?"

"No," Bodine said. "I want everyone alert until we have the money. We'll take the money. Then we'll leave her somewhere," Bodine said. "After," he added.

"After what?" Meeker asked.

Jarvis laughed. "You ain' payin' no attention at all, are you? He means after we have a little fun."

"Yeah," Meeker said. He smiled at Cindy, showing a mouth full of yellowed, blackened, and broken teeth. "I'll just bet you ain't ever even had a man, have you, girlie?"

"Hey, which one of us gets her first?" Jarvis said. "I know, we'll draw straws to see which one of us is first."

"Shut up, both of you," Bodine said. "Someone's comin'."

"How many?"

"Just one," Bodine said.

"That may just be someone ridin' by," Meeker suggested.

"No. It's the one we are waiting for," Bodine said. "It's Paul Nelson, and he is carrying a sack."

"Sum bitch!" Jarvis said excitedly. "I didn't think we could do it!"

"We ain't done it yet," Meeker said. "Let's wait until we have the money in our hands before we celebrate."

"What's he doin' now?" Jarvis asked.

"He just dismounted," Bodine said.

Although Tom and Gordon had both come with him, Paul had them dismount, and stay hidden, just beyond the bend in the road. He had come this far alone, and he was going to negotiate alone.

Looking toward the barn, Paul reached down into the bag, then pulled out a handful of money. He held it up so that anyone who might be looking at him from the barn could see it. Then he returned the money to the sack he was carrying, and tied the sack to the saddle horn.

"Bodine!" he called toward the barn.

"That's pretty good, Nelson," Bodine called back. "How did you know it was me?"

"Because the young lady who brought the message described you to me. And you are the only walking maggot I know."

"I don't like being called a maggot," Bodine called back.

"Here's the money. Send Cindy out," Paul called.

"Leave the money and ride away. Then we'll send the girl out."

"Bring her out. You've got the advantage."

Bodine was quiet for a moment, then he called back, "All right. Take your pistol from your holster and throw it as far as you can. If you do that, we'll bring her out. But if you try anything funny, we'll kill her right in front of you. Then we'll kill you."

Paul pulled his pistol from its holster, held it up so Bodine could see it, then he threw it away.

"Untie her feet so she can walk," Bodine said.

"You ain't really goin' to give her to him, are you, Bodine?" Jarvis asked.

"Just until we get the money," Bodine said. "Then we'll kill 'im."

"What about the girl?" Meeker asked.

"What about her? We won't need her then."

"I mean, we ain't just goin' to let her go, are we? Before we—uh, you know." Meeker rubbed himself.

Bodine smiled. "We'll use her before we let her go," he said. "But there ain't goin' to be any drawin' of straws. I'm first."

"Don't make me no never mind who's first," Jarvis said. "Just as long as I get my turn at her." Jarvis was untying Cindy, and he reached up to squeeze her breast.

"Uhmm!" Cindy squeaked in pain and fear. That was the best she could do with the gag in place.

"I'll be damned. You like that, don't you, girlie? Yes, sir, I believe you're goin' to have as good a time as we are."

"Get her down the ladder," Bodine said. "But don't nobody step out of the barn until I give the word."

"What's happening now, Tom?" Gordon asked.

"I couldn't hear what they were saying, but Pa just threw away his pistol," Tom said.

"Wait, there's Cindy."

* * *

Paul saw Cindy step outside the barn. She was gagged, and her hands were behind her back.

"If you want her, bring the money here," Bodine called from just inside the barn.

Paul reached up to get the sack of money, then started toward the barn.

"Do you remember, some twenty years ago, when I took some brats from that wagon train?" Bodine called. "You tricked me then. You brought sacks of rocks, with just a few gold coins."

"I remember," Paul said.

"Well, you ain't goin' to trick me again. This sack better be full of money, real money. 'Cause if it ain't, we'll be killin' you and the girl."

"The money is all here," Paul said.

Paul crossed the distance to the barn. Then when he was no more than twenty feet from Cindy, Bodine told him to stop. Three men stepped out of the barn, though Paul only recognized Bodine.

"Meeker, hold your gun to the girl's head," Bodine said. "Jarvis, go get the money sack. Before we make another move, I intend to see that the bag is filled with real money."

Meeker stepped up to Cindy, cocked his pistol, and held it to her head. Jarvis came, warily, toward Paul. Jarvis was holding his pistol in his right hand, and he reached out with his left.

Paul gave him the sack.

"Look inside, Jarvis," Bodine said. "What do you see?"

"Money!" Jarvis said with a broad grin. He stuck his hand down into the bag, then pulled out a bound packet of money. "It's all money and it's all real!" he said excitedly.

"All right," Paul said. "I've kept up my side of the bargain. Let the girl go."

"Not yet," Bodine said. "First I need to make certain you ain't goin' to give us any trouble."

Bodine took the shackles from Cindy's hands, and she brought them around front and began rubbing her wrists. Bodine started toward Paul. He clamped one side of the shackles around Paul's belt.

"Now, give me your right hand."

Paul complied, and Bodine clamped the other cuff around his right wrist, effectively immobilizing his right arm.

"Now," Bodine said, smiling broadly. He stepped back from Paul, unbuckled his pistol belt, and let it fall to the ground. "You was a Texas Ranger once, wasn't you? They used to say that Texas Rangers are so tough that they could whip a man with one arm tied behind them. Let's me and you just see if that's true," he said.

He swung hard at Paul, and knocked him down.

"Ha!" he said. "I don't reckon it is true, is it?"

Bodine stepped over to Paul and kicked at him, intending to kick him in the head, but Paul caught Bodine's foot in his left hand, then jerked up on it, causing Bodine to fall.

As Bodine went down, Paul got up.

Jarvis cocked his pistol and aimed it at Paul.

"No!" Bodine said, holding one hand out toward Jarvis. "This son of a bitch is all mine!"

Bodine got up quickly, then raised his two hands in the stance of a boxer, and moved toward Paul. He jabbed with his left, then swung his right, but Paul managed to pull his head back quickly enough to avoid both attempts. Paul answered with a hard left jab that caught Bodine on his mouth. Instantly, blood began to ooze from Bodine's lip, the bright red contrasting sharply with the white of his skin.

Bodine swung again, and this time he got through, causing Paul's head to snap back. He followed up with a right that knocked Paul down for the second time, and once again he rushed toward him, intending to follow through with a kick.

Paul rolled out of the way, hopped up, then caught Bodine with a roundhouse left that send Bodine reeling backwards. Bodine swung, but again, Paul managed to lean away from him. Paul counterpunched, though as it was with only his left hand, he was able to inflict damage but not score a knockout punch. The damage began to be cumulative, though, because in addition to the cut on the lip, both of Bodine's eyes began to swell up.

Bodine was growing more and more frustrated, and the more frustrated he became, the wilder his swings, making it easy for Paul to avoid them. Finally, Paul managed to set himself and he threw a powerful left cross, with everything behind it, knocking Bodine down. This time, Bodine made no attempt to get back up and Paul leaned down, took the key from him, and unlocked the cuffs that had him shackled to his belt.

"What'll we do, Bodine?" Jarvis asked. "What'll we do?"

"You've got the money," Paul said. "Why don't you just take it and get out of here? Come on, Cindy, let's go."

Cindy came to Paul and hugged him in relief and appreciation. Then the two of them started walking back toward Paul's horse.

"What'll we do, Bodine?" Jarvis asked again.

Bodine got onto his hands and knees, then crawled over to where he had dropped his pistol belt. He pulled the pistol from the holster, then stood up and pointed his gun at Paul's back.

"Pa! Look out!" Tom shouted.

Paul shoved Cindy hard, so hard that she fell down and rolled away, just as Bodine pulled the trigger. The bullet hit Paul in his spinal cord and his legs gave way as he went down.

Paul tried to get back up, but found that he couldn't move from his waist down. He didn't even hear the second shot that crashed into the back of his head.

"No!" Tom shouted, running toward the three men. "No!"

Bodine, still smiling over having killed Paul, turned his pistol toward Tom, but before he could pull the trigger, Tom shot him, the bullet hitting Bodine in the middle of the forehead. He fell flat on his back.

Even before Jarvis and Meeker could react, two rifle shots rang out, Gordon operating the lever on his Winchester and firing rapidly. Both of Bodine's henchmen went down.

Tom took a quick look at his father and saw that he was beyond help. Then, he moved quickly to Cindy, helped her to her feet, and held her as she wept out loud. "He saved my life," Cindy said. "He gave his life to save mine."

Comancheria

There were far too many people for the church, so at least two hundred gathered outside under the spreading live oak trees, following the service as best they could through the open windows. And while they were unable to hear Father Sharkey's homily, they could hear the organist and the singing of the congregation as they sang the hymns: "Day of Wrath, Day of Mourning," followed by "Hail Sacred Day of Earthly Rest," and concluding with "It Is Not Death to Die."

When the church service concluded, the doors to the narthex were thrown open and the pall bearers— Gordon Forsythe, Billy Chapman, Ian McKenzie, his son Peter, Ralph Good, and Joe Travis—carried the coffin out to the hearse. If anyone had questioned the idea of Joe Travis, a black man, being one of the pall bearers, they kept their comment to themselves, for he had been specifically requested by Fancy Nelson.

From St. Paul's Episcopal Church at the eastern edge of town, the funeral procession made its way to the Garden of Memories Cemetery at the west end of town, a distance of just over one mile. The hearse bearing Paul's body was painted with shining black lacquer, with polished brass fittings that glistened in the sun. The purple curtains were pulled back so the coffin could be seen inside. The coffin was draped with the Lone Star flag of Texas. Billy Chapman walked along behind the hearse, leading Paul Nelson's favorite horse. The saddle blanket was gray and gold, with the wreathed star designating the rank of brigadier general in the Confederate army. Paul's boots were reversed in the stirrups, and his hat was hooked onto the saddle horn.

Behind the hearse and the horse came an open carriage, pulled by a matching team of black horses. Joe Travis was driving the carriage, with Fancy, Tom, Lucy, John, and Susanna as its passengers. Fancy and Lucy were dressed in black, and wearing black veils. Tom was wearing a black suit.

A line of drummers marched behind the carriage, keeping up a somber cadence on their black-draped, muffled drums.

Behind the drummers came a second carriage with Gordon, Gretchen, Cindy, and the other Forsythe children. After that, came carriages bearing Lucy Good and her family, Ian McKenzie and his family, Billy Chapman and his mother. Then, on horseback behind the Chapman carriage, rode every cowboy who had made the drive north, all of them in their newest and cleanest clothes, each wearing a black handkerchief tied to his left arm.

Hundreds of people lined both sides of Justin Good Avenue to watch the funeral cortege pass by, its progress measured by the soft fall of horses' hooves on the dirt road and the somber beat of the muffled drums.

Fancy, Tom, Lucy, John, and Susanna stood close by the open grave as the coffin was lowered by ropes. They listened, lost in their own thoughts, as the priest intoned the graveside litany. Then, at a nod from Father Sharkey, Fancy, Tom, Lucy, John, and Susanna held their hands out over the coffin and turning them, dropped earth onto it.

"For as much as it hath pleased Almighty God in His wise providence to take out of this world the soul of our deceased brother, Paul, we therefore commit his body to the ground—earth to earth, ashes to ashes, dust to dust—looking for the general resurrection in the last day, and the life to come through our Lord Jesus Christ, at whose second coming in glorious majesty to judge the world, the earth and the sea shall give up their dead, and the corruptible bodies of those who sleep in him shall be changed, and made like unto his own glorious body, according to the mighty working whereby He is able to subdue all things unto Himself.

"The grace of our Lord Jesus Christ, and the love of God, and the fellowship of the Holy Ghost, be with us all evermore. Amen."

"Amen," the hundreds of mourners at the cemetery repeated.

One year later

Tom Nelson, and his wife, Cindy, stood over Paul's grave. Cindy was holding her infant daughter.

"Pa, we want you to meet your granddaughter, Gretta," Tom said. "You never got to know her, but I guarantee you that Gretta, and all our other children and grandchildren, will know you. And they will be as proud of you as I am."

Amarillo—Saturday, June 15, 1912

"He saved my life," Cindy said. "He could have jumped to one side, or even dropped down to the ground and he wouldn't have been shot. But his last conscious thought was to get me to safety."

Cindy wiped tears from her eyes. "That was forty-five years ago, but not a day has gone by since that time that I haven't been aware that I am still alive because of Paul Nelson. And sometimes, I confess, I feel guilty about that."

"Don't be foolish, dear," Fancy said. "Paul did exactly what he wanted to do. There is no doubt in my mind that over these last forty-five years he has looked down on us, all of us. And I know that, if there can be the sin of pride in heaven, he is proud of what has followed him. You gave him grandchildren, great-grandchildren, and a great-great-grandchild."

"Ha," Gretchen said. "I know that your father just punched Paul on the shoulder and told him, 'She's my great-great-grandchild, too.'"

Later that evening, before they went home, Fancy asked Tom to take her out to the memorial once more. The bronze memorial was gleaming softly in the beams of crossing spotlights, and there were still several people present to admire it. Fancy stood there for a moment, looking up at Paul's statue. She was carrying a yellow rose, and she laid the bloom at the base of the statue.

"Death has not separated us, my darling," she said, speaking so quietly that only her son could hear. "You are my love, my life, and my salvation through all eternity."